FRACKIN' LIVES

A Novel

Sequel to Twisted Vines

Art Maurer

ISBN: 978-1-5151-8031-9

Cover Design by Anna Powell

Vineyard Terms – Abbreviated Descriptions

Training Vines – Directing growth of vines to trellises.

Phylloxera – Grape phylloxera is a tiny aphid-like insect that feeds in *Vitis vinifera* grape roots, stunting or killing vines. *Vitis vinifera* species are native to regions of the Mediterranean, Central Europe, Southeast Asia, plus others.

BRIX – Sugar content of an aqueous solution. Named after Adolf Brix.

Micro-oxygenation – A process used in winemaking to introduce oxygen into wine in a controlled manner to improve the wine … developed in 1991.

Microclimate – A local atmospheric zone where climate differs from the surrounding area … often near bodies of water which cools the local atmosphere.

Malolactic – A fermentation process in winemaking in which naturally present tart-tasting malic acid is converted into softer tasting lactic acid.

Lees – Deposits of dead or residual yeast carried to the bottom of the vat after fermentation and aging. The sediment is left behind.

Veraison – Change of color of the grape berries at the onset of ripening. Many changes occur at veraison.

Canopy – Canopy management is to provide proper light energy to the grapes through photosynthesis … not too much, not too little.

Terroir – the natural environment of the vineyard including composition of the soil, microclimate, contour of the land, orientation to the sun, prevailing wind … all contributing to the taste of the resulting wine … all beyond human control.

Prologue

"He'll get you pregnant, that Joey boy..." The words reverberated over and over in Jackie's head. She grabbed another errant shoot and snipped it off the vine; each click of the pruning shears punctuating her grand-mere's warning.

Jackie wore gloves with the fingertips cut off; but found the Upstate New York winter unrelenting, colder than she'd expected. She rubbed numbing fingers against her jacket to regain feeling. Pruning vines was not abating her anger as she'd hoped. Instead, trudging up the hill, boots squeaking in the cold snow, served to solidify it; like the ice and snow stretching down the hillside and across the frozen lake below.

Cold wind hitting full in the face pulled her back to France; only two weeks before, when Chloe's harsh words slapped her hard ... harder than ever before.

It all started seven months ago, when she found letters and cards sent by her American grandmother, Emma, over a period of 15 years. Expressions of love her French grand-mere, Chloe, kept from her. After her parents died when she was nine, Jackie grew up with her French grandparents at their chateau in the Medoc wine region of Bordeaux; attended boarding school to be taught by the Catholic nuns. She never heard from Emma; thought she just didn't care. When Chloe had a short stay in hospital and asked Jacqueline, her proper French name, to bring her some banking papers from her armoire. It was there Jackie found the shoebox of cards and letters hidden high on a shelf. They smelled musty from years of neglect. That was it! Jackie needed to get away, see her American grandmother; leave the suffocating French chateau and its vineyards behind.

But Chloe didn't make it easy for Jacqueline; she followed her to Emma's home in the heart of the Finger Lakes wine country. Convinced Jacqueline would return to France, Chloe hoped she'd come to her senses and marry Francois, the very successful vintner owning a neighboring chateau.

Jackie found a return to France complicated. While visiting Emma, she'd met Joey, a young man working hard to get a start in life. She was attracted to him even though he was starting a winery, a profession she'd had quite enough of in France.

She was shocked when shortly after arriving, Chloe met Norman, a free-spirited, successful American businessman, just retired. He was immediately enamored with her grand-mere, and Chloe led him on; made him feel it was he who enticed her to begin an on-going relationship, even allowed him to accompany her back to France. Jackie followed a month later ... with the understanding she'd stay at the chateau through the harvest and Christmas.

By January Jackie felt the need to get back to the Finger Lakes ... and Joey. Since that was her plan and understanding with Chloe all along, she was startled by Chloe's reaction when she made her flight reservation. Chloe stood, waving her arms, shouting a string of French words: "You never listen! You never will learn! Just like your father, headstrong American plunging through life. Self-centered, not caring who or what you hurt." Chloe stopped to catch her breath, but still kept her arms aloft, looking ready to pounce. "After all I've done for you, all your grandfather did for you before he died ... now this? You just pack up and go wherever you want?" She brought her face close to Jacqueline's, looking directly into her eyes, spitting her words, "He'll get you pregnant. That Joey boy ... no better than a damned dirt farmer ... and he'll force you into the slavery of that life."

Jackie felt at a loss for what to say.

Chloe backed away, saying in a guttural tone. "You have everything here. Go ahead, throw it away. God have mercy on your ungrateful soul!"

Norman heard the outburst and came in from the other room. Chloe told him "Shut up!" before he even had a chance to speak. "Don't listen to me, Norman," Jackie remembered Chloe saying, "just pour your money down that rat hole of a winery Joey wants to build."

"I have faith in Joey!" Norman said, "He reminds me of me when I was young."

Jackie tried to calm the waters with Chloe during the rest of her stay. But, Chloe only spoke to her in monosyllabic grunts, her body language frigid and unrelenting. Norman made sure Jackie got to the airport on time; the rift between Jacqueline and Chloe unresolved.

Emma and her husband Will greeted Jackie with warmth and quiet understanding. Joey joined them to meet Jackie at the airport. On her arrival he stepped forward taking Jackie in a full-bodied embrace. As they pulled apart, somewhat embarrassed in front of Emma and Will, the glance between them spoke of caution, shared feelings too deep to be trivialized. Will broke the tension, "Guess you really missed her, huh?"

The two weeks since had been a happy time for Jackie, spending time with Emma and Will, dinners including Joey … beginning to consider the future. But Emma and Will had made plans for a short southern vacation and Jackie urged them to seek that month of warmth. As soon as they were on their way, the need to face her reality with grand-mere Chloe began to vex Jackie. She called Chloe; the conversation was civil, but distant. Anger, like a slow moving fog, seeped in.

A gust of wind caught Jackie's attention. She saw a snow squall forming across the lake … and she was cold … *cold enough to freeze my brain if I let it!*

Joey, working in the vineyard below, waved. "Jackie," the wind carrying his voice, "It's after 3 … Storm's comin' … Let's go warm-up."

Chapter 1

Joey stood at the high end of his vineyard, near the road, looking down toward the lake. He was surprised how quickly early May had bloomed, the soft green of budding trees in the distance framed by a cloud lifting off the water. Spring was a favorite time of year, all the new growth sprouting quickly; his other favorite being fall when it all succumbed in a blaze of glory.

From his vantage point, he could see across the whole vineyard, the alignment of the vine trellises stretching clearly before him. He remembered how he'd stood with his grandfather just after planting them ten years ago, row after row of trellis posts standing in formation, each placed perfectly next to its neighbors. No more. In the center of the vineyard, where the freak tornado of last summer had slammed into the hillside, yanking vines burdened with late summer growth upward and sideways, pulling everything askew and apart, there in the center, after much work to right the harm, misalignment still marked the damage. Joey was concerned for his vines.

An old Chevy pickup approached from the south. Its green paint faded by decades of standing in the sun; 'Kober Vineyards' spelled out on each door.

As the truck pulled to a stop, Joey shouted, "Hey, uncle Nic, morning!"

"You're out here pretty early." Nic stepped out, his overalls and worn boots making him look more like a farmer than a respected vintner. His face weathered by decades of working outside.

"Just checkin' the bud growth. Guess I'm screwed on a lot of these vines. Maybe too many!"

"Ah, Joey, on some, but I'm sure you'll be surprised at how many survive. Nature is pretty resilient, a lot'll come back. Just look at the vines, greening up pretty good I'd say. You're actually pretty lucky."

"Thanks to you. Without you and your crew helping set things straight last summer, this vineyard would be lost."

"Well, it was part of the old man's legacy after he retired. I didn't want to see it go."

"Nor do we. Jackie and I've been talking about your offer to guide us through the growing season. We want to learn."

"No more shortcuts?"

"I can't do it. Harry was the chemist. He was sure he could find a breakthrough to save a couple of years in fermentation. So we took advantage of the lab grandfather left me and experimented. But, now, with the tornado burning the lab to the ground, and Harry gone, I'm lost. Don't understand Harry's formulas; the chemistry. Don't know where to start."

"Well, you know, I'm old school. Only one way to make wine … the hard way. And you've already learned a lot working with me this past winter. Now we can get on with the growing. You know, that's why your grandfather left you this vineyard. He saw a lot of promise in you. I'm glad to hear you want to follow through."

"Yeah, without tornados."

"That was a first, hopefully a last. You need a break … you've had enough excitement to last you years."

"We expect some more when Jackie's grand-mere comes back from France."

"Oh, that's just family stuff … always happens. Anyhow, where is Jackie?"

"Sleepin' in I guess. I expect her later."

"Well, you know Joey, gettin' out in this early chill, the ground wet and muddy; not the most appealing thing for a young woman to do. You're lucky to have her. Most women wouldn't be as interested as she is. I never found one."

"Oh, I know. She's really into the new section where she's training the vines to the trellises."

"She's good at that. Learned well in France."

"Her grand-mere's vintner taught her."

"He did a good job. Let's check on some buds, assess the damage and see what we can expect this year. Jackie can catch up later."

          ℰℴ   ℭℬ

At the bottom of the hill, Will looked out the front window of the Carriage House toward the lake. The fog was lifting and bright sunshine tempted him to go for his first canoe paddle of the year. But, it being May, he dared not chance a rollover. He'd tipped once in spring, years before, in chest deep cold water, and was astounded by the rapid cramping of his muscles, how hard it was ... the struggle to walk to shore. Now, in his 70th year, a rollover in the frigid water could easily be fatal.

Instead he substituted a walk, taking Prince, a mixed-breed Shepherd with him. They both relished a brisk pace along the shoulder of the road.

When they returned, Emma was in the kitchen. "Cold outside? It feels chilly."

"Beautiful day, but only in the 40s."

"Good day for a waffle?"

"Sure. Is Jackie up yet?"

"I don't know. I don't think Joey picked her up. She may still be sleeping. They sure are spending a lot of time up in that vineyard."

"And they'll be spending more. Joey told me while he's working on the older vines, Jackie's taken on the young vineyard further up the hill ... pruning and training the vines to the trellis wires ... whatever 'training' means."

After feeding Prince, Will returned to the front room to again scan the lake. He leaned forward and craned his neck looking northward across the lawn of the stately home next door, affectionately called the 'Manor'. The yard was large enough to anchor the 120-year-old classic revival white brick building. Floor-to-ceiling windows, forest green shutters, and French doors opening to a lake-facing veranda on each of its two floors hinted gilded age elegance. Will and Emma's home had originally been the carriage barn of the small estate ... hence its refurbished name, the Carriage House.

Will was surprised to see Seth, his next door neighbor's six-year-old, standing on the shore on an outcropping of shale. *That's odd. Shouldn't he be off to school? And he's in his pajamas. Even with the sun out, it's too cold for that!*

Will walked through the kitchen to grab his jacket and hat off their peg. "Seth's standing out by the shore with no coat on. Just hold my waffle until I see if everything is okay?"

"It's already in the iron. Maybe Vicki's just late in getting him to school this morning."

"In his pajamas?"

"He's out in his pajamas? I'll throw some clothes on and join you."

Prince ran across the driveway and lawn to Seth, but Seth pulled away from his playful tail-wagging nudge. And he didn't acknowledge Will's approach. He just threw a piece of shale in the lake. Even from the side, Will could see he'd been crying. Bending down next to Seth, putting a hand on his shoulder, Will asked, "Is everything alright?"

Continuing to look straight ahead, across the lake, Seth picked up another piece of shale and threw it. He made no answer.

Will tried again, "Seth, why are you out here?"

"Throwin' rocks."

"Oh, but aren't you cold?"

"Nope."

"Okay. So if you want to throw rocks, why not skip 'em like I showed you?"

"Forgot."

Will picked up a piece of shale and held it between his thumb and forefinger. "Here, remember, hold it like this and then throw it flat across the water." Seth took the shale, held it as he'd been taught and threw it, but the angle was downward and it dove into a shallow wave. Will picked up another piece. "Here, Seth, watch." He threw the shale, putting on a backspin; it hopped several times across the water before sinking from view.

Seth frowned, "Easy for you."

Will held out another piece of shale. "Try again."

Seth took it, held it properly and moving his arm in a circular arc like Will had, let it fly, even got some backspin on it. The shale scampered across the water.

"Nice shot." Will looked at Seth, "So, Seth, now tell me, what's going on?"

"Mommy doesn't want me."

"Why do you say that?"

"She yelled at me."

"Yelled. What?"

"'Get out!' And a glass broke."

"A glass broke?"

"Yep."

"Where is she now?"

"Sleeping."

"Seth, can you tell me what happened?"

"After my cartoons I went upstairs. Maria and me ... get ready for school. But mommy's asleep. I touched her arm ... she screamed at me."

"Oh ... well ... how about we go and see what's what? It's too cold for you to stay outside without some clothes on."

"Okay. If you come with me."

Emma was coming out of the Carriage House and shouted to Will and Seth as they approached the Manor door. "Is everything okay?"

"Not really. Sounds like Vicki's angry with Seth. Seems she's not up yet."

"Let me go in and talk with her." Turning to Seth, Emma smiled and said, "Hey, I just made a waffle. Do you want to eat it while it's warm?"

Seth smiled, "Yup!"

Will asked, "You want to take this on yourself?"

13

"Probably better woman-to-woman."

"Well, check on Maria, I'm not sure where she is."

Emma walked up the brick steps of the Manor portico, the grand side entrance facing the driveway framed by two columns. The door was slightly ajar. She stepped inside and hearing the TV walked across the Great Room to the small family room. Four-year-old Maria was curled up on the sofa, thumb in mouth, eyes fixed on the TV screen.

Almost in a whisper Emma said, "Hi Maria."

Maria lost in the cartoon images didn't respond.

Emma went to the base of the stairwell and called, "Vicki?" Hearing no response, she walked up. The door to the master bedroom was closed. Emma knocked softly and opened it just enough to look in. She saw Vicki in bed, curled under a blanket in a fetal position. She also saw shards of glass lying on the floor. Walking to the bed, careful not to step on any glass, she whispered "Vicki?"

Waking, Vicki straightened out to lie on her back, blinking her eyes. "Oh, Emma. What are you doing here?"

"Well, Seth was outside down by the lake in his pajamas. It's too chilly for that so I was afraid something was wrong."

"Oh." Vicki continued in a stronger voice, "Yes, there is something wrong. I'm a terrible mother! And now, not only my husband, but now, my son hates me."

"What happened?"

Vicki sat up as she said, "Oh, Martin, he's up and all energy and drive before 6:00 and I know he expects me to get going. But I'm so tired. He tells me to 'buck up', 'get a grip'. Then Seth comes in later while I'm asleep and he just stands by the bed. He does that when he wants me to get up, just stands and stares without moving a muscle, like I'm some kind of Exhibit A. He startled me and I yelled at him, told him to get the hell out ... even threw the glass."

"At him?"

"No, no. Just in his direction ... to make a point." Vicki put her head in her hands, moving it from side to side. "I don't know, Emma. I just don't have any energy. Nothing to 'buck up' with. Martin can't accept that. Doesn't even listen." She looked up. "They're having a problem with that new press he bought, so he's at the damned printing plant most of the time. When Norman was running the place he used to rein Martin in. But, Norman, he's off in France with that relative of yours. Now it's like do or die."

"Chloe's no relation of mine." Emma's response was stern. "She may be Jackie's other grandmother, but she kept her from me for 15 years ... 15 years!"

Vicki stared straight ahead as if talking to herself. "I just don't see what Norman sees in that bitch. Talk about being smitten!"

After a moment, Emma leaned over and extended a hand placing it over Vicki's. She softened her voice, "But Vicki, what about the kids? I know, I know. Caring for children and a husband can be hard ... seems to be never ending. But the kids will grow and your husband, well, maybe Martin will mellow a bit. You're in the midst of those hard days we women sometimes just have to ride out."

Vicki kept her eyes down saying, "Even this 'Manor on the Lake' ... might as well be in prison." Vicki looked into Emma's eyes, "Damn it Emma, it's black, getting blacker, and nobody pays any attention to me, how I feel, what I want to do."

"What do you want to do?"

"I don't know. Haven't the slightest idea. I just don't want to keep doing this!"

Emma lightly squeezed Vicki's hand and drew a silent deep breath. "Well, Vicki, are you getting any help?"

"Yeah, the cleaning lady comes once a week."

"No, no. I mean professionally ... like counseling."

"Oh, I've tried that. I talk and cry. Martin who always has something to say sits there, stoic, like a goddamned indian. He's a judgmental male chauvinist, that's what he is. And then I'm supposed to take some antidepressant ... drives me crazy because I can't think straight.

"I'm awake now and I'll get up, get breakfast for the kids. I guess it's too late for school, so they'll get a day off."

"I can help with Maria and breakfast, and I'm sure Will is willing to drive them to school. Then you should get outside. It's turned into a beautiful day with the fog burnt off. Get some sunshine, take a walk. I'll go with you if you like."

"I'll put some clothes on and come downstairs. But first, just give me a couple of minutes. Can you hand me that pack of cigarettes over on the table by the chair?"

"Only if you promise not to smoke in bed."

"That's why I keep them on the table."

Emma raised her eyebrows, "Then, I guess, you'll have to get them yourself."

When Emma came back into the Carriage House, Will and Seth were sitting at the kitchen table, plates with the remnants of waffles and maple syrup pushed aside. They were contemplating the back and forth mechanism of the perpetual motion clock Will had gotten down from the fireplace mantel.

Will looked up, "You okay?"

"Yes, fine. Seth, you need to go home and get dressed for school. It's still early. Will can drive you and Maria to school."

Seth, leaned back in a stretch showing discomfort. "Do I have to?"

"Yep. Now get a move on."

As soon as the door closed behind Seth, Emma said, "Not good, Will! Vicki's depressed, really depressed, and I don't think Martin's being any help. Apparently problems at work."

"Yeah, I saw him the other day and he indicated Norman will be back from the Mediterranean soon. As he put it, 'He won't be happy.'"

Emma said, "I saw it in his face when he pulled in the other night. It was after dinner. Looked like he was ready to kill somebody."

"So what do we do?"

"I don't know. Let's go back over and get these kids off to school."

Jackie woke up a few minutes after her grandparents left the Carriage House. She sat up on the edge of the bed and quickly dashed into the small bathroom. Her second time that morning.

Chapter 2

In Rochester, Martin sat at his desk catching up on emails. He'd come in early but was held up when he walked through the pressroom by a production problem unresolved by last night's second shift ... a common occurrence lately. Since the installation of the new digital press, nothing was going as smoothly as planned. His father had often told him, 'You make a plan, then life happens.'

With Norman returning from France in the next few weeks, Martin was trying to get as much accomplished as possible; hoping to stave off Norman's anger over lack of progress coupled with tepid First Quarter financials. He knew Norman would not be happy.

Fran, Martin's secretary, walked past his door, stopped and came in. Martin looked up as she said, "Oh, you're here."

"Yeah, been here for a couple of hours ... well, down in the plant."

"So you heard." Fran said, sitting down on the edge of a chair.

"Heard what?"

"Norman's back."

"What? No, not 'til the end of the month."

"I just saw Denise and she told me she saw him at the airport last night"

"What? When?"

"Around Midnight. Says she was picking up her brother."

Martin sat back, glancing at the ceiling. He exhaled, saying, "Yeah, her brother..."

Fran sat down on the edge of a chair. "So you think?"

"Think what?"

"Oh, come on boss. We all know what was going on last summer. Denise damned near killed Norman ... she's too young for him. It was a blessing when he took up with that French woman, the way she got him the hell out of town."

"Yeah, I guess. A mixed blessing. I just hope she doesn't kill him in other ways."

"What's her name again?"

"Chloe. French name. And all that comes with it. Well, if you hear Norman's on his way in, give me a heads up will you."

"Always do. You'll know as soon as I do."

"Know what?" Norman said as he walked into the office.

Startled, Fran and Martin stood. Martin said, "Norman, we didn't expect to see you for a couple of weeks. How was France?"

"I enjoyed it." He smiled, turning to Fran, "Would you believe I actually got bored with the Mediterranean ... all that sun."

Turning back to Martin, "After we returned to the chateau, those French bureaucrats held up Chloe's property deal for months. I'd hoped to be back in January, but selling a vineyard over there is like transferring a national treasure ... she's still there waiting for the final papers to sign.

"But I'm back ... and concerned. My attorney just returned my call and he can squeeze me in, so I need to get over there. I'll come back in a couple hours so you can show me the new press, then let's catch lunch."

"Yes. Sure. Whatever works for you."

Again turning to Fran, "As always, Fran, good to see you." Norman turned on his heal and was gone.

Fran and Martin stood, looking at each other.

"Are we in trouble?"

"Well, he sure changes our plans. Before he gets back, make sure the production log is current and give me a copy of the financials we emailed him."

"Be glad to. Anything else?"

"No, that'll be enough."

"And your meetings this morning?"

"Let's have the Sales meeting as planned; we'll be done in time. But production control, move them to mid-afternoon, I don't want Norman sitting in."

Fran began to walk out of the office and turned back toward Martin. "And, boss, Denise wasn't picking up any brother. She was picking up Norman."

"Now, don't speculate."

"Oh, that's no assumption. She's hangin' all over him this morning."

"How can you say that?"

"His eyes, his step, his body language. He leans over and speaks to me. Besides, I'm a woman, we need to read you men … to survive."

ℂ   ℓ

The morning sun warmed Joey and Nic. They were in the center of the vineyard, the area where most of the tornado damage had occurred, crouching low to inspect the root of a vine. Joey hoed the soil Nic had hilled up against it last fall, exposing American rootstock in the ground spliced to a European vine … the vinifera technique essential to producing quality dry wines. Nic ran his finger over the splice. "See, Joey, this one was strained pretty hard." He looked up at the vine, "But the buds are alive. And they don't look too bad. It'll be interesting to see how many survive the summer heat; be viable enough to produce."

Nic and Joey checked several more splices. Many with the same 'wait and see' conclusion. As they moved along Nic stopped to inspect buds, most about a quarter inch long. When the surface was a fuzzy gray, he frowned. Other buds had popped tiny green tendrils reaching toward the sun. He smiled, "These look good. Let's hope for a few more days of this warmth."

"And no frost." Joey said.

Standing up, Nic said, "The vines they forgive. Amazing. We abuse them and still they come back. Like all the land, just give it a chance. Kind of like Jesus, just give Him a chance…"

"You keep telling me that."

"Yeah, I have to … you young people need to listen."

They walked toward a corner of the vineyard, untouched by the storm. After inspecting root splices and buds in that area, Nic asked, "Is Norman still going to invest, that was the plan wasn't it?'

"As far I know. I talked with him a few weeks ago and he asked how I was doing. But the call was on Skype with Jackie and Chloe part of the conversation, so we didn't get into any detail. Said he'd be in touch as soon as he got back. I expect he and Chloe to come home in a week or so."

Nic ran his hand over his head, through the little hair he had left. "I hope he follows through. For now, I need to get the plow down here and get this hilling off the roots. Otherwise the vinifera vines'll think they should grow their own. Don't want any pylloxera."

"But, will Uncle Tom be okay with you using the Kober Vineyards tractor again?"

Nic looked down, hands on hips and chuckled, turning his head side-to-side. "I'll handle Tom. Being my older brother he thinks he can order me around. He comes nosin' around, tell him to talk to me. He'll try to intimidate you, but I'm off limits – not if he wants those award winning vintages.

"You know, "Nic looked back at Joey, "he's a tough businessman … stubborn as the old man was. But he don't know jack shit when it comes to making wine. I inherited the feel of it, the 'nose', from your grandfather. All those harvests working beside him; he was demanding you know."

"Oh, I know, just the short time I had with him."

"But it sticks doesn't it. He handed his talent down to me. Can't tell you why I select any particular day to pick, what I taste and smell. Oh, I take all the measurements, the BRIX and all, but mostly I just know when the time has come and what needs doin'. Don't tell Tom that though; he knows everything."

Joey smiled, "Hey, uncle Nic, just keep doin' it…"

21

"Oh, I intend to. And when your crop is picked we'll take it over to Kober's and press it. Tom'll just have to live with that. If there's enough for your own vintage, come up with a label and I'll place it in the Kober Tasting Room."

"That'll really help. Take some of the pressure off."

"Has to be vintage wine though. Always remember, when a connoisseur swirls, sniffs and sips, the wine better speak to him. That's reality. Don't matter what else went on, whether I picked on the right day and called the right shots through the crush and fermentation. The wine-lover, glass in hand, our wine better be sensuous to him … have character and mystery. The French call proper aging *elevage.* I call it 'soul'." Nic looked up at the sky. "That's what counts … sensuous … soul."

Nic smiled and put his hand on Joey's shoulder. "We'd better get back to work so we have some grapes to press this fall."

Chapter 3

Late morning Martin and Norman spent over an hour touring the printing plant. Long-term employees greeted their old boss with respect, expressing hope he was enjoying his recent retirement. Technicians explained the speed and flexibility of the new digital press. Norman asked a lot of questions - as if he'd taken a course on the new technology. Satisfied he'd learned enough, he stepped back taking in the full length of the machine, "It's a damned sight larger than I envisioned it."

"Yeah, even I was surprised." Martin said, "You've got to come when we're running at speed. It's a thrill seeing finished work coming out at well over a thousand pages a minute."

"I want to see that."

Martin looked at his watch, "It's 12:30. What say we walk over to Flaherty's and grab some lunch?"

They sat in a tall booth in the Irish-American pub, offering a menu from substantial burgers to excellent corned beef and cabbage. The large room was anchored by a bar along one wall. Booths along the other three walls provided a degree of privacy due to their high sides and the fact that hardwood floors and a high tin ceiling provided no sound absorption, making the chatter in the pub create a curtain of noise. Each man cupped a small glass of single-malt scotch in his hand.

"So, you're getting the quality and sometimes the speed, but you still have to stop and restart too frequently?"

"In a nutshell … software, that's the problem. Once we can keep it running, we'll get the throughput we need."

"But, damn it Martin, you're losing too much ground. I couldn't stay any longer in France knowing you're in trouble."

Martin asked, "Well, yes, trouble with the press, but beyond that what trouble?"

Norman took a sip of scotch. "Your last quarter financials. The delay in getting the new press up to speed is costing us dearly. I don't want to see you run out of headway before we get this thing off the ground."

"I agree, Norman, we hit some speed bumps ... particularly with the new press, but I don't understand your alarm."

"Listen, I worked my ass off for forty years and now I need to cash out over the coming three, as we agreed. I need the money for the vineyard."

"I'm not even thinking of delaying your payments."

"Well, you may not be, but we've got finite resources. If you keep going the way you have since I left, it won't be long before thinking won't help. There just won't be enough cash to handle everything."

Martin leaned closer to Norman, setting his tumbler of single-malt, untouched, on the table. "Listen, I'll get this thing back on track. The software upgrade is being installed on the press next week, so we'll be able to finally get in full production. We've got work lined up for it. My problem has been that we sold production counting on it, then ran into the software glitch. We oversold our capacity, and at low prices. Without the digital press running properly, we had to keep using our old presses. Cost me dearly in overtime; even had to farm some work out to satisfy customer deadlines ... all on a *Rush* basis. But we're getting there...

Norman looked Martin in the eye, "You better get there!" He glanced away repeating almost to himself, "Yep. You'd better get there."

Martin held his gaze toward Norman, "You'll be amazed at the throughput when we do."

"So," Norman said, looking back at Martin, "what can I do?"

"The sales guys, in addition to bringing in work for the new press, they're running into new specialty jobs, shorter runs. Looks like new opportunity for us ... an indication of how the business is changing."

"On the old presses?"

"For now. But if we grasp it, we'll have to think of some new pre-press gear and presses better suited to the specialty papers. I'm looking into it."

"Jeez, Martin, we don't even have the new press under control and you're taking a stab at something else?"

"Don't worry, I won't make any commitment until you approve a plan with some solid numbers."

"Damned straight! We need to be careful so we don't run this company into the ground. Just know, now that I'm back, I'm willing to help."

"Give me this month. Once we get the press fully on-line things will be changing and then you may be able to help."

"I'm just concerned that even with you working harder, there won't be enough hours in the day to cover everything. Hell, you must be working 80 hours a week now?"

"Yeah, I guess … that's about right."

"Just let me know. Whatever I can do."

Norman leaned back, took a sip of scotch, and changed the subject, "So how are Vicki and the kids?"

"Fine, fine. They're fine. Thanks for asking."

"Vicki's hangin' in there okay?"

"Oh, yeah. She's okay. I mean, Vicki's Vicki, you know. She's fine. Come over for dinner some evening and see for yourself."

"Your dock in yet?"

"Hoping for this weekend."

"I'll tell the marina to get the Chris-Craft in the water, let the wood swell a few days … then run it to my place. So, I'll come across the lake in a week or so, when it warms up a bit."

"Okay. Just give me a call." Martin took his first sip of his scotch. "But I've gotta ask, how did you like France?"

Norman looked askance. "France is a mixed bag. Those goddamned French vintners in the Medoc can be a pain in the ass. But the Riviera is nice … if you're filthy rich. Luckily Chloe knows her way around or I'd never have been able to afford it."

Norman sat back, looking toward the ceiling ... thinking. "But the French ... ugh!" He looked back at Martin, "That François Chloe was always talking about, what a piece of work he is. Wears that Bordeaux Classification on his sleeve."

Martin looked perplexed.

"Oh, ah..." Norman continued, "You know, back in the 1850s, the French classified wines of certain vineyards as being the best."

"Oh, yeah, First Growth, Second Growth..."

"That's it. Francois kept saying, 'since 1855, since 1855', like running a Bordeaux Classification château that's over 150 years old means he can do no wrong. Lords it over everybody.

"So after a couple of days at Chloe's château ... nice, but needs a lot of work ... we start meeting François at his office. Palatial is the word; dripping in French tradition. He and a couple of associates, they sit there acting gracious as all get out, smoking up a storm and sipping their Bordeaux. After making sure I understood that they still appreciate the United States liberating France in World War II, they talked on and on about the vines. How they nurture them ... marrying them to the soil to mingle light and air and energy. To them it's a..." Norman raised his hands and eyes toward heaven, 'Divine Collaboration'. They consider the grapes their newborns; *les enfants* they call them. It's all about the centuries they've been making world-class wines. Yet, they're unwilling to share anything useful.

"And French manners. Hell, one guy even flirted with Chloe ... right in front of me. Get the picture?"

"Sounds like a bad dream."

"Chloe's husband, Maurice, had an appraisal done years ago and it was way high. The problem was Chloe thinks her vineyards are worth that ... like they're already part of the Bordeaux Classification. Francois, he's a shrewd businessman ... he starts low realizing he'll probably have to invest some to bring things up to his standards. He comes across like he's doing Chloe a favor taking on her vineyard. When he doesn't agree with something he shrugs his shoulders and sucks air in between his teeth, then looks you in the eye puffing his cheeks before he blows it out. Aggravating as hell after a while.

"He knows damned well he can add wine made from her grapes to his classification as soon as he buys the vineyard. Labeled as Classification wine it will sell at many times above what Chloe could ever get. So that's where it started. Big gap. And the last person those Frenchmen wanted to hear from was some damned American who shows up in an obvious relationship with Chloe. They think I'm taking advantage of Chloe ... like I'm after her money! What money? There ain't none."

"I thought she was loaded?"

"Maybe years ago. But all she has left is the vineyard. I couldn't get Francois to budge. Still he offered her what I guess he considers a fair deal, probably out of respect for her husband's family. I mean over 100 years of being a neighbor is a long time. But Chloe wasn't happy. She kept looking to me to get some leverage. Couldn't latch on to any ... pissed her off. Then we had to wait for some documents to clear the bureaucrats, so as soon as Jackie left I got Chloe out of town ... south to the Med. At least that got her back to being tolerable. But more delays after we got back."

"So, all these delays kept you there." Martin smiled, "I thought you were just having too much fun."

"Yeah, some fun! The French ... they pass the papers from one bureaucracy to the next until the owner has trouble figuring out where anything stands. You know Chloe's late husband was some kind of minister in the French government, so she's not used to being brushed off like that."

Norman polished off his scotch and signaled the waitress to get another. "Want one?" Martin put his hand over his glass.

"Let me tell you ... am I boring you?"

"No, no ... Please..."

"Well, Martin, as I always say there are a lot of assholes out there. This guy, François, he's pure grade."

"So Chloe sold out to him?"

"She's selling ... everything except the house. Some papers are still held up, so she can't sign yet."

Norman paused again, took a sip of scotch from the new glass placed in front of him. "I'm sorry. I guess I've got stuff bottled up for months. When we first got there François was all graciousness and concern, stroking Chloe's feathers, building her up - like she's been gone forever - talking about his concern when she left so quickly to come here and see Jackie. Pure bullshit and she didn't see through it.

"He's probably about the age of Jackie's parents. I read it as a mother-son relationship between Chloe and François ... nothing sexual. In fact, I doubt there's been anything sexual between Francois and Jackie..."

Norman leaned closer to Martin, speaking softly, "...a little light in the loafers, if you know what I mean." Norman sat back. "But he is smooth. I distinctly remember sitting there thinking, 'son of a bitch, how did I ever get into this'. Let me tell you... It *is* fucking stressful!"

"Jeez boss, sounds like running a printing business is a piece a cake. Not to change the subject but should we order something?"

"Yeah, corn beef on rye for me. I need to get away from all that French cuisine."

After the waitress took their order, Martin sat up straight. "Can I ask, will Chloe be coming back?"

"What kind of question is that? Of course she'll return. After all her granddaughter is here ... and, oh, Jackie's visit to her grandmother over Christmas at the chateau, that became a fun time. Chloe urging she stay in France, and Jackie insisting on coming back here. You know, Chloe is a very interesting woman ... just don't get her mad."

"I see Jackie and Joey together a lot."

"That's the problem. Even though Jackie and Joey kept in touch by Skype every few days, Chloe doesn't accept him as a good match. Considers Joey beneath her granddaughter."

"What? He's part of our local wine dynasty."

"Maybe so. But to Chloe, he's the bastard heir, with dirt under his finger nails … low class."

"Well, let me know when she's coming so we all can brace ourselves."

Norman smiled, taking his last sip of scotch. "Hey, watch it! She's my woman."

"I hear ya." Martin took the opportunity to pull his leather portfolio from the bench to the table and flipped it open. "Getting back to business, let me show you some production numbers. I think you'll be impressed with what we've been able to get through the plant."

Norman listened while Martin described the Herculean effort all had made to cope with the delayed startup of the new press. He let Martin finish, then leaned forward and said, "You and the crew have done a great job. I'll give you that. But you're spending too much ... you've taken your eye off the crucial factor."

"What's that?"

"Profit, Martin, profit! You can bust your butt 'til the cows come home but if you can't make it on the bottom line, it don't count for shit. Get those profit margins back Martin. That's all that counts!"

꽁   ಆ

Joey was replacing rotted floor boards on the deck of a customer's cottage when his cell phone rang. The screen displayed NORMAN.

Joey answered tentatively, "Hello, Norman?"

"Joey. How are you?"

"Norman. Surprised to hear from you. Fine. I'm fine."

"How about having an early dinner with me? We can meet at the diner in town, near the marina. That's right on my way home."

"Um. Yeah. Sure. You're back?"

"Got in last night. Printing problems. I couldn't stay away any longer. Chloe's still there ... in France. I won't tie you up very long ... startin' to feel jet lag and time change. So, can we meet, let's say at 5?"

"Sure. I'll be there."

As soon as he hung up, Joey called Jackie, "Norman's back."

"No. Grand-mere Chloe said they weren't coming back for a couple of weeks at the earliest."

"Well, he's back. Says your grandmother is still in France."

"Did he say why?"

"I think he came back due to problems at the printing company. But he wants to talk with me ... over dinner. Want to come?"

"No, best you two talk."

"Maybe he's having second thoughts .... or his money's dried up. I hope he isn't gonna back out on helping us."

"Or, he just wants to find out how you're doing."

"Maybe. But I'm not prepared."

"Oh, you are. It is all in your head. Just tell him the progress you're making. What you need."

Norman arrived before Joey and sat, his hand cupping a warm mug of coffee. He regretted having lost the stamina of his younger years when he could tackle the evening with the same energy as the morning. No more.

Joey rushed in, laptop case under his arm. "Sorry if I'm late."

Norman looked up, smiling, "No, you're right on time. Sit. Relax."

A waitress came to the table and took Joey's order for a cup of coffee.

"So ... how's France?"

"France is France. Arrogant, hard to get along with, tough negotiators. But the wine… It *is* good, particularly the reds. Nothing like a few centuries of experience."

"And Chloe?"

"She's good. Probably can use a break from me. Had to stay back for some legality on the sale of her chateau. How about you? Jackie okay?"

"Wonderful. She's getting more comfortable here. Started tutoring a couple of days a week at the community college across the lake ... students taking French. Making a few friends."

Norman smiled, "She ought to be good at that." He looked around, "The only problem with this place is you can't get a drink. The food's good though."

Looking back at Joey, "Okay, so tell me, where are you on your plans."

"The vine buds look good this year. We'll get some harvest from the mature vineyard in spite of the damage from last summer's storm. Amazing how resilient they are. The new vineyard; that's not ready, needs at least a year, maybe two. But, Jackie's being a big help training the new vines to the trellises; helps them mature as fast as nature allows."

"Do you expect any revenue?"

"Some, not much."

"Any progress on the winery?"

"I met with the architect you mentioned in Rochester. He referred me to an independent located in the Finger Lakes; name's Bruce Atkinson. He's worked with wineries, recently built one focused on being energy efficient."

"So he has a track record?"

"Yeah, he's completed several. I met with him a few times and we sketched out a building adequate for winemaking, along with a tasting room. The building is big enough to start; but we're positioning everything so we can add on if we need to."

"You mean, when you need to. So this architect was recommended by my guy?"

Joey nodded.

"Okay, I still want to see a portfolio of Bruce's work."

"No problem, he knows you'll need a presentation."

"Do you have a drawing of the building?"

"A rough one." Joey pulled out his laptop and turned it on. He displayed a colored sketch and turned the computer so Norman could see it.

Norman leaned over, studying the building concept carefully. "Pretty spartan look if you ask me."

"I told Bruce to make it energy efficient, but keep it as inexpensive as possible."

"I appreciate that. But when customers drive up the road the first thing they'll see is the front of the building. That has to be more dramatic than this. Entice them to stop in and check you out."

"Well, the rear part is a metal building, outfitted with everything we need…"

"That's good, but, frankly, I've gotta leave the winemaking to you. Just do it right."

"Okay, you are looking at the front, the Tasting Room. It uses post and beam construction with timbers exposed on both the inside and outside."

That's good, can be very attractive; but we need to invite customers to come inside. What I see here is too flat. Some kind of entry … portico. That's what I'm thinking of."

"Over the entrance. Good idea … but it'll add to the cost."

"What I'm getting at I learned from advertising people as I printed their stuff. They were always talking about "Branding'; creating an impression from the first contact and keeping that consistent. I think we need to think of that, not just in our labeling and advertising, but even in the design of our building. You and Bruce take a crack at it.

"Okay we'll rework the front."

"How about overall dollars? Any budget yet?"

"Yep. As soon as I listed the requirements, we detailed costs."

"So how much?"

Joey gulped. "Including the two buildings, vineyard equipment, lab, crusher, tanks, office … everything for the first year … it totals $755,000.

Norman didn't flinch. He leaned forward, "Do you have a detailed list?"

Joey pulled a spreadsheet out of his case. "This is a summary."

Norman scanned the list. "You fit a lot on here." He looked up at Joey. "Pretty complete. But where did the last $5000 come from?"

Joey looked perplexed.

Norman held up the list. "Your total is $755,000; why not $750,000?"

Joey started to say "Well, I can make a few changes..."

Norman smiled, "Relax! I'm just joshin' ya. It's been a long day. You'll have plenty of time to make changes. But I don't see any contingency."

"Contingency? I'm trying to be realistic with the estimates."

Norman leaned toward Joey, "Yeah, but stuff gets fucked up. Reality is like a headwind … slams into your plan, slows you down, throws you curve-balls. Happens all the time. Add in a contingency line, say eight percent. That'll give you some flexibility when you need it."

Norman sat back, "And smile, will you. You're much too uptight. What say we order?"

After ordering dinner, Norman asked, "Have you developed a timeline?"

Joey opened another screen on his laptop showing a rough schedule including dollars needed at each stage.

"Okay. Looks like you're on the right track," Norman said, "But, where can we meet?"

"What do you mean"

"As we build this winery, where will we meet? You live in town with your mother. My place is on the wrong side of the lake, and I get the impression Jackie's grandparents, Emma and Will, have been gracious in letting you use their kitchen table, but that's only because of Jackie. Let's get a trailer up on our building site, get some power to it so we can meet and lay things out right."

"So we can get going?"

"Damn right! Talked to my attorney and accountant today. Just give me your estimate of cash flow. I need some time to move things around. Don't worry, I'll have the funds when you need them. You concentrate on getting that vineyard in shape and starting on the building.

Chapter 4

Jackie had dinner with Emma and Will. As soon as the meal was finished and the kitchen straightened up, Emma said, "Jackie, we're going next door. Vicki wasn't her best this morning and we want to see if there's anything we can do. I'm worried about the children. We'll be a while."

"Oh, let me know if I can help. I expect Joey. *Ici* ... here, we will be here."

Jackie went into the great room and sat in what now was her favorite spot ... in front of the hearth. The setting sun washed the walls in soft warm light. Prince, sensing an opportunity to be petted, lay down beside her. Placing his head on her thigh he gazed up into Jackie's eyes. She petted him with gentle strokes across his coat.

Her thoughts went back to that afternoon in early February, so different from today, when she and Joey had come back to the empty Carriage House for relief from the harsh cutting wind blowing across the vineyard. Emma and Will were away on their winter month-long trip to Florida. Joey set a warming fire in the hearth while Jackie, still shivering from the vineyard chill, made strong coffee.

Joey held Jackie close for a few minutes trying to warm her. When the coffee was ready they sat on the floor, side-by-side, close to the flames, their hands tight around the mugs of hot liquid. They talked of the progress made on the pruning, with plenty left to do.

After a lull in the conversation, Jackie said, "I called grand-mere Chloe this morning. She spoke to me in a civil tone, but I can tell she is still mad at me. She makes me so angry."

Joey set his mug aside and looked directly at Jackie. "You know she's not gonna change. So, let it go. When I was growing up, my grandfather and the Kober family all but shunned my mother. She set her anger aside and got on with our lives. Taught me anger saps our energy and creativity. Limits what we can accomplish. Just let it go and focus on what you want to do."

Instead of dying down with the afternoon twilight, the wind picked up, swirling snow past the windows. Jackie stood and looked outside. She couldn't see anything, confirming a white-out. "*D'accord.*" she said, "Best to let the anger blow away like the snow with the wind." Turning toward Joey, Jackie said, "Stay and have something to eat. I do not want you driving in this."

Joey sighed, "Yeah, I guess. Better I stay here than end up sitting in a ditch."

"I can make an omelet."

"Okay, or I can whip something up."

"Joey, you cook more than I do when we're together. And, you're good. But I am French; we French need to cook."

"But all your great chefs are male."

"*Oui.* Males ... demanding to have control."

"You make a good omelet?"

Jackie smiled, "Joey, you know so little about what I can do. And just like the vines, I will surprise you."

Before leaving for Florida, Emma made sure the cupboards and freezer were well stocked. Finding feta cheese, spinach and olives, Jackie made a simple omelet, more Greek than French.

Tasting his first mouthful, Joey said, "This is really good." After a few more bites, he asked, "So, you don't mind doing all the work up in the new vineyard?"

"*Non*, only the cold and wind when I am pruning. With spring, it will be better. I need to get those vines trained to the trellises."

"That's crucial to the first harvest."

"New vines are like children. If you want them to succeed, you need to work with them, guide them, show them the way. They will learn."

"They will ... you're a good teacher."

"*Voila! C'est moi* ... I guess ... on better days."

After dinner, Joey prodded the fire back to life. The flames dancing soft light around the darkened room and radiating heat from the hearth, drawing them back to the spot they'd found so comfortable before. This time Jackie dragged Emma's afghan along with her. Joey put his arm around Jackie, giving her a gentle hug. Jackie turned it into a caress.

A few minutes later they looked at each other, smiles on their faces, and Joey leaned over and lightly kissed Jackie. She responded, but with a fervor that surprised them both. Normally they would have backed away at this point ... talked and cooled things down a bit. But that night touch replaced speech, gentle at first, each stroke erasing months of restraint. The barriers of winter garments were slowly removed, satisfying long-felt cravings ... until raw physical passion led each to grasp for the other. The conviction behind Joey's strength carried Jackie to a place she'd never been, to a feeling of security she hadn't felt since childhood.

Joey kneeled up over her, taking in the full view of her body in the firelight. Smiling, he whispered, "You are so beautiful." When he eased himself down and into her. It took the little breath she had away. She felt one with Joey, beyond the moment, confident in a future when nothing would come between them ... ever. Her joy exploded into a stifled scream at the very moment Joey stiffened giving his all to her; he managing only to utter, "Jac..!"

She was thankful Joey held still, hugging tight.

The memory of 'Man-and-woman-become-one' taught by the nuns in the boarding school came to Jackie. But that was in marriage to have kids; the nuns never said anything about the pure ecstasy she was feeling, followed by a peacefulness totally new to her.

Joey eased off her, "What?"

"Oh, nothing." She pulled him to her in a kiss.

They lay back, side-by-side, catching their breath.

Joey gently brushed his fingers across her forehead, moving errant strands of hair back in place, then softly caressed her neck. Easing his body against her, he cupped her breast ... a tender gesture of sexual closure ... and confirming a bond into their future.

Jackie had never so trusted another since her parents died. And all the stressful conflict she'd been living with in recent months: coming to the United States, going back to France, being drawn to return to Joey, having to ignore Chloe's demands she not return; the tension inside her just fell away. She turned to Joey who seemed so quiet, then realized he was near dozing off. How could he do that? But she didn't care, she was at peace.

Prince raised his ears and stood at attention, ending Jackie's memory of that February evening. Now, in May, Jackie realized she had to deal with stark reality. And Prince, tail wagging, stepped quickly toward the door he knew Joey was about to walk through.

Joey greeted Prince by taking the dog's head in both hands, then patting his flank. He stepped to Jackie and gave her a hug before taking off his coat, barely giving her a chance to ask, "So how did things go?"

"Great, Norman wants to go ahead. I just have to give him a calendar of when we'll need money so he has time to, as he says, 'move things around'. But he's anxious to make progress.

"Think of it Jackie, we can get the building under construction, we can take this year's harvest and make our own wine. Uncle Nic will help me with that, let us use the Kober press and winery. Seems like we'll be off and running. And that concern you've had with not having a job ... well, now we'll be plenty busy establishing the new winery ... the permits and approvals, the naming and labeling, maybe even some advertising. I've been making a list and it just keeps getting longer and longer."

With Joey's enthusiasm unchecked, Jackie saw the single-mindedness of the vintner surfacing ... the focus on the vines and winemaking she'd experienced for so many years in France. She tried to interject, softly saying, "Joey, I..."

Joey didn't pick up on it. "Yeah, Norman is really happy with the sketch of the building I showed him; just wants us to work on a more appealing facade. And he didn't even flinch at the cost. Are Will and Emma here?

"They went next door. Some problem with child care."

"Anything serious?"

"Vicki had one of her bad days."

"Oh ... well. Anyhow, we can have a good year, at a big loss; but at least get some wine in production. Then next year, then we'll have our own operation, and the Tasting Room ... what a view that'll have ... we'll get some customers tasting our wine. And, thanks to your work, the new vines, the following year."

Joey hugged Jackie again. "We're gonna be busy. You're still with me, right?"

Jackie took a step back. "Well, *oui*, you know that. But, Joey, listen!"

"Good, because the Tasting Room ... you know that's your domain..."

Jackie almost shouted. "Joey, *ecoutez-moi!* ... listen to me!"

Startled, Joey stopped and really looked at Jackie for the first time.

Leaning toward him, holding his gaze, Jackie said softly, "Joey, I am pregnant."

"What?"

Jackie repeated, forcefully, "Pregnant Joey, *pregnant!*"

He'd heard but failed to comprehend; couldn't fit Jackie's, 'I'm pregnant!' into the rush of ideas he'd just been sharing. He stepped back as if taking a mental breath, then leaned forward and smiled, reaching his hands toward Jackie's. "You're, you're pregnant? Are you sure?"

"The doctor is. *Novembre*. He told me November."

He drew her close, slowly saying, "Oh, my God. But, but how? We've been so careful."

"Think cold night, snowy blizzard, warm firelight ... same way it has happened for eons. We fell off our ledge, out of control."

Joey gently kissed her on the cheek.

"Joey, I am pregnant, not fragile." She kissed him on the lips ... hard.

"So, so that's why you've been sleeping in."

"No, not asleep ... *c'est* morning sickness."

Joey began to laugh.

"It is not funny Joey."

Joey pulled back to face Jackie. "No, no. I'm laughing because driving here I was figuring it all out. With Norman's support we'd get the winery established this year, then after the building's completed, in the idle season, we'd get married. I was trying to figure out how to get you out of here so we could live together."

"You mean live together, then get married a year from now?"

"Well, no, actually, the marriage would be, like, two years from now, just after the harvest and all."

"*Deux ans...*"

"Yeah, we can get the winery finished this season, what with permits and all. So, it'll be next year. We'll get married, what? Eighteen months from now."

"Oh, a year and a half. Glad to see I am so high on your list of priorities."

"No, no ... now don't be getting French on me."

"French, what does that mean? Unreasonable? Stubborn? You just said, once we get all the important winery list completed, you will make some time, in the idle period, to marry me. It makes me so happy ... *Voila!* ... I rate at the bottom of your list."

But Joey was not to be deterred. He raised his arms as he said, "And, now ... Jackie, as you say ... Voila! ... you are at the top of the list. Norman mentioned ... how did he put it? Oh, 'the headwind of reality disrupts our carefully made plans' ... something like that.

"Oh," Jackie raised her voice, "Now I am a headwind, a perturbation, ah, disruption?"

Joey raised his hands, palms out, "No, no no! Jackie you and that child of ours, the baby you're carrying, you are the most important. Remember that long timeframe we agreed upon to make sure we'd get to know each other; to be sure you're comfortable staying in the United States, getting Chloe used to the idea. Well, my love, that timetable is null and void." Joey stepped closer, "I don't have a ring in my pocket, but I'll ask you, "Will you marry me?"

"*Pourquoi!* Because I am pregnant? I could go back to France and raise our child myself, you know. I do not want you to marry just because... You were not in a hurry before I told you. Now, *Voila!* ... we are to be married? *Non, non*, I want out of love to be married. Only out of love ... not, uh, uh, necessary."

"Necessity..."

Joey reached out to embrace Jackie, but she stepped back – extending her arms toward him, hands open and upright, in the universal gesture of 'Back Off!' Joey retreated. put his hand to his chin, lowered it and said, "Jackie, I love you." Then louder, "I love you." Almost shouting, "You!"

"But you are already married?"

"What?"

"Yes. To the vines. They absorb you, the vines and the wine. You bring your damaged vineyard back to health like it is your ... your lover. *Oui*, yes, and the new vines ... they are your *les enfants*. Oh, you are so like the Medoc vintners!

"Uh, well ... yes ... I do pay them a lot of attention. But, Jackie, I thought you were with me on this. I mean, now, they need a lot of work, but not always. It's not the vines; it's you working beside me."

"*Oui*, today it is this bringing back vines to be healthy. What will it be next year? The fermentation, the racking and casking, the bottling? And the year after that? The Tasting Room, the bookkeeping? I assure you, it will always be something. Remember, I grew up in a French chateau. Probably, I know better than you."

Joey stood looking into Jackie's eyes, the silence of the pause becoming deafening.

Then he stretched out his arms, almost shouting, pleading "What do you want me to do? I need you! Don't you see? You are the most important person in my life … and I want to spend the rest of mine with you. I love you!"

Jackie crossed her arms over her chest. "Joey, in school the nuns warned us: 'Be careful with men … always stop and think'. They repeated that many times."

"Really? The nuns. You're bringing up the nuns?"

"*Oui*. With you ... with you I did not listen to them."

Jackie threw her arms in the air and spun on her heel. Striding into the front room she shouted, "*Mon Dieu!*"

Prince glanced toward Joey with a quizzical look, as if asking, "What happened?"

Joey pulled out the nearest kitchen chair and sat down … dejected. He reached over, petting Prince softly as if answering, "I don't know, I don't know."

Seeing golden twilight outside, Jackie went to the front door and stepped onto the patio. The sun, just setting behind the crest of the hill across the lake, outlined the ridge in a line of brilliant orange light; leaving the hillside in deep purple shadow. The lake, calm ... still water ... mirroring deep oranges and pinks off broken clouds. The vivid contrasts of the scene made Jackie stop … stop and look ... and breathe.

The brightness framing the ridge ... *so like my joy having this child ... and by Joey. Yes, Joey!* The colors on the lake, interrupted in the distance only by the dancing ripple from a gentle off-shore breeze ... *Why can't we be so peaceful?* The hillside in shadow ... *Mon Dieu, the unknowns of vineyards ... the challenges ... now a child!*

Jackie remembered a Sunday morning last summer, up in the vineyard, shortly after she'd discovered Joey was the owner ... a vintner who would live from vintage to vintage. She recalled her anger after trying to abandon everything about wine in France, then wandering right into it in the United States. That morning Harry, Joey's partner, saw her and walked over with some advice. *What did he say? A man with a woman who shares his passion becomes so much better.* 'The vines have Joey. But, Jackie, they also have you. Why not grow with them beside a man who loves you?'

And, who knew Harry would die in the fire a week later.

Taking one last look at the waning scene she was about to go back into the Carriage House when Joey opened the door and stepped outside. "Jackie, are you okay?"

"Just look at that ... so peaceful ... the way I had hoped we could be."

"Why can't we ... be peaceful?"

"Il est si belle!"

"That's why we call it 'God's country'," Joey said. "God'll help us out ... always does."

"D'accord. I feel She is with us now."

Standing side-by-side, watching the silent scene soften toward dusk, Jackie took Joey's hand in hers.

Jackie was the first to speak. "You know Joey ... all jumbled ... my thoughts ... feelings I never had before ... so strong ... my need for you. Sometimes you make it so I cannot think straight."

"You're not alone."

Jackie smiled, "You also?"

"Yes, really ... me also."

"I was just thinking about Harry. Remember I was so angry when I found out you owned the vineyard?"

"I won't forget that."

"Harry saw me up there, it was a sunny morning. I was crying ... and so angry I was shouting. He came over and tried to calm me down ... told me, like it or not, I am connected to the vines. I will not be able to stay away from them. So why not give you a chance? He saw you loved me even then."

"He got that right ... urged me to not give up. Thought we'd make a terrific couple. And we can, Jackie, we can do this.

We'll work together and figure it out. You won't be second fiddle to anything. We'll be side-by-side on everything."

"I just need to be sure. But, maybe we cannot be sure; that is not how it works."

"What can I do to convince you?"

"Honestly ... I do not know."

Jackie paused; Joey sensed he should wait.

Jackie continued, "I am beginning to realize I made my decision months ago when I returned from France. Grand-mere Chloe demanded I stay there. But, I came back ... to be with you. And I do not want to go back."

"Does that mean you'll marry me?"

She stepped closer to Joey, looking into his eyes. *"Oui ...* Yes!"

Joey pulled her to him, hugged her, kissed her - smiled as he pulled away, repeating, "Yes ... *Oui!"*

"We will have our child." Jackie said, "And the vineyard, I guess we are already married to it."

"We probably are."

"You have no idea, Joey, no idea how nervous I was to tell you. What if you did not want our child?"

Joey quietly responded, "That's not me, Jackie. I grew up without a father. I won't do that to our child. We'll figure it out. It'll be easier once we're married. No need for excuses about being together anymore."

"But France," Jackie said, "I am not sure what will happen with France."

      ℰꙮ   ℭꙮ

Across the driveway, the discussion in the Manor was not going well. When Emma and Will first arrived, Martin answered the door. "Oh, hi, come in." As he led them through the foyer, he said, "Will, I didn't get your voice mail message until I was driving home. Norman's back from France, showed up unexpectedly, out of the blue. He tied me up so long I had to play catch-up the rest of the day. So I'm sorry I didn't respond. But, I'm glad you're here."

"Yes, Jackie mentioned Norman's back," Will said. "More pressure on you?"

"Wants the new press in full production. Can't blame him. So yes, more pressure."

Emma said, "Well, we don't mean to intrude, but we're concerned for the kids"

"Vicki is just putting them to bed, she'll be down in a minute. Need a drink or anything?"

"No, we're fine. We just had supper."

In the living room Martin picked up toys and a blanket that had been left on the couch, giving his guests a place to sit. "So what happened this morning? Vicki had trouble getting the kids to school?"

Emma quickly recounted the events of that morning and Vicki's dark mood, finishing with her concern for the care of Seth and Maria. She finished just as Vicki strode into the living room.

"So, the posse's here. Going to take me to the judge for one of those damned parental competency tests?"

"Oh, Vicki," Martin said, "Stop it. Emma and Will only want to help."

"Yeah, well there's help ... real help to take the pressure off. And then there's the fuckin' help of busybodies who end up having kids separated from their parents. So which are you?"

Martin almost yelled, "Vicki!"

Emma held up her hand stopping Martin. "Now Vicki, we're here to help with the kids ... if you need or want help. Nothing more."

Still standing, Vicki said, "Well, Martin certainly isn't any help. He's married to the damned printshop. And that new press he bought, what a disaster that is ... never works right. Now he tells me Norman's back from France."

"As I said, showed up unexpectedly."

"So, now, more pressure on me," Vicki interjected, "More 'just buck up lady' … 'be quiet and do your part!' That's what I'll get."

"Vicki I never…"

"Shut up Martin, our neighbors want to know what's going on. Not your usual 'Oh, everything's just fine' bullshit."

Emma said, "Vicki, we know it's not easy. Sit down for a couple of minutes."

Vicki took the chair furthest from Martin, looking at Emma to continue.

"Will and I live close enough to know you and Martin have some differences. We know it's hard on you right now. But what…"

"Oh, Emma, everything's fine, just fine," Vicki said. "I don't think there's anything you can do."

Vicki looked at Emma, as if to say 'That's it!' But then leaned forward and continued, "Well, it's not fine. He expects me to stay locked up in this damned prison he calls his Manor, like he's some fucking feudal lord or something, And every day he takes off, goes into the city doing his thing where everyone prunes his feathers telling him what a great guy he is. Like I told you, a self-centered egotistical bastard.

"You know we used to live in the suburbs, at least there I wasn't so isolated, except for those country-club soccer moms that wanted everything just so. Didn't get along with them at all. But out here," Vicki raised her hands, her fingers gesturing quotation marks, 'in God's country' … even though we're on the lake, talk about being in the sticks."

Emma asked, "Vicki, were you ever happy?"

"What kind of a question is that?"

"Well?"

"How can I be happy living with Martin? He lives in his own fantasy world.

When I first met him … we got married awfully fast … I had all his attention then. But it didn't take long before he was the man and I his wife. All his old fashioned thinking came to bear. The model little woman, that's what he expects. Model slave is more like it."

"What we're your parents like?" Emma asked. "Were they happy?"

"Oh God, no! They only became tolerable after they separated. My father was very moody, alcoholic; my mother couldn't cope."

"So, your childhood and teen years were difficult."

"What's that got to do with anything? Now's the problem. Don't be goin' into my past tryin' to tell me I'm the one who's all fucked up. That damned shrink Martin dragged me to tried that. No, it's Martin who won't bend. He and his agenda … has to be his way. He never listens.

Will asked, "But Vicki, Martin, what about the kids?"

"Probably what keeps us together." Martin answered. "It'll be a disaster if we split-up. I won't let the kids go. Vicki can't raise them on her own anyhow."

Vicki interjected, "Oh, yeah! Just watch me."

Emma held up her hand, "Okay, okay. Let's not get way off-base. Will is just asking, what can we do to help with the kids?"

Vicki sat silently, as if considering her last remark. Martin sat, his eyes focused on the floor.

Emma asked, "Vicki?"

"Right now," Vicki softly said, "I don't know. Maybe if you watch them a few hours after school one or two days a week. It'll give me a chance to get groceries and go shopping. You know Seth can be a lot to handle – takes after his father. And when he and Maria are in the car they start squabbling; in a store it's a disaster."

"Okay, let's set up a couple afternoons each week. We'll pick Maria up after pre-school, then Seth from first grade, and keep them 'til you get back. That'll give you more time to run your errands. You won't feel you have to rush."

෨   ෬

47

In the Carriage House, Prince stood and walked, tail wagging, to the door. Emma walked in, with Will right behind her. "She needs help," Will said, "but not what we offered. Don't you see? I mean watching the kids so she can go shopping? The kids are in school all day, what about that for free-time?"

"Well, we'll give her more free-time. Let her feel like she's more in control."

Seeing Joey and Jackie standing side-by-side holding hands, Will stopped. "Oh, Joey. Hi. Hope we didn't interrupt anything?"

Both Joey and Jackie smiled, "No... no ..."

"Well," Will said, taking Emma's coat from her. "We just had a wonderful time next door."

Emma cautioned, "Now, Will, be nice."

"Yeah, well," Will continued, "I don't know how much to tell you but there are problems over there. And with those two little kids involved, you should be aware of what's going on. But, please keep this confidential."

Emma asked as she started to set up the coffee maker, "Everybody in for a cup of coffee?" Without waiting for an answer, she continued, "Vicki had a bad day and we we're hoping to help out."

"Fat chance of that," Will cut in, "you should know the woman is crazy – probably getting worse. Not really open to getting any help."

"Will, how can you say that?"

"Easy ... she's closed off to any advice, Martin's, ours... even a shrink."

"Don't say shrink. She needs a psychiatrist."

"Or a good kick in the pants. Emma, can't you see how she's manipulating? All the focus on her. She hardly acknowledged she has two kids sleeping upstairs."

"Well, that's what depression can do ... perception and judgment get distorted."

"Maybe so, Emma, but talking with her is like listening to an alcoholic. All the focus, everything, centers on them ... it's all about the woe-is-me troubles they've had all their lives. And with Vicki, all the trouble she said she's having with Martin. Then saying she's trapped ... trapped! ... living in that beautiful Manor, and on this lake. Give me a break!"

"But can't you see? She's in pain. Just trying to hold it all together. You know, Will, sometimes you can be a hard man."

"That may be so," Will said, "but she isn't the only one having to hold it together. Didn't you see the stress on Martin's face?" He turned to Jackie and Joey, "With Norman back the pressure's on to get that new press in full production, probably wants to see some profit from it. I don't blame him. Anyhow, Martin has a full plate to contend with at work. He doesn't need Vicki acting up just now. And she's totally insensitive to it."

"Oh, Will, don't make this bigger than it is."

Emma looked over her shoulder toward Jackie and Joey, "So you two... You're smiling. You find some levity in this?"

Jackie shook her head "*Non, non.*"

"Then why the amused look on your faces? What Will and I are talking about is serious."

"Well, uh," Jackie hesitated.

Joey said, "Jackie, go ahead, tell them."

Emma turned to face them. She asked, "Tell us what?"

Jackie shrugged, "Well...," then glanced at Joey.

"Emma, Will," Joey said, "I guess there's only one way to say this, Jackie's pregnant!"

Emma dropped the spoon she'd been using to scoop coffee grounds; a look of alarm crossing her face, quickly changing into a smile. "Really! Oh, Jackie... I, I ... don't know what to say." She opened her arms and put them around Jackie. Releasing Jackie, Emma began to ask, "But..."

Will cut in, laughing, "Well, Emma, you called that one right." Looking at Jackie he said, "Emma told me she was pretty sure you were pregnant."

Jackie just smiled and caved back into her grandmother's arms exhaling a long sigh of relief, but bracing for Emma's question.

"Now Will, just hush. But, Jackie, how do you feel about it?"

"I want to have my baby, our *bebe*."

Will turned to Joey, "So, Joey, where are you on this one?"

Emma released Jackie asking, "On this one? What does that mean, 'On this one'? My granddaughter just told us she's going to have a baby. Jackie, I heard you right? You are going to have it?"

Jackie looked at her grandmother, smiling, "*Oui*, Yes!"

"Emma," Will said, "I'm asking the father what his intentions are. Since there are no shotguns in this house, I can only ask."

"Oh, Will, don't be so dramatic ... so old fashioned."

Joey smiled and took Jackie's hand in his. "When you all calm down I want to tell you what my intentions are."

Will and Emma looked at Joey ... waiting. Joey glanced down, then looked directly at Will. "Jackie and I are getting married."

Will smiled, clasping Joey's hand. "Joey, congratulations! I'm sincerely happy for both of you. This calls for a celebration. Wine ... let's have some wine."

Emma leaned to Joey and gave him a hug ... smiling as she began to tear up. Then she pulled back. "Will, Jackie can't drink wine. She's pregnant." Turning to Jackie she asked, "But Jackie, what about Chloe? Isn't she still in France? Have you told your grand-mere yet?"

Chapter 5

The following morning, Nicholas was using the plow to move away dirt he'd hilled against the vine splices last fall. A necessary step in preparation for the new growing season. Finishing a row, he pulled the tractor around to start another. Bright sunshine warmed his back. He paused and let the engine idle. The tension of his ire with his brother slowly ebbed, relaxed in the scenery before him. *How can anyone stay enraged with this view ... the deep blue lake ... the delicate silver-green of the trees budding on the hills? Beautiful ... Thank you, Jesus!*

An hour earlier he'd been driving the tractor out of the Kober Vineyards equipment yard just as his older brother, Tom, was pulling in, heading toward the office. Tom pulled up next to him and rolled down the window of his pickup ... a four-door extended cab model outfitted with every luxury option available.

"Which vineyard ya working this morning? I thought you were all done with the outtake a couple weeks ago."

"I'm headin' over to Joey's."

Tom turned off his engine, opened the door, swung out, and walked toward his brother. Tom being the taller of the two, Nicholas stayed up on the tractor seat. He wanted Tom to be looking up at him, instead of the other way around.

"So you're gonna keep helping Joey. That's it?"

"Yep! That is it!"

"Damned, Nic, can't you see the kid's a looser. Tryin' all that crazy formula stuff, and now he's gettin' funding from some guy who doesn't know crap about wine. He ain't gonna make it Nic. No way. He'll only sully our name."

"How do you figure that? His mother's our half-sister, not his father. His name is O'Donnell and he'll probably not even use it ... too Irish."

"Don't matter. He's our neighboring vineyard and people'll figure out he's related."

"Which is precisely why we should help him out; make sure his wines are up to par. What's the matter, can't you stand the competition?"

"Competition on what?" Tom raised his hands, palms up, for emphasis. "Quality? Not a chance. But if he's successful it'll be one of those knockoff gimmicky vineyards, selling cheap wine along with God knows what to make a buck. And by the time the wine tasters get to us their buds will be shot and they'll find our medaled dry vintages boring." He pointed north, in the direction of Joey's vineyard. "Havin' him over there, with a better view I might add, is like livin' in an upscale neighborhood while the white trash moves in next door."

"Tom, Joey's our nephew, our blood."

"Yeah, just like our cousins think they're our blood … also entitled to a piece of Kober vineyards."

"Well, Dad's brother did work with him for years; helped get all this started."

"Listen, our uncle screwed up somehow. Probably the booze. Anyhow, he bought that 170 acres up top of the hill. And to his credit made it into a pretty good farm. But who's to say Dad didn't help him out … financially?"

"Maybe, maybe. But farmin's gettin' harder these days … costs, regulations…"

"Nic, you're always for the other guy. Why not us? Screw them! Whatever deals our father and uncle made are far past. We gotta look forward … and contend with Joey."

"Don't forget, he's our blood."

"But only Dad's blood; not our mother's. And, don't forget, the old man and our step-sister never did get along. Then she got herself pregnant by that alcoholic potato head and the old man all but abandoned her. So why do we have to put up with her son?"

"Because her son is still our blood, Tom. He's family, like it or not. And, he's a serious guy. Joey reminds me of the old man."

"Oh, come on Nic. How can you say that?"

"Because our father took him under his wing and taught him, just like he taught us; and then, Tom, and then, he left him that vineyard."

Tom raised his arms in disgust, almost in anguish. "Oh, shit, Nic. How could he do that? And that damned estate lawyer still says we ain't gonna be able to get it back. No grounds to establish the old man was senile."

Nic leaned over and spoke softly. "Give it up Tom. The old man knew what he was doin'. And he wanted to give Joey his chance. Probably felt it was the least he could do after leaving us Kober Vineyards outright."

Tom glared toward Nic. "I still think it's bullshit. The kid got to him, somehow."

"Oh, I think he did. I think Joey showed the old man enough creativity and gumption that the old man figured he should have a chance too. A couple of years before he died, he walked into our cask room. I was checking pH or something, along with tasting and sniffing. He walked up to me and jabbed me in the ribs ... remember ... his way of demanding attention. He jabs me and leans in close, almost whispering even though no one else is around. He says, 'Nicholas', never called me Nicholas unless he was serious. He says, 'Nicholas, listen ... your nephew, Joey. I been workin' with him. He's got our taste buds, Nicholas, he's got our talent. Don't you forget that ... he can carry our tradition on. Time comes, you help him.' That was our old man's take. Thought Joey'll improve viniculture because he thinks differently than we do. What do they call it, 'beyond, beyond...' Something like that."

"Out-of-the-box. You're saying the old man thought Joey thinks out-of-the-box. Well, if he keeps screwin' with all those formulas he'll be sellin' his wine in boxes. Give us a bad name."

"Listen Tom, the old man had faith in Joey, so I'm helpin' him. For God's sake, brother, he left him the last vineyards he developed. His experimental vines, they're good vines, mature. Closest to his heart after he turned everything over to us. He nurtured those like a mother with a newborn baby, like raising another child. Then that new vineyard they planted together just before he died - planted it right, too. All the limestone soil, bordered by the two ravines sucking warmth from the lake ... ideal terroir. I want to make damned sure the wine those vines produce would make the old man proud. Because, you know, he's watching over us. And we'd better shape up and just thank Our Lord, Jesus, that tornado last year didn't hit one of our vineyards."

Tom spun around on his heel, and shaking his head, waving his hands in disgust, stomped over to the office, leaving his truck in the driveway. Nicholas figured he'd struck a nerve in Tom and his brother was seeing 'red'. *No sense trying to reach him now.* He put the tractor in gear and went on his way, angered by Tom's obstinance.

Now, an hour later, Nic was at peace ... the sunny spring morning helping to calm his nerves.

He was about to start plowing a row when he saw Jackie jogging up the dirt road to the vineyard. She waved to him and he returned the gesture, turned off the tractor engine, climbed down and walked between the rows toward her.

"Well, good morning," he shouted as they approached each other. "You even brought some sunshine."

"Oh, uncle Nic, the sunshine got here long before I did." Jackie walked up to him, and gave him a kiss on the cheek. "Where's Joey?"

"He was all fired up this morning, talkin' a blue streak about Norman's okay to start on the building. He said he'd called Mosbey, the contractor he used to work for ... see if he had an office trailer we can use. Mosbey told him to get on over before he took off on a job. So Joey high-tailed it out of here."

Jackie smiled. "Oh. Well ... I guess I'll keep working on training those new vines, pick up where I was yesterday."

"Yep, they're waitin' for ya. They're not goin' away."

Watching Jackie walk up the hill, he wondered if something was happening between her and Joey. They both seemed to be in unusually good spirits ... as if in tandem. *Something's up!*

An hour passed before Nic finished plowing and pulled the tractor up onto the road. Just minutes earlier he'd seen Joey drive his pickup past the place he normally parked, over close to where Jackie was working. Then Joey sprinted between the rows of vines, hugged Jackie and was talking to her.

As he was about to turn off the engine, Nic saw Jackie and Joey beginning to walk, almost skipping, from the far end of the new vineyard toward him. He drove to where they would walk out of the vine row, turned off the engine and climbed down. He also noticed the couple was tightly holding hands.

"So," he said, "what makes you so bright and cheery this morning?

"Hey, uncle Nic, who can't be happy on a sunny day like today?" Joey grinned.   Jackie walked up to Nic and giving him a peck on the cheek, whispered into his ear, "We have something to tell you."

Nic pulled away to look at her. "Oh, really! I would never have guessed. I mean you two are almost jumpin' for joy this morning."

"Yeah, well," Joey said, "Mosbey has an idle trailer so we can get it up here later this week." Joey pointed. "Set it up right over near the corner across from where the building will be. Run some power to it and we're all set to go."

"Good. That's what's got you both so excited?"

Jackie and Joey smiled at each other.

Joey led, "Well, we decided to get married."

Jackie noticed Nic glance toward her ring finger. "I don't have a ring yet."

"So, Joey, you ask a girl to marry you and you don't give her an engagement ring? This some new younger generation cuttin' corners thing?"

Joey glanced down, scuffing his shoe on the ground. He looked up, saying, "Um... I didn't realize I'd be proposing quite so soon."

"Uh, Uh. Anything that caused a change in plans? I mean, it's not like you, Joey, to be rushin' too much."

"Yeah, that's about it. A change in plans..."

Jackie interrupted, "Oh, uncle Nic, we might as well tell you. I'm pregnant."

Nic raised his eyebrows. "Ah ha! So that's it." He reached over and gave her a hug and grabbed Joey's hand, smiling, "Well, congratulations! This really does make me happy. I've been watching you two; you make a great couple. Getting married ... usually not a good idea when a girl gets pregnant. But, for you, I think it's smart.

"Be careful, though, listening to an old batch like me. You know, no woman has been able to stand me. Last one said I was already married ... to the vines. I propose and she says that!" Nic smiled, "Kinda cooled our relationship. Anyhow, I know you don't need it, but you have my blessing.""

"Thanks uncle Nic," Joey said, "Your blessing means a lot to us."

"Well, you certainly have mine... Have you told your mother, Joey?"

"Haven't seen her today. But when I do, she'll be okay with it."

"I hope so."

Nic turned to Jackie, "And young lady, what about your grandmothers?"

"Grandma Emma, she knows. I think she was shocked. But, she quickly became supportive." Jackie grimaced, "But, Grand-mere Chloe, I don't know."

"She doesn't know yet?"

Joey cut in, "I only proposed last night."

"Well, a piece of advice from me, don't blindside her on this one. She's gonna need some time to get used to the idea."

Chapter 6

In the Medoc wine region of France, near Bordeaux, Chloe drove up to her chateau, noticing its drab appearance in the cloudy afternoon light. *Yes, a coat of deep burgundy on the shutters will freshen things up ... and in a week or so I'll have the euros to get it done.* Feeling the fatigue of mid-afternoon, she immediately went to her bedroom for a nap.

The afternoon light was beginning to fade when Chloe woke up. She walked into the kitchen and poured herself a glass of red wine; one of her vintner, Horbst's, better vintages. Feeling a spring dampness in the darkening room, she lit the paper under the stack of kindling she'd arranged in the small corner fireplace that morning in anticipation of the need to stave off the late day chill. Chloe sat at the table, firelight dancing on the stucco walls, thinking back to the fall months of the last harvest followed by the Christmas holidays; remembering the energy, warmth and joy Jacqueline and Norman brought into the room. Now, the Château felt stark, empty ... lonely.

Looking out over the vines, a shiver went through Chloe. The finality of selling the vineyard was settling in ... and she found it exhausting.

The drawn out negotiation with Francois had become much more tedious, more contentious, than she'd ever expected. And François, always so gracious and understanding, was distant and cool as the final terms, not to Chloe's liking, were agreed upon. Even Norman proved to be of little help against the high rank of Francois' chateau. She now wondered if she would have been better able to manipulate Francois to her point of view had Norman not been involved. But once she introduced Norman into the negotiations, she'd lost that opportunity. It became so contentious, Chloe now worried that she'd lost her neighbor, Francois, as a friend.

The firelight flickering on the kitchen walls, becoming more prominent as the natural light waned, did nothing to lift

Chloe's spirits. Her emotions were focused on the loss of the vineyard enshrouded in the gloom of nightfall.

She thought of her husband: *I am so sorry Maurice ... selling the vineyard ... an insult to you and your family. I stuck it out ... finally just slammed against the wall. Our savings gone ... couldn't find a way to make it work.*

And Jacqueline ... fickle ...cannot count on her. Just a year ago content to stay here ... now, who knows? Why did I ever keep those letters to her from Emma? Once Jacqueline found them ... ran to the grandmother she did not know she had. After all I did for that girl ... no listening to reason ... just up and left.

Chloe poured more wine into her glass, becoming aware the vines could no longer be seen.

And François, why could he not realize Jacqueline would be a wonderful wife? Marvelous if those two married ... the problems it would have solved. Why no spark? How could he ignore her? I thought I understood men. François ... No! ... makes me wonder about him.

Chloe smiled, as her thoughts shifted to Norman, that Nordic man so sure of himself; masculine and full of energy. The one who brought her unexpected fulfillment after she had given up on finding a man.

So different ... rough around the edges ...yet able to enjoy life. Sometimes distant, but I can reach him ... get his attention ... raw sex ... works every time. He must be kept busy ... learned that in the Mediterranean ... easily bored.

Chloe looked around. The Château just seemed so hollow. Tears welled up in her eyes. *Damn you Norman, a small problem in your business, and you are gone! How can you leave me alone ... now ... like this?*

Sitting there Chloe wondered if keeping the Château was a good idea. Would she actually continue to live there? With Norman in the States? But, did she really trust herself, and Norman, to move across the Atlantic to be with him? After all, she lived in France all her life, in this chateau since she was twenty years old.

But, then, Jacqueline, once your infatuation with Joey wears off, you will come back to France. Oh, you can do so much better than Joey!

Chloe firmed her jaw. She knew she could convince Jacqueline of that.

It is up to me. I will make sure she comes to her senses. No way she will be happy with that bourgeois dirt farmer filled with notions of grandeur. Going to make European class wines ...never happen. And now, Norman is backing him! And Jacqueline, as stubborn as her father. Damned Americans ... aggressive, arrogant. No! Jacqueline is French ... like her mother, tender and loving. She needs a husband who understands the culture of her birth.

Chloe took another sip of her wine, sitting in darkness now, thinking that although it being dinnertime she wasn't hungry. A break in the clouds let shafts of silver moonlight shine on the vines. Chloe stood and put on her jacket. She and Maurice had often walked in the shimmering beauty of the vineyard at night. She needed just such a walk, hopefully calming her nerves.

Had she waited five minutes she would've heard the ringing of the telephone shattering the silence of her chateau.

Chapter 7

Will turned into the driveway, invigorated by his hour-long walk; Prince following close behind. Beyond the Carriage House the surface of the lake was calm, steel grey; a cold reflection of early morning overcast. It being June 1st, Will hoped late spring sunshine would warm the lake enough to let him canoe soon … *maybe next week.* Walking, good exercise, just didn't give him the peace of mind of a quiet morning paddle on still water.

He noticed Seth standing on the shore in front of the Manor throwing flat pieces of shale across the water; getting a good number of skips on each throw. Prince ran up beside Seth, tail wagging. As Will approached, he said, "You're up early this morning."

Seth answered, still looking at the lake, "My dad got up. Done sleepin'"

"We call it being 'slept out'."

"My mom, she sleeps all the time. My Dad never sleeps."

"Pretty busy… your dad."

"Yeah."

"So, school today?"

Seth turned and patted Prince on the head, "Guess. I take a peanut butter and jelly sandwich. So does Maria."

"You make them?"

"Yeah. Sometimes. Mom, she forgets. So I just make 'em. Then she won't yell at me for not remembering."

"Well, I'm sure your mother has a lot on her mind."

"Yeah. Must be thinking about somethin'."

Seth is getting old for his years … Growing up fast! Will asked, "So Seth … had breakfast yet?"

Seth brightened at the mention of eating and looked up at Will, "Nope!"

"Well it's early yet. Let's go into the Carriage House and see if we can find something good to eat. Maybe we can get Emma to make us some pancakes."

A shrill yell pierced the morning's peace. "Seth! You get the hell in this house right now. You aren't s'posed to be outside." Will spun around and saw Vicki leaning over the railing of the porch off her bedroom, both hands gripping tightly. She was in her nightgown, her hair bedraggled as if she'd just gotten out of bed. She glanced at Will, then shouted in a more civil tone, "Damn it Seth! You never listen to me. Who said you could go outside?"

Without a word Seth ran toward the Manor.

Will said softly, "Vicki, he was just throwing some stones in the Lake."

"I don't give a shit what he was doin', he shouldn't be outside."

"Okay, okay... You're right. Just settle down."

"Settle down! How can I with you people lookin' over my shoulder all the time. 'Is Vicki doin' everything she's supposed to?' 'Why can't Vicki handle it all?' 'Damned Vicki, she never gets anything right!' And that husband of mine ... off again without a word. Came home late last night and never woke me up. Now he's just gone again. And I'm stuck here."

"Well, let us know if we can help with anything..."

"You can help by buttin' out. I can take care of my kids. You're getting' them so they don't pay any attention." Vicki looked from side-to-side like she'd just awakened. "Damned, it's chilly out here." She turned and dashed back into the Manor leaving Will to shake his head.

He turned slowly and walked toward the Carriage House. *"Nice way to start a day!"*

ɕ૭   ෬

Joey was in the construction trailer placed on the edge of the vineyard. The power company took almost two weeks, until the day before, to run in a temporary electrical line. Opening a few windows to let in fresh air, he heard the groan of a diesel engine grinding in low gear on the climb up the road coming from the lake. Looking out he recognized Mr. Mosbey's 'Honey Dipper' truck.

Once next to the trailer, Mosbey cut the engine. The stub of an unlit cigar in his mouth as always, he climbed down from the cab; nimble for a man of his age and girth. Joey met him at the door.

"Come on in. This trailer is gonna work out fine."

"I sure as shit hope so." Mosbey said, taking the cigar from his lips. "I told ya, it's a little old and tired, but it'll do." He carefully navigated the steps to walk inside.

"I just opened a few windows to air out the musty smell."

"Well, I didn't notice that. Can't smell worth shit after pumpin' the crud for years. I remembered we never checked to see if the window air conditioner's workin'. Have you turned it on yet? You're gonna need that sucker in a month or so ... these trailers get hotter 'en hell."

"Just got power yesterday. All the outlets and lights work."

Mosbey set his unlit cigar stub on the edge of the window air conditioner and turned the dial. It was only seconds before he and Joey felt a rush of cold air.

"Yep, that's what you want."

Joey turned the unit off. Smiling he said, "Thanks for helping me out ... with the trailer and everything. And having this desk and stand-up drafting table in here is great."

"Yeah, these angled tables come in handy when you got a sheaf of construction prints to deal with. I owe ya for helpin' me last year. Plus, you're gonna need some help with what you're getting' into."

"I'm sure it'll turn into a big job ... particularly doing it right."

"No, I'm not talkin' about the new building, you'll handle that fine. I'm talkin' about you ... you bein' a daddy." Mosbey smiled, "That's the word around the lake. True?"

"Where'd you hear that?'

"Just heard it yesterday. You know how it is, the ladies don't have a lot to do except gossip. And, you, single; they have you in their sights. Probably pissed, the young ones, that it's not them's pregnant by ya; and by some Frenchie to boot.

"I don't blame ya, Joey. That girl, Jackie, she is a beaut. And I think I told ya before, when we were workin' together, 'every a good erection deserves respect". Trouble is, while you young bucks are tryin' to figure out *Where* to put it, the women, they're figuring out the *Why*? It's the *Why* that causes the problem. Places all kinda strings on a good fuck. And don't you think the women don't think 'o that. Get pregnant and expect the one who plugged 'em to do somethin' about it."

Joey stood tall, shaking his head, "Mr. Mosbey, it's not like that. I asked Jackie to marry me."

Mosbey stood back. "Oh, hadn't heard *that*! Guess I'd better shut up."

"And, just for the record, when I asked Jackie to marry me, at first she wasn't sure she wanted to."

Mosbey stepped forward, raising his right index finger, " Aha! Yeah. Damned if they don't do that. Make you fathers feel you aren't such a sure bet. Put you on the defensive. Sets the ground rules for years to come."

Joey looked straight at Mosbey. "Maybe you can tell me. Why are older people so down on marriage? When Jackie told her grandmother, Emma dropped a spoon; and Will, he broke out in nervous laughter. I mean they're supportive, but I saw the look of doubt cross both their faces. And you, you sure aren't encouraging."

"Oh, don't mind me ... or them. I guess it's experience talkin'. Too often marriage don't work out so good." Mosbey picked up his cigar stub and put it between his teeth. Then, grasped it out again and pointing it at Joey said with conviction, "They change damn it! The women, they change." He lowered his hand and his voice. "But you Joey," Mosbey smiled, "you're old enough and savvy enough … you'll be fine."

There was a knock on the door and Norman stepped into the trailer. "Good morning. Hope I'm not interrupting anything?"

Mosbey held out his hand. "Olsen, right?"

"Yes, and you're Mosbey. Recognized your truck."

"Yep. Installed that new pump in your holding tank couple years ago. But you were in a hurry so we never got to talk. Hope it's workin' okay?"

"Yes … fine. And thanks for finding Joey this trailer."

"Yep. Least I can do after all the help he gave me last year. Bad ankle sprain and Joey kept things goin' for me."

"Well, we both appreciate it."

Mosbey reached up putting his hand on Joey's shoulder. "Yeah, Joey, here, 'Daddy Joey'. He's gonna need his friends…"

"You can say that again." Norman said. Turning to Joey, "Has Jackie told Chloe yet? I've done as Jackie asked and kept it to myself … but there'll be hell to pay if she doesn't know soon. I'm sure there'll be hell to pay anyhow."

Joey looked down, "Jackie's been tryin' to call her, but I don't think she's talked to her yet. Today … I'll make sure Jackie calls today."

"Better hurry, Chloe's flying back next week."

Changing the subject, Mosbey asked, "The other reason I came up here is to ask Joey if any landmen been pokin' around?"

"Who?"

"Landmen. You know, those fuckers preyin' on landowners to sign gas drilling leases. Makin' the landowner feel like he's gonna be rich for doin' nothin'."

Joey asnswered, "No, haven't seen any."

"Yeah, sure. Stands to reason they won't approach a vineyard,"

"Why's that?" Norman asked.

"Hydrofracking!" Mosbey said, "You musta heard of hydrofracking?"

"Sure, in PA..." Joey said, "the Dakotas, Texas and Oklahoma. But not around here."

Mosbey waved his cigar in the air. "I'm hopin' the drillers stay away. Leave our water alone. You do know, don't ya, we got about 20 percent of the fresh water on the globe in the Great Lakes? Plenty o' gas under other parts 'o the country. More than we ever want to burn with climate change and all."

Joey said, "I know my uncle Nic is concerned. Hates the idea here in the Finger Lakes."

"I hope he's not one of those 'tree hugger' types," Norman said, "They hate everything progressive. Hell, we drill enough and the United States could become energy independent."

"That may be," Mosbey said, "But you two better agree with Nic and hate the idea too ... if you hope to make and sell wine. The landman'll promise a pile a scratch, some upfront, then lots once the well hits. Course after the lease is signed you'll never see him again. I haven't seen any new Cadillacs drivin' the roads, have you Joey?"

Joey looked perplexed.

Norman said, "You don't sound encouraging."

"I'm not. Too much risk! It's all David against Goliath, the individual landowner up against the big oil and gas companies. And what makes it hard is landowners lookin' at all the money ain't aware of the problems. Like holdin' candy in front of a kid."

"But," Norman asked, "haven't gas wells been drilled around here for decades? Extraction can be very profitable."

"Yep, but for who? The landowner or those fuckers down in Texas and Oklahoma?"

Joey cut in, "You're right. Drilling has been going on, vertically, for 30 or 40 years. But hydrofracking is new. They drill down about a mile, then spread out horizontally. Using pressure a mixture of water and chemicals is shot against the rock. It fractures and releases the gas."

Mosbey chimed in, "But the fluid is toxic, nobody except the drillers seem to know what they're using. It comes back to the surface and has to be stored or taken away. Millions of gallons."

"But, I haven't heard of anyone round here…" Joey said

"Schmidt!" Mosbey cut in.

"Who?" Norman asked.

"Schmidt. Joey's neighbor up top of the hill. If you haven't been up there, you should go. It's flat land. His farm's at least a couple hundred acres. Rumor is he's signed a lease. Seems anxious to start. Talkin' about placing the well pad by the edge of your property. That'll put the waste water pond next to the crest of the hill … right above your vineyard. They do that and the sucker ever let's go, you'll have toxic water goin' all over your vines."

"Don't they need some kind of zoning and environmental approval?" Norman asked. "Businesses can't just barge in and go ahead."

"Normally I'd agree, they can't. But we're talking oil and gas companies out of Texas. They're used to doing whatever the fuck they want. And to make matters worse, most of the members of the county commission that has to grant approvals, they're landowners who wouldn't mind some income from a lease themselves."

Norman turned to Joey. "You know about this?"

"Apparently not enough. I guess I'm about to learn a hell of a lot more."

"You bet your ass you are!"

Mosbey again waved his hand in the air, his voice rising. "Yeah, yeah, they drill down about a mile, then go horizontal … right underneath you … and the damn law doesn't give you any way to stop 'em. Of course, if something happens that affects the aquifers or the lake, it's all over. Fuckin' contamination everywhere. Not a damned thing you or anybody can do about it. Yep, Joey, you'd better get on this right away."

Continuing to look at Joey, Mosbey softened his voice, "Well, just wanted to be sure you were aware of what the fuckers are up to. You really need to pay attention on this one." He nodded toward Norman. "Mr. Olsen, glad you came along."

"Norm, please."

Mosbey turned back to Joey, smiling, "And Joey, regardless of what I said, Congratulations! You'll make a great husband and father ... sure as shit." With that the cigar went back in Mosbey's mouth. He left the trailer, climbed into the cab of his "Honey Dipper' tank truck, started the engine and drove off on the road heading south, toward the Kober vineyards.

"Whew!" Norman said. "He always so sure of himself? Sucks all the oxygen out of the room."

"You should see him when he's pissed. But, he's always given me a fair shake. This hydrofracking, though. I just haven't heard of anything going on around here."

"Well, sounds like it's happening. Go to the town hall and see what kinds of permit requests are being filed, and by who. Do you know anybody with their ear to the ground on what's goin' on?"

"Other than Mosbey, not really. But uncle Nic might know. I'll ask, see if he knows anybody."

"Ask your mother too."

"Why her?"

"She's a nurse at the Clinic, right? Sometimes emergency care facilities, they have 'regulars', men who hang out at bars a lot and find themselves in need of help from time-to-time. They often hear things long before it surfaces. Just ask her if she knows anyone ... and if the guy's older, let me make the contact. We gotta figure out if this hydrofracking is good or bad for us."

Norman turned toward the drafting table, pointing toward the laptop and roll of prints. "Okay. What have you got to show me?"

Joey pulled an image onto the screen of the laptop and turned it so Norman could see. "We've added an entry portico and deck onto the front of the building. The portico will be 16 feet wide, coming from the building out to the edge of the deck. The deck will also be 16 feet wide.

"So the portico will be 16 feet square?"

"Right. And the deck will span along the front as long as we want to make it. Our thought is to have tables outside. With the portico roof being as wide as it is we'll always have tables in the shade, others in the sun."

"Sounds good. We have a great view from here, might as well capitalize on it."

"Exactly. Hopefully the vineyard and the lake will encourage people to linger longer ... help sell more wine. Let me point out a couple of other features. As you can see the roof of the portico is supported by two beams on each front corner; they'll be anchored up top by a curved arch, the same as we're using inside across the expanse of the Tasting Room. It's going to be impressive."

"I see a stairs from the deck down to the ground. What about ADA regulations?"

"The stairs is for convenient access from the lake side." Joey reached for the roll of prints and spread them open. "Here's the plot plan. We've laid out the parking lot on the side of the building with no view of the lake. The parking will be level with the building and we've put a double-door entryway there. No problem with access or wheeling cases of wine in and out."

"How much more for the portico and deck?"

"Probably more than you want to spend."

"Maybe not."

"Bruce is completing an estimate. I'll have it in a couple of days."

"Well, at least I'll be able to see this and enjoy it. A lot of my money you're spending will be going into stuff I can't see and enjoy ... that is, until you make some of that outstanding wine."

                ℰꙮ   03

Jackie held the kitchen phone to her ear, listening to the abrasive buzz of the European ringing signal. Just when she was about to hang up, Chloe answered.

"Grand-mere, c'est Jacqueline."

"Mon Dieu! Jacqueline?" Chloe continued speaking in French. "Jacqueline! Finally you call. Where have you been?"

Jackie was relieved to hear Chloe's tone of voice, without the rancor of her last conversation. She responded in French. "Right here, grand-mere. But, where have you been? I've called several times."

"Since I'm coming to the United States for an extended time, I've been visiting my friends. Sort of a saying goodbye. Still I missed talking to you. I became worried when you didn't call."

"I called several times, mid-day."

"Just the time when I would have been out. You must make more effort to keep in touch. I called and talked with Emma a few times. Did she tell you?

"Yes. I've been tutoring students at the local college. I was there every time you called."

"Tutoring, what?"

"French ... the only subject I know. It's fun and I've made some friends."

"Did Emma tell you I'm coming over next week?"

"She said you were coming, but not when."

"Next week. Didn't Norman tell you?"

"I haven't seen him lately. I know he's met with Joey a few times. And he didn't mention anything."

"Men! They never communicate. Keep everything close to their chest, as if it's a sign of courage. The cowards."

Jackie hesitated to respond.

"Well," Chloe sighed, "the sale is finalized. Now we have a house surrounded by a vineyard owned by Francois. Not much of a chateau. Your grandfather would not be pleased. He so wanted to preserve the whole chateau for you. And it would be such a blow to his pride to have to sell the vineyard,"

"I know grand-mere. He often told me of his plan for keeping it all for me."

"He loved you. But that Francois. He showed some colors as we were closing the sale that I've never seen before.

Perhaps your instincts were right. What he was willing to pay for the vineyard is so much less than it's worth. The only good thing he did was keep Horbst on so he'd have a job during the few years until he has to retire."

"I'm glad to hear that. Horbst is a good vintner."

"Yes, well listening to Francois one wouldn't be too sure in this era of new techniques. Micro-oxygenation, indeed!"

"What?"

"Never mind, Francois was just throwing around new terminology to confuse Norman and me. Norman advises me we both, you and I, must move on. But I hope you appreciate our single acre and the chateau, the little left of it. You know you can return to France anytime … this home is waiting for you here."

"Oh, grand-mere, I do appreciate that, but…"

"But what?"

"It's a lot to take in."

"Shouldn't be. You grew up here. Tell me, how are you?"

"Me … I'm good … Very good actually. I need to tell you something."

Chloe laughs, "I hope it's not that you're pregnant."

Jackie hesitated to answer, leaving the circuit void of sound.

"Oh, no, Jacqueline… No! You are *not* pregnant!"

Jackie leaned against the wall, physically deflated by Chloe's reaction. But she caught herself, stood straight, and forcefully said, "And what of it grand-mere? What of it?"

"How far along are you?"

"About eight weeks."

Chloe hesitated, then said almost under her breath, "Well, there's still time."

"What does that mean?"

"After I taught you of protection. I do not accept this. It could only be worse if you told me you want to marry that Joey. It is Joey, right?"

"Of course it's Joey. I'm not promiscuous!"

"I told you to be careful with him. Did he rape you?"

"No, no. Joey didn't rape me. I love him. "

"Oh, don't say that!"

"Well, I do. And to answer your question … Yes, we are to be married."

Chloe's voice rose into a keening sound, "Good God… no, no. Jacqueline I must sit down. You overwhelm me."

The line became silent.

After several seconds, Jackie hesitantly asked, "Grand-mere, are you still there?"

Chloe sounded deflated. "Yes, Jacqueline, yes. You've knocked the very breath out of me." Her voice became strong. "Now you listen to me. I will be over next week, staying at Norman's. Don't do a thing … not one thing … until I get there. Do you understand me? Nothing…understand? Nothing!"

"But, grand-mere, I'm going to have my child. And keep it. No abortion, if that's what you're thinking. And no giving it up for adoption. And, and, I'm going to marry Joey."

'And throw your life away! This is exactly why, after Christmas, I did not want you leaving France. No, Jacqueline, you are better than all this … You know that, I know it. Even Joey knows it. You stay put and I'll see you in a week."

"Listen … I'm getting married!"

"Yes, you will. But, not in the United States and not to Joey. You will marry someday … in France … and in a Catholic Church. That's how you will be married."

"You want me married in the Catholic Church … and then you suggest abortion?"

"*Non, non* … Not that!"

"Grand-mere listen…"

"No, you listen. Don't do anything until I get there."

71

"But, grand-mere…" Jackie heard a click and pulled the phone away from her ear. Listening again she realized Chloe had hung up. After replacing the handset on its cradle she put her hands to her face and shuddered as if she were going to cry. Then, she again caught herself, stood tall with a look on her face that would have commanded the attention of everyone in the room … if anyone were there.

Chapter 8

Skimming at full throttle across the lake from his home to the Manor exhilarated Norman, the wooden hull of his Chris Craft almost out of the water at 41 knots. The wind in his face as he scanned forward to assure clear passage, the sky reflected on the rippled surface ahead, and the early spring greens upon the hills. Everything as it should be. And such a release from the restraint and forced politeness he'd felt necessary in France. Yes, he was home again. And life was good, with the best days of summer ahead.

He throttled the speedboat down to make a wide circle as he approached the shore. It being his first outing of the season he felt a little rusty docking alone. Giving two blasts of his horn he hoped Martin would hear and appear to help him safely moor the classic boat.

Crossing its own wake, the hull sprayed chilly water into Norman's face. He wiped his eyes to better focus and saw Seth and Maria run out of the Manor toward him, with Martin following quickly behind. The children stopped at the end of the dock, waiting for their father to catch-up.

Martin shouted, "Norman, come on in. I'll catch ya."

Norman turned the wheel hard left and aligned his boat with the edge of the dock. Just as he threw a rope to Martin he shifted into reverse … expertly coming to a stop inches from the boards, proving he could have moored it himself after all.

"Nice approach. You haven't lost your touch."

"Hey, thanks for the invitation to dinner."

"We're glad you can make it."

"Well, with Chloe not due back until next week, I'm pretty free." Norman looked at the kids who had walked out onto the dock, standing near their father as he secured the lines. "Hey, kids, how are you?" Norman asked, "Being good?"

Not having seen him for six months, Seth and Maria both hesitated. Then Seth smiled, and Maria followed his lead.

Norman asked, "Want to come aboard?"

Seth responded by jumping into the cockpit; Maria stepped carefully on the foot pad at the edge of the deck and down onto the seat. Norman hugged them both, gently swinging them from side to side. "I've missed you two."

Vicki came out of the Manor and shouted. "Norman, you're here! Come on, all of you, dinner is almost ready."

Martin lifted the kids out of the boat, turned to give Norman a hand, but found him offering a bottle. "A Grand Cru by Francois, already aged. Pretty good wine, actually." He easily stepped onto the dock. "Save it for a special occasion."

Vicki met Norman half-way across the yard, arms open offering a warm hug. It became too warm ... more like a lover than the wife of a business associate. Last year, Norman had been Martin's boss, now he was the retired partial owner of the firm. He wondered if this changed anything in Vicki's attitude toward him. He enjoyed the moment. What man wouldn't, an attractive younger woman, her arms embracing his shoulders, pressing her breasts and abdomen tight to his body? He always enjoyed it ... women casually seeming to come-on to him. It happened many times before ... as if he were some form of magnetic yin to their yang. Most recently Denise, his ex-mistress from the printing plant, calling and leaving him a voice mail, then insisting on picking him up when he returned from France. She drove him all the way home and as soon as the door was closed and a drink poured, came close and offered, "We can do it ... for old times' sake ... no strings." Standing close to Denise, Norman gave Chloe, still in France, a thought. But he didn't stop Denise, young enough to be his daughter. For him, sex had often been 'no strings attached'; until he got married. His wife demanded the exclusive string he was not able to provide over the years; leading her to become his 'Ex-'. Denise offering 'no strings' brought him back to younger days.

Now, Vicki's hug was too tight, Norman sensed something different. She whispered, "Norman, oh, Norman. Where have you been?" ... urgency in her breath... instead of being seductive, more like a cry for help. Was Vicki grasping to deal with some chaos her life had become?

Norman gently returned Vicki's hug, then placed his hands on her forearms and slowly backed her away to look into her face. Seeing the pain in her eyes he softly said, "Vicki, I've been too long gone. But I'm back now and I'll do whatever I can to help."

Vicki smiled, "Well, you certainly were missed. How is that other woman anyhow?"

Norman wasn't sure if she was referring to Chloe or Denise. He decided to take the easy way out. "Chloe's fine. I expect her back here next week."

"Well that's good. She'll keep you out of trouble. Hell, keep us all out of trouble."

Martin, standing next to them, said, "Vicki, be nice."

Turning to Martin, she said, "I'm always nice." Smiling at them both, she continued, "Now let's go in and have a nice dinner, with our nice children, in this nice Manor situated so beautifully by this nice lake. And, you two, both of you, you remember to be nice."

Vicki turned on her heel and headed for the door of the Manor as Norman and Martin glanced at each other with raised eyebrows.

Vicki finished preparing dinner while Martin poured Norman straight-up Glenfiddich. Seth and Maria helped their mother carry the meal to the dining room table. Vicki called to the men, "Since you two are into the good stuff, bring your glasses with you."

Norman asked, "Want one?"

"That stuff?" She scrunched her face, "Ugh! No, I'll pass. One more thing and dinner's ready." Vicki darted back into the kitchen.

Norman turned to Martin, "Never saw her turn a drink down before."

Martin shrugged his shoulders, "Neither have I. Don't know whether this is good or bad."

Vicki called as she carried plates with shrimp salad to the table. "Come on guys, we'll start with these, then we have broiled chicken breasts with mashed potatoes; simple American style." Looking toward Norman, "Figured you'd like to get away from fussy French for a while."

Norman smiled, "Yeah, I need some good down-home cookin' for a change."

"Hope you like it."

"I'm sure I will."

As they sat down, Seth made faces at Norman and got silent movie-type mugs in return, making him laugh.

Vicki smiled at them both as she sat down. She said, "Well, unless someone's for saying grace, dig in."

Norman picked up his knife and fork, responding with the word 'Grace', making Seth laugh again. He took a bite and said, "Vicki, this is really good." Martin nodded in agreement.

Vicki cut into her chicken, "Amazing what can be done with a recipe off a mayonnaise jar." Then she asked, "So, Norman, Give ... what's the scoop?"

"Well, as I told Martin before, France is a mixed bag. Chloe managed to sell her vineyard after a damn drawn out negotiation ... took forever. That's why I'm only now getting home. And I found a lot to catch up on here. But those French..."

Vicki interrupted, "No, Norman, not the French. We want to hear about Chloe? You two getting on?"

"Vicki," Martin said, "... behave."

Vicki responded, smiling, "Oh, Martin, can't we be honest? Everybody's so damned polite, we never get down-to-earth ... share the truth. I'm sure Norman wants to share," Turning toward Norman, "Don't you?"

"Sure, Vicki, sure. Chloe's good. She's been under a lot of stress with the sale of the vineyard, but that's behind her now. So she's coming our way next week."

"To stay ... for good?"

"We haven't come that far yet."

"Well, how are things really? Like in the boudoir?"

"Vicki!"

"Oh, Martin, you're such a prude. If the sex holds up, Chloe will be probably stay with Norman. If not, she's back to France. Don't you see the connection, how important it is?"

"Well, "Martin said, "I think a relationship is based on a lot more than that."

"Yeah, easy for you to say … or wish. But, Norman, you do understand what I'm asking?"

"I think I do and right now, with the kids here, I'm going to enjoy this wonderful chicken you prepared."

Seth asked his mother, "What's a boudoir?"

"A bedroom, Seth, a bedroom." Turning back to Norman, "You're good Norman, really good. Compliment and insult the hostess in the same breath. Enjoy your chicken."

Vicki paused, looking at Norman she continued, "Men always want it and talk about it…"

Martin asked, "Want what?"

"Really Martin, are you that dense? Norman knows what I'm saying."

"Yes," Norman said, "So?"

"Well, you men always demand it on your own terms."

"Oh Vicki," Norman said, "I don't know about that."

"Okay, let's just drop the whole thing!" After taking a breath, Vicki continued, "Eat up, but leave room because I have a terrific cheese cake for desert." Vicki turned to her children, "You kids didn't hear anything that bothers you did you?"

Both Seth and Maria shook their heads 'No!'

Norman said, "I've been meaning to ask you two, have you heard anything about these new hydrofracking gas wells being proposed around here?"

Martin said, "I've seen some lawn signs that say 'No Frack' and read a short article in the weekly local paper, but nobody's said anything."

"He's been so friggin busy at the plant, he hasn't had time to pay attention to much here."

"So you don't know of the lease at the top of the hill to put in a gas well?"

"What? Joey?"

"No, not Joey. Above him, the farmer up on the flat land beyond the crest of the hill."

"Not a word. I didn't even know of a farmer up above Joey, thought it was all overgrown scrub land. Vicki, have you heard anything?'

"Norman, you're the first to mention it. I wonder why Emma and Will haven't said something? I see them every day."

"Maybe they don't know either. Joey was surprised when he found out about a lease."

Martin asked, "So, what's with these wells?"

"Not much, but Joey and I are gonna find out."

Since the kids were finished eating, Vicki took them into the family room to watch TV.

On her return she brought a pot of coffee from the kitchen, poured some in each cup and sat down. "So, okay, Norman, now that the kids are gone ... how's the sex?"

"Vicki!" Martin almost shouted, "Can't you get off that? Anyhow, we're still talkin' about gas wells."

"Martin, can you make life any more boring? Come on Norman, tell me, is Chloe a keeper or not?"

"Have to ask her that Vicki. You know Chloe, she has her own mind."

"But where's your mind Norman? You certainly were over the top last year when you two first fell for each other." Vicki sat back and began to quietly laugh, putting her hand to her mouth. "Like a smitten teenager..." She moved her hand from her mouth and laughed out loud. Pointing at Norman she said, "Oh, Norman, you were a stitch, especially when she got mad." Vicki bent over in laughter, while the men just watched, seeing nothing to laugh about, glancing at each other in concern over Vicki ... the laughter being too long, too deep.

Vicki stopped and sat up straight, saying, "Oh, you men, you never get the point. Okay, okay, I promised to be nice tonight. I won't get excited ... I won't swear. I'm just trying to be sure you don't get fucked ... financially that is."

"Don't worry. Everything's under control." Norman chuckled, glancing toward Martin, "As long as you keep the presses rolling. But, Vicki, this dinner is so good I'll tell you this: Chloe is a fascinating woman, very complex, and since you seem to need to know, I'm still very, very interested."

"So have you seen Jackie?"

"No, I've met with Joey a few times but Jackie hasn't been with him."

"So … what does Chloe think of the "Good News'?"

"There's good news?"

"Oh, come on, Norman. You must know about the pregnancy and the marriage plans?"

"Oh, that! Yeah, I heard something about that."

"But you haven't told Chloe yet?"

"Not my place to. But I wish Jackie'd hurry up and tell her."

Vicki scoffed, "I'm sure Chloe'll just love Jackie's predicament. Welcome a marriage to Joey with open arms. And you know who's gonna get the brunt of her anger when she finds out you know and didn't tell her."

"I just told you, it's not my place to tell her. Jackie needs to do that. Besides I'm not privy to any details. You know Chloe, a thousand questions."

"Yeah! Try that logic on Chloe when she gets her hooks into you. I'm surprised she hasn't been in touch … you know, women's intuition."

"Well, I missed a call from her mid-day today, but by the time I saw it and rushing to get over here I decided to wait until tomorrow to call her back. It's the middle of the night over there."

Martin cut-in, "Okay, let's leave Chloe and Jackie to Chloe and Jackie … and you Norman."

Vicki sat back, arms folded, "Martin, you know, you kill all the fun. What are you some kinda referee? I'm just getting' warmed up."

"If I didn't know you'd had nothing to drink, I'd say you're drunk. But as I think I said before, Norman is our guest … he's not on trial."

"It's okay Martin, Vicki hasn't seen me in months and just needs to have some fun. I understand."

"What a patronizing couple of bastards you two are. Well, go on, talk about all your man-stuff. I'll get the cheese cake out so the kids can have some before going to bed."

After Vicki left the room, Norman turned to Martin, looking down at his empty scotch tumbler, "She's right you know. Chloe is really going to be pissed ... and I'll catch hell for not telling her as soon as I found out."

"Ah, women, they freak out just to keep us on our toes. Want another scotch?"

"Yeah, I'm gonna need it ... after dessert."

Vicki followed Seth and Maria into the dining room carrying an uncut cheese cake. "Here we go," she smiled, "Everybody want a piece? We all need one ... have to build ourselves up for when Chloe again graces our shores."

As she served pieces on dessert plates she said, "Norman, you're a good sport putting up with me tonight. It's great you being back ... and a wonderful evening, a perfect time for some lighthearted fun. Please forgive me."

"A small price to pay for being with you all and for a wonderful dinner. But I can't stay too late, want to get back to my place before the twilight's gone."

Martin said, "You know Norman, I usually don't say things like this, but I think Chloe may have mellowed you just a bit."

"Either that or old age comin' on."

Seth finished his cheese cake first, followed quickly by Maria. Vicki used their haste as a cue to get them up to bed.

As Vicki and the kids walked upstairs Norman asked, "Is she okay?"

"She gets like this. She'll be okay. Probably over-tired or something."

Martin got up, poured another couple of fingers of straight scotch for Norman and himself. He handed Norman the glass motioning toward the warm light of the sun coming through the windows. "Let's walk outside."

Walking to the porch railing, Norman said, "I envy you these sunsets. I get the sunrise at my place, but I have to be up and ready to catch those."

"Kinda puts things in perspective doesn't it. I always find the last moments of sun very calming."

The two men stood in silence as the sun receded behind the far hill. Once it was gone, Martin looked at Norman smiling.

Norman asked, "What? What's so funny?"

"You're good, Norman. Got to hand it to you, you're good."

"You mean about Chloe … what?"

"Oh, just how you handle things with the women. You seem to have an answer for everything. Keep them coming … without getting hysterical. I can't seem to do that."

"I certainly didn't learn it."

"Not with all the risks you take."

"What are you talking about?" Norman paused. "Listen, if you're referring to anything else other than Chloe, I'm sure you'll keep it to yourself."

"Don't know what you're talkin' about Norman. But, yeah, one man to another, I wouldn't spread any rumors. Just be careful because you may have met your match in Chloe. You don't want to screw that up." Martin raised his glass in Norman's direction. "But, still, I gotta say, *You are good!"*

℘   ℃

When Vicki came downstairs the men drained their last sips of scotch and walked back into the Manor.

Norman said, "Well, I need to get going … catch the last of the light." He walked over to Vicki and brushed her cheek saying, "Thanks for dinner. We'll have you all over once Chloe gets settled."

The three adults walked out the main door of the Manor into the soft glow. Joey's red MG was just turning into the driveway. Jackie, in the passenger seat, glancing at Joey, her head thrown back in a hearty laugh, apparently responding to something very funny Joey said. Seeing the adults Jackie closed her mouth trying to stifle the laugh. Joey pulled up next to them, smiling, "Norman, hi."

"You two seem happy. It's a good night for the MG."

"Perfect. We just took a spin over by some of the Kober vineyards. Wanted to check out the early growth. But it's so nice we just kept going."

"So how does it look, the growth, that is?"

"Great. A good start."

Norman looked at Jackie, "I've seen Joey a lot, but I've always missed you. I hear congratulations are in order. It looks like Motherhood is agreeing with you … there's so much color in your face. Or maybe it's just the light."

Vicki leaned into the conversation, "Oh, Norman. What a thing to say."

"Look at her. She's radiant."

"Now that you've made her blush."

Jackie looked at them both, smiling. "I am happy. Just happy."

"I'm glad you came along." Norman said, "Your grandmother is flying in next week and I wonder if you'd like to come with me to meet her at the airport?"

Jackie looked down and when she raised her head there was no remnant of happiness left on her face. "Oui. Yes. I will come."

"Okay, I'll call with the exact time. Now, I'd better get going so I can cross the lake before it gets too dark."

Vicki and Martin walked Norman toward his boat.

Vicki said, "So, Norman, when you pick up Chloe, you're using Jackie as a shield?"

"Vicki," Martin said, "Must you be so crass?"

Norman interrupted, "Well, you must remember I may become Jackie's step-grandfather."

"Oh, it's that serious. Wow, I thought you and Chloe were just shackin' up together. What do they call it, 'friends with benefits'.

"With two countries, taxes and visas to worry about, the decision to get married, or not, becomes pretty complex. We're trying to figure out what's best."

"But you're keeping that woman satisfied?"

Martin interrupted, "Vicki, stop!"

"Oh, Martin, stuff it! I just asked the question." She followed them to the dock in silence and stood waiting while Norman started the engine and Martin helped him push off. Once clear of shore, Norman gave a final wave and gunned the engine to full throttle creating the deep exhaust note distinctive to the wooden hulled speedboats of the '50s era.

Martin turned toward Vicki to walk off the dock, "Nothin' like it."

She blocked his way, "I ought to knock you in the lake right now. You, you egotistical prude. Every time I tried to lighten up with Norman tonight you insulted me. Damned you Martin, you tell Norman I have a problem. I don't have a problem."

Vicki turned on her heel, "You, you are my problem!" Walking toward shore she shouted over her shoulder for all to hear, "Go fuck yourself, because you won't be fucking me tonight."

Martin stood watching her march up to the Manor. *As if I'd want to!*

He turned back toward the lake and watched the receding view of the Chris Craft skimming across the water. *One of these days I'll have to get one of those.*

            ဢ   **ଔ**

Emma had the kitchen window of the Carriage House open a crack to catch the sweet smells of spring as she emptied the dishwasher. She heard the last of Vicki's outburst, shouted for the benefit of all within earshot, 'Go fuck yourself!'. *Why does that woman do that to Martin? He tries so hard and she just goads him on.*

Emma would never say that, or anything like it, to Will. She had too much respect for him. She loved him. Five years earlier when she and Will fell in love, their intimacy touched deep hurts he couldn't hide, from years of anguish caused by his wife's depression ... 'a shadow disease I could never get my arms around' Will told her. It took months of tenderness before Will could cope with the depth of Emma's feelings toward him, months for Will to build enough trust to allow himself to abandon his fear to love another. It took that long before he could share the fact that 15 years earlier his wife had legally purchased a handgun then sat alone for hours in their car, before joining the thousands who commit suicide by firearm every year. Will cried as he told Emma, 'She hurt our four sons so deeply ... and wounded me for life. Why did she do that? All I knew to do was put my head down and raise the boys until they were grown ... and then I just felt empty, wasted, nothing left. Until I met you.' *And now, Vicki, next door, her antics resurfacing memories in Will of those dark days.*

Emma couldn't figure out what happened only minutes before. She'd seen Jackie and Joey pull up in the MG and greet the three adults coming out of the Manor. Jackie seemed very happy. After a short discussion, she'd come into the Carriage House telling Emma she needed to grab her jacket ... it was starting to get chilly in the MG. She and Joey were on their way into town, she'd be back early. Minutes later Vicki is shouting to the hills, *Martin ... Go fuck yourself!*

Emma walked into the front room where Will was standing looking out at the lake.

"Did you hear that?"

"What? I didn't hear anything other than the boat."

"Oh, nothing." Emma put her hand on Will's back, lightly rubbing. *There are advantages to having hearing problems.*

"Norman's Chris Craft just may be the last on the lake," he said, watching the classic boat headed to the far shore.

She moved her body close to his, coming to face him without blocking his line of vision.

"Kind of like us," Emma smiled, "the last classic lovers on the lake."

After a few moments, Emma asked, "You know how they wonder if a tree falling in a deserted forest makes any noise when there's no one to hear it?"

"Yeah? But it still makes a sound."

"But no one hears it."

What are you getting at?"

Emma kept her hand stroking Will's back as she moved her legs against his. "Well, Jackie just went into town with Joey, so maybe we could go in the bedroom. We can be noisy. But no one will hear us. So it'll be quiet at the same time."

Chapter 9

Joey drove his MG along Main Street of the village at the north end of the lake. Dimming twilight darkened the bright red of the long hood into a rich shade of burgundy. Turning into an alley sandwiched between two buildings; narrow even for the small roadster, he commented to Jackie, "I'll bet this block was built during the horse and buggy days, before cars." There were potholes in the alley, so Joey drove slowly, to protect the undercarriage of the classic car.

"We're going into Benny's, the neighborhood bar ... been here for a couple generations. Benny was a classmate of mine in high school; but the bar is named after his great-grandfather, the first Benny. I think he started the whole thing just after World War I, then Prohibition came and he earned quite a reputation for himself. The man to see for liquor from Canada. Are you following all this?"

"*Oui.* But I'll understand better if I know this Prohibition?"

"That's when all liquor was outlawed through the 1920s and early 30s."

Jackie laughed, "Really. Even wine?"

"Yes, even wine. Except for religious purposes. But, a lot of wineries went out of business."

"Not in France. Riots, there would be riots."

"My grandfather told me the do-gooders continued the ban until well into the Depression."

"The what?"

"The Depression. It started when the stock market crashed in 1929 and lasted about ten years. Money became very tight, even for governments. In the early '30s, the politicians realized they could make a lot of money taxing liquor, so they ended Prohibition. By then Benny's family was one of the most trusted in town. Folks around here don't forget. They're loyal."

Joey pulled into a parking space in the lot behind the bar, a tight space no one else felt comfortable using … just right for the MG.

As they walked through the rear entrance, Jackie looked down a long bar running the length of the room. The warmth of its wood, enhanced by decades of wiping, was highlighted by soft hanging lights, all under an original tin ceiling. A green pool table dominated the space in front of a picture window at the far end, overlooking Main Street.

A tall burly man waved and strode toward them. "Joey, it's been a while. Thought you'd fallen off the face of the earth. Heard you were tied up with a young lass." Looking at Jackie as he came close, "I can see why you'd be distracted."

Joey smiled, "Ben, this is Jackie."

Ben's broad face matched his shoulders; his goatee protected what otherwise would be a receding chin. He smiled, extending a hand toward Jackie. "Hi, I went to school with Joey; we were on the wrestling team together." Ben winked, "Anything you want to know about Joey, just give me a call."

She smiled, "*Oui…*"

"Jackie, a nice name. From France? That's what I hear. You're pretty enough to be from France."

Jackie couldn't think of what to say. She tried not to blush.

"Okay, Benny, cool it man. Did you get my message?"

"I did. Tried to call you back but you must've been out of range. Anyhow, you're in luck. See the guy at the end of the bar? Name's Hank … worked the gas wells in PA. Been here the last few nights, don't know why, but seems like a nice enough guy. He's a vet, too. Come on, I'll introduce you."

Ben turned and taking long strides walked quickly on the service side of the bar toward Hank, while Joey followed on the customer side. Hank was a man of slight build, about 30, with a pockmarked face covered with several days of unshaven growth. His jeans were worn, but clean; topped by an AC/DC tee shirt, too thin for the evening chill outside.

Ben said, "Hey Hank, this is Joey, the guy I told you might drop in; the guy that owns the vineyard."

Without moving his body on the bar stool, Hank glanced toward Joey, not looking particularly interested. "A vineyard owner, huh? So, Joey, is it? Why're you interested in yakkin' with me? I'm a little short on time."

Jackie caught up to the men and Hank noticed her for the first time. He swung around toward her, ignoring Joey. "Well, H-E-L-L-O … and you are?"

Ben answered, "Jackie, meet Hank."

"You didn't mention any Jackie. I expected some wheezened old vineyard owner, not some guy that looks ten years younger than you along with his girlfriend."

"I just met Jackie myself."

"Well, Jackie, Ben told me somebody called about gas wells. I wasn't excited about gettin' into it, but now, I guess I'm your man." It was evident Hank was no longer in any hurry. "Let's move over to a booth where we'll be more comfortable. And Ben, hit me with another sour mash, make it a double. I'm sure Joey won't mind pickin' up the tab."

"You got it. Joey, Jackie, what would you like … first one's on the house. I've got some last year Kober Riesling."

Joey answered, "Okay … Jackie?"

Jackie nodded, "*Oui.* Riesling, *tres bien*. But water for me."

"Ah, so you *are* expecting." Smiling Ben turned to Joey, "You really done it this time." Ben shrugged his shoulders. "Small town … word's out." He paused. "I'll bring the drinks over."

Hank slowly eased himself off the bar stool, his body moving with one side stiffened up, his face making a slight wince. He motioned to a booth in the back corner. Jackie slid into the booth, followed by Joey; Hank eased himself onto the bench on the opposite side of the table.

Hank looked at Jackie saying, "I move kinda funny … Afghanistan. Caught shrapnel from an RPG; knocked me outta kilter on the left side … for life I guess." Hank noticed Jackie's quizzical expression, "A rocket propelled grenade … explode into a thousand pieces of white-hot metal; no way the medics can get all the fragments out. But hey, I'm alive ... Marine next to me, he wasn't so lucky."

"Oh, I am sorry."

"Shit like that … nothin' anybody can do. Now, on top of it, I got this rash on my back and that ain't from no RPG … that's chemicals from the drillin'. But you didn't come to hear about me…"

Hank looked at Joey, "So, you own a vineyard. You're young for that, aren't ya?"

"My grandfather started it."

"Ah, you inherited a vineyard. Must be nice being born with a silver spoon in your mouth."

"Well, it wasn't quite like that. My mother was a single Mom raising me on her own. When my grandfather realized I had a knack for working with the vines he kept me busy. But we don't have any silver spoons lying around."

"Okay, so you're a struggling vineyard owner. And Jackie, somehow you don't look like you're from here."

"France, I grew up in France."

"Ahuh. Jackie, that's a strange name for a French girl."

"Jacqueline, in France I am called Jacqueline. I come here, people call me Jackie."

"Typical … lazy Americans. You like it here?"

"*Oui,* I hope to stay."

"Well, good luck with that … all the new Homeland Security crap."

"Joey and I, we are to be married."

"Well, if I were you, Joey, I'd hurry up before somebody comes along with a better offer."

Joey answered, "The sooner the better …"

Ben approached the table placing a glass of water in front of Jackie, a Riesling in front of Joey and a whiskey tumbler almost filled with bourbon for Hank. "You want it straight up, no ice, right?"

"Perfect!"

Ben also placed two bowls on the table, one filled with nuts, the other chips. He looked at Hank, "You'd better munch on some of these so you'll be able to walk out of here. And if you want something more substantial to eat, I can make that happen too."

Hank looked at the couple across the table as he said to Ben, "We're fine."

As Ben turned and left, Hank said, "Okay, what are you lookin' for?"

"We're trying to learn more about what's going on with hydrofracking around here. Any plans to start. We don't know much about it, yet."

"Haven't worked around here, but I've been a roustabout on wells in a few states, the latest Pennsylvania. I'm currently out of a job, so you're in luck. I can talk. If I was still on the payroll, they wouldn't want me talking to you, actually still don't. But they let me go, told me I move too slow ... somethin' about being a hazard to the other six guys on the team. Full o' shit, if you ask me! But the bastards won't admit anything tied to the rash on my back, so I'm outta gettin' any disability."

Hank sipped his bourbon and glanced toward the ceiling, "Damned twelve hour shifts were killin' me. The boss, arrogant Texas bastard, wouldn't let me work shorter hours. I even offered to split the day up. Fuckin' retard.

Hank sipped his bourbon, looked around checking for eavesdroppers, "Has a landman visited you?"

"No, not me. But, I hear the farmer higher up the hill is looking at a contract."

"Shit man, no landman is going to visit a vineyard owner. They're warned to stay away because you're passionate, like the tree huggers out west. You guys only care about your grapes, not, as the gas companies say, the good of the country."

"What do they mean by that?"

"The gas companies, they're patriotic, all about gettin' us out of the Middle East. What a crock of shit. But, you ... you stand in the way of progress ... and their profit."

Joey still looked perplexed. Before continuing, Hank took a sip of bourbon. "There's so much natural gas trapped right under our feet. Drill, baby, drill! All you vineyard types do is bitch and slow everything down. Keep us from becoming energy independent.

"Don't you see man? You protesters are keeping jarheads like me fightin' your wars. But your neighbor, the farmer, he's patriotic ... he'll fight to frack. Forget the fact he's gonna feel like a rich man for a while."

There was a loud crack as one of a group of four pool players took the break shot. Hank visibly flinched leaning over to his right. Straightening up, Hank said, "Reflex action after being under fire. Probably just a game of eight-ball."

"Yeah, it's hard to get back, isn't it?"

"Has its moments."

"But, Hank, what do you mean rich for a while?"

"Big payout up front. When the gas company comes in, sets up its pad for the well, along with a flowback pit, like a small pond, it's all neat and tidy on the surface. The landowner, he's finally got money in his pocket, more than he's had in a long time. So he pays off any debt he has and goes out and buys a new pickup, maybe even a Caddie. Oh, there's a lot of construction gear and it gets noisy with the compressors running all the time, but he's happy ... he's got that first payment with more promised when the gas starts flowing."

"It's that simple, some construction and a pond?"

"Hell no man! That first payment makes the landowner blind to the wide dirt road being cut across his land to the well pad. And he doesn't realize there may be several wells, as many as 10 on the site with trucks coming and going day and night."

"For what?" Joey asked.

"Sand and water. They need sand and a couple million gallons of water per well. The landowners overlook that. Also, the fact that a gas pipeline is going to be built out from the pad to wherever. Lots of scarred earth."

Hank looked at Jackie as he continued, "Below ground it's a whole different story. In PA the drilling goes vertical, probably about 4,000 feet, depending on the shale; then it fans out horizontally. It probably won't be so deep here. Geologists say only about 3,000 feet.

"That's when the fun begins, Jackie. They'll be frackin' the shale right under Joey's vineyard. No problem, right? I mean they're so deep, way down below everything else what harm can be done. Wrong! To free up the gas, fluid is injected along with sand under high pressure to fracture the shale. And, Joey, you can't do a damned thing to stop them."

Joey asked, "I thought they drilled deeper?"

"Yeah, they advertise that. But not in the Finger Lakes area; the Marcellus play, what we're sitting on top of. That's shallower. I was out in the Dakotas, they're a mile down. Different story."

"This fluid they inject, what is it?"

"Water mixed with sand and chemicals."

"Sand? Why sand?"

"The sand holds the fissures open just enough to release the gas. They call it slickwater … pretty nasty, toxic

"Well, making wine I've studied a little chemistry, what do they use."

"Aha! There's the rub … the gas companies won't tell us, not even the team I worked with. We were handling fluids; we didn't even know what's in them. But we figured out benzene, toluene, naphthalene … God knows what else. We also learned not to ask questions, not if wanted to keep our jobs."

"You're kidding me. I have to register every chemical I use at my vineyard; the type, manufacturer, quantity, date applied, it all gets reported to the state."

"We're talking about oil and gas companies here. Whole different world. And remember Dick Cheney. Before he was vice president he ran Halliburton, so when he's VP he invites his oil and gas buddies into the White House. They get an exemption from having to share the details of what they were going to use on this exciting new horizontal hydrofracking. We call the exclusion the 'Halliburton loophole'. The environment and clean water be damned."

"What about the ads I see that say hydrofracking has been used for 60 years … in New York State."

"That's true. Vertical fracking on the old wells … with no injection, no toxic shit. But the new technique drills horizontally, uses high pressure. Developed in Texas in the '90s. And there's problems with fracking near old wells, but I don't want to get ahead of myself."

"So this is all new…"

"And unproven. Look, they argue they're working so far underground, any aquifers, wells, ground water, none of that's affected. But the nasty little secret is, they are. Remember, a couple million gallons of water mixed with chemicals and sand is pumped into each well … and there may be as many as 10 wells per site. That's a lot of water that all has to be trucked in. And the waste water is extracted and poured into the flowback pit, eventually trucked away. But they can't capture all the waste water; some stays underground, and it affects the environment. You can see the result in PA now."

"I've heard some talk about that. Guess I should have paid more attention."

'Nothin' you could do about it. Even now, they lift the ban on frackin' in New York State and you're screwed buddy. Just bend over and spread 'em wide." Hank glanced at Jackie, "Sorry, guess I should clean up my act."

"*Non, non.* You tell as you see. Forget I am here."

"Oh, I don't think I can do that. You're far too pretty for that."

Hank looked back at Joey. "So what else can I say?"

"Tell us more about the hazards."

Hank took a sizeable swig of his bourbon, "The hazards, where do I start? I worked mostly in the Endless Mountains of northern PA. The bastards have drilled over a thousand frackin' wells there in the past ten years … too many. Just know, everything I'm gonna tell you is happening.

"On the surface it starts with a lot of heavy construction trucks on the local roads; when the drilling starts the compressors run all the time … noisy and diesel fumes. Once frackin' starts they need water … as much as 400 truckloads per well; then they need to haul away the flowback. But in PA the reclamation sites are several miles away so truckers often just dump the waste water along the roadways, right by farmers' fields … and I suppose any vineyards in the area."

Joey asked, "And you don't know what's in the water?'

"As I said, we don't know. But it's probably different from well to well, given what's happening underground, and who knows what's being picked up from the shale; sometimes the water's radioactive. Even though there are flowback pits at the well site, there's little concern for waste water other than to get rid of it.

"And, oh, pits have been known to leak. If your neighbor's up the hill springs a leak, you're probably going to get flowback on the surface. Maybe a whole lot if the damned thing bursts."

Jackie almost shouted, *"Non, non, non*! The soil, the terroir, it cannot be violated! Toxic waste water; it will rape the land!"

Hank raised his hands, palms open, and slowly lowered them, signaling her to keep it down. He said, softly, "Not me Jackie, I'm out of it. But you're right, no one knows how to make it right, get rid of the contamination."

"So," Joey said, "the roads are congested and take a lot of wear and tear, there's noise pollution, a lot of diesel exhaust, and there's a good chance the soil is contaminated and can't be reclaimed. That right?"

"You're a quick study Joey. Yeah, that's about right."

"That's awful! I agree with Jackie, our vineyard would be raped."

"Plus, with the traffic and noise you can kiss your tourists goodbye. The gas company'll frack for several months, then extract gas more quietly for months, then come back and frack again for more."

"My grandfather worked fifty years convincing people to come to the lakes, taste some wine … finally we're getting a lot of activity. We could lose that fast."

"Probably. But I'm not done yet. We need to go underground."

Both Jackie and Joey nodded for Hank to continue.

"The casings of the wells, the vertical concrete and steel, they're critical. Any flaw in the casing … concrete, steel, the welds … and chemicals leak at that depth. It's a real threat to aquifers and groundwater. Look, the guys I worked with, they worked hard to get everything right. But mistakes happen, accidents, and they're afraid to report it to the company. And if the company does know, they cover up because they don't want the liability. Just like my rash … they ignore me to sidestep liability."

"Nice," Joey said, "No see, no problem."

"You got it. But, stay with me. Once the horizontal drilling is setup, the compressor on the surface is putting 15,000 pounds of pressure per inch on the frackin' fluid to break the shale apart ... to fracture it. This releases the trapped gas. The problem is, shale being as stratified as it is, all the gas and wastewater don't come back to the surface. Some stays below and finds its way elsewhere. Methane and the waste of frackin' has been found in aquifers and wells close to the surface … making the water unusable, certainly not potable.

"Can the experts predict any of this?" Joey asked.

"Only that it's a possibility. And since most work for the oil and gas companies they don't have a lot of incentive to point out the hazards."

"What about our lakes?"

"They're vulnerable. Contaminate a lake and how do you reclaim it? Nobody knows. It's gone, probably for a generation."

A man, a little over six feet tall, still handsome even though showing the telltale signs of creeping middle age, approached the table.

Hank looked up saying, "Hey, the landman himself. How's the family?"

"Fine, I guess. Been up here all week."

"You need to get home to those kids more often."

"Lotsa luck on that."

"So, you celebratin' another signed contract?"

"Introduce me Hank. Who you talkin' to?"

"We were just talkin' about you … our fearless landman who sells refrigerators to Eskimos." Hank looked at Jackie and Joey, "Meet your local landman, Captain Contract." Hank looked back at the landman, smiling, "Not that it's any of your business, these folks, Jackie and Joey, they own a vineyard."

"You know damned well, Hank, you aren't supposed to be talking with any vineyard people."

"Last I heard this is the USA, a free country. First Amendment rights and all."

"Bullshit, you know the company rules."

"Yeah, it's like, the company can take their bullshit rules and stuff them up their bullshit asses. They fired me the other day … without any disability or anything."

"Well, you probably aren't entitled. Or are you still crying 'I'm a wounded vet'?

"You damned asshole! If I could move faster I'd clean your clock … right here and now. You bastards sit over here in your comforts and glory not even realizing there's a war going on and good guys are gettin' killed. Then we come home, broken, and you treat us like shit. So get outta my face."

The landman looked at Joey, "So what's he been telling you, all the fear mongering stuff about hydrofracking?"

Hank cut in, "Fear mongering! I been sharing all the good stuff. Why if I had a contract he'd sign it right here and now to frack directly under his vineyard. Good thing I got to him first because if you tried to sell him, you'd have to pull in that woman you use to sweet talk the old folks."

"Who?"

"You know who, the who you were pokin' all last year, 'til her husband found out and broke your fuckin' nose."

"Why you little…" The landman raised his fist, but it never moved forward because Ben was right behind him with a hammer lock on his arms. "Hey buddy, either too much to drink or far too uptight. I think we'll take this out front." Looking at the trio at the table, he said, "You all stay right where you are."

Ben stiff-walked the landman out the door, keeping his arms locked all the way. Joey leaned toward Hank, who was sucking down the last of his bourbon. "Wow. You guys put on quite a show. Is it always this interesting?"

"Only when that asshole shows up. He thinks since he's the advance man he can tell everybody how to, as he says, 'Prepare the ground for signing'. But he's finding you folks up here not so gullible. More and more landowners are organizing and hiring lawyers. Contracts are harder to come by … with more payout, a lot more payout. I imagine his commissions are pretty low right now."

"Well, thanks for all your help. I think Jackie and I have had all we can absorb in one night. Can I buy you another?"

"No, it's probably best if I just get the hell out of here. Nice to meet you both … but Jackie, you may just be too pretty for this town."

Ben walked back in rotating his shoulders as if fending off a bad chill. "Where'd he come from? I look up and see he's about to grab Hank. Not in my bar. You're always welcome man. Need another or all set?"

"I'm set. I'll come by again."

"Thanks for helping these folks out. And Joey, stop by more often; bring Jackie along."

"We'll do that. What do I owe you?"

"It's on the house." Ben smiled, "Least I can do since you're gonna be a daddy."

Jackie and Joey walked behind several men seated at the bar to reach the back entry. One tapped Joey sharply on the elbow, speaking with a liquored-up voice, "Joey O'Donnell!"

Startled, Joey spun around, facing the protagonist. "Yeah!"

"Joey," the middle-aged man smiled, extending his hand, "Joey, Fred Kober. Your shirt-tail cousin. We met at your grandfather's funeral."

Joey took the offered handshake. "Oh, yes … Fred. Yes, I remember."

"I hear you've got a vineyard now. Hear the old man treated you well."

Joey wasn't sure how to respond, "Yes, I guess you can say that."

"Guess! God damned man. He treated you a hell of a lot better than he treated his own brother, my grandfather. Forced my side of the family out of all the good vineyard land with the lake microclimates. Left us to hoe the soil on the flats …up top 'o the hill. No damned good for grapes there."

"Sorry, I don't know about that."

"No, I guess you wouldn't. Don't imagine your grandmother spends much time talkin' about the black sheep side of the family. Just remember your grandfather didn't start Kober Vineyards alone. He had help. Worked his brother to the bone, then screwed his ass out of any share of the business. Left him flappin' in the breeze."

"Well, I…"

Fred looked down, speaking to himself, "Aw, fuck. What am I doin'?" He looked back at Joey, "You get on out of here, your gals waitin' for ya by the door. Hell, all happened decades ago. No sense harborin' hard feelings now."

Walking to the MG, Joey put his hands to his forehead. "Whew!"

Jackie asked, "You okay? Who was that?"

"One of my distant cousins. He's drunk. From the pissed off side of the family."

Joey lowered his hands, "But enough of them." He looked at Jackie, "Listen, nobody's gonna frack under our vines!"

After a few more paces, he put his arm around Jackie and pulled her close. "You know, love, I really appreciate you being with me. But I think from now on I'm going to leave the research done in bars to Norman."

"And miss all the fun?"

"You and Norman will have all the fun you can handle when Chloe gets here next week."

"And you will not? Remember Joey my love, she holds you responsible ... for everything ... the way you overpowered me." Jackie smiled at him, clutching his arm, a skip in her step, "So, *Voila*, let the fun begin."

Chapter 10

Chloe repeatedly checked the video screen mounted in the seatback in front of her. Although she knew the Airbus was flying over the Atlantic at 500 knots, the little plane shown on the screen hardly moved, tightening the tension building inside her.

Chloe had hoped once all the legalities of the vineyard sale were completed and the repairs to the chateau were addressed, her nerves would settle. But delays with the contractor had forced leaving the final work under the direction of Horbst, her long-time vintner. It was convenient for him, since he continued to work the same vines he had for years … just on Francois' payroll. Happily Horbst's penchant for detail assured quality repairs would be made.

As the hours went by, sleep eluding her, Chloe focused on the real driver of her frayed nerves … not the vineyard sale to Francois and the urgent repairs to the chateau … no, it was Jacqueline's pregnancy by that country-boy. *How can he possibly be the love of her life?* Chloe knew changing the mind of an impulsive 25-year-old girl, one just as stubborn as herself, *and pregnant!,* would be just about impossible. She knew head-on reproach certainly wouldn't change Jacqueline's mind. It would just embolden her more.

And then there was Norman, and the reality of her love for him. He certainly would make her comfortable financially. *But where is this heading? And, where, where will we live? Must we marry if I decide to stay in the United States? Will he drop everything for me and move to France? If I convince Jacqueline to return with me, will Norman come too?*

Chloe reclined her seat position to get more comfortable and put her eye shade on to get some sleep. It never came.

ഇ   ൙

Chloe's plane was over an hour late arriving in Rochester. She rushed up to Jacqueline, giving her a warm hug and kisses on both cheeks. Speaking in French, "Mon cheri! How are you my dear? I am so worried about you."

"Fine, grand-mere, as good as ever. No more morning sickness. I feel the best I have in months."

"Well, we must be sure you are getting the proper care."

Turning to Norman, Chloe embraced him. "And you, you are behaving yourself?"

Norman returned Chloe's hug, saying, "Missed you, Chloe. Good flight?"

"Just too long."

"Well, it's getting late. Let's get your luggage."

Norman was surprised when he held the passenger door of his sedan open for Chloe. Instead of getting inside she opened the rear door and slid onto the back seat, motioning Jacqueline to follow, saying, "Norman you are our chauffeur tonight."

As they pulled out of the parking lot, Chloe ran her hands beside her head to assure no strands of hair had fallen out of place. In French she said, "You did not call, Jacqueline ... and when I called you were out. So everything goes well? Joey, Emma, Will, how are they?"

Jackie also spoke in French, "Fine, they are all fine. Joey has been very busy with the vines. He is also working on the plans for the winery. The Tasting Room building will be of wood ... 'rustic' is how he describes it ... with a beautiful view of the lake."

"And the winter? How was the cold and snow?"

"Harsh, more than I thought; we are happy to have spring. The winter was cold and long. And the snow, I am told deeper than usual. The hills get the most snow. But Joey took me out and we enjoyed it."

"Oh, I am sure he did. How so, did you enjoy?"

"He took me skiing. I like cross-country the best, so peaceful. And we ice skated on the lake. Even made a big snowman one day."

"You play … no work?"

"We keep busy up in the vineyard and with the plans. Norman has been helping us with those since he returned."

Norman, hearing his name, said over his shoulder, "You know, if you spoke slower, or even better in English, I could be a part of this conversation."

Chloe leaned forward. "Norman, don't interrupt. I talk with Jacqueline." Sitting back, she again spoke in French, "Yes dear, go on…"

"Joey's uncle Nicholas invited us to the Kober winery to learn some techniques he uses in wine making. I learned a lot about fermentation … a process called malolactic. It softens the taste of the acid. And the white wines, so much to learn, particularly the Rieslings that are so famous here. Then we helped stir the lees of the Burgundy. It was fun."

"Don't you already know this?"

"Oui, about the Burgundy. But going away to school I missed so much at the chateau. And there is so much more to learn."

"I suppose. I just hope this uncle Nicholas knows what he's doing. The wines from this region have never been held high by the world. The winter though, it sounds so difficult. Are you sure you want to live here?"

"Grand-mere, I love Joey. I want to be with him. And he has been wonderful about having the baby."

"Being pregnant you may feel that way more than you would otherwise."

"I felt this way before I got pregnant."

"That my dear is neither here nor there … you did not know Joey long enough before. You are still young.

"You mentioned on one of your calls that you are tutoring?"

"At the community college, across the lake. I enjoy it. Even made a few friends."

"French? You tutor in French?"

"Only the basics. No one is advanced."

Chloe paused a few moments with Jackie and Norman savoring the silence. She may even have nodded off.

Chloe brought them back to attention by asking, in English, "You will have the baby in November, right?"

"*Oui*. Early in November."

"And you plan to marry before that? So, you are planning the wedding?"

"During the summer, sometime, grand-mere, Joey and I will be married. But no plans are finalized."

"What about the Church?"

Jackie was taken aback. She and Joey hadn't considered a church, any church.

"We haven't decided yet."

"You must make up your minds. Talk to a pastor, get on a schedule…"

"If we decide to marry in a church."

"But, there will be the Church … yes?"

Jackie didn't answer.

"You hope for a wedding in just two or three months, and no plans are made?"

"It will be a very simple wedding."

"No wedding is simple, believe me. And, remember, it is a very special day. Do not let Joey take that away from you!"

Norman said, "Yes, Chloe, but the kids want to keep things very low-key."

Chloe raised her voice to be heard over the road noise. "As you men always want it, you are all so lazy. No, Norman, it cannot be low-key, as you say. Leave weddings to the women, we know what we are doing. And, please, do not interrupt."

After a moment, Chloe said, "It is late, and I have been up for almost 24 hours, so perhaps we should just ride quietly for a while."

When they pulled into the Carriage House driveway, Will came out to the car. Seeing Chloe in the back seat he opened that door. "Chloe welcome back. Would you like to come in?"

Chloe got out of the car, and gave Will a light hug, air-kissing him on both cheeks. "Merci, but I am tired, so we must go."

"Emma thought you might say that after your long day. How about lunch tomorrow, you and Norman?"

"*Oui*, that will be nice."

Chloe hugged Jackie, wishing her to sleep well. She walked around to the passenger side and Will opened the front door for her.

Norman leaned over and said, "So, okay. About Noon?"

"Noon's great."

As Norman slowly pulled the car around, Will lightly put his arm around Jackie's shoulder. He felt her shiver.

"Cold?"

"*Oui*, a little. It is chilly now." She looked at Will. "I am scared. She needs to control. To her I am only a little girl."

"Jackie, you're not. You're about to be a mother. Don't forget that! Emma and I will help you."

Norman drove in silence, allowing Chloe to doze off again. After a few minutes she broke the silence. "That girl … thinks she knows everything. Definitely will not listen."

"Sounded to me like she's got things pretty much in hand, the little I could decipher with you two speaking French so rapidly."

"Defiant! Telling me to keep my nose out of her pregnancy and her wedding."

"How do you figure that? I didn't hear any defiant tone."

"You need to take a course in French. She's got her mind made up. Definitely being misled by that Emma … the loving American grand-mere."

"Now Chloe, let's not set up the battle lines just yet."

"Listen Norman, the battle lines never came down. Jacqueline has her mind made up. And I intend to unmake it."

After a moment, Chloe added, "Oh, I am so tired of all this, I don't even know if I want you next to me tonight."

"That bad, huh."

Norman waited for a response. Glancing at Chloe he realized she was asleep.

A half-hour later, Chloe walked into Norman's living room. "A scotch would be nice; might settle my nerves."

"I thought you were exhausted?"

"I am, but the chilly air outside wakes me up."

As Norman turned on a few lamps she looked around the room "It intrigues me how an old printer, up to his elbows in ink, had such very good taste."

"Thanks, but as I told you, I had help."

"Yes, that first wife of yours; and then, you said, the art director of a client was your color coordinator. Thank God you had antiques to add some counterpoint." Chloe walked close to Norman. "I never asked you, was she good in bed?"

"What?"

"Was she able to satisfy you, really satisfy you?"

Norman handed a small tumbler of scotch to Chloe. "I thought we agreed we weren't going to delve into our history."

"Yes, we did, but I become curious."

"Just to satisfy your curiosity, I will say she was a very creative art director."

"Oh, that helps. Just opens up a Pandora's box of questions."

"Chloe, my love," Norman held up his glass to her, "It's wonderful having you home."

Chloe stepped closer to Norman and looked him in the eye. "So how was she, the recent one?"

"The art director, I haven't seen her in years. Heard she got married ... one of those office romances ... to a vice president."

"Nice deflection. You should play football."

"You mean soccer." Norman clinked his glass to Chloe's. "I'm glad you're home."

Chloe took a sip of scotch, held up the glass, saying, "*Tres bien.*"

"Shall we sit and talk?"

Chloe ignored the question and remained standing. "No, not the art director. How was the woman you were with since you came back here, since we were together? I mean Norman, it is only a month."

"Woman?"

Chloe stepped closer to Norman, repeating her question, forcefully, "*Oui*, the woman you slept with?"

'Well, uh…"

"Norman look at me! Do not lie to me. I can tell by your hug at the airport … you have had sex. But, you forget, being French I can deal with your need … better than American women."

"Yeah, that president of yours, who died. His wife and mistress sitting next to each other at his funeral. I like the French."

"Mitterrand, it was President Mitterrand. A long and deep relationship."

"Doesn't that give me some slack?"

"Perhaps. After all you are a healthy man. And all my life I have had to deal with the yearning of men … your need for other women.

"What I cannot deal with … what wastes too much of living … is lying. So, do not lie to me! Since you bring up presidents, look at your Clinton and what a mess his lies got him into."

Norman took more than a sip of scotch. "Okay, okay … an old friend."

"How old?"

"We've known each other about five years."

"No, no. How old is she?"

"Oh, I don't know, maybe fortyish."

"Or maybe more like thirty … the mistress from your company."

"My company.   Why do you say that?   Is Martin spreading rumors?"

"Oh, that a man should break your sacred male trust of always protecting each other … as if keeping women in the dark gives you some advantage. *Non*, Martin has not said anything. No need to be mad at Martin. He is very loyal to you."

Chloe sipped her scotch. "But we women, we have ways of knowing."

"Oh, really … intuition, or are you just psychic?"

"Much more direct…"   Chloe looked back at Norman. "Let's get back to Denise."

A flash of recognition in Norman's eyes assured Chloe she'd hit her mark. Norman said, "Wow. You think you know her name. Someone must have loose lips."

"Not loose … concerned. Stop playing with me Norman, you just gave yourself away."

"So what about Denise?"

"I was told that she left you in a bad state last summer … angry, drinking far too much, almost disoriented. You became a topic of gossip among the women." Chloe took a step closer to Norman.   "We also protect one another. When they saw us making plans to go to Europe, they warned me about Denise. They were concerned that your feelings for me might just be you taking a break … to catch your breath … she being so much younger."

"No, that wasn't it. She stood me up to go off fuckin' with some yahoo hick. Young guy with no job and a big dong. She's the one who broke it off. Then, thank god, you came along and grabbed me back; no more than that, gave me a new life. But now, you think I slept with Denise?

"Stop avoiding my question."

"Denise, yes, Denise."

"So, with me in France the desire for her came back?"

"Yeah, I guess. Somehow she'd heard I was coming home and called me. With all the frustration of the last few months in France it was like a boomerang effect."

"She called you? I do not like that."

107

"She called me to find out when I was flying in and offered to pick me up at the airport."

Chloe stepped up against Norman and looked up into his face. "I believe you. My love … is it still my love?"

"Of course."

"Or would you rather be with her?"

Norman pulled Chloe tight against him, his lips almost touching hers. He whispered, "Not a chance. I need you Chloe. Being with Denise confirmed the deal."

Chloe pulled away, "The deal … the deal. *Sacra Bleu!* You call what we have a deal? Like you can sell it."

"No, no, Chloe…"

Chloe stepped back against Norman. She spoke softly, "You know, at our age, maybe it is a deal. What more do we have to accomplish? We can only hope for some years of good health, perhaps some quiet moments. You must realize, Norman, you are beyond being able to attract women young enough to be your daughter … you just aren't rich enough, or won't be with that vineyard you've placed around your neck. As we get older we won't have the energy we once had. We'll need each other more … in different ways."

Norman tightened his embrace. "And we do care for each other." Norman paused, then added, "I love you … understand that. In all ways…"

Chloe leaned closer, putting her weight against Norman. "I am so tired. Can we just get some sleep?"

Chapter 11

Early morning mist was still on the vines when the door to the trailer opened. Joey, standing at the drafting table examining prints of the proposed winery, was surprised to see Jackie climbing the few steps into the doorway.

"Hey, love. I didn't expect to see you up this early. I should have picked you up."

Jackie walked over, accepted Joey's hug and kissed him. "The walk, it is good. A nightmare woke me ... terrible. Grand-mere grabbing me by the wrist and dragging me from you ... I could not break her grasp. You slipped away, *disparu* ... faded away."

Joey held her tight. "So, things didn't go well last night picking Chloe up? Don't worry, it's just a dream."

"*Non, non...* Grand-mere's plane was late and she was, how you say, cranky. She quizzed me on everything we plan. My answers made her ask more ... and angrier."

"Well, you knew she wouldn't be happy."

"*Oui*, but she brought up the Church, demands we be married in the Catholic Church."

"Are you against that?"

"Grandma Emma has hinted ... but she leaves it to us."

"Even though I don't go to church, you know, I'm not against it."

"But if, like France, the Church will complicate ... delay. And, Joey, I want to marry before our baby comes." Jackie clasped her hands behind Joey's neck and smiled, "He or she is not going to wait."

"Okay, okay. Let's think through what we want to do. Then we'll just do it."

"Not that easy, my love. Will and Emma invite Chloe and Norman to lunch today. We are to be there."

"You maybe, but why do I have to be there?"

"Me alone ... *non, non.* I need you to help."

"Oh," Joey chuckled, "I think you'll do better without me."

"Not funny Joey. I do not want to be saying, 'I will have to discuss with Joey'. *Non,* we make a stand and that is it! Besides, Chloe says I should not let you steal my wedding day from me."

"What?"

"She said men are lazy; want to find the easiest way."

"To get married? Really?"

"So you be with me. Show her your interest, your enthu…, what's the word?"

"Enthusiasm?"

"*Oui,* your enthusiasm in our wedding."

"Good point. You do know, my love, you're tough."

"Joey, I do not ask much … this I ask." Looking into his eyes, "*S'il vous plait.*"

"Well, since you say please."

There was a knock on the door of the trailer and it swung open as Nicholas peered in. "Am I interrupting anything?"

The couple stepped apart. "Nic, come in. What brings you here?'

"Just driving by on the way to the winery. Been keeping my eye on your vines. They look good, won't be long for some new growth pruning."

"I've noticed. Even those damaged by the storm."

"You'll be surprised at how those vines heal, how resilient they are. Can't stop Mother Nature. Did you notice, just now, the sun punchin' through the fog? Look out the window."

Jackie and Joey both turned to view the vineyard. "Beautiful!" Joey said, "Never the same."

Jackie turned to Nic, "How important is it, uncle Nic, to be married in a church?"

"Wow! Heavy question for first thing in the morning." He paused, looking away in thought, then back at Jackie. "I guess I gotta ask, 'Do you want to?' If it has meaning to you, why not? In fact, then you probably should. But, if not, you'll just be going through the motions."

"You would do it?"

"Me? I wouldn't want to be married if it wasn't in a church or at least by a minister. But that's me. You know I see our Creator in nature. And marriage is tough some days … having help from the Lord sure doesn't hurt. But, being single, I really can't give advice to anyone, especially you two."

Joey asked, "Why do you say that?"

"It's the two of you. You're a couple, close to the Lord already … working hand in hand to bear the fruit of excellent wine. And you are so right for each other. You've already bonded, and, now, you're having a child together. Whew! So, where and when you get married may not matter. But still, for me, I'd invite Jesus to the wedding."

"*Merci*, Uncle Nic, *merci*. The way you say it. Much to think about." Jackie looked at Joey, "…to discuss."

Joey took a deep breath and looked toward the floor. "Okay, okay." He paused, seeming not to know what to say. Then looked from Nic to Jackie, "Yes, yes. It's not just Jackie and me … we have a child … and we're part of much, much more."

Nic said, "Am I that profound? But, yes…"

"Wow! You're right Jackie, a lot to discuss."

Jackie and Nic both looked at Joey, their smiles confirming he was beginning to understand the breadth and depth of what it means to be a father.

After a moment of silence, Joey turned toward the drafting table. He cleared his throat saying, "Well, okay… While you're here, Nic, take a look at this plot plan for the new winery. I just got it from the architect yesterday."

Jackie said, "You see, Uncle Nic, Joey is as bad as you … wrapped up in the vines and winery." She smiled, "I must live with this as long as we are together?"

Nic returned her smile, "'Afraid so!"

"*C'est la vie…*" Jackie turned to Joey, "You are coming to the grandmothers' lunch?"

"I'll be there."

"*Merci.* I must go and help prepare." Jackie gave Nic a light kiss on the cheek saying 'Thank you'. Walking out the door, she said, "Joey, please do not be late."

"See you at 12 … sharp."

Nic turned to Joey, "How're you coming with the building plans?"

"I was just looking at them, right here on the table. The winery building will be in two sections. A wing in the back will take advantage of the lower elevation of the land on the ravine side so we can have high ceilings for the tanks and barrel room, It'll be energy and operationally efficient for making wine."

"Want me to come back when we can work on the equipment layout?"

"Yes. That'll help me check to see I have the building dimensions right."

"I'll call you later today. So, what's in front of that?"

Joey turned to the next drawing. "The Tasting Room … it'll be by the road. Post and beam timbered construction with a cathedral ceiling."

"That'll be impressive. Make sure the view is the same as from here. Set it at an angle so customers look toward the lake. Invite the beauty of nature to enhance all their senses. Your wine will taste all the better."

"You think it makes that much difference?"

"Revere and respect the land, that's my motto. Goes back to the Senecas; they honored the beauty of this land … how it sustained them. To them the land was sacred. Some even claimed it talked to them. It was a matriarchal society with the women in charge. They were concerned to preserve the gift of these lakes and hills. Made their decisions with concern for the next seven generations. Seven generations!

"Don't ignore that heritage as you think about the visitor's experience. The view can draw them out of every day cares, ease their stress. Who knows, the land may even speak to them … enliven their souls. People just have to slow down and relax enough to listen."

112

"You really think the view from here, vineyard and lake, can do all that?'

"I know it can."

Nic leaned closer to the table studying the details of the drawing before him.

ॐ   ॐ

Hoping to keep the conversation over lunch as informal as possible, Emma dressed casually in a pair of mulberry colored jeans topped by an off-white blouse. She prepared a simple lunch of sandwiches and iced tea. To take advantage of the warm day, Will suggested eating outside on the patio. A few minutes before Noon, he was just finishing sweeping when he heard Joey's MG pull into the driveway. It was quickly followed by a second car.

Will walked from the patio around the corner of the Carriage House waving to Joey, then Chloe and Norman, "Hello. Glad we can all get together." He gestured toward Chloe, "Seems you had a very long day yesterday."

Chloe, dressed in a light green long sleeved sweater and tailored beige slacks, stepped out of Norman's Mercedes convertible. She loosened the scarf she wore over her hair to protect from the wind and fingered her simple gold necklace and earrings to be sure they were in place. She came to Will and air kissed him on both cheeks, turned to Joey and did the same. "Oh, the airlines," she said, "do they ever get you to your destination on time? But, of course, I was held up in France all of last month, much too long. Finally, I am here"

"Well, you made it." Will held his hand out to Norman, "Thanks for coming." Norman took Will's hand in the tight grip of one embarking with another into battle. They held each other's gaze, knowing they were walking into an argument among their women that neither wanted; that each would have trouble controlling.

"Come around to the patio," Will said, "we'll have our first outdoor luncheon of the season. Just look at that lake. When the sun's out it shimmers; must be the cold water temperature … it just isn't the same once everything warms up."

Emma was making final preparations on the patio. She walked toward Chloe, arms outstretched. "Welcome back to America. I'm glad to see you."

The two women embraced, lightly kissing the other on both cheeks. "*Merci*. It is also good to see you."

Jackie came through the door carrying a water pitcher. Seeing her grandmothers, she set it down and threw her arms around both of them, saying, "All of us together. *Agreable*, this is nice."

The two older women gave a quick response to Jackie's tight squeeze, but then eased off, making it clear there would be no drawn out expression of closeness between them.

"Come," Emma said, "Everything's ready. Let's sit down and eat."

Norman turned to Joey, "Anything new on hydrofracking?"

Chloe said, "Norman, we just arrived. Must business be talked of even before people are served?"

"Oh, sorry. I haven't seen Joey, and I'm just curious. He talked to a gas field worker from Pennsylvania a week ago. Just wondering if there's anything new."

"I'm trying to find out more about our neighbor up the hill. He's pretty secretive, so I don't have much."

Will looked at Norman, "Jackie and Joey told me what they learned and I called an old friend who teaches in the SUNY system. He gave me the number of a geologist who has studied this area for years. Over the phone he didn't go into much detail, but in a nutshell he said, the shale in this area has fissures going in all directions. He's concerned the Marcellus gas is so shallow, only about 3,000 feet down, that the water being pumped in will migrate to fresh water … aquifers, wells, even our lakes. Problem is, once a lake's contaminated, no way to reclaim it."

"So this university professor, is he a tree hugger?'

"Oh, I'm sure he's accused of that. But he sounds pretty credible … no bullshit."

Norman put his hand to his chin, "Hmm… My concern is all the push-back to fracking by the green people. I mean there are significant dollars to be made from the gas trapped under us."

"That may seem so, but at what cost?" Will continued, "I got the date of a lecture he's giving later this month. I think we should go."

"Good idea."

Chloe held the platter of sandwiches in front of Norman, as if patiently waiting for him to take one; actually a physical expression of her frustration at being ignored so quickly after her coming back to the States.

Norman took the platter, selected a half sandwich and silently passed it on. His gesture of 'No comment!'

Once everyone had food on their plate, Emma started the polite conversation with, "So, Chloe, all is well in France?"

"Finally, yes. I have sold the vineyard; while keeping the chateau. And repairs, long overdue, are all but complete. So, *oui*, I can say all is well in France. I became anxious, though, to be here, given the situation Jacqueline finds herself in."

Jackie said, "Grand-mere, I wish you not say 'the situation'.

"Well, my dear, we are all in our own situation. *C'est la vie!* Some are just a little more challenging than others. And yours I am afraid has a time frame attached. If you do not notice it yet, give it a few weeks and you will see it in your mirror."

"Yes, "Emma said, "but everything is under control."

Chloe turned to Emma, "How can you say that? A child is on its way and they are not yet married, with nothing planned. I am not aware of how it works in the United States, but I assume Joey could leave Jacqueline to fend for herself. If they do stay together, where will they live? Everything I hear from Jacqueline is centered on the vineyard up the hill, and how infatuated she is with Joey … I think you call it starry-eyed. Nothing she says gives me comfort that real-life plans are being made. That would be fine if we had time, but Joey got her pregnant, so we must stop dreaming and, and…get things done."

Norman whispered to Chloe, "I thought you said you were going to be nice."

Chloe responded with a not so gentle elbow into his side

Joey, sitting across from Chloe, leaned toward her to get his face as close as possible. "I'm not going to leave Jackie in the lurch as you say … I love her. And we are making plans, probably not as elaborate as you'd like."

"As easy and as cheap for you as possible, I am sure." Chloe said.

"Well, we don't have a lot of cash … and things here in the States don't have to be as fussy as in France."

"Crude is more like it. We can discuss that later. Where, pray tell, do you intend to live? Here, with Emma and Will? Pretty small place for that."

"I'm glad you asked. It happens my grandmother, living in the lake house my grandfather built, is finding it difficult to continue to live alone. So my mother is going to move in with her leaving her cottage in town, where I live now, free for Jackie and me to rent. Jackie can move in next month and we can rearrange it any way she wants."

'Ah, so you will live together, still unwed. You are a pragmatist Joey, never considering all the aspects of life, of moral society. No, no, my granddaughter deserves more than an arrangement of furniture in a rented cottage. She would be treated so differently in France."

Jackie said in French, *"Grand-mere, stop! You cannot speak for me. I must find my own way."*

"And, Voila! You have all the answers?"

Emma interrupted, "I'm sorry. I thought this conversation was going to be in English."

"Oui, I mean yes. I was just trying to make a point." Jackie continued, "So, since that is settled, what else can we discuss?"

"Settled?" Chloe said, "Settled? Nothing is settled. If I agree with you, Jacqueline, living with Joey, up in town, then I must ask if you two intend on marriage, or is that just a possibility …something for consideration?"

"*Oh, non, non, grand-mere*. We will be married. Right Joey?"

"Of course, there is no question on that, just how."

"What do you mean, how?" Chloe asked.

Joey looked at Jackie as he spoke, "Probably small, and focused on our love for each other. Some sort of celebration after for the few people we know well."

"It amazes me that you plan your vineyard probably down to the centimeter, but you're adrift when it comes to your own wedding. What about the Church? You are Catholic aren't you?"

"Baptized, yes."

"But like most young people you do not go to church?"

"That's about it."

"But you do believe in God? I hope you believe in God."

"I've always believed in a Creator … I'm reminded of it every day in the vineyard. The beautiful gifts given to us. And if I forget, my uncle Nic reminds me. He's very much into the gifts of the Creator and how the land sustains us."

"Sounds to me," Chloe said, "like you are some sort of naturalist … probably not a real Catholic."

"Chloe, really!" Norman said, "Must you be so direct right out of the box?"

"Oh, you just be still. I was cooped up in France for months and then you leave me on the pretext of business. I just do not want Jacqueline making the same mistake her mother made, marrying a self-centered American who considers himself so damned exceptional."

Emma almost shouted, "What … that's my son you're talking about!"

"And Joey is just like him," Chloe said. "Only he is focused on vines and does not listen to anyone or anything, let alone God."

Jacqueline raised her voice, "That's not fair! Joey is tender and kind and I know he believes in God."

"That may be so Jacqueline, but you must realize you take after your mother ... stubborn and knowing it all."

"My memory is of happiness ... until I was nine when they died. I want to be that mother to my child ... loving, happy."

"I think," Chloe responded, "you do not remember..."

Will raised his hands, "Okay, okay. Let's all take a breath. I don't know how we got into the hurts of the past. Can we just focus on the future?"

"Good idea, Will. And just for the record, Chloe, I did not abandon you in France on a false pretext. I needed to get back to my business."

"Or your mistress..."

Norman smiled, "Chloe, you never cease to amaze."

Chloe, turning toward Norman, smiled and raised her water glass as if she'd just won an advantage in a chess match.

Jacqueline said, "Can we get back to the wedding, please."

"*D'accord*. Let me remind you, Jacqueline, in France we have two ceremonies. The civil wedding ceremony, then the Church wedding. I understand over here marriage is all in one ceremony. So, you are either married in the Church, or not."

Chloe continued, "Do you forget all those years I sent you to the convent school with the nuns ... oh, the expense? Now you disregard, abandon, all they taught you?"

"We have not decided yet. A church will slow us down."

"When you say church, I hope you mean the Catholic Church. Ah, yes, a heavy burden the Roman Catholic Church. That's a mirage. Or, are you just too lazy to be bothered? I am sure they will be happy to marry you. But you must contact them ... and soon."

Turning to Emma, Chloe asked, "You must know someone in the local parish?"

"Of course."

"Then why do you not urge these two to contact them?"

"It's their decision Chloe. Frankly, I find it very hard to restrain myself as you pressure these two."

"Pressure … pressure! They think they want to get married. Does that not require some pressure?"

"They've got enough on them already."

"Nothing like they would have contemplating a marriage in France. No, if they are to be married, we must do this right. So, first, Jacqueline, you and Joey must go to the parish church and talk with them. Once we know when the Church will marry you, we then can begin to make specific plans. And, as to cost, Emma and I can figure out ways to help. Right, Emma?"

"Well, yes. I always intended to help out. With the wedding and after the baby comes."

"Yes, well, good … I'm not so good with babies."

Chloe looked at Jackie, "Do you agree Emma should call the priest?"

Jackie glanced toward Joey and responded in a flat tone of voice, "*Oui,* Emma, please contact the priest."

Chloe turned toward Norman and Will, "Well, do you men have anything to say?"

Will held his hands up, palms out, saying, "On, weddings and babies … No, and I think Norm will agree with me … We'll pass."

₨   ₳

Once Joey's MG was headed out the driveway, Emma leaned over the table toward Chloe. She spoke with a low but determined voice, "Now that they've gone, I must ask. Why are you placing so many strictures on the kids? You're going to make them just elope or something."

Chloe responded, "They are not children. They need to be treated like adults. He got Jacqueline pregnant; he is responsible!"

"But," Emma said, "your requirement that they be married in the Catholic Church?"

"As it should be. I was married in the Church. Our children were married in the Church. So our granddaughter

119

should be married in the Church. I have bent on so many things with this Joey … the Church is not negotiable."

Emma stood, "You know Chloe, you are a sanctimonious pain. You … you who got terribly lucky when Maurice came along … in Paris. He got you off your back."

Chloe stood, saying, "I do not know what you are talking about."

"Need I say it, Chloe? Your life in Paris … what polite name did the French give it?"

"You have your facts wrong."

"I don't think so. When Lou and I were in Paris after Jackie's parents died, when we were searching for you and Maurice, your husband's associate spilled the beans. Chloe, you must have been good, very good. Why, you were a legend in your own time; the men remembering you decades later."

"Rumor is all. Trying to destroy my husband's reputation."

"Not him! No, the nostalgic gleam in the eye of the Frenchman we talked with made it clear he'd tasted your forbidden fruit. And was proud of it. Like Norman, he was smitten."

Chloe raised her voice, "Norman, must I stand here listening to this? *Non!* Emma, you think what you want. But be attentive to the fact that Jacqueline will be married in the Church. She will, or I will go to the immigration authorities and make sure Jacqueline is deported."

Will asked, "Really Chloe, you would do that?"

Chloe strode to the car. Norman shrugged, mouthing a silent, 'I'm sorry', and followed. He pulled out of the driveway and gunned the Mercedes up to speed. Looking toward Chloe, he smiled, "Interesting how I learn something new every day. Now I know why you're so good."

"Norman, take me as I am … or shove off!"

"Okay, okay, calm down. But I must ask, why all the focus on the Catholic Church?'

"Why? Jacqueline is set on having this baby … getting stuck with Joey. She will not listen. So, I hope the Church over here has strict marriage preparation requirements. They can slow Jacqueline down … maybe even until after the baby comes. Then it will be months more before a proper wedding can be held. By then she will come to her senses."

Chapter 12

Joey kept his focus straight ahead as he drove the MG toward the college, saying nothing, his jaw tightly set. Jackie looked toward him and spoke loud to be heard over the noise of the wind rushing past the open car. "You do not need to hurry. My class doesn't start for 30 minutes."

Joey maintained his speed, continuing to look straight ahead … without a word.

Jackie also looked ahead. She asked, "Angry?"

"What?"

Jackie leaned toward Joey, "Are you angry?"

"Not at you. Frustrated as hell at Chloe. I don't buy all this business with the Catholic Church. I think she's up to something. Hopes to slow us down."

"Would you slow down a little, please"

"You think we should slow down too."

"No the car, just not so fast."

Joey eased his foot off the accelerator, letting the car coast to a safer speed through a cottage populated area. "I can't figure out why though. Unless she just hates my guts so much she wants to throw sand in the gears of us getting married. I thought she hoped we'd be married by the time the baby comes. Now, she just brings up stuff to block us."

"Oh, I don't think she feels that way."

"You're too trusting Jackie … too kind"

"Joey, she's my grand-mere. Who can I trust?'

"Me, Jackie, me … and Emma and Will. I trust you and them, and beyond that Nicholas … and maybe Norman when he's not listening to Chloe. But that's about it … and, oh, my mother."

"With all those people you trust, what is your problem?"

"Chloe, Jackie, Chloe. Your dear grand-mere. In her eyes I'm not good enough for you. So, don't trust her."

"But I feel I must obey her. She raised me."

"Yeah, and kept Emma out of your life from when your parents died; what were you, nine at the time? So, why should you trust her? No, I think you feel a need to obey. You've been obeying all your life. Then, last year you discovered Emma and came here. But what did Chloe do, she came right after you. She's a control freak Jackie; don't trust her."

Joey took advantage of a stretch of open road, away from a populated area, and depressed the accelerator of the MG. The noise of the engine and wind signaled he'd made his point and the conversation was over.

ॐ   ☙

Prince chased after the Frisbee Seth and Maria threw to him, over and over. On each well placed throw, the dog caught the plastic disk in his mouth. His antics to reach the Frisbee in mid-air made them laugh. And then he ran the disc back begging for more.

Will enjoyed these good weather afternoons, after he picked up Maria from pre-school and Seth from 1st grade; watching them play in the yard out by the lake. He turned as he heard a car pull into the driveway. Vicki parked in her usual spot and walked toward him. He was surprised to see her smiling, not her usual expression when she arrived home late in the afternoon.

"Norman told Martin that Chloe is back; anxious to get the wedding planned."

"I guess you might say so. Anxious … a polite way to put it."

The kids rushed up to their mother and gave her hugs as high as they could reach. Vicki bent down putting her arms around both and held them for a second, saying, "I love you two."

She released them and stood up, looking at Will. He said, "You're in a good mood this afternoon."

"Aren't I always? But, listen, if no plans have been made, Martin and I would like to offer the Manor for the wedding, or the reception, anything that will help."

"Well, thanks. You're right. I don't think any plans have been made. And having the use of the Manor, it could be a big help. I'll tell Emma and Jackie to come over and talk with you."

Vicki smiled, "That'll be nice."

"Things must be lookin' up for you … you're so happy."

"Oh, I so love weddings. A wedding gown, bridesmaids dresses, flowers, the men decked out in suits and ties for a change … all the love and hope … promise of a bright future. I mean, you know, my marriage isn't going so well. But Jackie and Joey … they'll make it happen."

"Oh, they will. I have very positive feelings about those two."

"Too bad Jackie is pressured by the pregnancy … Chloe givin' her grief about that."

'Could be for the best," Will said, "make Joey commit. Otherwise he might concentrate on the vines and leave the wedding for later."

"Yeah, on that score, Joey is like Martin, he'll do anything for those damned grapevines. Martin, he can't see beyond the printshop." Vicki smiled, "He doesn't like it when I call it that, 'the printshop'. Told me I'm not showing proper respect for, as he puts it, 'the scale of the business'." She looked down and scoffed, "Whatever that is…" Vicki raised her eyes again looking at Will, "You men just can't seem to get your priorities straight."

"I used to be just like them. But, hey, we need to make a lotta bucks … make it all happen. I mean just look at this Manor. Martin worked pretty hard to be able to afford this."

"He goes overboard and you know it. All the attention that new press gets. Norman got the best of that deal. When he made Martin president, he left me with the dregs."

Will looked down, using his shoe to scuff away a couple of loose stones on the driveway. "I don't know, Vicki …"

Vicki leaned toward Will, "Oh, you sure do know. You're pretty smart, acting dumb all the time like you don't know. Dumb like a fox, I call it."

Vicki pulled back, then reached over and put her hand on Will's forearm, and smiled. "Anyhow, the wedding. It'll be wonderful. We'll have flowers, lots of flowers, an open bar and either a buffet or sit down dinner, a trio playing soft music in the background. If a lot of young people are coming we'll have a DJ for later."

"Whoa, Vicki!" Will smiled, "Think small, a handful of people ... and we have to remember there isn't a lot of money. No twenty thousand dollar wedding. They can't afford it."

"Well, Will, just how much can they afford? I mean we have to send them off in style. Can't cut corners on the wedding. Tell you what, I'll get a figure from Jackie and Emma; probably better include Chloe, too? And Martin and I will pick up the rest. But don't tell the women that just yet. I need to be sure Martin understands before someone else tells him."

"So he doesn't know?"

"Oh, I mentioned it."

Will smiled, "Yeah, probably when he was saying something else. Then later you can say, 'But, I told you!'"

"Oh, Will," Vicki said, smiling, "You're so smart ... and like most men, you don't know shit. Right now, I'm gonna go and play with Seth and Maria."

Will watched her almost run to her kids. *Haven't ever seen Vicki in such a good frame of mind. Maybe she's on some kinda new medication.*

Will was anxious to tell Emma, but found her lying on the bed asleep. *A well-deserved nap, after that luncheon with Chloe.*

Emma rolled on her side toward Will. "Oh, hi. I guess I nodded off."

Will sat on the edge of the bed and shared his surprise at Vicki's bright smile and happy disposition. When he got into her offer of the Manor for the reception, Emma's face darkened. "Oh, I don't know. That'll lead to some complications."

"Well, Vicki'll be in touch with you … just hear her out."

"It's just that it adds one more variable to the planning fire. I just hope it doesn't become so hot it burns itself out."

Halfway home from work Martin's bluetooth connected an incoming cell call to the speakers of his SUV.

"Martin, it's Vicki. How long before you get home?"

"Twenty, maybe twenty-five minutes. Why?"

"Oh, I'm just cooking dinner and want to have things ready when you get here."

Since this seldom happened, Martin asked, "What's the occasion?"

"Oh, nothing, just want to have a pleasant dinner … served warm for a change."

"Okay. I'll come straight ahead."

"Thanks for letting me know about Chloe and the wedding."

Immediately Martin's arms tightened, his hands firmly gripping the wheel. "Ah, Vicki, what does the wedding have to do with us?"

"I don't know. I just thought maybe we can help out a little."

"Yeah, well I'm so busy make sure it's not a lot."

"Oh, Martin, relax. Come home, we'll have dinner, then talk."

Martin knew he was in trouble. "I'm comin'. But I can't say I'll be relaxed."

They both avoided the subject over dinner. Vicki being unusually attentive to Seth and Maria; Martin playing along, hoping the subject of the wedding had blown with the breeze. But once Vicki sent the kids upstairs to play, his hope was dashed. Vicki smiled as she said, "Martin, just think … a wonderful formal wedding right here in the Manor."

"Vicki, I don't think you understand how pressured things are at the plant these days. Norman is after me for more production on the new press so we can cut down on overtime, and get back in the black. I just don't have time to worry about all the arrangements for a formal wedding … in our home. I mean why do we have to be so involved?"

Vicki stood up, her voice rising to a shout, "Son-of-a-bitch!" Her mood swinging 180 degrees. "You crap all over every idea I have. What do you mean you don't have time? I'll work out all the arrangements with Jackie and Emma. All you have to do, your royal-assed highness, is show up. Damned you, if it's your idea fine, let's pull out all the stops. Gonna have another company Pig Roast this summer? That sure took some doing last year. Yeah, you'll do that, it's your idea. But my idea, NO! You can't be bothered. You make me feel like a damned slave in your house, not our house. Like this place is a prison I'm stuck in just waiting for the honor of cooking you dinner … then letting you fuck me 'til you get your rocks off. Ever ask me if I'm satisfied? Ever do that? Huh?"

Martin spoke softly, "Vicki, you're blowing this thing all out of proportion. Just think…"

"Oh yeah, I should think. But I feel Martin…" Vicki began to cry, "I feel, and I don't feel good. The hole just keeps getting darker."

"Okay, okay, as always it's me at fault." Martin stood and stepped toward Vicki, his arms extended as if to take her in his arms. "If you want this wedding here, go ahead. I'll do what I can."

Vicki stepped back, beyond Martin's reach, "Of course, half-hearted as usual. Well, Martin, you just go fuck yourself…" Vicki turned and walked upstairs toward her children while Martin stood, hoping they hadn't heard their mother's outburst, wondering how the discussion had gone so wrong.

଼ଠ   ଔଃ

The following morning when Vicki saw Emma come out of the Carriage House, she hurried out of the kitchen to meet her in the driveway. She nearly ran, calling out, "Emma, has Will said anything about having the wedding at the Manor?"

"Yes he did. Thank you for the offer. We'll have to discuss it with Jackie. I know she wants to keep the ceremony and reception simple. But I have no idea when. As you know, Chloe's back and she's putting some pressure on the kids for a church wedding, the Catholic Church. So, I guess, they have to work through that to satisfy her. Then we'll be able to get on with our plans."

"Why does that woman always have to make life so difficult? She sticks her nose into everything. And the men, they act like they could care less. Mention wedding and a man either freaks out or goes brain dead. So, Emma, looks like we women need to come to the rescue and help Jackie out. It'll be a fine wedding, we'll see to that!"

"Now, Vicki, let's not get ahead of ourselves. We need to let the kids find out if they're getting married in the Church. Then we can make some definite plans. But we've got to let Jackie call the shots ... and maybe even Joey. He doesn't say much about the wedding, but I can tell he's thinking on it."

"Don't worry Emma. I'll keep on the sidelines, be there for whatever we need."

Vicki took a step back and looked toward the lake, speaking with a wistful tone Emma hadn't heard her use before. "This lake is so beautiful, and the Manor will make such a perfect setting. I know I bitch a lot about being so isolated and lonely here, but a wedding, that's what this place is built for." She looked at Emma, smiling, "Just what we need to liven things up."

Vicki's intense elation led Emma to fear she was experiencing one of the highs of her bipolar condition. Emma asked, "You did mention all this to Martin, right?"

"Of course I did. I just told you, men either freak out or go brain dead over weddings."

"So which did Martin do?"

"What do you mean? Oh, he did both ... first yelling about how busy he is at the printshop, then clamming up and not saying a word."

"So Martin's not on-board with this?"

"Don't worry, he'll be. Just leave Martin to me. I've been handling him for over ten years; a little wedding isn't going to stand in my way. In fact, if we get Chloe helping with the plans, she'll get Norman on board, and Martin'll do whatever Norman tells him to. No problem ... as the yachtsmen say, 'smooth sailing'".

"Well, Vicki, as I said, we need to talk with Jackie. Right now, I've got to get to a dental appointment."

Emma drove along Lake Road toward town, a headache she'd not had when she walked out of the Carriage House coming to the fore. *Oh God, Chloe ... and now Vicki!*

Chapter 13

A week later, Jackie and Joey were both surprised when the door of the parish rectory was opened by a young man. They'd expected a priest near retirement age. Of slight build, standing shorter than Jackie, with a high cheek-boned face and an engaging smile giving him a boyish look … too young to be a priest. His black cassock topped by a pure white Roman collar seemed out of place. "You're here to see Father Roy?"

Joey hesitated, "Yes … Father Roy?"

"He isn't here. Had to leave on an urgent matter. He told me he tried to call but couldn't reach you."

"Oh, well, I guess we must reschedule."

"No, no. That won't be necessary. I'm Father Steve. Father Roy told me you are planning to be married." He stepped aside welcoming them in. "I'm sure I can be of help." He led the way to a small room with a table and six straight-backed office chairs. Jackie and Joey sat beside each other.

Sitting across from them, Father Steve picked up a sheet of note paper from the table. "You are Joseph O'Donnell and you are Jacqueline Beauveau, correct?"

"Yes, call me Joey."

"I am Jackie."

Leaning over the table, extending his hand, Father Steve said, "Nice to meet you both. I've only been here a couple of months and haven't met many parishioners." After shaking hands, he continued, "I took the liberty, Joey, of looking in our baptismal record. You were baptized here at St. Mark's a month after you were born?"

"Yes, that's what my mother told me. I've lived here all my life."

"So you were raised as a Catholic? But I couldn't find you in our parish directory. Are you an active parishioner?"

"Not exactly."

Father Steve raised his eyebrows, waiting for more.

"My father was the Catholic. He left when I was a baby. My mother brought me to the church here on occasion, Christmas and Easter."

"Oh…"

"My mother's Lutheran. She continued to practice her Protestant faith … I just kind of tagged along."

"Ah, conservative … lots of bible studies. Did you study the bible?"

"Not much. My mother made sure I understood the lessons, but I never studied it much."

"Let's go back to your father. You say your father left when you were a baby. When did he return?"

Joey leaned forward as if to make his point, "We never heard from him, at least that I know of."

"Sorry to hear that. So, your mother made you aware of the Catholic rituals … somewhat."

"You've got that just about right."

"Hmm. And, your father, he was the Catholic. Unfortunate…"

Turning to Jackie, Father Steve said, "And you Jacqueline … Father Roy mentioned you are from France?"

Jackie sat up straight, at attention, as she'd been taught by the sisters. "*Oui* … yes."

"You are also Catholic?"

"Yes, my parents were Catholic. After they died, my grandparents took me to church … Catholic Church."

"I'm sorry to hear you lost your parents. How old were you when that happened?"

"Nine. Then my grandparents sent me to a Catholic boarding school."

"So your teenaged years were formed by priests and nuns."

"Sisters, *oui.*"

"And since leaving the Catholic school, you practice the Faith … weekly Mass, frequent confession, observing Holy Days of obligation?"

"Well, I do some."

"Oh," Father Steve raised his eyebrows again, "only some."

The priest looked toward Joey, "As Father Roy left he mentioned you want to discuss being married in the Church. How long have you known each other?"

"About a year."

"When do you hope to be married?"

"Soon … by the end of August."

"Oh, only a couple of months away. You know, we, the Church, have PreCana marriage preparation that takes months. What's your rush?"

Jackie looked down. "I'm pregnant."

"Ahh … there's the rush."

Jackie looked at the priest nodding her head, 'Yes'. There was a pause with no further response from her.

Father Steve stared at Jackie, "So, you only observe some of the Commandments?"

Jackie looked up, directly at Father Steve. "My pregnancy, it is out of love. Joey and I are in love."

The priest exhaled, glancing toward the ceiling. "Yes … Love. So much is based on love … when it's only infatuation. Like so many claim inspiration of the Holy Spirit; being motivated by the Spirit. Yet, I'm afraid sex outside of marriage is a sin; fornication … pure and simple.

"But, back to you practicing the Faith. You go to Mass weekly?"

"Yes, I go to Mass."

"With Joey? Or with your grandmother?"

"My grandmother, sometimes."

"Sometimes, not every Sunday? When it's convenient?"

Jackie's voice hardened, "I go frequently, usually with my grandmother, Emma."

"When it's convenient, I'm sure."

Father Steve smiled, kind of like a cat having cornered his prey. Even though it looked like Jackie was being bludgeoned to tears, Joey sensed her rising anger. He thought of what Nicholas would say and interrupted. "Father, I have a vineyard; we both tend the vines. The beauty of nature, you know, working with the Lord's creation. We feel close to Him."

"Do you make wine? Does your vineyard have a name?"

"Not yet. A storm started a fire last year, and we lost the winery. My partner was killed."

"Ah, yes, I heard about that. Some tie to the Kober family as I recall."

"My mother is a Kober."

"So, the vines, the wine ... it's in your blood. Well, the fire, that was a tragedy."

"And Jackie, she's from a chateau in France."

"So, the vineyard is the center of your lives?"

Jackie responded, "We do not look at it like that."

Father Steve sat back, his hand to his chin, in thought. Jackie and Joey glanced at each other, each with an expression of concern.

Leaning forward, Father Steve addressed them both. "Fortunately, the Church is not into quick marriages. Pregnancy puts on just too much pressure.

"But let's step back. There is a great tendency among lay people to pick and choose the teachings of the Church they like, then ignore the rest. But the wisdom of Mother Church must be taken as a whole, one truth building on another until the true beauty of the Faith shines through. And since Mother Church is never in error, always right, there's no room for debate.

"You, Joey ... you are a Catholic by Baptism only. That's not an insignificant fact, but as an adult you don't practice the Faith. And, Jackie, you're what we call a 'Cafeteria Catholic'.

"A what?"

"It's calling on the Church when convenient, but ignoring a consistent presence at the celebrations, particularly at Sunday Mass. I'm sure the nuns taught you better than that."

Jackie almost shouted, "That's unfair!"

"It's neither fair nor unfair, Jackie." Father Steve spoke in a steady, cold tone, devoid of emotion. "Mother Church teaches based on lessons learned over 2000 years and the laity must follow, it's as simple as that.

"You are both people of the secular world … not living the Faith. Given your situation, I see no reason to suggest you pursue being married in the Church. I suggest you look elsewhere. You are so attached to the vineyard … nature; perhaps you should be married standing among the vines." Father Steve paused, then raising his hands with a new idea, saying, "Yes, perhaps just after dawn, in the bright sunshine."

Joey stood, grasped Jackie's elbow urging her to stand. "Thank you, Father. We'll find our way out."

Whatever Father Steve said as they rushed out of the rectory, neither bothered to hear. There was silence between them as they got in the MG and Joey drove out of town. As he sped along the Lake Road, Jackie leaned toward him, almost shouting to be heard over the wind noise. "He is arrogant! In France, I know some hard priests. That guy…" Jackie shuddered, clenching her fists and grimacing, "*Pouah!*"

"Yeah, an arrogant bastard! Great idea, talking to the Church. So what now?"

"What now, how do I know? Jackie threw her hands up in disgust. *Mon Dieu!* He rejects us; throws us out. As if detritus … ah, garbage. Unnerving, he is unnerving!"

"Okay Jackie, calm down…"

"Just take me to the vineyard. I need to canopy some vines."

Joey put his hand on Jackie's knee as he eased off on the accelerator to bring the MG back toward the speed limit.

ഇ   CB

Late afternoon shadows were forming when Jackie and Joey pulled into the driveway of the Carriage House. They found Emma in the kitchen preparing a salad for dinner. Looking toward the door, Emma said, "Oh, I thought you were Vicki.

She's late picking up the kids. They're in the front room with Will."

Joey walked to the opening and waved "Hi" to the kids and Will.

Looking at what Jackie was wearing, Emma said, "Jackie, I hope you were better dressed than that when you went to the rectory.

"I had these up in the trailer. I needed some time with the vines after talking to that priest ... to calm down."

"Tell me what happened? But first let me tell you, Father Roy called. He is so sorry he missed you ... there was some emergency and it couldn't be helped. But he never intended that Father Steve get involved. How did it go?"

"It was terrible." Jackie said, "That Father Steve, he quizzed both of us ... and then refused to marry us. Told us we are so much into vines, we should be married in the vineyard."

"Yeah," Joey added, "Critical of everything."

Will walked in from the front room, "So, the Holy Roman Church throwing its weight around, making you feel guilty. That's how they keep control."

"Control," Joey said, "...or just piss people off?"

Will continued, "As if the bishops don't have a lot to feel guilty about, what with the priest scandals. And now, they criticize the nuns for not listening closely enough to them. It's almost comical, the bishops who covered up all their pedophiles for years have the gall to criticize the women who actually live the gospel Jesus taught."

"I don't know about that," Joey said, "but, Jackie, maybe we should take that SOB's advice and get married in the vineyard."

"You must be referring to Father Steve," Will said, "I've only heard him preach once ... that was enough. Likes to harp on 'Mother Church'."

"He came down on me for not going to Mass and then says the fact my Irish Catholic father abandoned my mother is 'unfortunate' ... that's the word he used, 'unfortunate'. No recognition that maybe my mother was bitter because her husband left never to return. My father screws her life up, and then the Church hangs its rules about no divorce around her neck … and for some reason she listened to them. Never let another man get serious about her. Some Church!"

"Oh," Emma said, "you probably don't want to meet Father Roy. He offered to see you both. He said he'll start from the beginning, and listen to what you have to say. He's very sorry Father Steve got involved."

"Who is this priest?" Jackie asked.

"Father Roy, he's been pastor for many years. He's due to retire next year."

"No, no, this Father Steve. He gives me chills … scary."

"He's new to the parish, came last month." Emma answered.

Will cut in, "I hear he's been ordained just over a year. Came out of one of those conservative seminaries teaching the Church has to purify itself, go back to the basics, and if it becomes a much smaller church in the process, so be it."

"Father Roy," Emma added, "he's completely different."

"Yes, Roy has been a good pastor. But Father Steve, I think they sent him here to get him out of the city. Too much controversy over his rigid conservative approach. Go see Roy; he's a pretty common-sense guy."

Joey waved his arms in the air. "It's just a waste of time. Why would we want to be married in the Church?"

"Because of the sisters," Jackie said, putting her hands against the side of her head.

"The sisters, what sisters?" Joey asked.

Jackie lowered her arms, looking at Joey. "It's your uncle Nic. He got me thinking about the Lord's blessing on our marriage. And I've been thinking of what the sisters taught me at school in France. That Father Steve, he tells us to go away. Well, Joey, you are Catholic, I am Catholic. Why should we go away? *Non*, we will be married in the Church, if not here, somewhere. I cannot ignore the heritage I grew up with, all the lessons I had to learn. No priest is going to tell me we cannot do this!"

Joey looked at Will, hoping for a comment. But Will only raised his eyebrows, saying nothing. Joey looked back at Jackie, "So, you're telling me we go back to the mat with this Father Roy?"

"*Oui*. That is our next step."

"Oh, Jackie, I love you, but you're a glutton for punishment. Just don't get your hopes up too high."

"This is not hope. It is what is right, Joey. And you are going to help me convince this Father Roy I am right."

Emma saw Vicki's car drive up next door. "Oh, Vicki's back, thank God. Hopefully in a better mood."

But, instead of coming over to the Carriage House to pick up the kids, she rushed, head down, directly into the Manor. "Uh, oh. That's not good," Emma said, "I may have some hand holding to do before dinner."

"You go," Jackie said, "Joey and I will cook tonight."

Emma walked into the Manor. Soft reflection of sunlight from the lake created a warm glow in the living room, patterns moving in slow motion caused by gentle late day waves. Vicki sat in a leather wing backed chair, her head in her hands. Emma walked over and quietly said her name, "Vicki."

Vicki raised her head removing her hands and Emma saw that she was beyond crying, her face a mask of terrified grief. 'Oh, Emma...," she croaked instead of said. Then she bolted from the chair, almost knocking Emma over as she ran to the downstairs powder room, choking up vomit just as she reached the bowl. Emma followed, not sure how to help her. Once the bile was out of her, Vicki regained her breathing, stood, rinsed off her face and stepped back into the hallway, hanging onto the door jamb ... unsteady on her feet. She staggered back into the living room, sat down where she'd been, looking at the floor.

"Vicki, are you drunk?"

"Never could hold my liquor. Guess it doesn't mix well with those pills the doctor ordered."

"What pills?"

"Oh, some kind of anti-something or other that's supposed to make me happy. Some 'happy', makes for a living hell is what it does. I thought a drink would calm my nerves. But that just led to another and the next thing I know I'm here upchucking my whole life."

Emma stood over Vicki, putting her hand on her shoulder. "Do you feel better now?"

"I don't think I'll be sick again, if that's what you mean. Beyond that, I just can't feel. Damned doctors and their pills. What the hell do they know?"

"Why don't you lie down and get some sleep. I'll keep the kids until Martin gets home."

"Oh, he'll be late. Another crisis with that fucking press."

"He's having a tough time isn't he?"

"I wish he had a real mistress. Then I could go pull her hair out. But what do you do to a printing press? Throw a wrench at it. He loves the damned thing … comes home, eats, sleeps, then Wham, he's heading back to the fucking printshop again. Thank god Jackie and Joey won't be like that."

"Let's not worry about them right now."

"Just give me a while; I'll come get the kids."

Chapter 14

Early morning rain eased off to fog under an overcast sky. Will walked out on the dock to check the lake temperature. Finding it still much too cold for canoeing he called to Prince and set off on an early morning walk with his dog.

Up in the vineyard trailer, Joey studied schematics of the winery ... preparing for a meeting with the architect. Nicholas knocked as he slowly opened the door. "Hey, coffee must be on."

Joey turned toward the door. "It's just brewing. Come in."

"Only had a cup of left-over from yesterday and need some fresh." Nic ran his fingers through the little hair he had left, hoping to straighten the tangled strands. "Can't jump outta bed like I used to. Hafta kinda ease into the day. But, hey, it's another day..."

Joey pointed back toward the drafting table holding the sheaf of building prints. "I had a call from Bruce, the architect, yesterday. Somehow he got the building permit approved. That was fast, a lot faster than I expected."

"Well, he's designed for vineyards all around the lakes. I'm sure he knows the town engineer; oh, what's his name? Anyhow, Bruce probably gives him everything up front." Nic put his hand over his mouth in thought. "Come to think of it, I think those two played basketball together in high school. And they probably trust each other. So, your project goes to the top of the pile ... one advantage of getting a local guy."

"You know Norman suggested an architect in Rochester. But when I mentioned winery to him, he backed away, referred me right back locally."

"You know why? The regs can drive someone not used to them right up a wall. Too much to learn. A wise move on his part. Like it or not, you're pretty small bananas for a large firm. They need the corporate and school projects."

"Bruce tells me we can get started right away. So Norman's coming this morning."

"He's a driver, makes things happen."

Joey turned and grabbed two mugs from the shelf, then poured coffee from the carafe. He handed one to Nic. Pointing toward the drafting table, he said, "Do you have time to go over these with me again. I just want to make sure I've got all our questions on my list."

Nic took a sip of coffee and smiled. "Sure. Be glad to. Where's Jackie, is she gonna be part of this."

"Given the weather, she may be sleeping in. I'll bring her up-to-speed when she gets here."

"You'd better. You're blessed to be marrying a woman who has winemaking in her blood. Be sure to make her your equal partner. Don't do anything to jeopardize her passion."

Joey laughed, "For me, or the vines."

"You know that's a good question, Joey. Does she love you for you, or does she love you as part of the larger picture." Nic immediately followed with, "I shouldn't have said that, my mouth getting ahead of my brain."

Joey was silent a moment, "No, Nic, it's actually a good question. Frankly, I don't know the answer. I wonder if she even knows."

"Since we're talking about this, Joey, you know, you can turn that question around. What about you?"

"Me?"

"Would you love Jackie as you do if she wasn't passionate about vineyards?" Without waiting for a response, Nic continued, "You're lucky to have found each other. Every woman I loved just couldn't live with my attention to the vines and winemaking. They were jealous ... got mad. But, it's my life. You have something very special."

Nic turned toward the table to stand next to Joey. "How are these plans shaping up?" Looking over the winery wing, a metal building to be attached to the back of the main building, he was surprised to see all the suggestions he'd made two weeks before incorporated into the revised drawings. He found the design across the front of the Tasting Room building most impressive. Working together Jackie, Joey and Bruce had taken Nic's suggestion to focus on the view down the length of the lake and developed a much more dramatic design with a wide deck out front, partially covered by a portico supported by a pair of massive wooden beams at each corner.

"It's beautiful Joey. Really sets off the post and beam structure." Nic smiled, "It'll be an eye-catcher to customers driving up the hill from the lake. And, once here they'll enjoy the view. You listened to me."

Nic took a sip from his mug, "It's not the same way down the road you know. Your Uncle Tom challenges me at every turn. Thinks he knows everything."

"You guys are pretty successful."

"Oh, Tom's a good business man, don't get me wrong; but a terrible wine-maker. He has no patience for it. And he doesn't have the nose."

Nic looked at Joey, "Smell, Joey ... it's so important. Working with you in the winery last winter confirmed my suspicion that you have my sense of smell; actually your grandfather's sense of smell ... I got mine from him. As we did barrel checks on fermentation you were asking me questions on problems that even I didn't detect. That's what sets you apart. And, Jackie ... don't ignore her ability to taste. I set her up one day with a bunch of samples and she picked out the fruits like a pro."

Joey smiled, "That's really encouraging. So what do you think ... of the building?"

"I think you should go ahead. Get the shell of the building up this season. Any further suggestions from me will only be internal refinements; won't affect the structure."

"You're welcome to stay for the meeting."

"No, I'd just be a third wheel. Anyhow, I need to get over to discuss a few Kober Vineyard issues with Tom. I'd rather stay, because dealing with Tom'll probably turn into a shouting match.

Jackie and Norman were sipping coffee in the trailer when Bruce showed up, right on time. After being introduced to Norman, Bruce laid the role of architectural drawings he was carrying out flat on the drafting table, then plugged in his laptop. With Jackie, Joey and Norman gathered around, he reviewed all the recent changes, answering questions as they came up. Bruce explained how lucky they were to have the approval of a building permit moving along quickly; but took little credit that his working relationship with the town engineer had anything to do with it. He cautioned, "As far as I can tell we've satisfied all the conservation regs. But, Jackie, please double check so if we've overlooked something we don't get blindsided by a delay."

Jackie opened her laptop. "I'll check it this morning."

Bruce said, "Finally, the septic system leech field. Joey, you're working with Mr. Mosbey on that, right?"

"Top of my list."

Norman said, "Okay. Sounds like we're gonna have a green light to start construction soon. Get me the specific estimates with how much is needed and when. I'll make sure the funds are available."

Joey looked at Bruce, "We can work that up together in a day or two, right?"

"Sure. I'll make some time tomorrow if you're free."

"Oh, I'll be free."

Norman asked, "Bruce, while you're here, have you run into anything on hydrofracking?"

"Like everybody else, I'm learning. One of my partners went down into the Endless Mountain region of Pennsylvania and poked around. Not good. The well pad installations are industrial, noisy, thick air pollution. Lots of trucks on the roads. Ground water has definitely been contaminated. One problem is the density of wells ... the gas companies, once they got the go ahead, put in hundreds of wells, many too close together.

"Being architects, we pride ourselves in building compatible with the environment ... and, to, ah ... bring some of the charm of viniculture into the structural design. Everything about fracking runs counter to that. So we're very concerned.

"So," Norman quipped, "it's safe to say you architects are not in favor of fracking."

"We hate to have the landowners who can profit from it mad at us. Some are our customers. But we just see too much damage. Much of it to the wineries.

"My partner also saw a social deficit. Quiet towns challenged by overcrowding, with drunkenness and fights spilling out of the bars, more traffic and noise than ever … we don't call them roustabouts for nothing. And neighbors become adversarial as some make money from the wells while those next door have to put up with the inconvenience and noise, and gain nothing."

"Did anybody warn 'em, the neighbors?"

"Oh, some did. But it was 'I gotta see it to believe it' situation. Now it's too late."

ℰↄ   ৪৪

The skies had cleared by late afternoon when Jackie and Joey again pressed the doorbell of the parish rectory. They were surprised when a man dressed in chinos and a soft green oxford shirt answered the door. His shining blue eyes and warm smile offered an instant welcome.

Father Roy extended his hand, "You must be Jackie and Joey. I'm Father Roy. Please, please come in." They were ushered into a small parlor across the hall from the meeting room of their first visit. Father Roy motioned them to sit down. The chairs were upholstered, comfortable.

"I got somewhat different perspectives from your grandmother and Father Steve as to what happened when you were here last week. So, let's start from the beginning. Tell me a bit about yourselves.

After Jackie and Joey summarized their upbringing and the months since they'd met almost a year ago, Father Roy smiled, "I'm impressed. You've accomplished a lot in a very short time. But, I understand, there is cause for some urgency … you're expecting a baby?"

"*Oui*, yes. Late November, around Thanksgiving."

"You want to be married before you have the baby. Right?"

"It'll be best." Joey leaned forward, gesturing with his hands, "Having our own home, being able to care for our child without having to be apart. Rather than just live together on a long term basis, we'll be much more comfortable being married."

Father Roy looked from one to the other. "Good thinking, provided you're both sure you want to be married?" Jackie and Joey glanced at each other; the smile they shared answered Father Roy's question.

"*Oui*, and we want to be married in the Church. But Father Steve told us to forget the Church, we are not good enough Catholics."

"Yeah,' Joey interrupted, "he told us we'd best be married up in our vineyard."

Father Roy sighed, "Yes, I heard. It's not a question of being 'good enough' Catholics … you're Catholic … period. But, by Church law I can only marry you in a church.

"So you don't agree with Father Steve?"

Father Roy sat back, putting his hands together as if praying, raising them to his lips. After a moment he lowered them. "You see there is tension in the Church. Many conservative clergy believe the Church should be protective of its tradition and past. Rigid adherence to the rules. They see the modern world as a threat to the Church's integrity. That's where Father Steve is coming from. I will talk to him because he goes too far."

Joey leaned in, toward Father Roy, his voice intense. "We tried to explain to Father Steve that working with the vines, we see the beauty of God's creation; it brings us closer to God."

Father Roy leaned forward, smiling, "Yes, yes. The reality is that Jesus reaches each person where he or she is …

married, raising children, at work … whatever their purpose in life. You prune the grape vines. I've found over the years that life prunes our conscience … makes us who we become. That's the key, an individual's conscience can't be violated; goes all the way back to Thomas Aquinas."

"But didn't he live hundreds of year ago?"

"That's true, Joey, in the 1200s. But his teaching has been upheld by modern popes and Vatican Council II."

"So, we're good enough Catholics?"

"Oh gracious, yes. Absolutely! You and Jackie are good Catholics."

"But what about the rules? Why do so many ignore them?"

"I'm hoping our new Pope Francis can bring the Church along … make it more relevant to younger generations. But it'll take years … decades. I mentioned that to the father of a large family recently. He said, 'Probably too late for my kids. When I needed the Church to help me as a parent, the Church retrenched … still doesn't make much sense to my kids. The Church just left us parents to fend for ourselves'. And he's right."

Jackie waved her hand, indicating to stop. "All this is good … interesting. But, what is the meaning for our wedding?"

"Oh, I'll marry you … if you're willing to have it in the church."

"Do we need to go through any special marriage preparation?" Joey asked.

Father Roy sat back, thinking. "You need a marriage license, of course. And with Jackie coming from France you should apply for that as soon as possible. Normally, it doesn't take long, but who knows with all the new Homeland Security." He leaned toward Jackie, "One other thing, Jackie, I need either a copy of your Baptismal certificate embossed with the seal of that parish; or, if that's not available, a letter from the parish where you made your First Communion."

"My Baptism, I do not know. But, I know where I made my First Communion. I will contact them."

Father Roy sat back looking from Joey to Jackie, "We have a program called PreCana and while I recommend it, I won't make it a requirement in your case. I can use discretion when special circumstances warrant."

"We have special circumstances?"

"Your timeframe … it's very tight. I must confess, though, I did some research on you two. I called your uncle Nicholas. I hope you don't mind. I've known him for years and respect his judgment. He thinks a great deal of you both and fully supports you being married."

"Uncle Nic … he's being a help on everything."

"You're lucky to have him. He even gave me some advice. He told me after I'd met you both and listened to your stories, seen your love for each other," Father Roy smiled, "He said, 'Don't get bogged down in the rules. Just do what Jesus would have done … marry them.' And talking with you two, I can see he's right. You're mature, focused … definitely in love. You'll make excellent parents.

"But," Father Roy smiled, "the Church has some minimum requirements that must be satisfied. Instead of PreCana, over the next couple weeks, I'd like you to meet with our lay pastoral associate and his wife. They'll discuss various aspects of marriage with you and the Church's view of marriage as a life-long covenant. So many view marriage as a contract; it is so much more than that. Two meetings should be enough. Then we'll meet again so I can complete the Church's paperwork."

Joey asked, "Can this all be done by August?"

"Oh yes. We'll make it happen. Having met you both and listening to Nic I see no reason for delay. In fact, it's probably best we set the date, so we have a firm goal to meet.

"*Merci*, Father. We will be glad to meet as you request."

"Before we look at the calendar, just let me make just one final suggestion. This being a small town, and the fact you'll be showing by August, it's probably best if you keep the wedding reasonably small."

"Not a problem, Father. We're thinking small already."

Before Joey started the MG, he exhaled, "Wow! What a difference. Jackie, you okay?"

Jackie smiled, "*Oui,* I am, how you say, fantastic! He is such a nice man." She leaned over and kissed Joey on the cheek. "And we will be married."

Joey said, "I feel like, 'What the hell happened?'. They're so different. How can they be in the same church … even live in the same rectory? I always saw the Church as being based on one message … these two probably don't agree on anything."

Chapter 15

Vicki and Chloe finally agreed on something. The wedding should be lavish with a gorgeous gown, formal dresses and tuxedos, a festival of flowers in the church and throughout the Manor. A formal French multi-course dinner accompanied by soft music would be served; upbeat rhythms later for dancing. And, the Manor being a private home, no guest should have to pay for a drink. Vicki and Chloe reached their concept independently; but soon conspired to tie down specifics. Emma, though, thought differently, on a much smaller, more casual scale.

The three women sat with Jackie at the dining room table of the Carriage House for the first discussion about the wedding. "I don't think there is much to be planned." Jackie said. "We will be married at the church in town; then we will all come back to the Manor for the reception. A simple affair, nothing fancy or expensive. And, thank you Vicki for opening your home. It makes everything so much easier."

"Yes, dear," Emma said, "And with a little help, I can cook food for whatever type of dinner you'd like ... a buffet or even sit-down."

Chloe cleared her throat and happened to look toward Vicki ... their eyes met ... a glance confirming they were of the same mind.

When Chloe received a call from Jacqueline informing her that Father Roy had agreed to the wedding and inviting her to a meeting to make wedding plans, her first reaction was to wash her hands of the whole affair. She kept that to herself, though, and agreed to attend, reluctantly. Upon hanging up, she walked into the living room of Norman's home, saying through clenched teeth, "That was Jacqueline. The priest will marry them!"

Norman lowered the newspaper he was reading. "You mean, without delay?"

"Oui. Voila! Whenever they want. So, no restraint from the Church. In France the Church practices more restraint. But, here, when we need the Church to say, 'No!', what do we get? Like everything else in America, loose … sloppy."

Realizing Chloe's hope to buy time had backfired, Norman had to suppress a smirk.

"Those two can get married on their own." Chloe said, "We'll see if they are up to it."

"Oh, they'll be up to it."

"And Jacqueline will be stuck with that dirt farmer."

'Chloe, come on. Joey's a lot more than that. He's developing into a vintner … working with his uncle, a good one. Give the guy a break."

"Oh, you just think so because you pour money into that bottomless pit he calls a vineyard."

"It will be a success, you watch."

"A disaster for Jacqueline, and for you, Norman." She threw her hands upward, "Ach, *c'est le vie.* No one listens."

"Chloe, listen to me. Jackie is carrying a baby. That baby is your only great-grandchild. Now, you can either get on board with this wedding or you can be obstinate and let Emma have all the joy. The choice is yours. Because like it or not, Jackie and Joey are going to be married."

Chloe sat down and put her hands to her face. She was still, saying nothing.

After almost a minute, Norman asked, "Are you crying?"

"No, Norman, I do not cry." Chloe clasped her hands in her lap. "You are right. I should focus on the baby. But if Jacqueline insists on being married, the wedding must be memorable. It must be in the French tradition … elegant. Maybe I should invite my friend, Beatrice; the one who lives in New York … you will finally get to meet her husband, the State Senator. We can show French elegance being imported."

"Well, just be involved. Don't get carried away." He lifted the paper to read. It crinkled as he lowered it again. "In fact, Chloe, since you raised Jackie, you should play the role of the parents of the bride and pay for this wedding. You know that don't you?"

"A wedding I do not want to happen. I should pay?"

"It's the custom … at least here in the States."

"Norman, you can be a real pain. How do you say … a hard-ass?"

Vicki's motivation was different. She loved weddings … but with her college friends all being married over a decade earlier it had been a long time … years dry of weddings. And a reception would bring the glum Manor back to life; even sweep away the black voids of her moods. Plus, after Martin's crappy attitude about being involved, she had to show him it could be done … and she could damned well do it.

Chloe looked at her granddaughter across the dining room table. "Jacqueline, we must plan – and carefully. A wedding is the signature of your whole married life. It expresses your hope for the future … sets the tone for years to come. It is not to be taken lightly."

"And," Vicki added, "we want you to have it just the way you want. No screwin' around cutting corners."

Emma leaned toward Jackie, speaking softly, "But, keep the focus on you and Joey. Forget the need for extraneous trappings; they just lead to a lot of needless stress and expense. Besides, it'll be a small wedding, right?"

"Joey and I discussed who to invite … we come up with 20 people."

"What? Only 20?" Chloe asked.

"Joey and I want to keep it small. Father Roy agrees, suggests a small wedding.

"What does a priest know about weddings … after the ceremony? They are so quick to make their own decisions without talking to anyone, then they tell everybody what to do. No Jacqueline, you are forgetting the family. What about all Joey's Kobers, and Emma's relatives? And all the friends Joey has? The people Joey does business with; even those in the community Joey knows well? No, the wedding cannot be so small. I am thinking over 100."

"Yes," Vicki added, "that's the scale we should plan for … with all the trappings: food, flowers, music, even an open bar. You know, go for the very damned best."

"You are correct, Vicki … the best, the very best." Chloe said.

Chloe was convinced Vicki, the brash, foul-mouthed next door neighbor, could be her partner-in-arms. As Madame of the Manor, Vicki would bring clout to make things happen her way … actually *their way*.

Vicki continued, "A wedding needs a theme, a color … the decoration in the church carrying through to the reception."

Emma looked at Vicki, "Whatever are you talking about?"

"I've seen it done, it's great. Take a word like 'hope', or 'love', or 'forever'; then select a color … build everything around them. They write the vows using the word repeatedly, and later in the lyrics of the music. The color is in the gowns and all the flower arrangements."

"And quality," Chloe added, "everything of highest quality – an air of elegance."

Emma sat back, upright. "Chloe, they're starting a life together, not making a movie. The love they have for each other … that's what's important. Everything else is secondary."

"Oh, you Americans" Chloe said, "so utilitarian. Cut corners, get the rings and the blessing, have a drink or two, then just rush off. Everything in a hurry. Do you take time to make love over here … properly … or just fuck?"

Jackie shouted, "Grand-mere! Must you two argue over *my* wedding? *Non, non* … a quiet wedding ... like our relationship, Joey and me."

Chloe crossed her arms over her chest and slowly moved her head back and forth in disagreement. "Quiet!" She raised her voice. "Quiet? Were you quiet when Joey got you pregnant? We wouldn't be planning this wedding now if he didn't do that, would we."

Instead of retreating into tears, Jackie flashed forward, "*Non grand-mere*," she shouted as she stood, "No, I screamed!" Right here in this room." She pointed, "Right in front of that fireplace ... on a stormy winter night. I screamed ... I shuddered ... a new life ... free of being so correct, so polite."

Eyes were wide as Jackie stood staring at Chloe. Then she sat down, saying softly, "Sorry. But you cannot mock Joey's love for me. Or, mine for him!"

In French, Chloe said, "Jacqueline, I apologize. I should not have been that way."

Emma asked, "Should we do this another time?"

Jackie shook her head 'No'. She said, "We need to get this done, and pick a date."

Chloe said, "Now, don't get mad by my asking this. Should Joey be a part of this? Where is he?"

"A problem came up with the new winery. Something about bed rock and elevations. He is with the architect and contractor now. He will come when they finish."

"Well," Vicki said, "men usually bug-off on making wedding plans; then they like to get the fuck involved approving every little thing. They still complain like hell about the stuff they don't like. We shouldn't wait. Can't we just move on?"

"Yes, move on ... I guess." Emma answered, "But with restraint. Even your language, Vicki, a little restraint ... please.

"First," Emma continued, "we'd better figure out how many are coming."

The next hour was consumed with reviewing Jackie's list and discussion of whom else should be invited. As so often happens, add one person of an extended family and it leads to ten. The threads of each family were explored ... both Jackie's and Joey's. But, many questions about Joey's family had to be set aside for his advice. Jackie listed friends to be invited. Finally, business associates were discussed. It was agreed, subject to Joey's approval, that at least 60 people would be invited; maybe even 70. Chloe and Vicki still thought that awfully slim, but whom else to invite? Except for two cousins and a few new friends Jackie had made at the college where she tutored, all her friends were in France.

"With 60, we'll have a sit down dinner." Vicki said.

"How will you seat 60 in the Manor?" Emma asked.

"Oh, we'll get a big-ass tent; put it on my front lawn. It'll be beautiful right by the lake. And, we'll have everything catered, so no one has to be stressed out cookin'.'"

"With drinks before dinner, a Champaign toast, and a proper vintage served with each course; just like in France." Chloe added.

"But, grand-mere, multi-course ... the cost."

"Oh, don't worry about the cost, Jacqueline. I will pay the cost."

"But," Jackie said, "we discussed paying for the wedding ourselves."

"Don't worry dear, it will be beyond you. Thank Norman, he confirms that by custom here in the States it is proper the bride's family pays for the wedding."

"It just seems so big ... 60 people."

"As weddings go," Vicki said, "sixty guests is small. And, Martin and I will provide the tent and tables ... so don't worry."

"Just remember," Emma added, "Everything we plan is subject to approval by Joey."

"Ah, yes. The male need to feel in control. We must feed their egos, how well I know. It is the same in France."

The discussion went on to the menu for the reception. Many issues regarding food could only be determined once a caterer was selected, and the cake ... a baker must be found for the cake. Jackie was asked what color she had selected for the bridesmaids' dresses so the flowers at the church and the reception could be coordinated. "I plan only on my Matron of Honor ... my cousin Carol. It is the custom in France, no bridesmaids." Chloe and Vicki advised there should be bridesmaids anyhow. Jackie stood firm, no bridesmaids.

Next, flowers were discussed. Vicki described so many that Emma cautioned, "Be careful it doesn't look like a funeral."

The women tried to select the music, but Jackie said she wanted that left to her and Joey. Chloe and Vicki looked at each other and shrugged. "Remember Jackie, soft during dinner, upbeat later."

After two hours, Chloe said, "Where is that Joey? Men, always distracted. Well, we have come a long way. Jacqueline, tell Joey everything we have planned. Then we will meet again in a few days. And, oh, your gown, when can we pick it out?"

Jackie looked at Chloe, "I have already found my wedding dress, grand-mere. No need to worry."

"White, I hope?"

"A more appropriate ivory. Goes with my, how do you say in English ... 'situation'."

"But you are getting married, making all things right."

"*Oui, oui*, I am." Jacqueline looked away then brought her eyes back to Chloe's, saying in French, "No, grand-mere, with all that has happened, I can go only as far as ivory."

Chloe quietly said, "*Oui ... D'accord ...* ivory."

That evening, Jackie walked into the Carriage House after Joey dropped her off. She found Emma alone, sitting in her easy chair near the fireplace, reading. "Hi. Where is Will?"

"He went to bed early. Said something about all that wedding planning wearing him out ... just the thought of it. So, how did things go with Joey? Is he okay with everything?"

"The important, yes. He is happy. The others, he shrugs and says, 'Go ahead'."

"That's often the way with men."

Jackie sat down in the chair closest to Emma and leaned toward her. "I am sorry this afternoon to shout about Joey and me here, in this room, during the winter. I did not intend to break your trust, in your home, while you were away."

"Jackie, I'm glad you were here ... when it happened. A moment you'll cherish always."

Jackie looked into Emma's eyes, "So intense ... so very intense."

Emma smiled, leaning forward, putting her hand to Jackie's cheek. "You became a woman that night, in every sense of the word ... and a mother. I know it's scary at times."

"*Non*, grandmother, *non*. I do not see being a mother scary." She looked toward the ceiling. "But planning this wedding with Chloe and Vicki ... *Mon Dieu* ... that is scary."

As soon as Jackie headed upstairs, Emma turned off the light and walked into her bedroom. Will rolled over toward her and extended his hand in a welcoming gesture. Emma slid out of her clothes and nestled herself against his warm body. Will encircled his arms around her and held her tight. After kissing her, he said, "Had enough wedding planning?"

"Oh, I never thought when we bought this place that I'd be in the middle of a wedding. It just shouldn't be this hard."

"Don't worry, we'll work it out."

Emma pressed in as close to Will as she could get. She knew in a few minutes he'd be back to sleep as she mulled over the many details swirling in her head, worrying all the more.

Chapter 16

Over breakfast Jackie told Will she was walking up the road to the vineyard trailer office. He asked if she wanted a ride. "I need exercise. Would you like to join me?."

Coming in sight of the office, they noticed Mr. Mosbey's tank truck parked next to the trailer. It was a steep climb and Jackie heard Will wheezing. Stepping off the road between two rows of vines, she said, "Let's check some grapes." Taking a cluster in her hand, "Look. Just about perfect."

Will wasn't sure how Jackie could tell perfection, the grapes were so small; except that like a newborn's hand or foot, all the detail of mature growth was present in miniature. "They look good to me, and so green. But I don't know anything about vineyards."

"These will turn red mid-summer. They are how do you say, 'Healthy and Hearty'. But we need to canopy so they get just the right amount of sunshine."

"So our cool spring has been good for them?"

"*Tres bien.* We avoided the late frost a few weeks ago because the ravine sucks the warmth from the lake up the hillside. The grapes were protected from freezing."

They heard a loud, scratchy voice coming from the direction of the trailer. "Yeah ... well ... Joey, you know the rock up here is gonna give us some grief. Hell, new construction near these ravines is never easy; but, jeez, you've really got a sucker's challenge on this one." Joey and Mr. Mosbey were walking toward them, looking between the road and the ravine at the area planned for the new winery. Neither one noticed Jackie nor Will, standing between the rows of vines.

"What do you mean, a sucker's challenge?"

"With all the limestone perc tests can be tricky; you can pour a lot of money into a leach bed and then find it ain't worth shit."

"Ironic that the limestone is good for the wine."

"Hey, I'm just tryin' to warn ya."

Mosbey took the unlit cigar butt from between his teeth; held it between his thumb and forefinger, and pointed toward some scrub growth on the slope down toward the lake. "There Joey, along there. Looks like soil's deep enough and it's wide enough between the road and the ravine for the leech field. We'll have to perc test it but good; satisfy all the regs so we don't have to pull the whole thing out. Yep, between here and over there by the ravine. We'll still have our challenges, but we got a shot."

Mosbey walked off the road toward the ravine, scratching his temple with his little finger, the cigar butt held high away from his hair. He stopped, started waving his arms and shouting, "Go on, get outta here." He looked at Joey, pointing toward the ground, "See that sucker, big damned snake for around here. Must like the warmth in that rock." Mosbey took a step forward, "I'll snap your damned neck... Oh, there he goes."

Joey, had caught up with Mosbey, "Yeah, bigger than usual ... but harmless. Just don't tell Jackie."

Walking toward Joey, Jackie asked, "Don't tell me what?"

"Oh, Jackie ... and Will. Just a snake. You aren't afraid of them are you?"

"Not when they go the other way."

Mosbey turned toward Jackie, "Good mornin', I hear there's gonna be a weddin'." He walked out of the scrub to the road. "Congratulations. Joey's the best..." Turning toward Will, he extended his hand, "We've met, but your name slips me."

"Will, just call me Will."

"Jackie's grandfather, right?"

"In a manner of speaking, yes."

"Ah," Mosbey smiled, "complicated huh? Life does that."

"Not so much anymore."

"Well," Mosbey turned toward the spot he'd just come from, "'we're tryin' to figure out where to put the septic field ...

gotta get that right." Mosbey turned to look up the road, again using the cigar between his fingers as a pointer. "The site for the winery, it's beautiful, but the rock's too close to the surface. And Joey, here, he wants to go first class … the Tasting Room with a big mother of a deck out front. Hell of a lot when ya got no wine to sell. Joey tells me it's somethin' to do with branding, whatever the hell that is. All I want, Joey, is just a damned taste of your wine."

Mosbey turned back facing Will, "But new vineyards, they're a fling at fate anyhow. So what's a few thousand more to have a stand-out building? Everybody's doin' it. Thankfully, plain or fancy, they all need septic systems."

Joey looked at Will, "You know … we started out simple. Then Norman explained branding and image. So Jackie and I worked with the architect. It'll be dramatic … take advantage of the lake view."

"Yeah, I know," Will said, "You showed me a rough sketch when you two were working at my kitchen table."

Mosbey looked up and down the road, "Joey, you own this lane, right? You ever checked for easements?"

"Yeah, my land goes to the center of the ravine … and maintenance on the road is up to me. Like a private drive."

"But, does the county have a right-of-way?"

"What do you mean?"

"Well, this goes from the Lake Road up to the high road … both county roads … and often the county has an easement for certain types of use on connecting roads."

"Why do you ask?"

"It's that damned frackin'. You know your neighbor up top, he's signed a lease with one o' them gas companies . If they start drillin' they'll need a lot of water. I've heard as much as a million gallons. And they never put in just one well, think several, maybe ten."

"Yeah. A million or more, per well."

"So where's the closest water source? And truckin' it, with those big rigs, they want the shortest way. If I was doin' it, I'd head right down the damned hill to the lake. Cut a road in from the top of the hill to get where your trailer is, it's only what … three, four hundred yards. Then this road'll make a shortcut to the friggin' lake. Otherwise they need to drive way around wastin' time and diesel."

"What's that got to do with easements?

"Joey, the county'll ask themselves why tear our pavement up with the big rigs comin' and goin'. Nope, they'll pull an eminent domain and get the direct route. Right past your nice new winery."

"But they can't just do that." Joey said, '"Can they?"

Will smiled, "Joey, we're talkin' a gas company here. Don't think the powers that be in the county won't be properly primed for a decision that goes their way."

"Yeah, Joey," Mosbey said, "think thousands of truck loads, hundreds per well, big rigs, laboring up this hill in low gear. The exhaust fumes'll be so bad you'll need to give your customers gas masks. Forget their taste buds; the diesel fumes'll knock 'em haywire. Noise and congestion all over!"

"So, I guess I need to check the county records."

"I'd get a lawyer to help. You know lake property records get all fucked up. Could be lookin' for some damned side entry somewhere."

"Or," Will added, "a blanket ruling that gives the county the right to use any private road connecting two of their roads."

"Damn, you two are ruining my day … really."

"Better now than later."

"Jackie, what do you think?'

Jackie looked down, then up at Joey, "In France, working at the bank, I saw some powerful men get their way. I suppose it is the same here. Not what is right; only what those with money, what they want to do. They find a way."

Will said, "Just follow-the-money. Who'll profit most … there's the lever for whatever action is taken. Look deeper and you may even find the political payoff that makes it legal."

Mosbey smiled at Will, "Jeez, a cynic like me." He turned to Joey, waving his hands to emphasize his message. "With this frackin' they'll tell you the local farmers profit and there'll be lots of jobs. But the good pay goes to the drillers from Texas and Oklahoma … that's where all the big money ends up anyhow. Then when they're done, they pull out and leave all their mess to the locals, with no future liability at all."

"So what are you saying?" Joey asked.

"I'm sayin', the oil and gas men, and don't forget the Wall Streeters, they all want to drill. So, you've got a battle to fight. Just be sure the damned frackers don't put you out of business … and, remember, they won't have paid you, a vineyard owner, a penny. You won't have one damned thing to sue for, either. They'll be sure there's no recourse. It's a damned war Joey."

"Injuste!" Jackie said, "It is unfair." She turned and looked at the vines across the road. "Today … I canopy the vines. The new growth is healthy and needs cutting back. Right now, it is what we must do. Let the sunshine in."

"Can I help?"

"Oui. Of course, Will. I will show you."

    ℰ   ℭ

Mid-morning the Carriage House phone rang. Emma immediately recognized Chloe's voice. "Emma, the priest, is he going to marry Jacqueline in the church in town?"

"Oh, Chloe … Hello. To answer your question: Yes, as far as I know. Jackie mentioned that he's not comfortable marrying couples outside of his church."

"Norman thinks he has several churches now … something about joining parishes together."

"Oh, that. It was caused by the priest shortage. But I know Father Roy is still most comfortable in the church of his old parish, the one in town."

"So it will be in town, not miles away."

Emma held in her breath to avoid being brusque. "I'm sure, Chloe."

"When, Emma, when?"

"What do you mean, when?"

"Are they talking about a date ... for the wedding?"

"Oh, that. They're discussing early August."

"That's almost two months away. By then, Jacqueline will be showing too much, too big. She will be too pregnant ... embarrassing."

"How can she look too pregnant?"

"To be stylish, in her wedding dress. She's so thin, she'll be showing way out. Have you seen the dress she picked out?"

"No, she hasn't shared that with me. She will when the time comes."

"The time is now Emma. We must get her to tie down these plans ... even move the wedding up so it doesn't look disgraceful."

"Chloe, it's not disgraceful. Jackie is a mature, healthy young woman. Thank God, she's getting married to the man she loves. What's disgraceful about that?"

"Oh, you Americans, you are so, so bourgeois."

"This never happens in France? A pregnant woman gets married."

"We conduct ourselves with more decorum in France."

"Oh, I bet you do."

"We must meet with Jacqueline again, soon. I suppose we need Vicki there too, since the reception is at her Manor."

"I'll talk to Jacqueline when she gets back."

"She is not there, Where is she?"

"Up in the vineyard. Said something about canopying vines. Will went with her. I'll have her call you later, but when she gets at those vines, she's always gone for hours."

"Just as I expected..."

ഇ   ൫

Preparing for day's end, the sun bathed the lake in a rich mandarin hue. Will carried two mugs of coffee from the Carriage House down toward the water. Emma was already

161

sitting on the bench by the shore, trying to enjoy the scene, anger in her eyes. Will handed a mug to Emma and sat beside her.

Emma took a sip, saying nothing. Then, almost to herself, said, "That woman! She's so exasperating."

"You mean Chloe or Vicki?"

"Oh, Chloe, of course. Vicki, she's depressed. I feel sorry for her. Chloe's ... well, I can't say what I want to say about Chloe nicely. Bitch isn't strong enough."

"So, have you women actually tied down the plans?"

"Ugh," Emma shrugged, "At least for today, until someone changes their mind, or comes up with another idea. You know dealing with those two is exhausting."

"You mean Chloe and Vicki?"

Emma exhaled in frustration, looking at Will. "Yes, Will, Chloe and Vicki. They feed off each other. Then they double team Jackie and me to get their way. What a tug-of-war. Jackie hangs in there though. No one's gonna run over her."

"Or Joey, I wouldn't think."

"Well, on wedding plans, Joey tends to stay out of it until he sees Jackie being badgered. Then he jumps in and tells us how it's gonna be. That, of course, gets Chloe all riled up."

"Yeah ... it doesn't take much."

Emma looked out over the lake. "Remember how peaceful this was a year ago, just before Jackie came. I was happy she came, don't get me wrong, but last spring it seemed we'd found our place ... this beauty, the peace and quiet."

"Jackie isn't the problem; she's calm."

"You're right, it started when Chloe came. The stress."

"Of course, and we had a minor tornado to liven things up." Will put his hand on Emma's knee, looking at her. "Then Jackie and Joey ... falling for each other."

Emma looked back at Will, "They're nothing like Norman and Chloe; that was another tornado. Those two are old enough to know better."

"Well, be thankful for Joey. Without him Jackie'd be back in France."

"I guess." Emma looked at the ground. "It's terrible to say, but I wish Chloe would've stayed there. She second guesses everything Jackie does. Doesn't like anything. Makes me wonder if she even likes herself?"

"I was surprised when you sent Seth up to get Jackie and Joey; at first we thought there was an emergency."

"Chloe just set me off. I decided, we'd just get this planning done and over with. Enough snide remarks from her."

Will chuckled, "What did she say?"

Emma looked out over the lake. "She called a couple of hours after you and Jackie left. Started questioning specifics, where the wedding will be, and when. She wants it soon. I told her Jackie was up in the vineyard and might be there for hours. She said, 'Just as I expected. Jacqueline', that's what she always calls Jackie, 'Jacqueline will have so much dirt under her fingernails she'll need a dark tan wedding dress'. Then she added, 'Appropriate for vowing her life away to that nobody farmer who took advantage'. She used some French term I didn't understand. Probably something about Jackie's pregnancy making her look like a peasant woman."

Emma looked back at Will, raising her voice. "I smashed down the phone so hard we're lucky I didn't break it. Then I walked over and Vicki was there with the kids. Since she was free I decided to call Chloe back and tell her to get her ass over here. But I needed Jackie and Joey. Luckily, Seth could run up and find them."

"Hey, don't be angry with me."

"You got lucky with your doctor's appointment; that sure was well-timed. You missed all the fun. But, you're the last person I'm angry at. Without you I'd be lost."

"So the wedding will be the first Saturday in August … right?"

"I called Father Roy, he said 4 PM works best."

"Reception here at the Manor, right after?"

"That's the plan. With a sit-down dinner."

"Are you still gonna cook?"

"We counted about 90 people to be invited."

"Ninety, I thought you were planning on 60?"

"It was a reach cooking for 60. The meal will be catered … we need to find a caterer and figure out the menu."

"So, it'll be crowded, even for the lawn."

"I just hope Martin goes along. I can tell Vicki hasn't told him much. Vicki's gonna get a tent, tables and chairs. But that leads to who sits where and Chloe even has her fingers in that pie … hardly knows anybody but wants to be sure everyone is properly placed. You'd think it's a formal state dinner."

"Probably gets that from being married all those years to Maurice. And you know French diplomacy, more protocol than substance."

"Anyhow, I think Jackie is somewhat unplugged from that. Other than the immediate family, she doesn't care where people sit … and Joey, he just smirks when Chloe starts pontificating.'

"So, what can we do?"

"I'm making a list. I'll need your help on a few things."

"That's no problem."

"There's a lot Jackie and I have to do together. She needs me. After the meeting she mentioned how she misses her mother; how if her mother were alive it would be so much easier. She's never said that before."

"Oh, I doubt it'd be easier. Chloe'd just be telling her daughter what to do. It could even be worse."

"Maybe so. Just don't make any plans between now and early August."

"I hear ya."

"And, oh, at the end of our meeting, after Joey left, Jackie showed us her wedding dress. It's not a gown; it's a very tasteful off-white dress, just below the knee, adjustable so it can be let out. I think that, with Joey and the best man in suits, it'll fit the occasion perfectly." Emma smiled, "Chloe nearly had a hemorrhage. She wants a formal wedding dress, a gown … with a train … something, I'm sure, that will make Jackie look much slimmer than she'll be by the time early August rolls around. So,

Chloe left in a huff … again. Probably haven't heard the end of that."

Emma glanced toward the lake. "Look at that…" A ball of deep red was just starting to go down behind the hill across the lake. She and Will sat in the silence of the setting sun.

The stillness was broken by the sound of breaking china coming from the Manor, followed by a string of words unintelligible through Vicki's near-shriek. Then Martin could be heard, although loud, more measured and controlled.

"I'll bet that's about the wedding plans." Emma said, "I knew Vicki hadn't told him."

"Could be, or maybe he just disagreed with one of her ideas."

"Think I should go over."

"Nope. I think we should just enjoy this beautiful scene as those pink clouds turn to purple. Intervene now and we're only enabling Vicki's irrational behavior. If they need us, they know where we are."

Chapter 17

On a sunny morning during the last week of July, Joey walked through his vineyard checking the veraison of the grapes beginning their change from vibrant green to the red color of harvest. A car on the county road just above the vineyard usually wouldn't attract his attention, but the light bar spanning the roof did. He recognized the 'Sheriff' script along the passenger door. The car didn't drive on past his property as he expected, rather pulled over next to the office trailer. He quickly walked out of the row of vines to the road so he could be seen. He raised a hand, waving a greeting.

The county sheriff, once a fit deputy, but now somewhat portly having suffered the political gatherings of several campaigns for office, acknowledged Joey's greeting with a wave and started walking toward him. Joey reciprocated by striding to quickly close the gap between them.

"Joey O'Donnell ... it's been a while. Your vineyard here ... it's really recovered. Hardly know anything happened. Can you believe a year's gone by since that storm?"

"Yeah, we've all been surprised. If the weather keeps cooperating we'll have a decent vintage this year."

"Good, that's good to hear. You deserve a break."

"So...?" Joey let the words drop in a question.

"Well, Joey, I'm sure you know your neighbor up top leased drilling rights on his farm to a gas company. Word around town is you've made it clear you're against any hydrofracking."

"Yes, that's true. Drilling there is a risk to these vines ... a great risk. One spill and the vineyard's worthless. Plus all the noise and trucks and smell ... it gets pretty ugly from what people tell me."

"Yeah, well, you know Joey, people have rights, property rights, and they can do with their property as the law allows."

"Oh, I know that. Don't agree the gas companies can just drill under my land, though. But what's the problem?"

There's a fella been cruisin' around our county on a small motorcycle, 'bout the size of a good sized dirt bike but set up for the road. He pops up here and there, and we haven't been keepin' track of him … no reason to.

"But I got a call from the sheriff in a county in northern PA … know him from some conferences we've attended. He's lookin' for a guy riding a motorcycle like we've seen. Used to be a roustabout on the wells down there, but got himself fired. Got some bone to pick with the gas companies. Plus, he's a vet … a crack shot; apparently a sniper who served in Iraq. They were chasing him after some well equipment got shot up; but lost him. Think he may've headed north … our way. You don't happen to know anything about this guy, do you?"

"Haven't seen him."

"How about a couple of months ago? I stopped at Ben's. He said a roustabout named Hank was hangin' out about that time … ticked off at the gas companies. Ring a bell?"

"Oh, yeah … Hank. He talked with Jackie and me about fracking … all the problems. Haven't seen him since."

"What's his last name?"

"If he offered it, I don't remember. Don't think he ever said."

"Let me know if you see him."

The sheriff looked toward the top of the hill, "You know if the gas company gets approval to proceed, they'll bring in one o' them thumper trucks."

"What?"

"Yeah, damnest thing … big contraption mounted on a truck. It thumps the ground hard and seismologists analyze wave patterns to determine where there's gas. This Hank fella, he likes to shoot them things up … make the gear inoperable. Not in my county, he won't! And don't you go gettin' any ideas."

Joey glared at the sheriff, his face reddening in anger. "Hell, only gun I own is a pistol. Locked up in my office just in case some critter needs to be dealt with. I'm not about to be shootin' up some gas company's truck. They can do too much damage to me."

"Okay, okay. Settle down now. Just call me if you see or hear anything." He held out his card. "You don't want to be withholding from the law. That would make you an accessory."

"I'll let you know."

"Well, I sure would like to talk to this Hank fella. Got any idea where he was staying?"

"Didn't say that either. I got the impression he was just passin' through. He'd just been let go from down in PA. I just talked to him the one time."

"Anybody with ya ... when you talked to this Hank?"

"Jackie was there. We both heard the same thing."

"What's her last name again?"

"It's Beauveau. Jacqueline Beauveau."

"Has that nice European ring to it."

The sheriff turned to go, then spun back toward Joey. "And, oh, your uncle Nic, what's he been up to lately?"

"Uncle Nic? What's he got to do with this?"

"Well, everybody knows he's outspoken against fracking."

"He's a pacifist! He's not about to go around shootin' at trucks. Besides, with Kober Vineyards, why would he risk getting into trouble with negative publicity from doing a dumb thing like that? I don't even know if he has a gun, let alone knows how to shoot it."

"I guess you're too young to know about his war record."

"His what?"

"In Nam. Crack shot ... long kill list. Came home to no welcome. I was a deputy in those days and we were worried about him. Had PTSD, but they didn't call it that then. Some months after he came back he was having a lot of problems readjusting. Then, he ran into one o' them 'born again' Christian types; priest or minister ... I don't know. Anyhow, he starts 'praising the Lord'. From what I hear he's been praising the Lord ever since."

"Oh, I can vouch for that."

"Well, okay. I just gotta look under all the rocks, see what I can find. Some days upholding the law isn't so easy. You know, I'm not so sure this hydrofracking is all it's cracked up to be."

Joey watched the sheriff walk back to his car and drive off. He turned back toward the vineyard glad his passion was among the vines, unpredictable given the laws of nature, but not as warped as human challenges to life.

ഔ   ೞ

Martin all but shouted, "No Vicki, just one. Got it! Not two, just one." before he slammed down the phone.

Fran heard his frustration and came to stand in the doorway to his office. "Everything okay?"

"Would you believe she wants two limos for this wedding now? It's a small wedding, why am I paying for two limos to get from the church out to the Manor?"

"You're into the hectic phase."

"The what?"

"The hectic phase. When all the last minute ideas bubble up and everybody gets a little crazy. Startin' early, with the wedding two weeks away."

"Yeah, well we aren't even related, so Vicki can't just go crazy spending money on this thing. I'm already on the hook for the tent, tables, chairs. The caterer, DJ, photographer … they all want to plug in at the same time. I may need to run more power out there. Thank God it's in August or I'd be putting in heaters."

"Let me know how I can help." She turned her head to the side and stepped into the office so Norman could walk in without having to squeeze around her. He smiled as he said, "Hi."

Martin flashed a concerned look of surprise. "Norman, are you psychic? What brings you here?"

He smiled, "It seems we may need to coordinate a few things about this wedding for Chloe's granddaughter."

"Well, I'll leave you two to it," Fran said.

"Don't go too far away," Norman said, "We may need some help with only 10 days left."

"I'll be right out here." Fran closed the door behind her.

Martin remained seated, looking directly at Norman with undivided attention.

"Chloe tells me Vicki's really been helpful putting this wedding together, but it seems there's an anchor holding her back."

"A what?"

Norman pointed his finger, "You!"

Martin, usually somewhat submissive to Norman, sat taller. "What's the problem?"

"Something about not wanting to decorate with flowers, pushing for the smaller tent, taking a chance on using extension cords instead of a proper electrical feed. I don't know, Chloe sometimes goes on and on, but now she's classified you as a banal pain-in-the-ass. Over breakfast she told me to get off mine and talk to you. So here I am. What the hell is going on?"

"Damnit! Vicki, you know, can get carried away. We were married with a very simple, low budget wedding. It's as if she's rethinking our wedding and adding in all the elements she'd demand if she was getting married again. Like she's trying to redo our wedding vicariously. She wants to spend over a grand on a florist to decorate the tent. Just now, this morning, she wants two limos ... for such a small wedding, two limos! Can't you and Will drive from the church to the Manor? Do we really need another limo?"

Norman chuckled, "You do realize that's Chloe's idea ... two limos. Anyhow, it seems Vicki is trying to do the best she can and she's offering to pick up all the additional costs. Emma sure can't; she doesn't have a lot of money to spare."

"I think Emma and Will had to stretch to buy their place."

"Probably. But, Martin, that doesn't mean you need to be holding the bag. You and I know it's a tough year here in the company financially, and that bonus in your contract, we both know it probably isn't gonna happen. That aside, I certainly don't expect you to pick up costs on this wedding.

"I mean Vicki's offer to use your Manor, that's really great. And it's more than enough. I told Chloe she should pay for the wedding, and I meant all of it. She's a little tight and hasn't offered Vicki near enough to cover your costs. Chloe's claiming she has limited resources. Well, she did, until a couple of months ago. Now she can afford it, believe me ... she made out fine."

"You mean in France?"

"Yeah, the vineyard. Hates to part with her money though. I'll tell you what, you let me know what your costs come to and I'll write you a check so you don't have to suffer the brunt when the bills come in"

"No, Norman, I'm not looking for a handout."

"Martin, Jackie may well become my step-granddaughter. Hey, I'm living with the bride's grandmother, so by default I'm much more responsible than you are. Don't let your pride in our business relationship cloud this one. I may need some time to get the money back from Chloe. Leave that to me. Let the women do what they want and stop worrying. Like all weddings, they'll freak out, spend much more than necessary, and talk about what a wonderful day it was for the rest of their lives. So just hang back, have a couple of drinks and enjoy it. With Jackie it'll probably only happen once ... Joey's a keeper ... with the child coming they'll be even more cemented together."

Norman walked around the desk and put his hand on Martin's shoulder. "Relax, my friend. Happily these weddings don't come too often."

Martin stood, saying, "Thanks for the offer. You do realize the flower arrangements for each table and the décor are over a thousand dollars? But if you pick up that and the limo, I'll handle the rest at the Manor."

"Okay. I appreciate that. But let's go over the list because I'm sure the family of the bride is responsible for more."

Martin walked over and opened the door a crack. "Fran, bring your pad in here ... please. We've got some expediting to do."

        ℘   ☙

It being a bright morning with the temperature moderate, Will had paddled a bit farther than usual. Instead of turning around in front of the cove where Joey's grandfather had built his lake home, a cove his lawyer had nicknamed 'Moot Point', a name that stuck, Will paddled along the shore. It was a beautiful setting, the property where Joey's mother, Deborah, had recently moved in with her mother. That allowed Jackie and Joey to rent Deborah's cottage in town ... a perfect place to start their married life together.

On the paddle home, the ache in Will's shoulders reminded him he wasn't as young as he used to be and maybe he'd gone too far; it was becoming more like work than pleasure.

As he pulled the canoe onshore, Emma came out of the Carriage House with a mug of coffee. "You stayed out a long time today. I got worried."

"Why? On a beautiful day like today."

"Well here, have a seat on the bench. I need to ask you something."

"Must be important." Will sat and took a sip. "You never greet me like this."

"Oh, it's just so nice out here." Emma sat beside him. "Why stay cooped up inside."

"So, what's so important?"

"Oh, it's the reception. Chloe and Vicki were making up the seating arrangement yesterday."

"There's a problem?"

"I don't know; I just have a bad feeling about it. There's a lot of baggage in that Kober family ... long-felt hurts over land or something. Put the wrong people at a table together and we've got an argument."

"Was Joey there?"

"Not while they did it. Jackie got him to look later and he made a couple of changes, but I don't think he knows much about some of his family's wounds."

"Well, what about Deborah?"

"You know, Joey's been very reticent to get her involved. She's going to hold the rehearsal dinner at the lake home, but other than that his mother hasn't shown much interest."

"Yeah, it seems Nicholas is the only one in good straits with her."

"I'm sure she'd be happy if Joey just had a small wedding. Deborah likes Jackie; but shies away from anything with her step-brothers or cousins."

"It's the old story of the unexpected baby-sister by the second wife," Will said, "Not much love lost in a lot of those families. Hell, I bet it wasn't long after the old man married his young bride that Deborah was born."

"But that was over 40 years ago!"

"Doesn't matter … not with that Moot Point lake property in the picture. It's worth a fortune … and the brothers still feel it should be theirs. So, now Deborah moves in to help her mother whose health is failing. Her brothers are blind to that fact; to them she's staking her claim."

"But they got the Kober Vineyard, the winery, the business."

"So why not have it all?'

"So they're the bastards, not Joey's mother."

"Emma, your insight is lucid and I love you for it. Anyhow, don't you worry about the reception. If any fights break out we'll stand back and watch the show."

Chapter 18

Promptly, just before 4 PM on the first Saturday in August, the wedding guests gathered in the pews of the old Catholic church. All were in a good mood; many greeting their only-seen-at-weddings-and-funerals relatives; some anxious to see this Jacqueline, the girl from France who Joey was about to marry.

The second limo Chloe had insisted on having pulled to the curb. Emma and Will got out, followed by Norman, who turned to give Chloe a hand, helping her out of the oversized back seat. Norman said, "You go in. I'm gonna walk around the side and see if I can find Joey."

"Make it quick, we've got to get in the church."

Joey and Ralph, his best man, were standing in the shade near a side entrance to the sanctuary. Norman approached saying, "How come you're out here? Isn't it cooler inside?"

"Yeah, but there's nowhere to stand other than up by the altar. We just figured we'd stay out of view for a few minutes, until they're ready to start."

"Well, Jackie was getting ready to leave as we pulled out of the driveway, so she shouldn't be long. You look good in a suit. All set?"

"As set as I'll ever be."

"Nervous, huh?"

"A little."

"That's healthy. Just remember, everybody's happy for you." Norman looked toward the street. "There's Jackie's limo. I'd better get going. Chloe'll be waiting for me."

Joey and Ralph opened the door to the church and walked in. Joey liked the tasteful flower bouquets on each side of the altar; white lilies and red roses in a bed of baby's breath. He recalled the plethora of flowers Chloe and Vicki wanted, followed by Father Roy's caution, "I have to say the Saturday Mass at 5, and while a few flowers will be nice, I can't have parishioners wondering who died." He appreciated Jackie's decision to keep it simple.

Joey's mother and grandmother were seated in the first pew. They stood as he walked over and he gave them each a hug, the gesture saying 'Thanks for everything over all the years'. Then he crossed the aisle and gave Emma a hug; he stepped toward Chloe as she held out her hand.

Back at the foot of the altar, Joey shared 'Hello' glances with many in the pews. He was startled when the organist began playing Mendelssohn's Wedding March, signaling the ceremony was about to begin. Seth, the ring bearer, and Maria, the flower girl, walked slowly down the aisle, side-by-side. The two young children glanced hesitantly at the guests, not quite sure of themselves in the new role they'd been pressed into.

In keeping with French tradition of having no bridesmaids, Jackie's cousin, Carolyn, the Maid of Honor, came into view, her blue dress cut just below the knee. She was escorted by one of the two ushers, walking confidently, her pace a bit brisk, as if to get out of the way.

Jackie started down the aisle, escorted by Will. Her broad smile heightening the tender glow of a pregnant mother ... excited in joyful anticipation ... as he, Joey, was taking her hand in marriage! Jackie looked so happy!

Jackie's choice of the ivory, simple, yet stylish, maternity dress acknowledged her pregnancy, but didn't emphasize the fact. The soft off-white shade complimented her natural color. Cameras flashed from many angles.

Will gave Jackie's hand to Joey in the age-old gesture of conferring life-long responsibility for the welfare of the bride to the groom. He smiled, "You take good care of her."

"Oh, I will! Of that you can be sure."

Taking her hand, Joey felt the slight tremor of nerves belying Jackie's outward calm demeanor. He gave a gentle squeeze. They looked into each other's eyes in a final assertion of "Let's do this!" and turned toward Father Roy. Joey felt Jackie's nerves ebb away.

Across the congregation many purses were opened, Kleenex being sought. Emma, standing next to Will, leaned against him. Chloe had tears streaming down her face; Norman, not sure why, took her hand in his. Across the aisle, Joey's mother and grandmother dabbed tissues at their eyes, their first indication of emotional involvement in the milestone taking place just feet in front of them.

Without a Mass the Catholic wedding ceremony was of short duration. At the conclusion, just before telling Joey, 'You may kiss the bride', Father Roy smiled as he quietly said to the couple, "Our former bishop, Fulton Sheen, used to say, 'Three get married' I really feel that applies here, the Lord *is* with you. May you have many years to grow in your love together and with Jesus."

The wedding kiss was a model of passionate restraint, polite and cool to the casual observer, but exposing deep mutual respect and bonding to those emotionally astute. Father Roy patiently waited, then raised his hand to give the final blessing. The organ came to life and the newlywed couple walked hand-in-hand, almost skipping, to the back of the church; laughing and sharing glances of greeting with their guests.

ℰᴓ　　　　ᴓℰ

It was at the reception that Chloe and Vicki's planning played out in full force. Under a clear blue sky the sweet light of late day sun began to shine on the lakeside scene. A large white tent stood on the lawn of the Manor with a welcoming arbor of grapevines leading to it from the driveway. The grape arbor motif was carried on across the ceiling of the tent. There being no need for protection from foul weather the sides of the tent had been stowed away, leaving one with the impression the grape arbor was authentic.

With over 100 people expected, the two women had spent the morning overseeing fourteen round tables being set with white tablecloths, China dinnerware, silverware, a Champaign flute, and a name tag for each guest. Vicki then placed three small glasses with red rose buds floating in water on each table. Chloe positioned the Wedding Party's head table along the north side; the bar along the east side, nearest the Manor. Toward the lake, she saw that no obstruction impaired the view of the late-day sun reflecting off the water.

A DJ played soft music as the guests assembled while the wedding party first had lakeside pictures taken by a professional photographer, then stood in a receiving line near the head table. Everyone offered their well wishes, expressed in the good mood and sage advice weddings bring forth.

When the last guests had been greeted, and Jackie and Joey began to circulate, Norman made for the bar. Chloe had instructed the bartender to have single malt on hand … hoping for Norman's best mood for the duration of the celebration. Norman saw Martin walking over and greeted him, a tumbler of scotch in each hand.

"Nice, Martin, very nice." He handed Martin a scotch. "This tent idea really worked out."

"Yeah, I gotta hand it to Chloe and Vicki; they know what they're doing. Too bad we didn't know what a beautiful day it was going to be … we could've just had a grape arbor and ditched the tent."

"Same difference … the way it's decorated."

"You do realize a crew was out here all morning making this happen?"

"Oh, yes, I know. I heard Chloe on the phone making sure everything was covered … except the bill. I can't wait to see that."

"Well, the Kober clan sure is out in force."

"Joey tells me he hardly knows some of the distant cousins, even though their grandfather started his farm just up the hill from the vineyards."

"Joey's vineyard, the farm leased to the gas company?" Martin asked.

"No, a ways south of that, right up above the Kober vineyards. I guess Joey's grandfather had a brother who worked with him for years, then bought land on top of the hill and farmed it. It's been passed on down, a grandson owns it now."

"So they're here?"

"Yep. The grandson, Fred Kober. I don't know much about him."

Nicholas approached the two men. "I see you two got a quick start."

"Nic, how are you?" Norman held out his hand. "Yeah, Martin got in early to avoid the rush." Shaking hands, they glanced toward the many waiting at the bar for their first drink.

Martin asked, "Can I get you something?"

"No, I just got here. I can wait. I only go soft anyhow."

"So," Norman said, "Any word on activity up on top of the hill?"

"Nothin' I can confirm. Rumor has it there's plenty of gas, so if the ban on drilling is lifted, expect a lot of activity ... fast."

"That fits with what I've heard."

Nic rubbed his forehead, "I don't know how we stop it. The environmental protesters are preparing an action for a local moratorium. I went to their last meeting; but I doubt the town will go along. It's tough when you've got leasing land-owners on the town board."

"We hear your cousins are here. The ones who own the farm up the hill?"

"Yeah, Freddy. Is he here?" Nic tipped up on his toes looking over the gathering of guests. "I don't see him, maybe later. I'll bring him over and introduce you."

"So," Norman asked, "This Fred, you have much to do with him?"

"Naw, haven't even seen him for months; grandson of my father's brother. Understand, there's been hard feelings ... for years. When dad died that side of the family felt they should inherit a share in the Kober Vineyards since their grandfather worked during the early years. They all thought they had some kinda claim. I guess the old man didn't see it that way. Weren't mentioned anywhere in his will."

"Shirt-tail relatives, always come out of the woodwork when the will's bein' read."

"This rift goes way back. Pretty hard feelings. Frankly, I'm surprised they were invited…"

Jackie and Joey walked up to the threesome. "Well," Nic said, smiling, "Look at you two, the happy couple. Listen the wedding was wonderful. I'm so happy for you." He leaned over giving Jackie a kiss on the cheek.

Joey said, "We want to thank you, all three of you, for everything you've done. Without you, we might never have made it."

Norman laughed, "Oh, you would've made it; our women just wouldn't be talkin' to each other."

"You know, Norman, you've got a point there." Martin said.

"And you, Uncle Nic," Jackie said, "You've been such a … an anchor, all along."

Nic blushed, "Well, Jackie, I try. Now stop thankin' us and go on and have a good time."

Since the dinner hour had come, the guests were invited to be seated. Happily the arrangement had kept the warring factions of the Kober family at separate tables. After a short grace by Father Roy, Ralph, the Best Man, clinked his Champaign flute signaling a toast. He'd decided to keep-it-clean, but saying, "…and during the past year Jackie and Joey have proven they can really work together," brought a smattering of laughter. Ralph's clarifying, "No, no, up in the vineyards…" led to an outburst of laughter. "Okay, okay. But seriously, you know Jackie seemed to pound some common sense into Joey's thick skull, I mean he really settled down shortly after he met her." Ralph paused, putting his hand to his chin and looking into the distance, then saying softly, "Or, was it getting hit on the head by the spar on my boat." He moved his hand down, "That was almost a first date for these two … and Joey, he takes her sailing … but he doesn't think to tell her he really doesn't know how to sail. Luckily, Martin and Norman came out and fished

179

him out of the middle of the lake, right off here." Looking at Jackie, "Anyhow, Jackie ... Jacqueline ... you are the best thing that's ever happened to Joey. And we all wish you two, and your baby, many loving years together." He held his glass up to acquiescence as everyone stood, raising their glasses. Jackie leaned in, kissing Joey on the cheek.

The dinner Joey had suggested much to Chloe's dismay, smoked ribs - the meat just falling off the bone, catered by the best ribs joint in the area - was perfect for the warm summer day. The music afterward, became more upbeat for dancing; somewhat incongruous with the orange orb moving toward a peaceful sunset across the lake. Nic, sticking to his ginger ale, was one of the few still sober under the tent.

Norman walked over, "So, Nic, having a good time."

"Sure am, don't get many weddings in the relation lately. The kids just aren't getting' married like they used to."

A man, in his early '30s approached. He spoke too loudly, "Hey, Uncle Nic, great to see you. It's been a long time."

"Freddy, how are you? Yes, it has been a long time." Nic turned toward Norman. "This is Norman Olson."

Norman held out his hand, Fred seemed not to notice.

"Freddy, I guess I should call you Fred. So, really, how are you?'

"I'm just peachy Nic. You know why?" He air punched upward, over his head, saying, "Pow!"

Nic could see Fred's face was flushed, his pupils dilated. "No," Nic said softly, "Why's that?"

"It's a damned gold rush Nic ... a gold rush! So, this landman guy, he comes over, offers me thousands per acre. And, Nic, I'm gonna sign. They'll drill, Nic; right on top o' your Kober Vineyard ... well actually under..." Fred thrust his body forward toward Nic, almost falling over, looking brashly in his face, "and there ain't one damned thing you or Tom can do about it."

"Maybe, Fred, maybe. You do realize the ban on drilling needs to be lifted first."

"Yeah, well, I'll be laughin' all the way to the bank with the first payment."

Looking toward the sun, Nic tried to see Fred's face better, but the reflection off the water was blinding. He moved to the side, came close, and said, "Fred, we should talk about this."

"Yeah, I'm gonna let you and Tom talk me out of it. No way…"

"Just be very careful. Read the fine print. Get a lawyer to look it over."

"Yeah, sure Nic, just like you and your brothers screwed my side of the family when your father died. I'll be sure and get that lawyer."

"You know, Fred, you've had a lot to drink. Is your wife here?"

"What's she got to do with anything? You leave her outta this."

"No, Fred, no. I'm just thinking you may need some help getting home."

"Oh, don't you worry about me. I always find my way home. Now, I think I'll just sidle over and get another drink."

"Listen Fred, no more. And I'll be glad to talk anytime."

"Yeah. Up yours…"

As Fred wove his way toward the bar, Nic caught the bartender's eye, pointed at Fred and slashed his finger across his throat, signaling there was one guest who should be shut off.

"Jeez, if looks could kill!" Norman said. "That guy, he's related? He really hates your guts. He's flyin' though. I think he's on a lot more than just booze."

"I don't know. Rather not get involved. He was a nice kid, not the brightest, but nice. Now, when it comes to land, just seems all the gloves come off. You know, the Senecas, they cared for the land, preserved it, and they shared it … this very land we're standing on. Hell, the whole Iroquois Nation. They shared this land, and they worried about protecting it for seven generations to come … everything they did, they considered that. We came along, enlightened Christians, and we said 'No, that's not right. We must show you how'. Once individuals claimed ownership all the greed set in. And now, how many give a shit about the next generations. Hell, most don't care about a decade down the road!"

"But Nic, you won! You're one of the land owners. You're not going to share your legacy are you?"

"Not with Fred... he just pisses me off. Even when he's sober."

Tom walked over.

"Norman, you know Tom don't you?"

"Yes, yes, we met after that storm last year."

After he shook hands with Norman, Tom asked, "Nic, I saw Freddy talkin' to you. What's he up to?"

"He's got a frackin' lease offer. Says he's gonna sign.

"Shit! I was afraid he'd take the bait."

"Yeah, well I was just saying to Norman how the Native Americans didn't have these problems ... they shared the land, no individual ownership." Nic smiled, "So maybe if we give Fred a share of the business, he'll back off."

Tom looked at Nic in alarm, "What the hell you been drinking?" You didn't say that to him?"

Nic laughed, "No ... but the look on your face."

"Damn. We should have bought that farm off him while we had the chance."

"You know he wouldn't sell ... to us."

"You're right, no way!"

The DJ stopped the music and announced, "I'm going to be quiet for a few minutes so we can all enjoy the sunset. Isn't it beautiful?"

Everyone turned toward the lake, except Seth performing the dance gyrations of a six-year old, impervious to the DJ's words. Noticing the music was gone, he stopped; adult conversation ebbed to silence. Tom nudged Nic, whispering, "Share of the business ... That's not even funny."

All eyes concentrated on the orange orb going behind the ridge on the far side of the lake. Couples stood, arms entwined around each other, with tighter embrace.

Just as the setting sun inched to rest across the lake, while silence still reigned, a loud voice shouted over by the bar. *"The fuck you won't! Another damned drink, that's what I'm having'. Open Bar Man, O-P-E-N B-A-R! Know what that means? I get as many as I want."*

"Oh, Christ...," Nic said, "Freddy's out of control." He rushed toward the bar. Fred was behind the bar when Nic approached, the startled bartender shoved to the side, grabbing for a bottle of gin. Nic went around the end of the bar, grabbed Fred by his collar. The quick jolt caused Fred to drop the bottle; it shattered on the wooden ramp behind the bar. Nic, a head taller than Fred, dragged him backwards to the end of the bar, turned him toward the grape arbor opening and stiff-walked him out to the driveway.

"Get the hell out of here Fred. You're drunk. Keep it up and the sheriff will have you spending the night in jail. Just go, damn it. And get a grip."

"Like hell...!" Fred tried to say.

"Listen," Nic brought his face directly to Fred's, "you aren't going to destroy this wedding. Just go! Before I really get mad. Don't be like your grandfather was."

Fred's wife appeared at his side. "I'll get him home. I am so sorry."

"Take care of him, will you. And get him some help!"

Emma and Will were standing on the dance floor watching the sunset when Fred's shouting shattered the silence. They swiveled around to find its source and watched as Nic collared Fred out of the tent.

"Well," Will said, "You knew something had to happen."

"Oh, right from the start I didn't like the idea of inviting the shirttail Kober relatives. Too much anger in that clan."

Chloe walked over to them, Norman not far behind. She asked, "Who was that ruffian?"

"One of the Kober cousins." Emma said.

"He certainly cannot handle liquor."

"Oh, I think it's more than that. What I was trying to tell you and Vicki when you insisted on a large wedding."

"You aren't going to accuse me, Emma. Just because you Americans have no savoir-faire." Under her breathe Chloe mouthed, '*petite bourgeois!*'

"So, you condemn us all based on one's man's being drunk?"

"Uncouth, Emma, Uncouth. That's a word you may better understand."

"Oh, I understand alright…"

Will stepped in, spreading his arms between them like a referee at a boxing match, "Okay, okay. Let's call a truce on this before you two make another scene."

The DJ announced, "Okay folks … a little surprise there. Let's start out with a slow tune so everybody, and I mean everybody, can dance."

As the volume of the music rose, Norman took Chloe's hand indicating he wanted her to follow his lead. She looked at him, smiled, shot one last harsh glance toward Emma, and followed.

Will took Emma's hand. "What a piece of work! Let it fall off your back Emma. Let's dance and enjoy the rest of this evening. There's really nothing to argue about."

Emma followed Will's lead, but added, "Easy for you to say."

Chapter 19

Night was coming quickly when Will walked out on the dock to see what Norman was doing on his boat. "Nic called it a night ... headed home. Apologized again for his cousin. Saw you out here. Just wondering if everything's okay?"

Norman, standing in the well of the back seat, turned toward him. "I just wanted to get this hatch open ... vent the engine compartment." He wiped his hand over his forehead. "Yeah, that Freddy ... sometimes it's better not having a large family. Anyhow, this morning I drove Chloe over here to help setup. She brought her dress for the wedding so she could change in the Manor. But after I went back and got changed myself, the day was so nice, I came over in the boat. It's a lot faster."

"Should be a pleasant ride home."

"I was hoping for a moon."

"Probably out of luck there; not gonna have one tonight. You able to see out on the lake on a night like this?"

"I just go slow; keep the spotlight pointed ahead. Chloe offered Jackie and Joey a ride down to the Bellagatto, so we'll be going a ways. But some of the cottage lights help guide me." Norman bent to pick up the glass he'd set on the edge of the seat, sipped the last of his scotch, then looked up at Will, "So, now that the cake's served and the garter's been thrown, what comes next?"

Will laughed, "I don't know. That's probably it unless these young folks have somethin' new."

"This cool breeze helps; keeps people dancin'. We were lucky it didn't get any hotter this afternoon.

"Jackie's still holdin' up ... they're havin' a good time. And young Seth, still showin' off all his dance moves."

Norman chuckled, "The energy of a six-year-old ... wish we could bottle it."

Will looked back toward shore. "The tent sure is pretty from out here. Who thought of those white pin lights mounted to the vines across the ceiling. That's a great idea."

"I think Vicki came up with that. I heard Chloe debating it with her. Just Christmas tree lights … cast a nice soft glow off the canvas."

"It was a nice wedding, Norman. The gals sure did a good job."

"Hey, when money's not a problem, great things can happen. I guess we men just have to keep smilin'."

Will chuckled, "I heard that somewhere about weddings … just keep smiling."

"And the checkbook open. With the wedding over, my concern is what Chloe'll do now. With her vineyard sold and Jackie married, I sure hope she doesn't start meddling. It's gonna be hard … she being so controlling as Jackie grew up. Be nice if she finds something that makes a few bucks."

"Well, she's got the vineyard, too."

"Joey's vineyard? No, no, she has no interest in that. Thank God! All I need is her muckin' around up there. She's givin' me a hard enough time just bein' an investor."

"Well, I'm sure she'll find her niche. She's got too much energy … not the type to be sittin' around."

"That's for sure..."

"Coming back in?"

"Yeah, I'm in no rush …whenever they're ready will be fine. I'll leave the hatch open … air things out."

Will reached his hand to Norman as an assist to step on the dock.

"So, you're coming back to the brunch at our place tomorrow, right?"

"That's what Chloe tells me. You ready for another drink?"

"Not right now, gotta pace myself. And, I'd better find Emma. It's so dark out here she won't know where I am. Probably wants another slow dance."

Will held Emma close as they slowly danced cheek to cheek. When the tempo and volume picked up, they walked to the side of the dance floor.

"At least he plays a slow number occasionally."

"That was nice." Emma said, "We should dance more often."

Dabbing sweat off his forehead with a handkerchief, Will said, "Well, Jackie and Joey sure like this beat … look at them go."

"Yes, "Emma said, "Forty years ago we'd have liked it too. I just hope Jackie doesn't overdo."

"She'll be alright. Never did get the knack of dancin' like those two; to this kinda beat. Always wanted to hold my partner, not jump around wavin' my arms."

They approached Norman, also a refugee from the dance floor, standing near the arbor entrance to the tent … about as far away from the speakers as he could get.

Will nudged him, leaning to be heard, "Too fast, huh?"

"I guess. The rhythm in my head doesn't find its way to my feet like it used to. Being twenty was a long time ago. And the sound level, too loud for Chloe."

"Tell me about it. More noise than music."

"It's the beat … that's what's important."

Chloe approached through the arbor leading from the driveway. She said to Norman, "Beatrice and Ralph have headed back to our place … getting tired."

"Good thing he drove the Jag over…" Norman turned to Will, "You met Ralph, the state senator … right?"

"Yes, at the church. We chatted with Beatrice and him after dinner."

"He has a new Jag. Drove it up from New York yesterday with the top down … rough, huh?"

Will smiled, "Yeah, life is tough, particularly for those of us driving Mercedes and Chris Crafts…"

Norman laughed, "Touche! But his is brand new. I think he wanted to drive it over here to show it off. Good thing with us taking the bride and groom to the Bellagatto after the reception; and the way these kids are dancing, this could go on for a while."

Will glanced at the crowded dance floor, "Yeah, you're right ... must be the beat. Do you happen to know where our newlyweds are going on their honeymoon?"

"Tonight," Chloe said, "I upgraded them to the Honeymoon Suite at the Inn."

"Yeah," Norman continued, "Top shelf all the way ... but after brunch tomorrow, they're on their own. Joey left his MG at the Inn to drive over here, then I guess they'll drive that wherever they're going ... haven't told us where to."

"Or us," Emma added.

"The MG?" Will said, "That's awful small. Can't be going too far away.""

On the dance floor, Joey saw them out of the side of his eye; headlights coming fast from the driveway toward the tent. The heavy bass of the music masked the noise of the pickup truck crashing into the entry arbor. Still under full power, it compressed the vines into a tight tangle, shoving them hard against the tent. Emma, Chloe and Norman were pushed aside by the compressed mass of vines. Will, hit square, was knocked backward and pinned under them.

Joey froze as he watched the truck ride up onto the tangled vines, lifting the tent roof off nearby poles, then tip over onto the driver's side. All the lights in the tent went dark; leaving only harsh headlight beams splashed across the ceiling. Poles and struts groaned under the pressure; level and square were replaced by angles askew in a garish nightmare.

The tent listed toward the lake. One pole split in two, hitting a couple standing nearby, knocking them to the floor. The whole construction was ready to collapse. The engine of the pickup raced on, making a racket as the exposed rear wheels spun against open air.

Women screamed as their men tried to protect them from falling debris. "Oh my God!"

Joey grabbed Jackie's arm and pulled her away toward the lake. He shouted, "Everybody out! Get out of the tent!" He turned toward the couple lying on the floor, a few others already by their side.

"Are they okay?"

One of the men kneeling looked up, "She's got a bad slash into her leg and he got hit on the head ... but he's conscious."

"Can you get them out before this collapses?"

"We're on it ... get Jackie out."

Once beyond the tent roof, Joey saw Martin, standing on the lawn looking toward the wreckage. He cupped his hand to be heard, "Martin ... Martin. Cut-off the breaker ... may be live wires."

Jackie asked, "Where are Will and Emma?"

"On the other side. I'll find them. We need flashlights. Run over to the Carriage House and grab as many as you can. Be careful, don't trip over anything ... and call 911. And, grab you're pruning shears."

Walking around the side, Joey looked into the tent. He saw Emma and Chloe standing by the tangle that had been the arbor; Norman was bent over, both hands grasping a vine, trying to lift upward. Rushing in, he yelled to be heard over the noise of the truck engine. "What's going on?"

Emma, her hands also around a vine, trying to pull, yelled, "It's Will. He's underneath."

"Oh, shit."

"I can't lift it." Norman shouted.

"Hey, Joey, that you?" Will's voice was strained, short of breath. "I'm pinned. This damned thing's all scrunched together."

"You all right?'

"Just a couple of scratches. Can't move ... God, it's heavy."

189

"Okay, okay … relax as much as you can.   We'll get some help."

Joey stood and looked around. He didn't see anyone in the tent; everyone standing outside looking bewildered, as if in shock, trying to understand what was happening.

The Manor spotlights came on, flooding the driveway in harsh light.   Joey saw Martin come out the side door of the Manor, shouting in his direction, "Tent breaker's off."

"Martin, over here." Martin hurried past the pickup toward Joey, stopped, turned and yelled, "Everybody stand back! This damned thing is leaking gas."

"Yeah, I can smell it." Joey said, "Get some guys to come in here for just a minute." Turning back to Norman, he said, "You'd better get out. Can you cut the engine on that damned truck?"

Six men, a few cousins of Joey, came into the tent. "Okay, we need to lift this tangle just a little. Enough so I can pull Will out?"

Ralph, who was up on the body of the truck trying to open the passenger door, shouted, "Hey, the driver's still in here."   He moved to get leverage on the door handle. "Goddamn! It's sprung. I can't open it."

Joey kept his focus on Will. "Okay, Will, we're gonna lift and I'll slide you out. Can you help me?"

"I think so. Nothin' seems broken."

"Okay, guys, on three. One … two … three!"

Six men stressed to the limit, and lifted the arbor … only inches.

"Joey," one said, "the vines, they're all smashed together and the truck's pressing against them. We gotta lift the truck to get him out."

Joey looked around, "It's too heavy. See if you can push the truck back just enough to get the pressure off … then we can lift the front edge. Damn, we need more light."

Martin shouted, "Does anyone know how to kill this engine, we're getting gas over here." Norman yelled toward Joey, "You gotta hurry Joey, this thing could blow."

The men stood beside Joey getting in position to push the truck back, carefully planting their feet to avoid stepping on Will. Giving all the strength they had, the pickup slid back about a foot.

Joey moved farther into the tent, to the other side of the fallen arbor. "That took some of the pressure off. Lift on this side and I'll slide Will out." He looked down, "Will, you ready?"

Will, out of breath, grunted, "Do it."

"Here..." Jackie held up a flashlight. "I have the shears, can we cut him out?"

"May have to, but we need to be quick."

Jackie knelt by Joey, "What can I do?"

"Hold the light and if you see a branch holding Will from coming, snip it off. Be careful, don't cut Will."

Jackie felt someone behind her. It was Emma. "Hand me the light so your hands are free."

Joey looked up, "Okay, guys. One ... two... three."

The twisted vines gave way almost two feet. Grabbing Will by the legs, Joey pulled; Will came toward him, but given the position of his arms he couldn't help.

Jackie saw that vines were holding Will's hand back, his arm at an odd angle. She snipped the vines in two to free him.

Slowly Will came free. He lay on the floor looking up, gasping for air.

"Thanks guys," Joey yelled, "Now get out of here, away from that truck."

Joey grabbed Will's elbow and helped him up. "We're gonna walk out, but be careful there's stuff hanging all over the place.

Emma stood shining the light, showing the two men hazards in their way. When they were outside, Emma flashed her light up and down Will's clothing. "You're bleeding."

"It's only a scratch."

"All the blood on your shirt says it's more than a scratch. Here on your head, you've been cut, there's blood all over your ear ... and scratches, you're all scratched up. You need some bandaging."

Will took Emma's hand and squeezed it, saying, "I need to help."

"Not now," She tugged his arm toward the Carriage House. "After I patch you up."

Careful to skip over the raw gas on the ground, Joey ran to the truck, still tipped on the driver's side. Ralph and a couple others were struggling with the passenger door. "It's jammed."

"Break the window." Joey said.

"But he'll have glass all over him."

"Better cut than dead. We've got to kill that engine ... now!"

Mr. Mosbey held up a crowbar. "Here, this fucker'll do it. Ralph, hit that sucker hard."

"Mosbey, I thought you'd left."

"Free hooch ... fat chance."

Glass shattered down into the cabin of the truck. Ralph broke away all the shards still in place and squirreled himself through the opening. The motor stopped racing, then shut down. The abrupt silence was alarming.

Ralph shouted out, "This guy's out cold. I'm tryin' to get the glass off him."

"Can we just right this damned truck to make things easier?"

"I guess, doesn't look like he's injured."

"Know who he is?"

"Yeah, it's Fred Kober. Your cousin from up the hill."

"Ralph, sit tight. We'll right this damned thing. It'll be easier than liftin' him."

The men who'd helped Joey on the tent rushed over and rolled the truck back to an upright position. But, the grape vines underneath made an unstable cradle so the righted truck wanted to tip the other way, then back toward the position it had been in.

Joey yelled, "Hold it steady so Ralph can get Fred out. Then we can let go and let it rest any way it wants. Be careful of that gas … let's not ignite it."

The truck was lifted upright and held there. Ralph worked his body around Fred's slumped under the steering wheel, and extended Fred's arms toward Joey. The two men quickly slid Fred across the vinyl bench seat and with the help of others Joey carried Fred to the edge of the lawn, setting him down on his stomach.

"Wa…" Fred mumbled. Joey bent over him getting ready to turn him over on his back when Fred hoisted himself up on his side and spewed vomit over those standing nearest. They jumped back, Joey not quickly enough, getting bile all across his white shirt and the front of his suit pants. He almost gagged on the foul smell.

"Oh, shit … sorry …" Fred groaned, settling face down on the lawn … then rising up just enough to croak up another disgusting mess. But the effort was too much and Fred fell face first on his own barf … unconscious.

"He's fuckin' stoned," Mosbey said, "Stupid shit's drunk out of his mind."

"Come on," Joey said, "let's carry him over on the lawn; it'll be safer." Joey and a few others grabbed Fred by the arms and feet and dragged him well away from the wreckage.

Along the way, Joey asked, "Damn it Fred, why'd you come back? Haven't you caused enough trouble already?"

"Anybody got a fire extinguisher?" Norman yelled. "Truck's set the vines on fire."

Martin ran back with a large extinguisher in hand. Norman yelled, "Everybody back, get back! Way back!"

Martin emptied the extinguisher on the blaze, trying to protect the gas tank. But the fire, fed by the spilled gas on the ground, crept under the front of the truck and then through the mass of tangled vines … upward to the tent ceiling. Although the dead vines fed the flames, the retardant treated fabric refused to burn.

Norman grabbed Martin's arm and pulled him away. "Come on, that damned thing's empty anyhow." They both ran toward the Manor. Seconds later the flames inside the truck crept to the gas tank. The explosive fireball blew a couple of the Manor's windows out; Martin and Norman found themselves sprawled on the ground.

The couple who had fallen in the tent were sitting on the ground, a safe distance from the truck. A friend was holding a cloth, a first-aid pressure bandage, against the injured girl's bloodied leg. Joey noticed his mother, kneeling next to the man, talking with him, apparently to assess his condition.

Joey saw a small crowd of guests, standing near the Lake Road, the reflection of the flames in their faces. They watched the fireball and flickering light with aboriginal fascination.

One man leaned toward another saying, "Best damned wedding I ever been to…"

"Damned straight! Fuckin' beautiful!"

Jackie was in the Carriage House helping Emma bandage Will. Hearing the explosion she came out and saw Joey walking along the edge of the fire. She rushed to him.

"Don't get near me, I'm a mess."

"*Mon Dieu!* You reek! Did you throw up or something?"

"My cousin, Fred."

"I thought he went home."

"He came back. Passed out. But, how's Will? Is he okay?"

"He has a bad cut on the side of his head; luckily not deep. And scratches … many scratches. Your mother told Emma she'll be in to help bandage him."

"Yeah, our very own nurse. Too bad we didn't invite a doctor."

"*C'est la vie.* Come in … let me get you cleaned up. I'm sure Emma can find a clean shirt for you."

"In a minute."

Jackie stood back, took a good look at Joey and started to laugh.

"You find this funny?"

"Not really ... just look at you. What a memorable finish to our ideal wedding!"

"Hear that? The fire department's coming. I better be out here."

The truck pulled in coming to a halt in the center of the driveway.

Joey yelled, "The fire's in the pickup and the tent. Can you get that out?'

By the time the firemen had squelched the flames, the sheriff's car was behind the pumper, with an ambulance beside it. The EMTs were immediately shown to the injured couple, the man holding his head in pain.

The sheriff saw Joey and walked to him.

"Heard you were gettin' married today. This the way you end your wedding? God damn you stink ... you had too much to drink?"

"No, no. It's one of the guests."

Jackie rushed up holding out a clean tee shirt. "Here, at least put this on."

The sheriff looked around while Joey stripped off his stained shirt.

"Okay... I see a burnt out pickup teetering on a tangle of burnt vines, pushed up against the tent so it broke the poles and beams. When the pickup caught fire musta ignited the inside of the tent, scorched the whole damned canvas." He turned back to Joey. "Looks like a war zone out here. This some kinda new prank, some new wedding ritual?"

"No, no, an accident."

"Anything else I should be seeing ... that you'd better show me?"

The sheriff put his hands on his hips, making a more imposing figure of his six-foot, 230 lb. frame. "You say an accident! Looks more like the booze got outta hand. That's illegal you know. Somebody drove that truck out-a-control? I'll ask again, anything else I should be seeing?"

"No," Joey said, "That's about it."

"Okay, so maybe you can explain how a two-and-a-half ton pickup ends up on top of a bunch of vines, damned near pushes the tent over, then the whole shebang catches fire?"

"I think the driver blacked out, hit the accelerator. That's what I think … not sure."

"And the driver … okay?"

"Yeah, I think so."

"You think so. Who is this driver?"

"Fred Kober, a cousin."

"Where is he?"

"Over on the lawn."

"Well, let's check him out." The sheriff then stepped back and shouted. "Listen folks, anyone who saw this happen … please stay. I need to get your eye-witness statements. There'll be a deputy here in a few minutes to speed things along. So a little patience, please. Much appreciated. And you, the fella with the camera, I see you're takin' pictures. Don't leave, I want to see those."

Fred had his eyes closed, trying to dampen his spinning nausea, and the pain he felt when he opened them to the harsh light of the Manor's spotlight. Some kind person had given him a wet rag to clean off his face. He lay on his back, not yet able to sit upright.

The sheriff stepped in close, moving Joey aside as he towered over Fred. "So, Fred Kober, we meet again. My deputy's just pullin' in and I'll send him right over with our nice new Breathalyzer; just calibrated … so you can't claim our equipment is at fault this time. And welcome, since I'm sure you've committed a few felonies, we'll give you another excellent accommodation in our bed and breakfast."

"So, you know Fred?"

"Oh, we're becoming fast friends. Listen, it's your wedding day, and I personally am sorry to have to be here. You go and say goodbye to your friends while we take some statements and get at the bottom of this mess. Don't worry about Fred, we'll give him a ride and take care of him."

Joey shook his head as he walked over to Jackie talking with a cluster of guests. "What is it about August?" He said to the group. "Last year the storm, and now this!"

"Hey, Joey," one of the guests offered, "you gotta agree, this will be *THE* memorable wedding reception."

"Well," Joey forced a smile, "I guess as soon as the sheriff is done with us, we've gotta wrap this up."

Jackie put her arm around Joey and gave him a kiss on the cheek. "I need to say, your family…" At a loss for words, she just shook her head. Then looked at Joey and smiled, *"Je t'aime.""*

Norman was surveying the extent of the wreckage. Martin came to his side. "Have you seen Vicki?"

"Not since before, on the dance floor. What about the kids?"

"The babysitter was putting them to bed, thank God, when all this started. But I can't find Vicki. I'm gonna check the house again. Can you look around for her?"

"Sure. I'll look on the beach."

Norman walked out to the dock, looked both ways along the shore. In the light from the Manor, he saw a faint silhouette near the far edge of the property; someone sitting on the ground, near the water's edge. Approaching, he quietly asked, "Vicki?"

She looked toward him, her cheeks wet with tears reflecting the harsh light.

Norman kneeled next to her, putting his hand on her shoulder. "Hey, hey, it's okay. Everything's under control."

Vicki slowly, silently, shook her head from side to side. In a deep graveled voice, almost a whisper, looking out over the black lake, she said, "Cursed! This goddamned place is cursed."

"Now Vicki, just a drunk getting out of control."

Again Vicki shook her head from side-to-side, saying nothing.

"Well, come on in. Martin's looking for you."

Vicki looked at Norman and almost yelled, "Yeah, well about time. Just tell that fucking husband of mine I'm out here. I'll come in when I damn well please."

"Okay, okay. I'd stay with you but I've got to get the newlyweds off to the Inn."

"Go, just go! Leave me the fuck alone, Norman."

He found Martin. "Vicki's down on the beach. She needs some space. Check on her in a while. But be careful, she's pretty pissed at what happened."

"Yeah, I guess. So am I. Can't wait for the first lawsuit."

"Well, at least you're insured ... aren't you?'

"Of course. I hope they cover it. I wonder if that Fred Kober's covered."

"From what the sheriff was saying I wouldn't count on it. I'll bet his license is suspended. Sue his damned ass, he'll be getting' money from that frackin' lease."

Martin sighed, "Yeah, I guess."

"No guess, he told Nic that earlier."

"What a way to end the prefect wedding reception."

"Listen, it was a great reception... Now, unfortunately, it'll be remembered for all the wrong reasons."

"Well, we tried..."

"I gotta go," Norman said, "Put my happy face on for Jackie and Joey. Then I'll have to listen to Chloe."

"It's gonna be a long night."

An hour later, the sheriff having finished with Joey, a gaggle of guests carrying flashlights escorted the newlyweds around the tent, out to the dock. Any bothered by the pungent smell of the smudged-out fire kept to themselves.

Emma had given Joey a white shirt and pair of Will's khaki pants ... both much too big. Jackie had changed into a pair of maternity pants and pastel blouse. Not the outfits they had planned. At the end of the dock, Jackie kissed Emma and Will; Joey embraced his mother. Chloe and Norman were already seated in the front seat of the Chris Craft; the guests helped Jackie and Joey climb in back. Once they were seated, the camera bug took one last picture. It would become the most memorable, the young couple, Jackie nestled in Joey's arm, looking at each other, smiling broadly. The pure joy of being together, shown in their eyes, caught by the camera in the bright light of the flash.

Chapter 20

A beautiful Sunday morning, sunshine and the lake mirror-calm. Norman saw only a few boats in the distance. He gunned the Chris-Craft to plane at top speed, the wind rushing through the thinning strands of hair warding off his baldness. Chloe ducked behind the windscreen, protecting what was left of her 'wedding' hairdo. When they'd first pulled out, she'd turned around, sharing a few comments about the lake with Beatrice and Ralph, seated behind her; but with the engine gunned and wind whipping up, she got down, placing her hands over the coiffure she'd spent so much to achieve. The guests sat silently, seeming to enjoy the speedboat ride ... the bright blue of the lake, the lush green of the hills ... a quiet Finger Lake on a sunny morning.

Norman really needed to vent some stress after the disaster at the reception, the slow boat ride in the dark to get the newlyweds to their Honeymoon Suite; then Chloe harping on the Kober family gene pool all the way home ... continuing late into the night. There was no therapy better than this classic boat at full throttle to bring his sanity back.

Beatrice and Ralph had driven their Jag back to Norman's place shortly after the reception dinner and were not aware of anything unusual happening until Chloe filled Beatrice in over wake-up coffee and croissants; but she spoke in French leaving both Norman and Ralph to wonder what was being said. The expressions on Beatrice's face, the pursed lips and bulging eyes made it clear the rendition was condemning ... Norman could only guess it all came back to Joey. He was tempted to interrupt, but kept still, fearing any challenge to Chloe would just encourage her to delve deeper into her anger, directing it toward him.

He crossed the lake heading just south of the Manor so a power turn could cap off his few minutes of flat-out euphoria ...and for a change Chloe kept her mouth shut.

Martin was standing on the dock, waiting, as Norman brought the boat aside. "I heard your exhaust note ... you've got the only boat on the lake with that."

"Maybe ... it's one of the few classics left."

Martin helped Chloe step out of the boat. As he gave Beatrice, then Ralph, a hand to step onto the dock, he said, "Nice to see you again. Sorry we have a bit of a battle zone on shore."

Chloe ignored Martin's comment and asked, "Is Jackie here?"

"Nope ... been quiet. Haven't even seen Will. Emma came over and asked Seth and Maria if they wanted to help get things ready. And, oh, Joey's mother came a while ago."

"I'll go help. Beatrice, come join me."

The three men walked around the tent, the frame askew, the fabric charred. Ralph paused and bent down to see the destruction inside the tent better. He closed his eyes, bringing his a hand to his nose, saying, "Whew ... charred wood and burnt rubber ... pungent!"

Coming around the corner to the driveway they were greeted by the hulk of Fred's burnt out pickup truck; an area ribboned by yellow tape. "And here," Norman extended his arms as if making a presentation, "is the crowning achievement."

Ralph exhaled, "Jesus Christ! This really is a disaster. I'm sorry we left early."

"Yeah," Norman said, "You and half the guests." He walked up to the police tape. "Damn! Can't we get this fucker out of here?"

Martin stepped to his side. "Not yet, the sheriff wants more investigation done ... in daylight. He was here about an hour ago, said he's sending someone out."

Norman continued to focus on the truck, "For what, to move it."

"No, some investigator." Martin looked at Ralph, "Could be State Police. He said once that's done, I can move it."

"Oh, that's big of him," Norman said, "Grab what he needs and then dump the problem in our lap."

"So what else is new? I've also got the tent to contend with."

"Yeah, well, I guess we gotta live with the eyesore today. It being Sunday nobody'll want to come out for the tent this afternoon."

The Marimba ring of a smartphone intruded on the conversation. Ralph reached into his shirt pocket and drawing it to his ear, said, "Hello." He walked toward the yard of the Carriage House.

Norman asked Martin, "How's Vicki?"

"She came in sometime, probably 3 or so. Just kinda collapsed onto the bed and fell asleep. I threw a blanket over her and she's still there … asleep."

"Did she say anything when she came in?"

"She mumbled something about everything becoming shit. Like '…the wedding was shit, this place is shit, you're a shithead..,' meaning me, then, '…I feel like shit…' and she went to sleep. I didn't dare disturb her."

"Probably a good decision. I had to listen to it all the way home and over an hour after … the disaster of Jackie marrying one of those Kobers. I was hoping she'd go to sleep, but Chloe was just hitting her stride about 2 o'clock."

"No offense, Norman, but we sure do have strange taste in women."

Norman put his hand on Martin's shoulder, "If you ever figure it out let me know." He smiled, "I can't, and I've been through a few."

Norman focused back on the truck. "But this … we need to figure out how to shove this mess right up Fred Kober's ass."

Martin gestured toward the Carriage House. "Here comes Will…"

There was a spring in Will's step belying a white gauze bandage taped to the side of his head. "Good morning. Looks like a good day."

"Beautiful." Martin said.

Norman added, "Even better out on the water. How are you?"

"Oh, I'm okay. As you can see, I took a blow to the head last night; luckily it glanced off me." Will raised his arm to have his hand wisp past his head. "Thank God, Deborah, Joey's mother, was here to patch me up. But it kept me awake last night, so I overslept this morning."

"Well, I gotta say, that bandage above your ear is impressive. Makes you look like you were in some kinda bar fight."

"Guess you might call it that. Felt like it, too. Now the worst part is convincing Emma I'm okay."

"You know," Martin said, "That's nice. Shows how much she cares."

"Yes, she woke up during the night and knowing I was uneasy just sat with me for an hour or so, it really helped. Then this morning she's up at the crack of dawn to get the brunch ready. Quite a gal."

Will walked toward the hulk of the pickup, a charred skeleton of steel. "I guess we're lucky this thing didn't set our homes on fire."

"Yeah, I've got a few broken windows. That's all the damage I see. I walked around the Carriage House; don't see anything wrong except I think you want to examine this side up close. Give the paint a careful look ... just to be sure."

"I'll do that. Any idea what we do with this thing?"

"Sheriff is sending someone out to look at it." Martin said, "Then, I guess it's up to me to get rid of it."

Ralph returned, saw Will and held out his hand. "Good morning, Will. How are you?" Seeing the bandage, he leaned closer. "I heard you took a blow. Are you okay?"

"Better than this damned bandage makes me look."

Norman asked, "So senator, everything okay?"

"Just a matter of State. Most people think we legislators just goof off when we're not in Albany, but that's not how it works. Downstate, you know, always something."

"Yeah," Norman said, "All the money gets sucked out of Upstate."

Ralph ignored the comment, "So, where were we?"

Norman smiled, "Well, we're stuck with the mess for now. Of course, Martin and Will could plant some flowers around the base, the burnt vines underneath kind of set it off; make it into some kind of memorial. How's that for an idea."

"You know, Norman," Martin said, "sometimes you're funny … that's not."

"Sorry…"

"No, it's probably me. With Vicki the way she is, there's damned little space for humor."

"How is Vicki?"

"Well, Will, you know how she gets when she's down. I think this put her way down … like in a deep hole. I'm not sure what I can say or do to help her climb out."

"That bad, huh. Remember, Emma and I are here to help."

"Thanks. It's like chasing shadows. Think you have your arm around one and it's gone. Anyhow, as soon as the sheriff releases Fred's truck, I'll get someone to come and haul it out of here."

"Maybe the sheriff will impound it. If not, shouldn't Fred be doing that?"

"I think it'll be a wait for him; he's in jail."

Norman added, "Serves the fucker right!"

"So, Martin, you'll get it towed away if the sheriff doesn't want it?"

"Unless we want to look at it for days … and I don't want Vicki seeing that. On the tent, I talked to the rental company. They're gonna get some pictures for insurance; then they'll get it out of here, probably tomorrow."

"God, "Will said, "And the wedding was going so well up until then."

Norman said, "Martin, you'd better get some pictures, too, for your own protection. Fred, he's gonna have a lot of claims to pay off. Cut into his good fortune with the hydrofracking lease."

"And a lawyer," Ralph said, "Martin you need one to protect yourself; I hope you're insured."

"Oh, I had a rider put on my policy to cover the reception … just in case. I hope they cover this. My agent's on his way out here."

"Good thinking, to get the rider. You know, something happens … the owner always gets sued along with everyone else. And Joey, he should be able to sue since his wedding was disrupted. Take it all back to that Kober idiot. Make him pay."

Will said, "Well, at least the couple that was injured last night seems to be okay. Deborah tells me Joey's cousin needed stitches, over 30, and was sent home last night. Her date has a concussion. He can go home today; back in for tests tomorrow."

Norman said, "That's a relief."

"Yeah, for sure," Martin said, turning to Ralph, "This Fred Kober. He doesn't have shit now. But if hydrofracking is approved, he'll have more than he knows what to do with. Do you think it's gonna get approved?"

"Yeah," Norman said, "too much damned money to walk by."

"Well," Ralph said, "the Wall Street bankers are really anxious to go ahead. They see millions passing us by. But, being a senator, I have to stay on the fence until all the studies are completed."

"But what about Joey's vineyard?" Will asked.

"What about it?" Norman answered, "A vineyard is a five-year proposition just to get started, with a promise to make money in the future … maybe. A gas well is immediate profit for the landowner, probably more than a vineyard will ever make. There's a 'romance' to vineyards; but hydrofracking … instant profit! And the landowner doesn't have to do anything. Hard to beat a gas well."

"But, Norman," Will said, "The environment – air quality, the roads, our lakes - the water."

"All those costs come later; long after the profit's been made. The landowners, they'll never need to pay; probably not even the gas companies. That's the way with all the extraction industries … energy, minerals. Meanwhile, those with wells have a fortune in the bank."

"And," Will said, "the local governments are left holding the bag. So, the taxpayers end up paying, years later. But, Norman, I thought you opposed fracking; agreed with Jackie and Joey?"

"I did at first. Until I looked into it. Then I realized what a constant flow of money a gas well can be ... 24/7 ... even while we sleep. Fastest way to make money."

"But, "Martin asked, "Where's the catch?"

"No catch. Even the tax code's rigged to hold onto profit. Hell, pipeline companies don't even pay taxes. With Joey owning all these acres with gas under them, all we gotta do is figure out how to plug into the flow. Profit gentlemen, that's what it's all about."

"But the vineyards ... and tourism, doesn't that ruin them?"

"Who's to say; nobody's done it yet. Listen, we need to get in on the ground floor; get a well next to the vineyard. Wait and the opportunity for the big bucks'll pass us by. Don't you agree, Ralph?"

"Well, as I said, there's pressure downstate to go ahead. Of course, any pollution won't affect them because the New York watershed is already permanently banned." Ralph stepped back and gestured toward the lake, "But being here, seeing the beauty of these lakes and the vineyards, I understand why so many are concerned. It's a valid concern. So, I'm going to wait until the studies are completed before I make any decision one way or the other."

Joey's red MG pulled into the driveway.

"Okay," Norman leaned in toward the others, "Let's not mention this now. I don't want Joey worrying about it on his honeymoon."

Jackie got out of the MG with the agility of youth; pregnant ... but not that pregnant. With a radiant smile she offered a cheery "Good morning!"

Will responded, "You're in a good mood."

Walking up to the men, Jackie offered her cheek for kisses and light hugs from each. Joey was right behind her accepting handshakes and pats on the shoulder.

"So," Joey said, looking at the wreckage in front of the wedding tent, "This is what's left of it." Turning to Jackie, "Kinda like a nightmare, isn't it?"

"Oh, for me, in a nightmare everything is not quite right and then, how do you say, All-Hell-Breaks-Loose. No, our wedding was perfect until this happened. Then, after ... Norman, you gave us that wonderful boat ride to our marriage bed. The gentle motion of the boat out on the lake, being held by Joey and feeling safe, alone together in the dark."

Her voice became softer, an octave lower, her eyes wide in wonder, "I looked up into the night sky and saw hundreds of stars. As my eyes adjusted I saw galaxies I've never seen before ... so far, far away... like thin silver veils deep in the heavens. I was dizzy, and let myself fall deeper into Joey's lap. I knew he'd hold me, protect me, never let go..."

Jackie paused, then almost in a whisper, "*Non, non,* to me, it was not a nightmare."

Jackie took Joey's arm in hers and kissed him on the cheek. "Last night" she smiled, "that is the dream I will remember."

Norman looked at Will, Will looked at Martin, and Martin looked at Norman. Three loquacious men left speechless, thinking of nothing appropriate to say.

But the senator had his voice. He smiled, "Jackie, you spin to the positive so well, you should become a politician."

Joey hugged Jackie, smiling, "No, no, I just got her. I'm not losing her to that."

"Well," Will said, "Let's leave this to the sheriff or whomever and head on inside. See what the women are up to. And, there were several gifts left here last night that you need to open. Luckily they found their way into the Carriage House before the fire."

Jackie led the way, with Martin and Will bringing up the rear. As Martin held the door for Will, he waited while Will eyeballed the siding of his home. "Yeah, Martin, I see what you mean. The trim paint, something's wrong. Must be the heat affected it, at least down at the other end, nearest the blast.

Emma had extended the square dining table with a long folding table that stretched into the living area of the Great Room; set for the dozen people expected for brunch. When Martin and Will came in, Chloe held Jackie in a tight embrace; closely, like she didn't want to let go. Releasing her grip, she looked directly in Jackie's eyes, her steadfast gaze saying, "You will always be welcome back home with me."

Chloe was irritated by Emma's cheery energy, all smiles and upbeat since the bride and groom had arrived; giving direction to everyone, even the children, as the last of the food was placed on the table. But when Emma glanced at Will, Chloe saw the dint in Emma's façade, the gauze bandage on the side of his head a beacon of his injury.

The food being ready, Emma directed everyone to sit down. She gestured to Chloe to leave the seat between them vacate, saying, "Let's save this, in case Vicki shows up."

Once everyone was seated, Chloe asked, "Emma, I thought you'd planned to have brunch out on the patio?"

"I did. But when I went out this morning, that smell made me decide to stay inside. It's so heavy, gets right into your throat. Let's not dwell on it." Turning to Will she asked, "Would you like to say Grace."

"Of course, unless Joey wants to."

"No, no." Joey said, "You can say the grace. But first, since a few have asked, let me tell you all … Jackie and I stopped at the Clinic on our way here. My cousin has many stitches on her leg but should be okay. Her date suffered a concussion. They kept him overnight, but he'll be on his way home today. We can thank God the injuries weren't more serious."

Joey turned toward Will, "So, Will…"

Will scratched his head, too close to the bandage for comfort, then brought his hands together. "Well, I guess we need to thank the Lord that Jackie and Joey are married, ask for their safe journey on their honeymoon…" He paused, then continued, "And we should thank the Lord that our injuries were relatively minor … could have been worse. And, to keep it short, Lord, please bless this food."

All said 'Amen', except Chloe leaned over to Beatrice saying in French, *"See, as I told you, the marriage will always be defined by the disaster."* Chloe saw Emma's disapproval with her speaking French and asked in English, "So, you two newlyweds, where you are going for your honeymoon?"

"Oh, grand-mere," Jackie answered, "It is far, and yet so near."

"You are not going to tell us, are you? You may be married, Jacqueline, but you don't have to be snippy with me."

"Chloe," Norman said, "She's not being snippy … just, ah, protective. Hoping she and Joey can be away, really away. I applaud them for that."

"Away, they can be away. But, really away … from what?"

Norman chuckled, "Why … away from prying grand-meres."

Ralph laughed, until he saw Beatrice's stern glance from across the table.

"All I can say," Emma said, "the Wedding was beautiful. The reception was beautiful; along with the dinner. Those ribs were a good choice, Joey. And I, for one, enjoyed the dancing. So, we had a problem at the end. Jackie, you just put that right out of your mind. By the time you get back, you'll not even know anything happened. Anyhow, then, you two will have to concentrate on getting ready for your baby."

"Yes, Jacqueline," Chloe said, "Don't forget you are going to be a mother."

"How can I forget … my baby is with me all the time. And…" Jackie took Joey's hand in hers, squeezing it and smiling as she said, "And, Joey is going to be a father."

"Oui, yes… Well…" Chloe said, *"C'est la vie…"*

"I'm a lucky man, "Joey said, "Jackie and me, we'll also make good wine this year. Limited production, but in a couple of years we'll be up-to-speed. With Jackie … and our children … what more can a man ask for?"

"Oh, you caught the prize all right," Chloe said, "A beautiful woman who will be a good mother … and an expert vintner. Do not forget just how lucky you are!"

After brunch, once the wedding gifts were opened and the honeymooners departed to their 'away', the guests said their goodbyes, suggesting Will take a nap.

Vicki never made an appearance.

Chapter 21

The three and a half hour drive to their 'Away' wasn't long by most standards, but far enough in the confines of the MG, particularly with Jackie five months pregnant. It was her pregnancy that led her to tell Joey to plan a short honeymoon, peaceful and quiet. They drove about a half-hour after passing the "Entering Adirondack Park' sign on the two-lane highway toward Old Forge, when Joey turned onto a narrow road and slowed due to bumps of repeated frost-heaves. Jackie began to see the blue of a mountain lake through the trees. They passed the occasional dirt road 'driveway' into a camp and kept going, staying close to the lake. Coming to a temporary sign drawn on poster board, its bright colored letters saying 'J & J', Joey geared down and slowly entered the drive, not much more than a dirt track. A hump in the middle of the road between two well-worn ruts coupled with the low ground clearance of the MG made it necessary for Joey to place one wheel in the center of the rise, the other skimming the side of the road. After a quarter mile they came to a small peninsula jutting out into the lake, with a rustic log cabin, not much larger than a big lean-to placed in its center between massive pines. Just beyond it was a natural sand beach with the lake stretching another quarter mile across to a shoreline protected by the unbroken forest of forever-wild State-owned land.

Joey stopped the MG and killed the engine.

Jackie looked in all directions, taking in the scene. "Ah … Joey, *c'est magnifique!* How did you find this place?"

"Oh, Love, I know a guy who knows a guy. He even offered to stock in some food, just for us."

They both got out of the car. Jackie came around and hugged Joey, holding him tight. Joey jumped, stepping back. "What was that?"

Jackie laughed, "Our child just kicked you." She took Joey's hand and held it on her belly. Joey almost jumped again as he pulled it away. "Oh my God, I never felt a baby kick before."

"Oh, Papa, you will be surprised for many years to come." Jackie put her arm in Joey's and walked toward the lake, out onto a short strip of narrow dock leading to a square platform just inches above the water. Standing on it, they looked down the lake, about a mile. Occasional cabins, nestled in the trees, hugged the shoreline.

Jackie held onto Joey's arm. "This is so peaceful."

"Yeah, not even any speedboats. No motors allowed."

"Do we have a boat?"

Joey stepped back, pointing, "A canoe, right there, on the beach. Nice huh? But, don't worry, there's plenty to do. If we get bored we can drive over to Whiteface Mountain and the high peaks."

Jackie looked down off the side of the dock "The water is so clear up here. Look! Little fish in the shadows?"

Joey leaned next to Jackie, "Yep, sure are. I wonder how big they get in a lake like this."

After focusing on the fish a few seconds, she stood straight taking in the scene. *"C'est parfait!"* She turned toward the cabin. "Let's go and see inside. I hope it has a double bed."

"Yeah, in the pictures it did."

"You haven't been here before?"

"I've never been to the Adirondacks before." Looking around he added, "But I think we'll like it here."

"Oh," Jackie laughed pulling Joey closer, "I am sure we will."

"As I said, if you get bored, there are places to go, things to do."

"Oh," Jackie guided Joey toward the cabin, "let us not worry about that!"

          ഔ   ഗ

It was Tuesday, under an overcast sky, when Will pulled into the driveway of the Manor and Carriage House. Emma, Seth and Maria were with him. They'd taken a short drive on the hot, lazy afternoon along the lake and then up into the vineyards, the last stop being the site of Joey's new winery. He wanted to show Seth the foundation just completed days before the wedding. Today the construction site was quiet; Jackie and Joey being away on their short honeymoon. Will was anxious to have Seth see the concrete work from the ground up before the walls were erected. But Seth's attention span only lasted a few minutes; so while Will explained how the winery building would look to Emma and Maria, Seth wandered off to explore the edge of the ravine. Will had only to shout, 'Watch out for the poison ivy!' to get him back on safe ground. Seth hadn't forgotten his encounter with the weed the prior summer.

Will stopped short of the fresh driveway patch to repair the damage done by the fiery blast at the climatic ending of the wedding. As soon as he stopped, Prince came over from the shade of a tree out near the lake, wagging his tail. Seth scurried out of the car and headed into the Carriage House, suffering from the thirst of the hot, muggy August day and the promise of the drink he had cooling in the refrigerator; Prince following on his heels. Emma helped Maria out of her booster seat, promising her a cold drink just like Seth's. Will opened the driver's door, but remained sitting in the car, watching Emma as she walked away from him holding Maria's hand; then stooping to inspect a bug Maria pointed at on the ground. Emma's movement demanded Will's full concentration. How young she looked, the fabric of her shorts casually draping her classic form, he was convinced among the most beautiful ever created! *Although we're both in our 70s, still, the magic!*

The wound on the side of Will's head was beginning to itch under the bandage, *hopefully, it's healing.* He had to restrain himself from scratching. He sat, pausing to look at the lawn, surprised at how well the landscapers had repaired it. He appreciated Martin's quick action to get the burned out hulk of the truck removed on Sunday, the tent on Monday, and finally, the lawn restored today.

He looked toward the lake and noticed someone sitting on the end of the dock, a woman, her legs drawn beneath her ... stoic, as if in meditation. *That must be Vicki?* He hadn't seen her since before the accident. Emma visited Vicki late in the day on Sunday, and again Monday morning. She told Will she'd found Vicki balled up in a fetal position on her bed both times, responding to queries in monosyllables ... speaking so softly Emma had to strain to hear. Just as Emma was about to leave on Monday, Vicki quietly said, "I know I'm supposed to get a grip; but, Emma, I've nothing left to grip onto. Nothing to grip with." Considering the funk Vicki was in, and Martin having to go to work, Emma took charge of the kids and brought them to the Carriage House. When Martin came home late Monday afternoon, Emma went over again and after talking to Vicki with little response, spoke to Martin about getting Vicki psychiatric help. Martin agreed, but suggested giving Vicki a little more time to 'pull out of it'.

Will sat looking at the figure sitting still on the dock, wondering, *What next!* Should he approach her and try to engage conversation, or leave her be to whatever was going on in her head ... just follow Emma and the kids inside. He sat a few more minutes. Vicki didn't move ... sitting in stoic, motionless, silence. *Maybe I'd better mind my own business.*

He decided to ask Emma's advice and stepped from the car. Out of the corner of his eye, he saw Vicki begin to slowly stand up. Will stopped, giving her his full attention. Vicki, her back to him, didn't notice Will. She kept her gaze straight ahead, focusing across the lake. She stood straight, her left hand hanging idle at her side. But, Will noticed something in her right hand. *No, no! Not a gun.*

Fifteen years collapsed for Will into an instant. He remembered that overcast day when a call came to rush to the hospital; his wife had been in an accident. He got to the ER ... too late. When he'd finally seen the blood spattered over the interior of her car, he was convinced it was no accident; the police agreeing it was a suicide. But a detective still came around asking questions, saying he'd gotten comments from neighbors about months of screaming arguments at Will's home, impossible not to overhear. Will was numbed by the questioning piled on top of his grief, deepening his bottomless void to wonder: *What did I do wrong? What should I have done to save her?* Questions that haunted him for years.

Vicki slowly moved her right hand upward. Will shouted, "Vicki! No, Vicki, *No!*" and ran toward her. *I can't let this happen. Not again.*

There was no reaction from Vicki, as if she didn't hear Will at all. Slowly she raised her arm, the gun pointing toward the sky; but, Will realized, bend her wrist and the barrel will aim at her head. Will ran, his 70 years taking his breath away.

Vicki slowly brought the barrel toward her. Will screamed at her ... she was deaf to it. He was at full tilt when he came onto the dock and he didn't slow down. He saw the barrel was still several inches from Vicki's head, so he just called on his old football days and rushed her. He held his arm up so he could force her arm away, similar to deflecting passes from the waiting hands of receivers. With an 80 pound weight advantage over Vicki, her body offered little resistance when Will tackled her. He heard the crack of a gunshot as they both flew toward the water.

Underwater Will immediately let go of Vicki; he was out of breath. But he was being pummeled, hard, each blow of Vicki's fists landing deep into his flesh. He got his head above water and gasped for air. She screamed at him, "YOU SON-OF-A-BITCH, BASTARD ... JUST LEAVE ME THE FUCK ALONE." Vicki attacked Will more, trying to punch his head, the water slowing the swinging of her arms. "MIND YOUR OWN DAMNED BUSINESS FOR ONCE ... JUST THIS ONCE!" Will couldn't touch bottom, and wasn't a good swimmer. Vicki, a good swimmer, dove under water; she had a definite advantage. Will tried to head for shore; Vicki grabbed his leg scratching it, then got a grip on the fabric of his shorts, pulling on the leg to pull Will down, and moved up grabbing his shoulders. She wanted him underwater. Will fought back, but not well. In the water he was blinded and impaired; Vicki was in her element ... agile, fierce and furious. She used her nails to dig into Will's skin, all she could reach: head, arms, legs ... even his torso since the water had lifted his shirt well above his waist. Will raised his hand to protect his eyes.

But Will was strong. As Vicki's fingers dug into the flesh of his shoulders, he managed to get his hands around Vicki's narrow waste, lifting her upward. She took advantage of the position to again bring her fingers to Will's face. Will closed his eyes to protect them. But their combined weight sunk them just far enough so Will touched bottom. He held on until he could bend his legs, then thrust upward. It gave him enough leverage to throw Vicki off to the side. Freed, he struggled to reach shallower water.

Vicki's scream was guttural, "YOU HURT ME ... YOU BASTARD. WHERE'S MY GUN?" She turned and swam away. She stopped and yelled back, "JUST LET ME DIE! FUCKER!!!"

Will grabbed the ladder at the end of the dock, choking on lake water, gasping for air, heart racing. He crawled up the steps and onto the dock, panting on all fours like a dog beaten and done wrong. His whole body in pain, Will slowly eased down onto the planks trying to catch his breath, to regain his bearings.

He felt Emma's hand on his shoulder. She brought her head close to his. "Oh, Will. What happened; I heard a shot? Are you alright ... your head's bleeding again."

"I'm not sure. Just help me get up."

Prince was beside Emma and moved closer, trying to lick Will's face. "Hey, dog," Will said, "back off will ya."

Emma said, "Oh, my God, you're all scratched up. What happened?"

"Where's Vicki?"

"Out in the lake ... swimming. Why?"

"Vicki tried to kill herself. Then, if she could have I think she'd have killed me. We've got to call 911. She needs help … far beyond what we can handle, or Martin. Emma, go in and call … now!"

"You stay right here! I'll be right back.' As she hurried toward the house, Emma called over her shoulder, "Don't even try to get up."

Will stood up. He felt everything in his pockets, wallet, key fob for his car, smartphone … all soaked. *Shit!* Then, he looked toward the lake and saw Vicki way out, still swimming the crawl, heading toward the far shore. He cupped his hands and yelled, "VICKI … GET THE HELL BACK HERE!"

Will wondered if she could make it. *She's so angry she can probably do it! But what then?* The moisture running down his cheek he attributed to lake water, then realized it was his own blood. He couldn't see the three jagged scratches across his cheek, one dangerously close to his left eye.

ℒ   ℘

Emma ran back out of the Carriage House after quickly calling 911 and helped Will into the kitchen, guiding him to sit at the table. She carefully wiped the blood oozing from the opened head wound, then the scratches to face, arms and legs. She almost cried, "Oh, Will … she really hurt you."

"Doesn't hurt as much as where she punched me. I was afraid I was gonna drown."

"Let me get some gauze for your head … but we need some help."

It only took a few minutes before Will heard the siren of the sheriff's cruiser. Will stood to walk out and meet the sheriff in the driveway

"Will, you need to sit while I tend to these scratches."

"I'll be right back." He limped as he headed toward the door.

The Sheriff pulled up and getting out of his cruiser, reaching for his hat, "I just happened to be down by the marina. But I gotta say, I'm over here too much these days." His first

217

good look at Will startled him. "What the hell happened to you? Your face, it's all bloody. What's going on?"

"Listen, the woman who lives here in the Manor, Vicki. She tried to shoot herself. I stopped her, but she swam off and now she's out in the lake somewhere. She needs help."

"Okay, okay, slow down. What happened?

Will grabbed the edge of the police cruiser roof to steady himself. He explained Vicki's attempted suicide, his intervention, and her attacking him. "But, sheriff, she's still out in the lake, or maybe she made it to the other side."

"Yeah, Vicki, Martin's wife. I know who you're talking about."

Emma, now standing by Will's side, said, "She's been very depressed."

"Let me call this in."

Will listened impatiently as the sheriff ordered his deputies to check the lake and the far shore. He listened to acknowledgements over the hash of radio static. Then the sheriff said, "And be careful. I don't think she's armed but she may be very agitated. I need to talk to her, so bring her in."

After he signed off, the Sheriff turned to Will and looked him over, head to toe. "You're bleeding man ... kinda leaking from all over. Those scratches, they're weeping. She really did a number on you. You probably shouldn't be standing." He pointed toward the Carriage House. "Let's go inside where you can sit down. You definitely need some medical attention. I'm gonna call the EMTs."

"Yes, sheriff, please. We need help. I'd take Will to the Clinic but I've got Vicki's kids inside and no one to care for them."

The Sheriff put a call in for an ambulance; then followed Will and Emma inside. He pulled a kitchen chair next to Will's. "So Vicki did all this damage to you? And on your face! It's gotta hurt."

Will winced, "Yeah, mostly my pride, though. Feel so damned old."

"Do you want to press charges?"

"Only if it'll help you keep her from hurting herself."

"I'll keep that in mind. Between attempted suicide and what she did to you, she'll go into a psych evaluation … that takes a few days. Many stay in the hospital for a few weeks or longer."

Emma said, "She needs help."

"I agree with that. But the gun, where's the gun?"

"It flew out of Vicki's hand when she fell into the lake. It discharged just before we hit the water."

"You two are lucky nobody was shot. Where's it now?"

"In the lake, probably some distance from the dock."

"Did either of you know she had a gun?"

"No," Emma said, "Martin and I were talking about Vicki yesterday and he said, 'At least we don't have any guns in the house'."

"Wonder where she got it? I'll take a quick look for it before I leave, but I'll probably have to send a deputy to dive for it."

The Sheriff's portable radio buzzed; he put it to his ear. "Yeah… Good… Is she okay? Take her in and I'll be right there." He looked back at Will and Emma, "My deputy has her in his cruiser over on the West Lake Road. Seems pretty subdued … that swim probably took it out of her. So, I'm gonna head back to the station and talk to her. Don't worry she won't be walking away. But, remember you can press charges regardless of how the next steps play out."

"Thanks for your help."

"Now listen, I know you're the independent sort, but let the EMTs take you to the Clinic. Those scratches may get infected; gotta be careful, particularly on your face up near your eye. And that gash on your head, I can see it's bleeding again."

He stood, heading for the door, "I hear the ambulance coming. I'll show them in."

Emma followed the Sheriff, saying softly, "Thank you. Maybe he'll listen to you."

"Hope so, I'll stay 'til the EMTs are all set."

Emma walked back into the kitchen saying to Will, "How are you holding up?"

"I'm fine. It's just a few scratches. I don't need all this fuss and bother."

"Well, you've got it. Do it for me; for my piece of mind."

Will just hung his head, slowly moving it up and down.

"Good." Emma said, "But, I wonder where she got that gun."

"Unfortunately, getting a gun isn't a problem. I learned that 15 years ago."

Chapter 22

Joey awakened to pre-dawn light on Saturday, the last day of their Adirondack honeymoon. The air was chilly. Jackie slept at his side, her breathing steady. He cherished these quiet moments, looking at her face holding the serene beauty of pregnancy. Raising himself on his elbow, Joey looked through the small window toward the lake ... the water was barely visible, mirror-calm, shrouded in mist. The motion of his easing back down roused Jackie. She opened her eyes, looking into his, "Are you okay?'

"After last night, terrific! Just woke up." He leaned, kissing her, lingering in her warm response.

Jackie said, "I am going to miss this place."

"Well, we've got the morning left, let's not waste it. In fact, that lake is going to be perfect as the sun rises, so let's take the canoe out."

"*Mon Dieu*. Did I marry another Will? You like to canoe so early in the morning."

"Best time of day. Nothing like it ... almost as good as sex. With the mist and the calm water ... extra special."

"Oh, you compare to our sex! Now, you wake and want me to get out of bed?"

"I'd sure love to have you with me."

"So, you will go without me?" Jackie smiled, "Did I marry 'Evening ... Passion; Morning ...Goodbye' ... that kind of man? The nuns warned me about your type."

Joey laughed, hopped to his feet, pulling the sheet with him as he walked to her side of the bed. Jackie's nude body lay exposed; no more so than his own standing over her. "Yep ... look at what you married ... impatient, inconsiderate, demanding." He stopped as if to catch his breath. Hard for him to believe this gorgeous woman lay before him, even more so now, being pregnant with his child. He exhaled, saying softly, "You are so very, very beautiful!"

Jackie reached up drawing Joey to her. Their kiss was passionate as he settled back down, their bodies forming in tandem to lay side-by-side. Joey eased into the warmth of Jackie and thought of what a terrific mother she'd be. His joy was tempered though … he doubted how good a parent he could be having never known his own father. Jackie looked into Joey's eyes, questioning, "What?"

Joey cast aside the thought and said, "Nature's not gonna wait for us this morning. Throw on some shorts and a top and let's get out while the water's calm."

There was a slight chill in the lake air as Joey eased the canoe from the dock into the water. His action caused the only ripple on the lake. As soon as she was seated in the bow, he handed Jackie a paddle, then got himself onto the stern seat and took a strong, slow stroke, gliding the canoe away from the dock. The mist was dense, obscuring any view of the far shore. With each stroke the near shore fell away into a dream-like haze of unfocused gauzy white.

Jackie stopped paddling and said, "It is all foggy out here."

"Just wait a while."

"I can't see a thing."

Each paddled quietly under the shroud of white silence surrounding them. After several minutes, the lonesome call of a loon punctured the silence. Joey spoke almost in a whisper, "Notice how it's lightening up." He raised his head backward to see directly above them and saw blue sky. They were under a hole in the mist still surrounding them.

"Jackie, look up."

"Oh … the sky, such deep blue … and the sun is out."

"Voila! As you'd say … and it is getting brighter. Now watch what happens to the mist."

Ever so slowly, Jackie began to see through the mist. What looked at first like just the outline of a point jutting out into the lake, a tall pine reaching upward its top still out of sight … all in a grayscale monotone. Slowly the scene came into focus, establishing itself as real … with clarity … and then changing into full color.

With the lake still shrouded in silence, the mist began to rise off the water in clusters, forming small clouds. Jackie and Joey continued paddling with gentle strokes, being careful not to make a sound. As the day brightened, looking down, they could see the rocky bottom … seemingly in motion as they skimmed over the surface.

The lone call of a loon led Joey's eyes to spot it gliding effortlessly on the surface near the 'Forever Wild' shore. He stopped paddling and leaned forward to point it out to Jackie, but the bird dove and Joey knew it would stay submerged until coming to the surface a distance away. He said softly, "Jackie, did you see the loon?" She shook her head 'No' and kept slowly paddling. "Well, watch for it ahead, along the shore." But they never saw it again.

As the sun shone through, Jackie and Joey began to feel it's warmth on their backs, clouds continuing to gather off the water just ahead. "*C'est magnifique*, Joey. This … this I will remember."

The sun took command and the surface of the water began to ripple in rapidly moving textures, the beginning of forming waves later in the day. When Joey guided the canoe back into shore most people staying in the camps around the lake were still asleep. He was ravenous for breakfast. Walking beside Jackie toward the cabin, he said, "Jackie, you know, a man can't live on love alone."

Jackie smiled, "No, but with me, I know you like to try."

Joey gave her light pat on the rear-end. "Touché!"

Later in the morning the trail that circled the lake attracted Jackie and Joey one more time. Since Jackie had been told to walk a lot for an easier birth, they'd trekked it twice before. Just one more circuit before the ride home seemed the order of the day. Then, Jackie took a short nap while Joey set everything in order before their departure.

They headed home early enough to still have late-day light for a stop by the vineyard. Jackie and Joey both needed to check the grapes maturing toward the coming harvest; grapes left under the watchful eye of uncle Nic. Joey was also anxious to again see the foundation of the new winery, the concrete poured just days before the wedding.

After circling the winery foundation twice, frequently squatting to inspect a detail more closely, Joey walked across the road between two rows of vines to where Jackie held a cluster of grapes in her hand; they were still attached to the vine.

"Everything looks to be right with the foundation. How are you doing?"

"Fine. The grapes need some canopying this week. We have had enough rain, now we need to protect from mold. Pray for more sun."

"Yes, but you be careful. I don't want you out here midday when it's hot."

"Early in the morning, I will canopy."

They stood side-by-side taking in their favorite scene, looking across the vineyard down toward the lake. The sun, having just set, sent orange across wispy clouds streaked high in the sky. Jackie entwined her arm in Joey's. "We are blessed to live in such a beautiful place. The mountains, they are nice; but this, here, I love."

She looked at Joey, "Our honeymoon ... such happy days for us! Now, back here, I hope all the crazy goes away."

"Want to stop at your grandparents on the way home?"

"Not now, I am tired. Tomorrow, we will see them."

They headed toward town and as soon as Joey turned onto the short dead end street of their home, Jackie told Joey she felt the urgency of a pregnant woman. So Joey quickly pulled into the drive and unlocked the cottage door without fanfare. It wasn't as he'd always dreamt it would be with the girl of his dreams ... just married and carrying her over the threshold. He had the girl alright, but she, at this crucial moment of arrival, had a more pressing priority. He shrugged his shoulders and stepped into the small living room.

When Jackie came out of the bathroom he motioned for her to follow him outside. "Hey, come out here a second."

"Why, what's…"

As soon as she stepped beyond the threshold, Joey took her in his arms and kissed her. Then he picked her up. "I've always wanted to do this." And he kissed her again.

Jackie laughed, her arm around Joey's neck, being carried over the threshold. "Oh, Joey, not French and you are so romantic."

Joey gently set Jackie down. "I married in…"

She teased, "You are not going to carry me up to the bedroom?"

"Oh. Yeah. Sure. No, my dreams of this moment only go this far. Maybe later."

"Your dreams? This girl in your dreams, she is more beautiful?"

"No way. She was okay, but kinda wispy. You're warmer."

"I bet." Jackie kissed Joey on the cheek, "And heavier."

"And getting hungry. We should have stopped at the store."

Joey released Jackie and followed her into the kitchen. She opened the refrigerator door. "Look! Milk, eggs, juice; even bread. Must be your mother."

"Gotta be. She's the only one with a key."

"I hope you appreciate how good Deborah has been to us. Do you think she really needed to move in with your grandmother to help care for her, or did she move just to get out of our way … so we can be alone?"

"I think my grandmother really needs the help. But, you're right, Mom likes you. She's supported our marriage when she easily could've gone the other way. "

"Too bad my family is not the same."

Joey flicked Jackie's comment away with his hand, "Oh, your grand-mere. I'll win her over; just gonna take some time."

Joey carried as much as he could handle to the table. "It's gonna be hard getting back into the swing of things."

"*Oui*. The winery to build, the harvest coming…"

Joey looked into Jackie's eyes, smiling, "And then the baby! We've got a busy three months ahead of us."

"*D'accord.* Just remember me when you start putting up that building."

"How can I forget you?"

"No, no. It is just that…"

"Are you scared?"

"Not really. So many babies are born. It is just new to me. So, *oui,* scared … a little. I need you close."

"Oh, I'll be close. With you every step of the way."

"But I need not to cling. I hate wives who cling."

Joey gave Jackie a light kiss. "I love you … and you can cling all you want. I'll probably be so close, you won't have to cling. You'll be begging to get some space. Come on, let's have one last meal before we take on the challenges of the real world."

"*Oui,* I have been so happy. I am almost afraid to get back to the Internet. But I see the message light on the phone. Let me check that." Jackie tapped in the number and then password. She looked at Joey, "The last message is from Emma. She asks us to breakfast tomorrow morning after Mass. Something she wants to tell us."

℘   ℘

Sunday morning, despite Emma's effort to hide worry as she hugged Jackie, hoping only to express joy at seeing her newlywed granddaughter, Jackie sensed disquiet. After a tight embrace, Emma held Jackie away, checking from head-to-toe, "You look wonderful, Jackie. The baby's grown; you're showing a lot more."

Looking down, her hand on her belly, Jackie smiled, "*Le bebe* … getting active. Even kicking Joey." She looked up at Emma, "You were not in Church?"

"Oh, we went early, so I'd have more time to get breakfast ready."

Will walked into the kitchen, a slight limp to his step. He offered a cheery, "Hello." Seeing the scratches on his face, Jackie was shocked; and he still wore a bandage on the side of his head.

"What happened? Is something wrong?"

Joey, waylaid by Prince bounding to him with a vigorously wagging tail, hadn't seen Will. As he walked in hearing the tone of Jackie's voice, he asked, "What?" His eyes widened as he reached out to shake Will's hand, looking at him for the first time. "Oh! What battle were you in?" was all he could think to say.

Jackie repeated, "Grandmother, is something wrong?"

"Well," Emma squeezed both her hands together, speaking softly, "Seth and Maria are in the front room watching TV. And, we don't want to burden you, but we want to be sure you know." Emma hesitated, glanced away, then looked back at Jackie, "Vicki tried to shoot herself on Tuesday. Out on the dock. Will saw her and stopped her. She scratched him ... badly. His face, and look at his legs."

Jackie put her hand to her mouth.

"She was arrested for assaulting Will; then they found the gun ... that was illegal. She's been placed in the hospital for a psychiatric evaluation. Will and I have been watching the kids during the day for Martin, and this morning they just came over as soon as they woke up."

"But why?" Joey asked, "Why would Vicki shoot herself?"

"The accident at the reception. She just went into some deep depression. Blamed herself somehow."

"The Camelot of your wedding," Will said, "Her dream of making the Manor sparkle for all to see. It all just blew up in her face. She was more than embarrassed."

"But," Joey said, "she's not responsible in any way."

Emma kept her voice down, "Her trauma goes far beyond the accident ... deep into her view of herself, her marriage, this place ... reaches back into her childhood. So, don't even think of blaming yourselves. Now, we can't see her; no visitors are allowed."

Will put his hand on Emma's shoulder, "Yeah, but Emma and I, we still hope for a peaceful last few years, just sitting quietly on the shore by the lake."

Emma turned toward him, "Will, we don't need your sarcasm."

"Even the sheriff tells me he's had it. First the reception accident and fire. Freddy Kober's still in jail by the way, his wife won't bail him out … says he's safer there where he can't drink and do drugs. Then, Vicki … lots of paperwork. He went on, something about some guy on a motorcycle they're trying to track down … something linked to hydrofracking up on the hill."

Emma raised her hand – open and upward. "Let's not get into all this." She reached out toward Joey, "Give me a hug." As she stepped back, she said, "Here, we've been burdening you with our problems and haven't even asked you how your honeymoon was. Where did you go?"

"Oh, grandmother," Jackie said, "to a little cabin on a lake up in the Adirondack mountains. It was the perfect place." The smile she glanced toward Joey and his reflected response answered Emma's next question of 'How did it go?' … the question Emma wanted to ask, but wasn't sure how to phrase.

"Looks like it was a good week." Again the answer captured in reflected smiles. "Good!" Emma said, "You two deserve a break."

Jackie said, "*Oui*, we didn't want it to end. But still we are anxious to be back here … the vines, the winery … you and Will."

"Jackie, you are so kind to say that."

"You know I will help anyway I can … with the children."

"Thank you. I may need to ask for some help. We have no idea how long they'll need us."

"Don't worry. We will assist."

"Yes, for a while. But, it won't be that long before you'll have your own child to care for."

228

Will asked, "Can a man get something to eat this morning? I imagine Joey's hungry."

"Oh, of course, what's the matter with me?" Emma said, "Let's get the kids away from that TV and have some breakfast."

Chapter 23

Sunday afternoon, Chloe called Jackie with an invitation to dinner at the Bellagatto. Jackie accepted out of a feeling of family duty, having just had breakfast with Emma and Will ... best to keep things in balance. From the threshold of the Bellagatto dining room, the newlyweds spotted Chloe and Norman seated at a table on the deck overlooking the lake, a bottle of wine chilling in a bucket beside them. Jackie entwined her hand in Joey's and paused, "So beautiful, late in the day." The lake was calm, in the 'sweet light' before sunset; a few sailboats catching the gentle breeze, a water skier skimming the surface near the far shore. At full throttle a jet ski cut diagonally across the scene, its raspy exhaust the only sound to be heard as it chased after some trophy that will never be caught. Jackie let go of Joey's hand and approached Chloe, who stood, open-armed, offering a hug.

"Jacqueline, are you alright? No trauma or woes from the accident at your reception?"

"Non, grand-mere. Joey took me to a beautiful cabin in the Adirondacks ... on a lake. It was wonderful."

"Well, I just hope you and the baby are alright. You look good."

"Fine, grand-mere, I am fine. I will go back to the birthing classes next week."

"I hope so. And, Joey ... he goes with you?"

"Of course..."

Norman stood to give Jackie a hug, then shook hands with Joey. "Glad to hear all is well. Here, Jackie, sit down." He held up the wine bottle, "A glass of wine? Oh, I forgot, you can't have wine. Well, whatever you want. Then, we can order dinner."

"Norman," Chloe said, "you press too fast. So American! Have you learned nothing from France? We savor the moment ... embrace it ... slowly and with feeling."

"Geez, Chloe, I was only offering Jackie a drink."

"Jacqueline, *si vous plais*. Her name is Jacqueline. Not your American slang."

Jackie sat down between them and looking up said, "Okay, you two, enough pecking at each other. Because, to be honest, I don't care which name is used."

"Just remember," Chloe sat next to Jackie, "...your mother named you Jacqueline."

"*Oui,* I know. But I am in America now."

A waiter approached. Jackie said, "A glass of water ... please."

Norman poured a glass of wine for Joey and refilled Chloe's and his glass. He sat down, putting the bottle back in the ice bucket.

Jackie leaned over to see the label. "And this is?"

"Oh, last year's Kober Riesling. Nic told me it's an exceptionally good vintage."

"The same as at our wedding," Joey said, "One of his best." He twirled his glass, then took a sip. He raised his glass and his eyebrows.

Jackie was getting used to Joey speaking only when he had something to say. She hoped he wasn't going to make her carry the whole conversation with her grand-mere.

"Jacqueline, your wedding was wonderful ... the reception, also ... unique."

"Does that mean the reception was good?"

"*Tres bien.* My friend Beatrice, from New York City, she was impressed. She and Ralph left before..." Chloe hesitated. Joey finished her sentence, "...a memorable finish."

Jackie asked, "The wine, or our reception?"

"The wine, I must say, on a par with the German Rieslings."

"*Merci, grand-mere.* To you and Vicki, the arbor and decorations were wonderful ... *tres magnifique.*"

Chloe sighed, "Try to remember it as it was before that idiot destroyed everything. I hope the photographer captured it all." Chloe paused, then asked, "Your week away ... what did you do?"

Norman laughed, "Chloe, what do you think they did?"

"Crass Norman ... that is all I think to say. You are crass."

Norman leaned over the table toward Chloe, "Just the opposite. It's none of our business what they did. That's what honeymoons are all about."

"You learned this, where?"

"Grand-mere ... Norman!" Jackie's voice commanded attention. She continued softly, looking at Chloe, "We had a cabin on a small lake. We hiked and swam, and canoed ... yesterday morning in the mist ... so peaceful and beautiful. And, yes, grand-mere, we made love ... tender and slow ... as in France." She smiled, almost whispering, *"Tres, tres bien!"*

Jackie sat up straight, her voice strong, "And, Papa, he feels our baby kick now." Leaning toward Joey, Jackie asked, "Do you want to add anything?"

Joey looked at Norman, "I knew I was a lucky man before. I'm luckier than I thought."

Norman laughed, "Perfect, Joey. Perfect response."

Jackie smiled and sat back, saying, "We walked our vines today."

Joey chimed in, "Looks like a good year. We just need sun for the rest of the month."

Jacqueline looked toward Norman, "I will canopy to give the grapes more air and a little more sun."

"Oh, Jacqueline," Chloe fussed, "should you be out in the vineyard ... the pesticides, the sun ... being pregnant?"

"We use very few pesticides and no fungicides, grand-mere. We rely on canopying ... it is important. And, I have not seen any warning about sunlight hurting pregnancy."

"Just be sure you don't get too much, or sunstroke, or..." Chloe turned to Joey, "you will be sure she doesn't overdo?"

"Of course," Joey smiled, "Jackie listens closely to me. She's not headstrong at all ... particularly when it comes to working on the vines. But seriously, she'll be out early. I'll make sure she quits long before the sun gets high. It'll just take a few days longer."

"And you cannot help her?" Chloe asked.

"To some extent. But we're starting construction on the buildings, the Tasting Room and winery. That'll keep me from concentrating on the vines, at least for the coming week."

"So," Norman asked, "the posts and beams … all ready to put in place?"

"Yes, mid-week. Hopefully finished by the end of the week."

Chloe asked, "What are they doing?"

"It's amazing," Joey said, "All the beams have the mortise and tenons cut by computer control in a factory. They put the whole structure on a flat-bed truck and use a crane to lift each part into place."

"Like my Erector Set when I was a kid." Norman said.

"We're meeting with the contractor tomorrow morning to make sure we've covered all the bases. He's an interesting guy, name's Aaron. My uncle Nic tells me his father and grandfather used to build post and beam by hand. Aaron helped out. When computerized machining of all the joinery came along about 10 years ago, Aaron teamed up with a manufacturer-builder. The dying art brought back to life."

Norman said, "Is he Amish."

"I don't know how Aaron can be. He uses trucks, cranes, computers."

"Probably shunned."

"What's that?" Jackie asked.

"Some leave, usually older teens or young adults. They've learned the skills, but don't want the rigid rules of the Amish community. Many are successful; adopting our modern methods."

"So," Joey said, "the best of both worlds."

"I don't think the Amish view it that way. The community breaks off all contact with those who've left. That's why the term 'shunned' is used. But, Amish or not, from what I saw in Aaron's proposal, he knows what he's doing."

"Are you gonna come tomorrow morning?"

"Got it on my calendar. Start about nine?"

Chloe said to Norman, "Enough about the vineyard! I sold mine, remember." She looked at Jackie, "You are settled in your new home? Do you have everything you need?"

"*Oui, grand-mere*. Since Joey's mother moved in with her mother, she left everything in the kitchen for our use."

"Anything, you need, let me know. And, what about preparing for the baby..."

Norman took the direction of Chloe's questions as liberty to talk with Joey. He leaned toward him, speaking softly, "Joey, that land your cousin Fred owns high on the hill, up above the Kober vineyards, there's gas under it, right?"

"Apparently, at least the gas company thinks so. Nic told me they're paying Fred quite a bit for his lease."

"So, once they get deep enough, they turn and drill horizontally."

"Yeah, I know."

"While you were on your honeymoon I did a little pokin' around. They can go anywhere off Fred's well pad, in any direction. I don't know if the drilling can reach as far as your vineyard, but let's assume it can. You have no mineral or depth rights. So, we're at their mercy. You might get a small royalty, but not much ... if any."

"I've got to learn more about that, because if it's true I sure don't like it."

"My adage is, if you can't beat the fuckers ... join 'em"."

"What do you mean?"

"Let's see if a gas company would be interested in drilling on your land. The geologists'll figure out the best location to drill."

"You mean in my vineyard? Why would they do that?"

"We give them a sweetheart offer for the rights to drill. Make it attractive. They only need six or eight acres to set up a well."

"But what about the wine? Customers coming for wine tastings?"

"Oh, you'll still have the wine. And customers, they'll still come. Once the drilling's done the site will be restored, just a quiet well-head above ground."

Joey's voice became tense, "I'm not so sure once a well gets going. Contaminated ground water affects vines. And an industrial environment on-site ... by a winery? Just doesn't make sense."

Norman glanced at Chloe and saw her still engrossed with Jackie in whatever 'girl talk' she'd started. He leaned closer to Joey, keeping his voice low, "For God's sake, Joey, you're sounding like a damned bleeding heart tree hugger." His eyes darted toward Chloe. "Keep an open mind."

"Don't worry; my mind is open ... to all the hazards. I went on the Internet a couple of weeks ago. Gas drillers inject chemicals like benzene, naphthalene, xylene; other crap I've never heard of."

"Well, you know, Joey, you can't trust what you see on the Internet."

"You're right there. It's hard to verify because when The Clean Water Act was signed by President Bush all the oil and gas companies were exempted from having to disclose anything. So a few million gallons of slickwater gets pumped into each well under high pressure and no one knows what's in it.

"And, that's not all Norman, when it comes back out, the flowback has radioactive material from the underground ... radium, barium ... who knows what."

"But, Joey, I'm told, in very small amounts."

"Maybe so, but in a vineyard we are sensitive to even the mist from a farmer's spray hitting our vines. Why would we ever invite exposure to all these chemicals, any one of which could taint our vintages for years?"

Norman, sat back, put his hand to his chin ... in thought.

Joey raised his voice. "No, Norman ... Hydrofracking is not a good idea ... not anywhere near a vineyard!"

"Yes, I agree, maybe there are long-term hazards. But short term there are damned big bucks to be made. No need to age gas like wine. Once it flows there's income; royalties as high as 18 percent. We'll be makin' money while we sleep."

"You do realize, you just ruined my dinner ... and I haven't even looked at the menu."

The tone of the men's voices grabbed Chloe's attention. "You talk of hydrofracking? Terrible idea! In all of France ... *Voila!* ... banned, it is banned across my country!

"What is the matter with you Norman? Must everything about you American men involve insertion? Into the land, under the sea, fouling the air ... and women ... oh, what you do to your women!"

Norman stared at Chloe, angered, but offered no reply.

Joey broke Norman's silence, saying, "I'm sorry, Norman. I usually try to go along. But on this one I have to say an emphatic 'No!' There'll be no fracking on my land!"

Norman set his stare on Joey, saying nothing.

Jackie looked at the two men, "What has gone wrong?"

Joey answered, "Nothing, Jackie, not yet." He looked Norman in the eye, smiled, picked up a menu and said, "Come on, Norman, we'll talk later. Let's order dinner."

Norman followed his lead, also picking up a menu and opening it ... in silence.

ॐ   ௭

Jackie walked into the vineyard at dawn to the sound of birds chirping their wake-up song. The view across the lake caught her attention, the bright orange-tint of the rising sun being reflected off the crest of the far hillside, the shore-line and water below still captured in pre-dawn shadow. Sun warmed her back, promising a hot day. She walked down toward the far end of the row, an area in need of attention. Bending to reach a ground creeping tendril, Jackie felt new constraint on her range of motion; pregnancy posing ever greater limitations.

It seemed only a few minutes before she heard Nic's greeting. "How's Mama?"

"Oh, uncle Nic. *Bonjour.*"

"You're smiling. Must have had a good week?"

"In the Adirondacks ... Joey surprised me with a cabin on a lake."

"That's my Joey. I see he's at it in the office already, but I decided to come see you first."

"*Merci.* The vines, like children ... need training."

"Yes, doesn't take long and they get out of hand. But should you be doing this ... all the reaching and stooping?"

"Oh, I will stop for the meeting."

"How about if I send a couple of my Kober men over? You can show them exactly what you want done. They're good ... and they'll listen. Always anxious to learn."

Jackie smiled, "And steal all my secrets?"

"Aw, you caught me ... and the sun just above the horizon. But, seriously, you want to protect your baby."

"You think it is bad if I am doing this? You are right that I begin to feel so big, heavy ... and it is hard to get up."

"That's what I worry about."

Joey walked up next to them. "So, Nic, I heard you telling Jackie she shouldn't be out here working."

"Ah, Joey, yes. Don't mean to intrude. Just some free advice."

"No, no, not at all. I was trying to tell her that yesterday. Then over dinner last night, Chloe goes after me ... like I'm heartless making my wife work the vines in her third trimester."

"*D'accord,*" Jackie said, standing up. "The way Nic says it, 'protect our baby', that I accept."

Joey smiled at Nic. "You're here five minutes ... I tried for an hour and in five minutes you figure out how to convince her."

"Hey, Joey, you convinced her to marry you. And from the smile on her face, I think your honeymoon sealed the deal."

Jackie laughed, blushing. "Uncle Nic, you are naughty..."

Nic held his hands up in defense, "What? What did I say...?"

237

Joey gestured toward the trailer. "Come on you two, I made a pot of coffee and it'll be gettin' stale."

Norman was the next to arrive, just after Joey had poured coffee for Jackie and Nic. He motioned Joey to step outside. "Listen, about last night. Understand I'm a businessman, you're the winemaker. To me, it's all about the bottom line. You … you worry about the character of the next vintage. With me, it's profit, money in the bank … as much and as fast as possible. So, Joey, on occasion we'll step on each other's toes. You can't take it personal, it's just the way it is."

"So, where are we?"

"You and me, we're okay. Have I given up on the idea of fracking? No! But, today we focus on building the winery. We need to be reading off the same page on that. I just want to assure you, no hard feelings. And I respect, I'm even glad, to see your passion … protecting your vineyard. But the need for income … it never goes away."

Two cars were approaching the trailer, a lone driver in each. Joey said, "Ah, Aaron and Bruce, right on time."

After greetings and handshakes, Aaron, the contractor, and Bruce, the architect, followed Joey into the office. Norman brought up the rear. With Jackie, Aaron and Bruce each using their laptop, most of the desk space was occupied; the top of the standup drafting table kept clear to lay open the large scroll of prints Bruce carried with him..

The discussion lasted over an hour. First, all the items on the job ready lists were checked for the Tasting Room and winery buildings; second, the schematics were reviewed to assure all electrical and plumbing needs were included. The group then walked across the road to inspect the job site. It was two tiered. The front portion nearest the corner of the roads was the highest, where the Tasting Room would be built. In the rear, a half story lower, attached to the higher building, a steel building for winery production and barrel room.

Aaron walked through the process to take place starting Wednesday morning. The setup of the crane and placement of the flatbed truck. Then, how the base sill of the Tasting Room would be set on the foundation, followed by the erection of posts and crossbeams, the top plate and braces. Finally, a ridge beam and roof rafters would cap it off.

Aaron said, "Each piece is precision cut at the factory by a computer controlled machine, so the joinery will fit exactly. But, the Tasting Room is a wide expanse, so getting everything absolutely level and true is critical and may take some time. You have to understand that my crew can't rush a job like this. If we run a few days more than we estimated, well, so be it. That's post and beam. The final erection is the key. As soon as the Tasting Room is up, we'll tackle the winery building. With luck, we'll be done no later than early next week.

Bruce described the wood panel assemblies to be used as walls of the Tasting Room; insulation sandwiched within to provide energy efficiency. "The interior will be dramatic with the exposed posts and beams. It'll convey warmth, along with a feeling of substance, tradition. Like your wine Joey, new wine made using the wisdom of the ages."

Joey glanced at Nic, knowing without him such vintages wouldn't be possible. Nic raised his eyebrows, smiling back.

"And Joey," Aaron said, "I'd like you available, on site, in case we have questions."

"Of course, after all these months of planning, I'm not gonna miss this."

Bruce added, "I'll be here, too."

Chapter 24

After the construction meeting, Jackie walked down the hill to see how her grandmother was coping with Maria and Seth. With Vicki still in the hospital, perhaps for weeks of extended therapy, Emma had taken on the responsibility of caring for the children during the day. Jackie knew the coming weeks wouldn't become the end-of-summer peace she'd hoped for. She'd envisioned spending the first weeks after marriage focusing on Joey; the two of them nurturing vines heavy with grapes maturing toward harvest. Then, just weeks before the birth of their child, using the Kober Vineyards press and tanks they'd work side-by-side producing their first vintage.

It being a sunny day, Emma had Maria and Seth eating lunch on the patio in the shade of the Silver Maple. Emma waved to Jackie, "Come join us. It's cooler over here out of the sun." The kids both ran to Jackie with smiles and traces of grape jelly on their faces. Prince followed, tail wagging. Jackie bent with hugs for all.

Seth asked, "Are you getting fat?"

Jackie smiled, "Yes, Seth. I am going to have a baby … and when a baby gets ready to come, the mother gets fat."

Emma saw Seth pondering his next question and quickly said, "Seth, it isn't polite to tell someone they're fat. And, that's enough of questions for Jackie. You'll understand better as you get older."

"Understand what?"

"How babies come. Your mother told you about the stork, didn't she?"

"Yeah, but that's for little kids. Storks don't bring babies."

"Do too!" Maria said.

"Yes, Maria… Let's just leave it for now that the stork brings babies."

Jackie looked at Emma, "*Mon Dieu*. You've got your hands full ... but different than I thought."

Emma poured Jackie a cup of tea without being asked. "Do you want some lunch?"

"In a few minutes. After the walk down that hill, I need to steady my breathing."

"Just let me know when you're ready." Emma put her arm around Seth. "This one here has a very inquisitive mind. Questions, all the time ... questions. And watch your answers, he asks follow-ups." She turned to the kids, "Okay, let's sit down and finish our lunch."

"Can we go swimming?" Seth asked. "Jackie, want to go swimming?'

"I can't just now, Seth. And you need to finish your lunch and then wait a while."

"Why is that?"

"So you don't get a cramp."

"What's a cramp?"

Jackie looked at Emma, who said, "See what I mean?"

Jackie looked at Seth, now seated at the table. "It's a pain in your tummy, Seth. And you won't like it. Cramps really hurt."

Seth, his mouth full with another bite of his sandwich, managed to say, "Okay."

As soon as they were done eating, Maria and Seth ran to the water lapping on the shore. Emma shouted her stern warning not to go in until she said they could.

Jackie looked at Emma, "How is Vicki?"

"I honestly don't know. Martin was over for dinner last night. He sees her, but visiting time is limited. He says that while they tell him some, he feels there's a lot they don't tell him. 'Like chasing shadows,' he said. "I'm not sure about Vicki, how she's going come out of this.' And, keep this to yourself, he suspects the doctors hold him responsible for what's happening. Anyhow, they aren't telling him much. But, I told him, maybe there's not much to tell right now. So, Martin isn't sure what the future holds. I feel sorry for him. Will tells me he's under a lot of pressure at the printing plant, too."

"Where is Will?"

"At the hardware, where else. He's been getting cabin fever, not wanting to go to town with all his bandages. But, this morning, he was antsy and said he needs some plumbing part. I think he goes just to have some other men to talk with."

Jackie laughed, "Funny how I see that in Joey, too. Loves me, but needs space ... time away."

Emma smiled, "I guess we're just too hot for them to handle. Can I pour you more tea?" She pushed a serving plate with a fly cover over it toward Jackie. "And, have a sandwich. You must be starved."

Norman played the role of an observer at the winery construction meeting. He wanted to keep Joey front and center and fully responsible. Since he was learning and found no need to insert new input, he held back on questions, only asking a few. No need to be in a command-control position, or to insert himself into in the critical path of decision-making.

Norman started back to his lakeside home, but when going through town, he decided he really didn't want to head there with little to do other than listen to Chloe's almost constant barrage of frustration. She'd always been short on patience, but much more so since the wedding. And lately he was too often her target. Instead of turning his Mercedes onto the West Lake Road, he pulled over and put the top down, then stayed on the highway heading north, toward Rochester. He felt a need to touch base with Martin, see how he was doing; hesitating to admit that his real need was to get back where he was the expert rather than the student. Deep down, though, he wanted to avoid the fact that Chloe's anger was driving a wedge between them.

He walked into the printing plant unannounced and startled Fran, her fingers flying across the keyboard before her. "Oh, Norman! Hi. Didn't expect to see you."

"Just in town. Thought I'd drop by, see how things are going."

Fran nodded toward the closed door to Norman's old office, now Martin's. "He's in a sales meeting. They should be about ready to wrap-up. Want me to let Martin know you're here?"

"No. Not yet. I'm just going to stroll through the plant for a few minutes. If he's still tied up when I get back, we'll interrupt."

As soon as Norman was out of sight, Fran grabbed her smartphone and sent a text to Martin, 'He's here!!!' Martin checked his phone when he heard the incoming text ping. As soon as the plant's production expediter, Denise, finished her sentence, he said, "We've got to cut this short. Norman Olsen just arrived and I need to meet with him. Anyhow, we're pretty well wrapped up. Let's match this new sales projection against production capacity and meet again on Wednesday. As I said, we need to be very aggressive, but don't promise customers what we can't deliver. Same time on Wednesday, okay?"

As Denise walked past Martin, she whispered, "You didn't tell me."

Martin mouthed back, "I didn't know."

"I'll find him and tell him you're free."

A few minutes later, Norman walked through Martin's open door. After coming around the desk to shake hands, Martin closed the door and gestured to Norman to join him in having a seat.

Sitting in the second of the two chairs on the visitor side of his desk, Martin said, "Good to see you Norman. What brings you here? In this heat, you should be down by the lake."

"Came from a long meeting on building the winery. You know, it's gonna be post and beam design. Hard to understand how they engineer all those cuts to fit the structure together ... the joinery's all computer driven. Had a yen to get back to something I understand. But, more important, I want to ask about Vicki. How is she?"

Martin sat back, ran his hand through a full head of hair just beginning to gray. "Oh, coming along, I guess."

"You mean making progress."

"I think so. They don't tell me much."

"Any idea how long she'll be in the hospital?"

"Too early to be sure. I see her as much as allowed, not much. She's pretty distant. I think some of it's from the drugs. She seems lost, unsure of everything. Totally focused on herself. Little interest in the kids, how they are and what they're doing. Guess she needs more time. Still very angry though; a lot of that comes back on me."

Norman put his hand to his chin. "Um, having a wife angry at her husband ... pretty common. I mean it seems we're held responsible for everything that's fucked up in their world."

"Yeah, that's Vicki."

"No, I was thinking of my first wife, and now Chloe."

"Really! Chloe?"

"Before I get a headache, let's talk about the plant. How are things going? I've been distracted the past several weeks with the wedding and all."

"Not much to report. We're in the midst of our late summer dip, customers holding off on decisions, trying to eke out the last of summer vacations; everybody promising to sign contracts come September. Lots of potential business ... you know how the end-of-summer slump goes. Come September, sales expects to sign almost too much work. We just met on scheduling, so we don't overcommit."

"Well, you know, Martin, we've got to goose the financials for the end of this quarter. You don't want to find yourself showing red ink. Our line of credit will cost too much."

"I hear you Norman, I know."

"That new press is still a boat anchor to you, isn't it?"

"It's a challenge to keep busy enough. Faster was always better. But that press is so fast, it creates overheads in backend and bindery operations that don't go away when they're idle. So, yes, it's much more challenging than I thought. But our new sales and pricing strategies will overcome that."

"Always the optimist, Martin. But now you're between the rock and the hard place. Too far in ... gotta go deeper ...

can't back out now. Like a pilot on takeoff, committed to become airborne, too late to abort."

"Nice analogy, Norman, nice. Particularly for a guy whose wife is confined to a mental ward without a clue as to what's next."

"I was talkin' about the press."

"Don't worry. Like I told you, we'll master the logistics of making that press profitable."

Norman put his hands in the air palms out, as if surrendering. "Okay, okay. I'll back off. Let you do your thing. Just don't run off the end of the runway."

Martin leaned over close to Norman, looking directly at him. "You know, Norman, you're a piece of work. My wife, who you say is a friend, tried to kill herself. Now she's in looney-tunes land for God knows how long." Martin stopped, sat straighter, sucking in breath; his face stiffening in anger. "I don't know if she'll ever be back. When she is discharged, she'll be on meds. Will she be able to be the same person? Will she be able to stand the sight of me?"

"Oh, I'm sure she'll…"

Martin cut in, speaking louder, "And, you come in here fuckin' me over asking bullshit questions on how poorly we're doing with the new press. How this quarter, just half over, is going to end up. Damn it, Norman … Damn it!" Martin sat back. "What the fuck gives with you. You tryin' to trip me up … or do you just enjoy the tension you create. What are you? Some kinda damned sadist?"

"Okay, okay…" Norman stood, "you're taking me way wrong here. I guess I needed to shed some nervous energy, but I didn't mean to put it all on your back." Norman stood. "Call me when I can buy you lunch and we can have a more relaxed conversation. And, oh, say 'Hello' to Vicki for me."

As he walked out of the building, the thought came to Norman that during the past 18 hours he'd managed to royally piss off the two men who were his hope for increasing his future earnings, Martin and Joey. He'd parked in the shade, but the sun now shone on the leather driver's seat. As he sat on the too-hot surface he recalled Martin's question, 'What gives with you?' He sat for a moment, to be sure the seat wasn't just too hot, before putting the key in the ignition. His mind shifted to Chloe. *Damn it, woman, you're the one puts me on edge. Well, we'll just see who's in control here.*

Will stood by the shore, shielding his eyes from the sun hanging low in the blue summer sky ... soon to set. He'd just warned Seth and Maria that they had 10 minutes more in the water, before getting ready for bed. Hearing the SUV pull in, he turned toward the driveway and waved for Martin to come join him.

Walking over the recently patched driveway and around the reseeded section of lawn where the tent had been, Martin shouted, "Sorry I'm late."

Will waited for Martin to come beside him. "No problem. Emma appreciated your call ... we went ahead and fed the kids. Happily, you made it before their bedtime."

Seth ran up, dripping wet and without saying a word, gave his Dad a watery hug. Maria, close behind, threw her arms around her father's legs. Martin responded as best and warmly as he could. After several seconds he said, "Okay, kids, I love you too." He slowly crouched down to their height and looking in their eyes, running his hands through wet hair. "You been good today?"

"Yep," Seth said, "and I can swim from our dock to the dock next door."

"Hey, that's a long way, Seth. Good boy!"

"And Maria, you have a good day?'

Maria nodded up and down, but offered no testimony of any new accomplishment.

"Okay," Martin said, "Get your towels and let's just watch the sun set."

Emma came out to join them ... the small group in silent ritual watching the distant orb slide slowly behind the far ridge.

As soon as the sun was gone, leaving its purple remnant across the few clouds in the sky, Emma felt the immediate change in temperature and said, "Okay, kids let's get out of these wet suits and ready for bed." Martin moved as if preparing to go in with his children, but Emma said, "I've got this. Sit and talk to Will for a few minutes ... he needs the company. I'll call you to say, 'Good Night'."

Once alone, Will asked, "Want a drink?"

"Thanks, but no. I'm good."

"Well, here, let's sit."

Both men sat on the bench by the shore. Martin looked out across the lake. "Stopped by the hospital. Tied me up longer than I'd planned." Thinking, he paused. Then, looking at Will, quietly said, "I am so sorry for all the pain you had to go through. You're one hell of a neighbor being so understanding. I mean, refusing to give any testimony to the Grand Jury so the assault charges were dropped. That meant so much to us."

"Listen, you've got your hands full as it is. Emma and I, we're just hoping Vicki's getting better. How is she?"

Martin looked away, sounding fatigued. "The same, far as I can tell. Don't see any change. Bad day at the office, though. Norman showed up unexpectedly and after a polite asking about Vicki, he was giving me a hard time about quarterly financials ... this quarter. We're only half through it. I lost it, told him to get off my back ... something like that. Hope I didn't say, 'Fuck off!'."

"Yeah, well ... Norman's shown me he can be a real pain-in-the-ass. Some days he reins Chloe in, but when he wants something, he gets just like her. They make a good pair. On the other hand, I don't think he's one to hold a grudge as long as things go his way. If they go against him, watch out. Be careful not to cross him."

"He's done a lot for me. But, this new press; shit, he expects it to be profitable right off. It's such a radical departure from the past ... so fast; it's taking months to iron out the bugs, to take advantage of the potential. He's been on my case since he got back from France." Martin lowered his head, looking at the ground. He spoke softly, "And, now Vicki, she just tore the guts right out of me."

Will put his hand on Martin's shoulder. "First of all, it's not your fault. Vicki isn't your fault. Take it from me, I've been there."

Martin swiveled his head to look up at Will ... a silent questioning of how Will could say that.

Will locked on Martin's gaze. "When I was about your age, my wife, my first wife, tried as Vicki did." He looked away, sucking in breath, "But she succeeded! Instantaneous, no chance for a reprieve." He looked back at Martin. "I'd like that kept between you and me ... and Emma. She knows."

"Oh, Will, what can I say?"

"Nothing. It was a long time ago. But same story, she got the gun herself. We never had a gun, but she got one, a small pistol. Apparently no problem getting her hands on one. Then she drove off alone, I was at work, the kids in school. She sat in the car, God only knows how long. Held the gun to her head ... pulled the trigger. End of story! Not really ... just the beginning. Slammed a wedge of suspicion between me and my kids ... they held my constant arguing with their mother against me. Yet, in their own way they helped me get through it all. But, I ended up blaming myself for years, actually until I found the love of Emma."

"So ... any advice for me?"

"When I saw Vicki out on the dock, gun in hand, I couldn't let it happen again. Not to Vicki ... not to you. Maybe, just maybe, you two have a second chance. All the scratches and bruises, I'm glad I have them ... proves to me how serious Vicki was. Without me being there, who knows? I just pray something works better for her, between you two."

"Wow! I really owe you. Didn't realize how much."

"You don't owe me a thing. My action was nothing more than my own need for survival. I couldn't live with myself doing nothing. No way."

Martin did something he was not prone to do. He half stood, reached over and put his arms around Will. After a moment he said, "Thank you, Will ... Thank you!"

Will returned the squeeze, then released Martin and sat back. Neither man spoke for almost a minute. Will said, "Okay, tell me something. Norman ... do you understand the man?"

"I think so, in business."

"Well, he confuses me. He's investing some major dollars in Joey's vineyard. I mean that building being designed using post and beam is costing a lot more than it has to, mostly for aesthetics ... not necessary for making wine, more for selling the stuff, attracting customers. Then, since the wedding, he's been suggesting some vineyard acres be leased for hydrofracking. Is he crazy?"

"Not to his mind. To him it's all about money in the bank ... that's all that matters. Bank as much as fast as possible; pick up the pieces later."

"Yeah, he sees a short-term hit with the gas wells, doesn't weigh-in the long-term harm for the vineyard and the winery."

"That's Norman."

"But what about the lake? Doesn't he consider the damage to the lake?"

"I'm sure he figures if a problem crops up modern science can fix it."

"I sure wouldn't count on that."

"Well, Will, neither do I. We live in one beautiful place, we need to protect it."

"So, you don't agree with Norman?"

"Not on fracking," Martin said, "anywhere near the Finger Lakes. No way."

"Has he given you his patriotic speech about how domestic gas wells can get us out of the Middle East?"

"We really haven't talked about it."

"Norman's argument is that if we frack, we'll have enough gas and oil in the United States to make us energy independent. Then we can get out of the Middle East. As he says, '...let those fuckers fight out their thousands of years old blood-cult tribal gripes. No need to have our troops slaughtered in meaningless wars...' He's right on that point. But if we have gas and oil all over the States, why threaten our fresh water lakes?"

"We shouldn't. If Norman argues we should be independent, he does so with a view of his own bank account swelling.

Seth shouted from the Manor House, "Dad … We're ready for bed."

Martin stood and leaned down toward Will, "You didn't only save Vicki's life. You probably saved mine."

"Not me … your kids will save you."

Chapter 25

Shortly after dawn on Wednesday, Will heard the growl of diesel engines coming from the Lake Road. They revved higher, as if shifting down, but didn't pass by. Instead, squealing brakes signaled they were coming to a stop. Already dressed, Will went out to investigate; Prince at his heels. A long flatbed truck loaded with square wooden timbers slowly turned into the dirt road leading up to the winery. The weight of the load, combined with the steep grade, forced the use of a low gear; the truck moving not much faster than a walk. A crane followed. The noise of the two engines shattered all that was left of the early morning peace.

Looking to the sky, Will saw high clouds promising an overcast day; he knew to be accompanied by the high humidity of mid-August heat. His immediate inclination was to go up to the post and beam raising he knew was to begin; become a 'sidewalk superintendent'." *But, better if I wait until mid-morning; take Seth up to see the skeleton of the winery actually being assembled.*

Joey was already on-site, offering any help he could be to Aaron, the contractor. Bruce, the architect, was also on hand, a print of the building structure laid across the hood of his car. "Thanks," Aaron said, "I'll keep your offer in mind. But understand my crew has done this before. And the beams are heavy, so it's important you stay alert to what's goin' on, and out of the way. I don't want anyone gettin' hurt."

"Oh, sorry," Joey said.

"Happens all the time, particularly when someone's building a home. They want to help, just don't know how." Aaron glanced toward his pickup truck, saying almost with a sigh, "Anyhow, I'll get you a hard hat." He looked down at Joey's feet, "And you've got steel toes in those boots, right?"

"Yes, these should be okay."

251

"Well, we'll be setup soon. I hear the truck coming up the hill now,"

Just minutes after the truck and crane arrived, Aaron directing them into position, a van pulled up with the construction crew of five men on board. One of the men, older, tall, had a head of white hair and an angular face framed by a full beard, also white. He wore a blue work shirt and black trousers anchored by black suspenders. Walking over to Aaron he extended his hand in warm greeting, clasping the younger man's arm with his free hand. Aaron smiled, turning to Joey, "I'd like you to meet my father. Whenever there's a raising, he comes and helps."

Aaron's father shook Joey's hand. "Thanks for hiring my son."

"We're glad we found him."

Aaron looked at Joey, "He's been doing this all his life; can't stay away. He can eyeball a misalignment with more accuracy than most using a level." Aaron pointed to a large square wooden mallet standing off to the side. "See that ... it's his 'Commander'. If a joint's a little tight, a few well-placed taps with that and it fits snug together ... perfect."

The older man smiled, "Some need a little convincing."

"So," Aaron said, "you'll find him wherever the next joint is being placed. Fitting the joint properly, making sure the pin's set is true; it's his passion. Next thing to religion."

Aaron's father addressed Joey, "This building will outlast you, even your children. It must be right ... and in making it so, the Lord is honored. Honest work, son, best way to honor the Lord."

"Sir," Joey didn't know what to say, "Thank you for coming."

It was nearing 11 AM when Will announced he and Seth were heading up the hill to checkout progress on the winery. Emma said, "Wait a minute. Maria and I will come with you."

"We're gonna walk, you know. But I'm gonna leave Prince down here … too much goin' on up there to be watching him too."

"He isn't going to like that."

All four were sweating by the time they neared the construction. Other than the crane and the flatbed truck there wasn't much to see; the sills and a couple of posts were in place, but the form of the structure hadn't yet taken shape. Will cautioned both Seth and Maria to "…stay away from the building area, the truck and crane; I mean it! In fact, Seth, you hold my hand, and, Maria you hold Emma's hand."

Jackie walked up to the group and clasped her hands together. "This is exciting! After all our planning, today the building will actually be built."

"It should go quickly now," Will said.

"*Oui, oui*," Jackie smiled patting her stomach, "It must because he or she will be coming soon. Then the harvest late in the month. The harvest, then the baby."

The crane's engine came to life and its long arm hoisted a beam off the truck bed and swung it toward the building. Experienced hands reached to grab it and guide it to its appointed mooring. Will was impressed with how easy it looked. He had to yell to be heard over the noise of the crane, "Looks good, Jackie. These guys seem to know what they're doing."

"We hope so." She shrugged, "Too late to turn back."

'Oh, Jackie," Emma said, "It's going to be beautiful."

"Yeah, well," Will said, "I was hoping we could see more. But, with all the work going on, best if we get the kids out of here. We'll come back later."

By mid-afternoon, Joey was impatient with how long it took for each beam to be anchored in place; he thought after the first few, the erection would progress at a faster pace. But, he was glad to see the care being taken, particularly by Aaron's father, to make sure each joint was set properly. *Hopefully they'll get the Tasting Room up today.*

Standing on the lake side of the building, focusing on a long crossbeam being lowered into place, Joey caught sight of movement in the woods up across the road. He squinted to see better. *A man? Who? No, probably just a deer. No, no, definitely someone.* But the figure was gone.

There was late afternoon sunshine when Emma, Will and the kids came back. The few vertical posts set in place just before noon, had grown into the skeleton of the whole Tasting Room building. Even with only a few roof rafters positioned at the far end, it was impressive with a wide expanse from side-to-side; the massive beams destined to expose the beauty of structural strength.

Will pointed to Aaron's father giving commanding taps with his oversized mallet, convincing the last mortise and tenon joint to seat solidly in place. As soon as he set the pin, the crane swung away, its engine shutting down. That brought a thankful silence, even over the voices of the crew wrapping up a day's work.

Will took the kids in hand and walked them over to the side of the building for closer inspection. The threesome received nods and smiles from crew members, happy to see their work being admired. Aaron's father introduced himself. He took the opportunity to guide Will, Seth and Maria in some of the finer points of post and beam craftsmanship.

Jackie came out of the trailer and walked up to Emma who was standing, arms folded, impressed by the skeleton structure before her. "It is beautiful?"

"Oh, yes, Jackie. Amazing to see it up so quickly."

"*Oui,* they come … and *Voila*! It is standing. And all the beams, they will be exposed, to be seen, not hidden."

"And this light … brings out the beauty of the wood."

"After they finish the rafters, they will mount the walls … all sections built in the factory."

Emma put her arm through Jackie's. "You know Jackie, you take Will and me to places we never dreamt we'd be … and right up the hill from our own dream house."

Jackie looked around, casting her eyes over the vines across the road. "This is my dream; one I did not know I had."

After a moment she turned toward Emma, "So much happens, grandmother. Joey, my pregnancy, the wedding, our honeymoon … so fast. Like a dream … it is flying by … full of life … love." She paused again, then turned to look at the new structure, "The strength of these beams. This building … it will last. Like Joey and me … we will grow strong."

"Yes, solid … not like the wisp of a dream."

"To me it means hope … in the future."

Emma clutched Jackie's arm tight against her. "Oh, you and Joey, you will have a long life together, you and your family. I just know it. Things will settle down, you'll see. When the routine becomes tedious, and it will, just look at this building and remember it is your symbol of hope. Hope for depth and stability in your life. You have a love that will just grow deeper and deeper. I can feel it."

Seth ran up, Maria close behind. Seth held up a long wooden peg, the type used to fasten the mortise and tenon joints of the frame together. "Look, Jackie, Will says these hold the beams so they don't fall down."

Maria was close behind, her arms outstretched, "Mine, Seth, give it back."

Will brought up the rear, "Come on, Seth, give it back. It's Maria's to keep."

Jackie smiled at Will's look of frustration as he said, "These two, they never quit."

"We'd better get back down," Emma said, "When you finish up, you and Joey stop down for dinner. Nothing fancy … come whenever you're ready."

"Merci, Joey is in the trailer finishing up with Bruce and Aaron. We will be down soon."

Jackie walked across the road toward the trailer, waving to Aaron, just climbing into his truck. Bruce was walking out, a roll of prints under his arm. He was saying to Joey, just behind him, "We should be okay. I'll see you tomorrow." He waved to Jackie and headed toward his car.

Joey came over to Jackie, putting his hands on her shoulders, turning her around to look at the Tasting Room, her back to him. "So, Mrs. O'Donnell, how do you like it so far?"

"I love it! Better than I thought."

Jackie turned her head around toward Joey to give him a kiss. She half-screamed, jumping sideways, "Oh!"

Joey looked downward thinking she'd seen a snake, but quickly raised his eyes realizing a man was standing 10 feet from them. "Hey!" he shouted, then lowered his voice. "Hank?" Hydrofracking Hank? Where'd you come from?"

Hank extended his hand, stepping forward. "Sorry, didn't mean to startle you."

Joey took his hand, but not enthusiastically ... unsure of why Hank suddenly appeared out of nowhere.

Hank then offered his hand to Jackie. "And you, Jackie, you've grown since we met."

Still catching her breath from being startled, her grip was uncharacteristically limp. Hank had been an enigma to her in the spring at the meeting in the bar, and, now, having him come so close without warning put her on edge. She noticed he wore the same worn jeans and black AC/DC tee shirt he'd had on when they first met ... except for the wrinkles of a day's wear, still clean.

Joey asked, "Were you up in the woods earlier? I think I saw you."

Hank gave a frustrated wave. "Yeah, I screwed up. Prefer to stay undetected. Gotta wear my combat fatigues."

"Like when you're shootin' up gas wellhead gear?"

"Really? Now, why'd anybody be doin' that?"

"Come on, Hank. The sheriff's been lookin' for you ... related to trouble down in Pennsylvania. He was up here askin' me about you a month ago."

"Just cuz I'm ex-military. They assume I was Special Ops ... sniper. Hell of a way to treat a vet."

"Well, aren't you ... Special Ops?"

Hank shrugged, "Maybe, maybe not. You know that's classified."

"So, can I ask, why are you here? Now?"

Hank waved toward the new structure. "I like this building you're puttin' up. Gonna be nice. I'm just concerned with the damned frackin' getting' closer and closer. Especially after that fire at your wedding."

"Oh, that was my cousin ...drunk and high at the same time."

"Maybe ... but even if they don't torch it, this won't be worth a shit once they ruin your land ... pollute your water. You know the damned drill."

"Do you know something I don't? I haven't heard of any fracking approvals yet."

"No, nope. Just a feeling. It's gettin' closer. The big money farts downstate, they ain't givin' up. It'll be just like Iraq, powers-that-be keep pushin' 'til they get their way. Then you watch, it'll be shock and awe all over again, only ravaging your hillside. You'll hardly see it comin', then it'll be too late."

"So, what do we, Jackie and me, what do we do?"

"Other than be insured..." Hank looked back at Joey, "you are insured aren't you?"

Joey nodded 'Yes'.

"Well, you can't do much except protest, I guess. Fight to keep the frackers out of here. But, I just want to let you know I got your back." Hank looked over Joey's shoulder toward the vineyard. "I like what I see, how you keep your vines, what you're building here. I'll be keeping an eye on it. So, if you get a glimpse of me now and again, don't worry. Anything amiss and I'll be here for ya."

Joey smiled, "We do appreciate your concern Hank. But I don't have any money to pay you."

Hank shook his head, "No, no. No money. I'm just fighting my own little war. Gives me purpose ... a man needs a purpose after being in combat. Gotta keep doin', even when nobody'll hire ya. Just sittin' around ... that can be lethal. Long as I have the damned rash from the chemicals ...those harmless chemicals they use for frackin' ... long as I itch like Poison Ivy with no cure ... I'm fightin'."

Jackie asked, "Can you see a doctor for help?"

"Tried that, nothin' works."

"What about the shrapnel, that pain?'

"Not so bad in the warm weather. Bearable."

"Where are you staying?"

"Best you don't know. " Hank smiled, "But, thanks for askin'. I'm okay."

Hank reached in his pocket, pulling out a small 8X12 cloth American Flag. "Listen, I'm gonna go. If you need me just hang this in the window on the other side of your trailer so I can see it from up the hill."

Joey took the flag in his hand. "Okay."

"I'll be in touch. And, Jackie, you take care with that baby coming."

Hank spun on his heel and trotted off, soon lost in the foliage of the woods.

Joey and Jackie stood looking directly at each other ...stunned. After a moment, Joey said, "Holy shit! He is scary."

"*Mon Dieu.* Can we trust him?"

"I hope so. But for what I'm not sure."

"He is ... what's the word?"

"Try 'Creepy'..."

"*Non*, just 'Odd'. I do not know why, I think we can trust him..."

"Yeah, I guess... He doesn't wish us any harm."

Jackie glanced around, "We need to get down to grandmother's. But no mention of Hank ... he will scare her."

"Hell, he scares me."

Sitting next to Will at the patio table, Joey talked about the progress made during the day, seeing his plans coming into reality ... just as planned. Emma set a fresh pitcher of iced tea on the table, the first having gone quickly ... victim to the heat of the day. Thankfully the heat and humidity began to ease off as evening approached. Almost in triumph, Joey said, "And, hopefully tomorrow, the walls start to go up. After that, the winery wing."

"The exciting days of construction," Will said, "…seeing buildings take shape."

"And this stretch of weather; thank the Lord for that."

"Aaron's father is an interesting character. Gives your project the flavor of a modern-day Amish barn raising. Wonder if that's his background. But the son, Aaron, he can't be Amish … not with all the machines they're using."

"I don't know." Joey said, "Never had reason to ask."

"Well, I'm glad his father's involved. He's bringing old-school attention to detail along with decades of experience. The old craftsmen, they strove for perfection … built to last. None of this just-good-enough thinking of today."

"You remind me, Will, of my grand-pere. He preferred traditional methods instead of the modern." Jackie leaned forward to get more comfortable.

Emma looked at her, "Are you feeling alright?'"

"Fine, grandmother, fine. Uncle Nic got a man to help with the canopying, so I stay out of the hot sun. Right now, there is little to do. But I worry that the buildings will need my attention just as harvest starts or when the baby comes. The fall will be busy."

"But remember, Jackie, we talked about this," Joey said, "most of what has to be done can either be covered by others or can wait. Don't get me in trouble with Chloe."

Emma raised her eyebrows. "Oh," Joey said, "Chloe thinks I'm a slave driver … that I work Jackie too hard."

"Well, we certainly know that's not the case."

"You know," Will said, "Chloe's gonna be a bit like a Pit Bull … she ain't about to let go. I sense she's never really dealt with the fact Jackie's grown up." He looked at Jackie, "That you can make your own decisions."

"Merci, Will. I was afraid it was just me."

"Oh, no, Jackie, not you. Chloe wears it on her sleeve. Norman even mentioned to me he's concerned she'll be butting into your marriage. And, Joey," Will laughed, "In her eyes you are one country hick."

"I'm just tryin' to figure out which is worse to her," Joey said, "the fact I'm learning to be a vintner in the north-eastern United States where it's just too cold, or the fact I've been born and bred in America, Or, or the fact I have the audacity to be in love with her granddaughter."

"Probably a little of the first two, Joey," Will said, "But, I'll put my money on the fact you stole Jackie away from her. She'll never forgive you for that. Your only hope is giving her a great-grandchild. In fact, between us kids, I think the baby may be the only thing that keeps her stateside."

"You mean Norman can't do it?"

"If I can say something?" Emma said. The two men nodded in her direction. "She eventually may drag Norman back to France … if they stay together, that is. Do you want to say something, Jackie?"

Jackie cast her eyes downward, in thought. "I always looked to grand-mere Chloe as someone to follow. She seemed so sure of herself." She looked up at the others. "But now, I am not sure Chloe knows who she is. Did she ever know? And, she's sold the one anchor she had, her vines. But she can no longer discover who she is through me. I did not know it then; how I was slipping away from her when I bought my first plane ticket to come here."

"You've come so far since then." Emma said, "Just a year ago, so shy, unsure of yourself; now, mother-to-be, a mature woman."

Will sat back in his chair, the look on his face telling Emma he was about to share what he was thinking. "Yes," he said, "Yes, and Chloe helped you become the strong person you are. With all the tension she brought to your decisions: to stay, to marry Joey, and then all the palaver over the wedding plans, she and Vicki. Poor Vicki with her own fantasies to play out. Through it all you were always true to yourself, Jacqueline Beauveau, now O'Donnell."

Will looked at Joey, "Sorry, but I don't think your Irish name works as well with Jacqueline as Beauveau. But I guess I need to forgive you for that."

"Anyhow," Will sat back placing his hands over his stomach, looking at Jackie. "You came here and it's as if you conquered. You even got your driver's license so you can go over to the college and tutor students in French. Did you have any idea how much tutoring would help you with English?"

Jackie shook her head, mouthing, "No."

"And you dove into helping with the vineyard. And, Jacqueline, I must say, you have brought joy to both Emma and me. You're keeping us young…"

Emma patted Jackie's arm, saying, "Yes, my dear, you have done that."

"I think," Will wasn't finished, "I think, well I've always thought, Jackie, you and Joey are right for each other. And now you're ready for all the challenges of being a parent."

Jackie was blushing being the focus of Will's praise. "*Merci*, Will." She leaned forward, "My grand-pere, Maurice, died while I was young. He was stern, so protective he sucked the joy out of our years together, and critical, quite critical. But I loved him and he taught me much. I always felt the need to satisfy him … and even after he died I did not feel free to be me. But, here with Emma and you encouraging me instead of criticizing, here I am able to be me. *Merci…*"

"And, Joey," Will put his hand on Joey's shoulder, "Swept the girl right off her feet. All this would never have happened without you. Jackie would've never come back from France."

Chapter 26

An hour after sunrise, on the last Thursday morning of August, Maria burst into Emma's kitchen. The broad smile brightened her four-year-old face. "Mommy come home!"

Emma asked, "What?"

Seth came through the door, Martin behind him … Will came into the kitchen from the front room … like actors making their entrance from opposite sides of a stage. Seth said, "Yeah, for Labor Day, Mom's coming home."

"No, no," Martin said, "I told you. Not just the weekend and Labor Day, we're hoping she's coming home for good … her hospital stay is over."

"Oh," Seth smiled. "Awesome!"

Martin stooped down to look his children in the eye. "Mommy's really anxious to get home … to each of you. But you've gotta be good when she gets here. No fighting, no screaming. And she'll be tired so you both need to help her out. Okay?"

Seth nodded; Maria copied his response.

Will said, "That's great, Martin."

Martin glanced at Will, then over to Emma He was relieved to see support written in the smiles on their faces. Standing back up, Martin said, "Yeah, they're discharging Vicki from the hospital."

Will put his hand on Martin's shoulder. "Just in time for the long weekend. We'll be sure to be here all day."

"Thanks. I wish I had a definite time but you know how hospitals can be."

"That's for sure."

Emma stepped over, stretching to give Martin a kiss on the cheek. "You take good care of her. You know we're here when you need us."

Emma and Will shared the bench near the lake, the shade of the Maple protecting them from the hot mid-afternoon sun. By the shore, water lapped lazily up and over flat shale, making the stones sparkle in the bright light. With no mid-day boat traffic, the lake seemed to be holding its breath, bracing for heavy use over the final summer weekend.

Seth and Maria walked in the shallows, bent over in their search for stones to add to the fort they were building on the beach. Even when they couldn't resist splashing each other, they did so quietly, with little force, in keeping with the rhythm of the languid afternoon.

Suddenly, Maria froze and stood tall; the first to see Martin's SUV turn into the drive. She ran headlong toward the spot where Martin normally parked, shouting, "Mama!" Hearing her, Seth spun around. He followed and caught up just as they came to stand beside the passenger door of the car.

Vicki opened the door and stepped out. She seemed unsure of herself, showing the hesitancy of reentering habitual surroundings, now somewhat unfamiliar.

Vicki bent down, arms opened to Maria. The young girl lunged forward so forcefully, she almost knocked her mother over. Embracing Maria, using her body for stability, Vicki regained her balance. She opened one arm toward Seth, inviting him to join in. "Oh, I'm so happy to see you two." Vicki's voice was strained, holding back a cry.

Emma and Will came near, but did not intrude, happy to see the intense joy of the children, answered by tears beginning to stream down Vicki's cheeks. Holding Maria and Seth tight, her body language informed everyone she did not want to let go.

Martin stood to the side, the happiness on his face reflecting the gratitude of seeing his children finally reunited with their mother. After several moments, Vicki stood, reaching out to Emma for that tender embrace women give each other so well. "Thank you … Thank you for watching over my kids." Stepping back, she quickly glanced at Will. Her face registered surprise at his warm smile. Will stepped into the void between them, bringing his face close to hers. "I am so happy Vicki, I can't tell you how much…"

Vicki glanced away, then brought her eyes back to his. "But, but … after all…"

"Vicki, just forget it. It's behind us."

She held his gaze. "Oh, Will, damn … I don't know what to say … to do…"

"Just get well my friend … and come to us if you hit a rough spot."

Vicki reached to Will for a hug and he engulfed her in a strong, protective embrace. He was surprised at how slight she had become, a woman of average height, approaching middle age, but much thinner than he remembered her.

Being engulfed in Will's arms, the flashback hit Vicki hard … memory she'd suppressed so well, now rushing back … painfully clear. Her struggle with Will in the water, trying to pull him under … anything to get him away from her … kicking, biting, clawing with her pointed nails to draw blood from deep scratches … an enraged feline determined to cause damage. If he'd just let her finish what she'd set out to do! But, where'd the gun go? Swimming far and away, running onto the shore and up that long dirt road. Completely out of breath …exhausted … the sheriff taking her in. By then she was spent. *Damn my mind. Why the memory? Now? When I need to cool it. Who the hell gives a fuck???*

Vicki responded to Will's embrace politely, slowly pulled away, then gave him a gentle reassuring hug. She remembered being questioned about a gun just after being taken to the hospital, told one was found, but it was never shown to her. *After what I've been through, the meds I'm on … Was there ever a gun? Can't remember…"*

Martin broke the silence. "I bought dinner … before I picked Vicki up. All I need to do is warm things up. So, at dinner time, I hope you two will come over and help us celebrate."

"But," Emma asked, "shouldn't it just be family tonight?"

"Emma, you are family."

Vicki walked through the downstairs rooms of the Manor, Martin by her side, the kids close behind. It seemed surreal to her, so neat, everything in its place ... and dusted; not the chaotic clutter and unkempt floors she'd left behind. On the refrigerator she admired a picture Maria had drawn in day-care, stick figures of a father, son and daughter lined up in front of a house similar to the Manor; coming to them from the side was the figure of a woman, more prominent than the others. Vicki caught the meaning and paused to admire Maria's work; she bent down and gave her a kiss.

After strolling through the rooms her comment to Martin was somewhat formal. "I'm surprised, frankly, at how well you've kept the place. Thank you. Now, I'd like to take a shower. Wash the hospital antiseptic stink off me, and have a nap ... I'm tired." Martin had hoped for a hug, a kiss, some sign of affection. Vicki left him standing at the foot of the stairs. By the time she awoke, Martin, with Emma's help, was ready to put dinner out on the veranda table.

During dinner, warmed by the late-day sun, Will was amused at how exceptionally well-behaved Seth and Maria remained, no sniping at each other, no arguing or raised voices. Vicki was polite, much quieter than he'd ever seen her before. He sensed it wasn't only out of effort on her part to be on good behavior, to make some sort of good impression. Rather, he saw a vacuousness in her, the quelling of her fiery spirit down to a smoldering ember ... a shadow of the person she once was. A new Vicki ... restrained, he assumed by her meds, refined even ... trying so hard to fit back into her own family, but in a much more peaceful way.

Will wondered if the new version of Vicki could last. She hadn't lost her figure; although slimmer, still attractive and sexy. *I hope she hasn't lost her mind!*

Will turned his attention back to the discussion over the dinner table. Vicki was saying, "...that's all well and good, but you have to understand what I've been through. People think I was just resting and relaxing. The therapies they put me through were hard, wrenching. They don't call the doctors 'shrinks' for nothing."

Everyone nodded in recognition. Emma said, "Rest dear ... now what you need is rest. A few weeks of rest will do wonders."

With Vicki seeming to have nothing further to say, Martin steered the conversation to Seth and Maria, how much they were learning in their day-care classes. The two children smiled, enjoying the attention.

Will glanced across the table at Vicki. He couldn't forget the pain, not just of the wounds, but that a friend would so viciously attack him.

Vicki also had trouble concentrating on the conversation, even though it was focused on her kids. She realized she was having trouble, more so than ever before. She also knew Martin would want to make love later ... of course he would, she'd been away almost a month. But she really didn't feel like making love, to Martin or any man. *Maybe just buy him off with a quick lay 'for medicinal purposes'. He'll come like a racehorse anyway.* She sat quietly, looking around the table. *Do they have any idea what I'm going through? The pain I've been in, am still in, masked by my meds.* Vicki sat up straight, smiling in agreement with what Martin was saying, whatever that was. *Oh, who gives a shit about what I'm going through? I mean really, does anybody care? Anybody give a fuck ... really?*

Chapter 27

After a week of late September rain, sunshine blessed the vineyards, increasing the sugars in ripening grapes. Joey and Nic agreed if the weather held, they'd have a good harvest. Construction on the winery was keeping to schedule. And Jackie wore her burgeoning pregnancy proudly ... aware of the beauty only expectant motherhood can bring. But she wouldn't stop canopying. "We need more airflow to dry the leaves ... keep out the mold."

Clear weather continued into the first week of October. Joey, in the vineyard early in the morning, felt his phone vibrate, signaling an incoming text. He palmed it, seeing a new message from Nic: *'You checked Brix'*

Joey typed, *'Doing now. Little low'*

Feeling the warmth of the morning sun on his back, Joey walked to another row of vines and pulled grapes from a cluster. Nic seldom used texting, so Joey half-expected him to pop-up between rows of vines ... a practical joke. Instead his phone vibrated again. *'How low'*

He replied, *'20'*

'Be over'

Joey handled his refractometer with care to avoid knocking it out of calibration. An accurate measure of the sugar content of his grapes, the Brix, was needed. But there was no sign of Nic.

A few minutes later the familiar old pickup came across the County Road from the direction of Kober Vineyards, green paint dulled from decades of standing in the sun,. Nic pulled up at the end of the row Joey was working in. Walking toward him, he shouted, "You're gettin' close."

"At least with the Rieslings."

"That's what the sun'll do for you. And thinning the crop a few weeks ago ... that really helped. But I expected a higher Brix by now." He stood hands on hips, looking across the vineyard, his lips tight against his upper teeth, "I'd like at least a 23 or 24. Makes a big difference in the wine; but you know that. Usually the Rieslings are in by now."

Nic raised the refractometer he had in his hand, "Let's see what I get." He squeezed drops of grape juice into the instrument with a like amount of water. While waiting the half-minute for the grape juice and water to mix, he put a couple of grapes into his mouth, tasting the juice. "Taste is just about there. And they look ripe, feel good. Gotta be time ... usually it's late September, early October is late, 'specially with the good weather we've had. But that rain and cold snap a month ago ... slowed 'em down a bit. In the south Kober vineyard we're ready. My pickin' crew's gonna start tomorrow."

"Seems I may need to wait several days."

"Maybe not. What I worry about is if this weather turns. I've been surprised in the past with unexpected rain lasting days; having a crop get fungus and rot. The annual guessing game, the gamble. So let's see."

Nic raised the instrument to his eye. Then held it out for Joey to take a look. "What do you see?'

'21'

"Yep, close enough to your reading. I say we check every day. Get everything ready. When these grapes hit 23 or 24, get the pickers over here and work your crop on the press in the lull between the Kober loads."

"How do you know there'll be a lull?"

Nic smiled, "I control the pickers. And, this vineyard is small enough it won't be that heavy a load. But, you know Tom, hell of a brother; he'll be goin' crazy if I slow things down. Even made me write up a Custom Crush contract ... wasn't happy when I entered zero dollars. I told him it's the Family Special this year ... belated wedding present."

"You know I appreciate all this. Just get me the best timing you can ... but let's not get in a big family feud. I've had enough of that with Freddy."

"Yeah, Joey, your weird uncles and cousins. Thankfully, we're coming to a Full Moon; let us see to harvest before sunrise, while the grapes are cool. Ever do that with your grandfather?"

"Oh, yeah. Had me sleep over so we could start early, be in the vineyard by 4 AM."

Nic smiled, "Should have been around the old man before he retired. Those were good days; just didn't know it at the time."

"I don't think he mellowed out much at harvest time, even in his '80s."

"Good point." Nic looked toward his pickup. "I gotta get back. Come over; we'll load up the crates, at least get 'em set out in your vineyard. Later, I'll be doing the final check on the press ... make sure everything's ship-shape. Once that crew gets goin' those crates come fast. You can help me if you want; might learn something."

"I've gotta touch base with the carpenters in the Tasting Room ... they're moving right along; then run Jackie back to town. She's down at her grandmothers for breakfast. I'll be over; but she needs the truck, so I'll have the MG."

"No problem, we'll use the Kober flatbed. Your pickup's too small anyhow.

As he always did, Nic stood tall and scanned across the vineyard; then down to the lake, early sun making the tips of the waves sparkle. "Yep, Joey, the Lord has been kind to us ... a wonderful place to work."

"Couldn't agree more."

'We gotta thank Him ... all the sun and rain, the soft lake air rising to our vines ... we wouldn't have the terroir without Mother Nature."

"You ever think of becoming a preacher?"

"Yeah, several years back ... once, for a couple a minutes. But couldn't put what I felt into words. Like the hack writer imagining vivid scenes, but his novel falls flat. No, I realized my calling's different ... bringing moments of calm to men through wine ... maybe even a whiff of God. Only a few of us can do that."

You're lucky."

"Not lucky, gifted. So are you, in many ways. You're a quick study on wine; and take that beautiful wife of yours. Jackie's getting' pretty close now isn't she?"

"Still about a month out. She keeps coming up here, checking on the grapes, but I'm trying to keep her away. She's so big; I don't like her walking the uneven ground."

"Yeah, I saw her the other day. Bending over grabbing clusters in the thick of it. Took one look at her and said, 'You're gonna have a boy'. She tell you that?"

"Yeah, she did. Something about the way she's carrying."

"Way out front. You can tell every time."

"Well, I don't want her twisting an ankle, or worse, hurting the baby."

"She's just gotta behave herself."

"I'm hoping to get all these grapes harvested before the baby comes. The reds will be ready by then won't they?"

Nic chuckled. "Yeah, a month, should be."

"What?"

"Oh, I'm just thinkin' how we make plans and then life happens. I shouldn't say that. You're plans make sense and I'm sure things'll happen, if not right on schedule, close to it."

In the Carriage House, Emma spooned the scrambled eggs she'd just made onto two plates. She carried them to the table, placing one in front of Jackie, the other at her own place.

Jackie was saying, "…so this morning, getting dressed, Joey ordered me to stay away from the vines until after the baby comes. Like I might catch something, or fall and get hurt. His tone of voice, I did not like it. But he may be right, I have to be careful when I sit down on a chair." Jackie shook her head, "Sit at home for a month, I do not think so! Instead, I come here … too early?"

Emma reached over putting her hand over Jackie's. "Lord no, Jackie. You know you're always welcome anytime … anytime. And with Will 'catching the dawn' as he says, I'm always up early. But, you must admit, Joey does have a point.

270

Having a baby changes your priorities. You've got to protect yourself; and after the baby comes, it won't be Joey making demands on you. You two will need to work together."

"The baby is different. I love Joey, but sometimes, just the way he says things, I get angry ... and now being so big and heavy ... oh, if only I do not have to wait a month."

"Things happen in due time. You're frustration ... part of being human. And, remember, Joey's stressed too. He's never been through this either ... and, knowing him, he's thinking ahead on all the responsibility of raising a child. But still, we women always say, 'If the men had to give birth, the human race wouldn't have made it.' After one they'd be done."

Jackie smiled, "Good point." She glanced toward the lake. "Will is out in his canoe?

"Oh, you know him. Since the weather cleared after the rains, he's been out every day ... cool mornings, sunshine, low humidity. October is such a pretty month. You missed it last year when you went back to France.

"Anyhow, Will always tells me he'll be back when he gets here. I just know with the sun starting to beat down and getting hot, he'll come paddling back. Always stop what I'm doing and make breakfast for him ... figure a long paddle is tiring. It's good he keeps at it; helps keep him in shape."

"I should be paddling with him."

"Walking is better ... as much as you can. It makes your labor easier."

'I do a lot of walking checking the vines ... between those rows ... a long walk."

"Well, that's for you and Joey to figure out. Any plans for today?

"Just a tutoring session over at the college this afternoon."

"It's good of you to do that. Are you getting paid this year?"

"Yes, not much ... the college wants me on a contract for insurance purposes."

"With the baby coming I'm surprised you signed up."

"It gets me out and I get to know some of the girls. Remember the two who came to the wedding? I tutor them in French. But what really helps is working with them in English. Have you noticed how fast my English has improved? I knew English before, but not to speak ... conversational. Helping students understand French, I have to use English properly."

"Your English has improved."

"So, Joey is going to pick me up in a while and take me back to town because I need the pickup this afternoon. I do not fit behind the wheel of the MG anymore. Even the seatbelt on the truck is too tight."

"Should you still be doing this ... tutoring?"

"Other than the driving, no problem. I have sessions this week and next, then no more until after the baby comes."

"Well, you know, we could give you a ride, Will and me."

Jackie waved her hand, batting the offer aside. "No. I am fine."

"Oh, I almost forgot, Chloe and Norman are coming over this afternoon. Probably stay to dinner. Do you and Joey want to join us?"

"We better not. I need a nap after tutoring."

"Well, they usually come early. Norman likes to stroll up into the vineyard."

"*Oui.* He comes unexpected ... walking."

"They come across the lake in his speedboat."

"Joey hates it; feels like someone looking over his shoulder. I tell him Norman asks questions to learn. Joey feels he is critical."

"Oh, Norman is a pusher. An innocent question from a man like him can easily be taken as criticism."

       ℰᴑ   ᴏℨ

Early afternoon became the high point of a gorgeous fall day with the oranges and reds of the vineyard leaves ablaze in bright sunshine. A deep blue of the lake provided contrast, making the colors even more vivid.

Nic kept Joey fully occupied during the morning moving the crates to his vineyard. After a quick lunch, they checked the operation of every function of the Kober wine press. Even out on the pressing pad, under a roof next to the Kober Vineyards winery building, the machine was noisy. Nic's mantra with all mechanical devices was 'check it works, then check again' ... a few more times. He had the motor running, making a fairly loud hum, when Joey felt his smart phone vibrate with an incoming call. He pulled the phone from his pocket and saw '*Deborah O'Donnell*' on the display. Since his mother never called him, he held the phone up and pointed toward the parking lot, letting Nic know he was taking a call.

"Mom ... Hello. Hang on." Once he got far enough away from the press to hear, he asked, "What's up?"

"Is Jackie with you; or is she at the college? Doesn't she tutor today?"

"She should be just getting there about now. Why?'"

"I'm at the Clinic. There's been a shooting at the college. We're prepping for multiple injured."

"What?"

"It's serious Joey. Multiple gunshot wounds. Contact Jackie and tell her to stay away."

Joey speed-dialed Jackie's cellphone. After several rings he heard her voicemail greeting, 'Bonjour. Leave a message, please.' After the beep, Joey said, "Jackie, if you're not at the college don't go there. Call me ... right away!"

Joey knew if Jackie was driving, she wouldn't pickup her cellphone and answer. *But, if it keeps ringing she'll pull over and answer.* He speed-dialed again and waited through the rings until hearing the recording.

He tried one more time, pacing back and forth now ... waited. No answer.

Nic hollered from the winepress, "Problem?"

"I hope not. Give me a minute."

Joey called again. The rings seemed to be taking longer. *Come on, Jackie ... Pick up!*

The fourth ring was cut short ... stopped. Joey clutched his phone, "Jackie?" He heard random background noise, people shouting, then a weak voice, hesitant ... more question than statement, "Hel ... Hello?"

Joey looked toward the ground, concentrating. He almost yelled, "Who is this?"

The voice, male, regained its strength. "I just found this phone."

"Is Jackie there?"

"Who? Jackie?" Breathing heavily ... hesitating to catch it, "No ... I don't know."

"Wait! Where are you?"

"The back parking lot. I heard this phone ringing. It was on the ground."

"Are you at the college?"

"Yeah, we've all been ordered up to the Field House. I gotta go."

She's at the college! Joey exhaled so sharply he felt dizzy. Grabbing control of himself, he sucked in air, then yelled, "No, no, don't hang up. Carry the phone with you. It's my wife's phone."

"It's crazy here. Some guy shot up the place."

"Where did you say you are?"

"Back parking lot, behind the main building. More police cars are coming in. Sheriff's waving to keep moving. I'll give the phone to the cops."

"No, no, hang on to it. I'm coming over. I'll look for you at the Field House. What's your name?"

The phone went silent to Joey's ear; all background noise gone ... the connection lost. He redialed with no answer. "Shit!"

Nic was standing by his side. Looking at him, Joey said, "I gotta go. A shooting ... over at the college."

Nic pointed across the lake. "Something's goin' on. Never saw emergency lights like that."

Joey turned and saw flashing lights coming from all directions; south, west, north ... all heading at high speed toward the college.

"Guy I just talked to ... found Jackie's phone. But she's nowhere in sight."

"Jackie? She's there now? We'd better get over there."

They jumped in Nic's pickup. He drove across the ridge line road toward Joey's vineyard. When they came to the new Tasting Room, Joey said, "Turn down here." Approaching the Lake Road, Joey could see over the roof of the Carriage House and the Manor to the lakeside. Norman's Chris-Craft was moored to Martin's dock. Joey said, "Nic, pull into the Carriage House. If Norman's here, he'll get us across the lake in minutes."

As the pickup stopped in the driveway Joey jumped out and sprinted around the corner of the Carriage House. The two couples, Emma and Will, Chloe and Norman, stood on the patio looking across the lake. Seeing Joey, Norman almost shouted, "Hey, Joey ... Will and I walked up to the vineyard. But you weren't there. Now there's some kinda commotion goin' on over at the college."

"Listen," Joey said, "there's trouble, some kinda shooting."

"But Jackie's not there yet. Isn't her class later?"

"Jackie's there, but I can't locate her."

"What?" Will and Norman both asked, almost in unison.

"She's at the college. Some guy found her cellphone in the parking lot. I need a ride over."

Norman stood, "Okay. Let's go."

Will said, "I'll come along."

Joey turned to Nic, "You better get back ... finish up the prep for the pickers. I'll keep you posted."

Chloe stepped in front of Norman. "And you'll call Emma and me too ... right?"

"Yes, Will," Emma said, "don't leave us in the dark."

Norman and Will both nodded, turned and headed for the dock. Joey gestured, acknowledging agreement, and sprinted past them. Lines were cast off and the Chris-Craft pushed from the dock in record time. Norman opened the engine hatch cover, powered the engine and put the boat in reverse; clear of the dock he placed it in forward and accelerated into a power turn setting a heading toward the far side of the lake.

Nic watched, smiling, saying almost to himself, "Kinda like the three Musketeers." He nodded to the women, "Don't worry, they'll find Jackie."

At full throttle, the Chris Craft planed across the lake at just over 42 knots ... a fast speed on the water. Norman set his course straight toward the broad light-gray dock of the college. More detail came into focus as they approached; the ancient Bell Tower atop the century-old Administration Hall, with two large bells silhouetted in its open arch. The single structure of the original teachers college was flanked by two classroom buildings built in the '50s, during the post-World War II education boom. Beyond the outer side of each classroom building was a green space and a relatively new dormitory. All faced a broad lawn to take full advantage of the lake view. On the lawn, several small groups huddled together, and many people were running in no discernable pattern ... either a macabre ballet or just unorganized chaos. The flashing lights of an ambulance gaining entry between the buildings, punctuated the scene.

As Norman began to throttle down, a sheriff's boat came into view, lights flashing. It headed in a direction that would bisect Norman's path. Norman took his engine to idle, letting the aft-wave come forward under the boat. The police boat turned toward the Chris-Craft, bobbing in the wake. A sheriff's deputy had a bull horn in hand, raised it and broadcast. "You must exit this area."

Norman shouted in response, "We're looking for this fella's wife. She's eight-months pregnant."

The bull horn again came to life. "Doesn't matter. This is a Crime Scene. Turn about and leave this area ... NOW!"

Norman raised his hands, palms up, asking, "What next?"

The sheriff responded, "Find a place to tie-up and go on land to the Field House. You need to go down the lake and walk back. You can't get there from here. Understand?"

Norman signaled a 'Thumbs Up!' He turned the wheel to head north and gunned the engine, pulling away from the police boat and out of the Crime Scene. He slowly went along the shoreline, saw a man standing on a dock, and throttled down. "You the owner?"

The man, distracted by the curved almost feminine form of the speedboat, hesitated, "Yes, of course."

"Can we tie up for a while? We need to get up to the college, but they won't let us in there."

"What's goin' on?"

"We're not sure. Some kinda shooting. We're looking for this young fella's wife. She's eight-months pregnant."

"Yeah, sure. Throw me a rope."

Norman said, "Joey, go ahead. We'll catch up to you."

The narrow county road into the campus was jammed with cars ... going both ways. A couple of volunteer officers were trying to control traffic so a lane would be open for ambulances to arrive and depart. Their efforts were complicated by foot traffic ...some going in, most streaming out.

Joey sprinted ahead toward the campus. Encountering yellow police tape, he jogged along its circumference, scanning the parking lot for his red pickup. In addition to cars parked in an orderly fashion, the lot was peppered with emergency vehicles, lights flashing: several state and county police, two fire trucks, three ambulances. People rushing about as if not sure where next to go. Not seeing his truck, he ran up the hill to the Field House.

The hubbub outside was hushed ... many hugging, wiping tears from their cheeks; several leaning on another, needing support just to stand; a few staring into space, seemingly oblivious to the chaos before them. The somber mood was shattered by a Mercy Flight helicopter rising from the lake side of the campus buildings, above the height of the Bell Tower, then setting a course of the north-west, toward the nearest hospital. Joey never experienced war, but the scene mirrored what he'd always imagined it to be. He grabbed his cell-phone and speed-dialed Jackie's number.

Answered after the first ring, the now familiar voice said, "Hey. This the guy I talked to?"

"Yeah," Joey said, "It's me. I'm here."

"Already!"

"Yeah. Where are you?"

"Over by the door on the far side."

"There are four sides. Which one?"

"The south side ... looking away from the campus. Can't watch it all."

"I'm on the other side. What are you wearing?"

"A blue sweatshirt. I'll wave my hand."

"I'm on my way. I'll wave too. Damnit, there are so many people up here."

A few minutes later, seeing a waving hand above the crowd, Joey walked up to a young man, slight of stature, looking to be hardly out of high school. A bright blue sweatshirt confirmed he had the right person.

"Hi. Thanks for waiting."

"No problem. No place to go. Can't get back in the dorms. Something about the police having to sweep every building; just to be sure." He held out Jackie's phone, the distinctive aqua case confirming it was hers. "Here it is. I tried to give it to the cop directing traffic, rushing us away from the parking lot ... he didn't want it. Told me to give it to a policeman up here. I decided to wait for you."

"Thanks. What's your name?"

"Paul."

Joey felt weak ... out of breath. Having made it across the lake and running up the hill, his total focus was on getting Jackie's phone. But, *What next!* He wasn't sure. With his adrenaline rush ebbing, he felt empty. He was ready to strike forward into the next stage ... but where? How?

He spoke softly, holding up the phone, "Thanks Paul, for this. What the hell happened?"

"Some guy with a gun got in the Bell Tower over the main building, up in one of the arches. Nobody noticed him. Then all the fire alarms went off. So everybody came out, most on the lakeside lawn. He starts shooting ... fast. He hit a lot of people. Everybody was running for cover. I looked up and saw him rapid-firing ..." Paul waved his arms apart, palms upward, "...we were screaming, but he wouldn't stop. Then blood splattered all across the bell behind him. He was gone."

"Where did you pick this up?'

"The back parking lot." Paul pointed. "I was running across the lot with everybody else and I heard it ringing. That's when I talked to you."

"Did you see a red pickup truck?"

"Nope. Don't think so."

"How about a pregnant woman; my wife's eight months along?"

"Didn't notice. You gotta understand, I was running for cover with everybody else. The fire alarm goes off; everybody gets out of the building. We're all on the front lawn looking for smoke and a gun starts shooting ... at us! People are getting hit. We ran toward the side of the building ... too dangerous to go back toward it. I look up at the tower, see him, the gun. Look again ... blood all over the place ... just kept running. Didn't realize the shooting stopped." Paul wrapped his arms around his shoulders, closed his eyes and bent forward, the images replaying in his mind.

Joey put his hand on his shoulder. "Wow! You saw that."

"Never forget." He looked at Joey, "They wouldn't let us back to help those who were hit." Joey thought Paul might begin to cry.

After a moment, Paul said, "But, your wife. I don't think I saw her."

"Oh, if you saw her, I think you'd remember." Joey held out his hand. "Well, Paul ... Thanks! If you happen to see her, her name is Jackie. Let her know I'm here, looking for her."

"Will do. I gotta go, see if I can find my roommate and some   friends."

"Yeah, and with TV stations arriving, let anyone worried about you know you're okay."

Joey turned around, all 360 degrees, scanning the crowd ... nothing. He walked to the campus side of the Field House.

Two ambulances, lights flashing, electronic sirens beeping, pulled out between the buildings, across the parking lot, and headed toward the state highway. Another chopper could be heard coming closer, but instead of preparing to land, flew overhead.

Norman and Will came up to Joey. "Any luck?"

"Nope." He held up Jackie's phone. "Talked to the kid that picked this up, but he didn't see her, or my truck. Picked it up in the parking lot," Joey pointed, "right down there."

"We tried to find who to talk to. The cop directing traffic told us to come up here. Going to fill everybody in on what's happening."

Will looked around, "Geez! I haven't seen anything like this since the '60s ... Nam!   Listen, let's inform the police Jackie is missing, get a bulletin out on your truck."

They were directed to an officer who took the details and promised to get a report dispatched. A police briefing was about to start, so he told them to hang-on, he'd come back to them for more specifics.

After the briefing, including the usual barrage of questions, Will said, "Nothing new there."

"Listen, I gotta stay here and talk to the police," Joey said. "Make sure they list Jackie as missing. They say they've checked all the buildings, but something may have been overlooked. Can you two get back over, fill in Emma and Chloe, then drive into town and check my house and the clinic yourselves... just to be sure Jackie's not there?"

"Sure ... right away." Will said.

"'Yeah," Norman added. "Within the hour, we'll be able to check it within the hour."

Chapter 28

It was past 6:30 when Will turned from Main Street onto the East Lake Road heading back to the Carriage House. Norman was at his side. Their check of Joey's home found nothing; a neighbor doing end-of-season yard work told them Jackie had been home until early afternoon, then drove off in the pickup truck. At the Clinic, Joey's mother, stressed by the overload, had little time to talk. "No, I haven't seen her. We've been triaging patients, sending those needing surgery to Rochester; treating everyone else. People are coming in like you, searching for loved ones. I'm worried about Jackie. Give me your number in case she shows up."

After leaving the Clinic, a ride around town, just to be sure, proved futile.

Norman called Joey on his cellphone to advise that nothing turned up in town. He asked Joey, "Anything new at the campus?" He listened a moment, then said, "What's that? ... They did a second sweep of the buildings ... and nothing was found?"

Will, hearing only Norman's side of the conversation, shook his head, gripping the wheel tighter.

Norman continued speaking into the phone. "Okay, so you're going to stay there ... What? ... work with the police." He held the phone tightly to his ear, trying to hear over the road noise, hoping not to have to repeat everything. "And the police, they put out a bulletin on your pickup ... right? ... Yeah, of course, that went out while Will and I were still there. But just check again ... okay? ... Yeah, I get it; you're working with them."

Norman listened for several seconds. "Chloe and Emma, we filled them in before. We're headed back their way now. Don't worry, anything new and we'll call ... Okay, Bye."

Norman took the phone from his ear. "Whew! These damned things. Can't hear on 'em. Nothing new."

The two men sat quietly, on the surface looking like they had few cares in the world; their internal turmoil demanding they logically collect their thoughts.

Norman broke the silence. "One more chink out of 2nd Amendment rights."

"What do you mean?"

"Every damned shooting at a school... Gets the bleeding heart liberals all fired up – pleading more gun control. Hell, we've already got enough gun laws, particularly in New York State. Cops can't enforce the ones we've got.

"Well," Will said hesitantly, realizing Norman was going down a path he hadn't seen coming, "don't they have a point? The liberals as you call them. Aren't they just asking for tighter controls over access to guns?"

"Hell, no! Gun control just makes it harder for lawful owners ... still easy for criminals to get their hands on 'em."

Will, just weeks away from knocking a gun from Vicki's hand, firmly supported more control. But, realizing Norman's stance wouldn't be changed by debate in the car; he reached over and turned on the radio. He was surprised to hear a 'Breaking News' update regarding the shooting at the college, a male voice saying: "...with authorities confirming three dead and four in critical condition ... presently in surgery. All others are believed to be in stable condition, their wounds non-life threatening. Names and ages have not been released."

There was a slight pause, then an aggressive female voice came on air: "'News First' has confirmed that the gunshot killing the shooter was not at close range ... placed from an undisclosed location off-campus."

Norman said, "Somebody was either a crack shot or very lucky. Just proves, your best bet in a shooting is a 'good guy with a gun'."

Will held up his hand, signaling Norman to be quiet. The announcer continued: "Witnesses have also described a semi-automatic rifle, equipped with a high capacity magazine, was used by the shooter. These facts have yet to be confirmed by the police. No information is available on the identity of the shooter." As more facts become available 'News First' will be first…" Will turned off the radio.

"And still no Jackie! Did Joey say he'd checked everything? I hate to ask, but she isn't among the wounded is she?"

"Joey told me he checked on that. And, they've searched that campus again … nothing."

"I wonder if she was abducted somehow."

"Damned, seems someone would have seen something. But with the pickup missing, hopefully she never got there, was turned away by a roadblock. She'll turn up shortly."

"I hope so. But how did her phone get into that parking lot?"

"You're right. My thought she never got there … doesn't hold up. Maybe she was there and rushed away."

"That could be."

"Well," Norman sighed, "anyway, there'll be hell to pay over that gun … semi-automatic. Unless the guy had it from before, must've purchased it out-of-state."

"That's why we need universal background checks."

Norman turned his head toward Will. "I just told you, already got them in New York."

"No, I mean uniform in all the states."

"Can't do that!"

"Why's that?"

"State's Rights and the 2nd Amendment."

Will slowly shook his head, "Oh, yeah. I forgot!' He drove on in silence.

When they turned into the driveway of the Carriage House, Norman asked, "Where to from here?"

Will sighed, "I don't have the slightest idea."

"What can we tell the women?"

"The truth … we struck out."

The sky to the west was bathed in recent sunset orange. On the far shoreline, flashing lights of emergency vehicles punctured the peace of twilight shadows. The men found Emma and Chloe seated at the table of the Carriage House patio looking as if in prayer. They were silent when Will and Norman walked from the driveway. Emma raised her head, eyes watered from crying, and asked in a soft voice, "Nothing yet? You didn't find her, did you?'

"Had we," Will sat down next to her, taking her hand, "you'd be the first to know. We checked the house, then with Joey's mother at the Clinic, even drove around town. Not a trace. A neighbor saw Jackie leave during the afternoon ... that's it."

"My poor Jacqueline," Chloe moaned, "that girl has been through so much ... and now this." She put her head down into her hands, slowly shaking it from side-to-side.

Norman, standing behind Chloe, put his hand on her shoulder. "I called Joey. The police have issued a bulletin to watch for his pickup truck. And, he's checked and rechecked ... although we don't know where she is, Jackie's not among the injured. In a case like this, sometimes no news is good news. No one recalls seeing her at the college. So, as I was saying to Will, maybe she arrived, saw trouble and rushed off. She might still be finding her way back here ... or home."

Chloe twisted to look at Norman, "Only in America can you say a shooting is good news."

"No, no, I'm not saying that. Just that Jackie being missing right now is perhaps better than the alternative."

"Norman," Chloe said, "you depress me."

Will interrupted, "We left a note on the door for her to call us."

"And," Norman said, "they didn't find any accomplice after sweeping the campus a second time. So, at least it's over."

"Oh, my Jacqueline," Chloe lowered her head again, speaking quietly as if to herself, "...her parents dying, all those years worrying for her safety, then her headstrong rush to America ... and now this!" She looked up at Norman, "Is nowhere safe?"

"I guess, not really. But, on balance, I think the United States is safer..."

"Than France!" Chloe shouted, "You must be kidding."

"Norman, how can you say that?" Will's words were measured, spoken between clenched teeth. "We have way more guns than any other developed country."

"Oh," Chloe said, "Norman's always defending your gun laws. What you in the United States allow to happen."

"Yes, Chloe, I do." Norman's demeanor was hardening, indicating he intended to hold his ground. "We have our Constitution and its 2nd Amendment ... the right to keep and bear arms."

"To anyone?"

"In some states. New York's pretty rigid now; they've gone too far ... violating the 2nd Amendment."

"Not quite," Will raised his hand to the spot on the side of his head where the scars from his recent stitches were still visible; his voice echoing the gesture. "Everything in New York's law has been judged constitutional."

"You believe that crap?"

"It's the law, damn it!" Will stood as if to better be heard, "Lax gun control, that's how Vicki got a gun ... damned near killed herself and me. We need tighter control like New York in every state."

"Ain't gonna happen." Norman said.

Will shouted, "Why Not?"

"I told you, 2nd Amendment." Norman's voice remained steadfast, uncompromising, "Gives us the right to buy and own, even carry."

"But you forgot the 'regulated militia' part of the 2nd Amendment. We already have that with the National Guard."

"Just look what happened, somebody blew the shooter away. Thank God, he had a gun."

"Yeah," Will snarled sarcastically, "and how many died, three, maybe more ... and how many injured? Hopefully none of them will die." Will pointed his index finger at Norman's chest, his face contorted in anger. "Listen, the 2nd Amendment was written to protect 'we the people', not subject us to wanton carnage."

Emma looked at Norman, exasperated, "Jesus, Mary and Joseph and all the Saints in heaven, can't you hear what Will is saying?" She stood, leaning toward Norman, flailing her arms, shouting, "People used to yell, use their fists. Now they just pull a trigger to injure and kill. It's the coward's way out!"

Before he could respond, Chloe grabbed the arm of her chair and screamed, "Damn it to God!" Standing, she stepped between the two men. "Damn it! Do you two not realize my granddaughter is missing?" She pointed toward Emma, "Emma's granddaughter." She turned back toward the men. "And you both stand here debating guns. *Mon Dieu!* Where is she?"

Norman said, "Its important ... gun rights."

Chloe turned toward Norman, her voice becoming guttural, low in register, "You stupid Americans with your guns. Devoted to them ... you are ... more than to God." She came closer, reached her face up toward Norman's, fists clenched by her side. Speaking slowly, the rasp of her anger punctuating every word, "You tell me ... you fucking idiot ... you tell me..." Then she screamed, eyes blazing at Norman's, spittle flying into his face, "Jacqueline! Where is my Jacqueline?"

Norman glared back at Chloe, wiping his hand across his cheek. His voice was soft, belying the anger on his face, "Calm down, Chloe, calm down ... we'll find her."

Chapter 29

Jackie sat on the lone chair in the room. The air hot and stuffy, late-day sunlight shining through a single dirty window pane highlighting years of dust floating aimlessly about. The chair, wooden, straight-backed, uncomfortable, particularly given her eight months of pregnancy. A dull gray pallor embedded in the planked floor confirmed decades of wear. The walls were a faded light green of a happier time, long, long forgotten; random patches having fallen away exposing naked lath of the era when plaster was hand troweled. Covering all surfaces, even the dangerously buckling ceiling, were stains of wiping down rather than washing; whatever had been splayed aimlessly about, in nightmarish spasms of mindless mirth or misery. The only saving grace was that it had happened long in the past, leaving a stale offensiveness, somewhat tolerable, enough so Jackie resolved not to let her rising nausea blossom into a pool of vomit. There was a bed in the room, worn dirty mattress and no sheets. *I can't lie on that!*

In the white-heat of anger at having been overwhelmed, car-jacked, she'd not been able to think. Now, in the silence of the room, her attacker on the other side of the wall, swearing to himself, loud and incoherent, his words unintelligible, she had time to reconstruct what had happened ... so fast.

The drive in Joey's pickup from town to the college was short, but with no air conditioning it was hot even with the windows open. Since the seatbelt didn't fit over her belly properly, it was left slack, the concern being that if latched, any accident would hurt the baby. Her light-weight cotton maternity skirt, with plenty of room to keep comfortable on a beautiful autumn summer day, had proven to be a good choice. But in the afternoon heat, Jackie doubted the need for the knitted sweater Emma had loaned her in case the air conditioning in the building proved to be too chilly … it lay on the bench seat, on top of her laptop computer. Parking behind the Administration Building was easy given the spot reserved in recognition of her pregnancy … just a short walk to the office used for tutoring.

It happened so quickly. Jackie remembered having just pulled into the parking space, picking up her cellphone, and beginning to open the driver's door. The handle lurched out of her hand and she dropped the phone as the door swung wide. The attacker shoved his body behind the steering wheel… forcing her to slide toward the center of the bench seat. She clutched the sweater to her belly, a reflex action to protect the baby; her laptop fell to the floor. Swinging the barrel of the long gun the attacker held upward to get it in the truck, the muzzle pressed against Jackie's cheek.

The attacker was a man of medium build, slightly paunchy, early '20s. "Stay out of the way," he shouted, "or I'll blow your fuckin' head off!" He started the engine, jammed the gearshift into reverse, and careened the truck backwards, almost losing control. Then into first with a tire screeching acceleration out of the parking lot.

Once on the road, glancing toward Jackie for the first time, he slammed his hand against the wheel. "Oh, fuck! Fuck, fuck, fuck! You're goddamned pregnant. I got no time for pregnant." He resettled the gun, next to his body pointing it straight up toward the ceiling of the truck cab, and looked at Jackie again. "Damn … shouldn't be happening like this." His face dissolved into an expression of grief, almost to the point of crying. "Damn it, Luke! Gotta be dead. All that blood up there. Shit!" He hit the wheel with each word, "Damn!" … "Fuck!" … "Shit!"

Grasping the wheel tighter and accelerating faster, the truck speeding down the two lane road faster than Jackie had ever gone, farmers' fields and verdant vineyards rushing by, the gunman's face tightened with concentration. The gun slipped sideways, its muzzle again resting against Jackie's cheek. As if talking to himself, he almost yelled, "Luke had the gripe … Not me. I just went along to help out. 'Just gonna shoot up the place a little,' he said, 'scare the shit outta them college brats.' Not kill 'em! I never signed on for any killin'.'"

He looked toward Jackie. "We gotta get to someplace. I'm not into hurting babies; so I'm not gonna hurt you. But don't try anything, or I will hurt you ... hurt you bad."

Jackie remembered just staring back at the stubbled face, unable to speak ... fearing anything said could prove fatal. But what, she wondered, what was happening ... a few minutes ago ... back at the college.

"Damned fire alarms," the attacker continued, "Luke says, 'All you gotta do, Lenny, is run through the buildings, pull the fire alarms ... get everybody out on the lawn. That's all!' As soon as I finish the kids are coming out; he's shootin' from the bell tower, but the kids ... fallin' down." He glanced at Jackie, "I'm trying to figure out why they're all fakin' it. Until I see they aren't! I yell to Luke but he don't hear, just keeps with the rapid fire. Oh God," Jackie saw her attackers face grimace again, "I see the top of Luke's head fly right off. Oh, Fuck! Fly right off ... blood and gunk sprayed all over the bell ... his brains! Fly right off..." The truck lurched over onto the shoulder causing Jackie to grasp the passenger side handle just to stay on the seat. It skidded back onto the road, came under control. The swaying back and forth drove the muzzle of the gun into Jackie's cheek. "Gotta get the hell out of here ... all's I could think." He glanced at Jackie, "And you, you just opening the driver's door. Damned ... Luke ... what were you thinking?"

The ride was a blur to Jackie's memory. Speeding down the narrow paved country road she felt moisture running down her cheek. Her fingers came away with blood. Instinctively she lifted the edge of Emma's sweater to act as a pressure bandage. Tightness across her abdomen became a distraction from the chaos. Then, suddenly, Lenny braked hard, forcing Jackie to place her hands on the dashboard to keep from falling into it. A tight turn onto a single lane track, paved for a ways, until a barn was passed, then just dirt, not much used, weeds growing in the center. Going slower, still too fast for the bumpy, rutted lane; rows of vines engorged with grapes nearing harvest on both sides. An old house, sized small, came into view ... paint worn, left to be, Jackie thought, probably since the last tenant worked the land. Creeping vines climbed the shingles as if trying to overwhelm, while what once was lawn had been replaced by aggressive weeds. Lenny headed straight for the front door, skidding to a stop.

He sat looking forward, then turned toward Jackie. "Did not see this coming. We were gonna have some fun is all, come back here and drink some beers, smoke some weed, celebrate. But, I gotta get out of here ... better not 'til it's dark. You be cool ... you won't get hurt. There's a bedroom in here, you're gonna stay there." He patted the rifle, still by his side. "Don't make me use this. I'd hate to on a pretty girl like you."

Jackie remembered being guided at gunpoint out of the truck, up the three steps of the porch and through the front door. The interior demonstrated just how abandoned the structure was, everything faded with age, worn from years of use. Now it was trashed, by the young men trespassing, beer bottles, discarded junk food containers and snack bags, soiled dishware, all left wherever they'd been dropped. Slept-in sleeping bags, unrolled on the floor. And a large gun case, hard-shelled, lying open ... empty.

Jackie hesitated long enough for the attacker to poke her with the tip of his rifle toward the lone bedroom. That's when she said her first words to him, "Please. Before I go in there I need to use the bathroom. Lenny, can I call you that ... Please!"

"How do you know my name?"

"You told me, in the truck."

"Oh yeah. Okay, pregnant lady's gotta pee. Be quick. I'm right outside. Try anything and I swear, you will regret it!"

What can I do? I'll get both of us, the baby and me, killed! The bathroom was a disgusting mess ... brown smudges on the walls, the smell of stale urine from the sticky floor, a faded full-color picture of a nude ripped from a calendar, her exaggerated breasts hanging over the back of the toilet ... it was a mess Jackie had no choice but to hold her breath and ignore.

Lenny followed her closely into the bedroom, rope in hand, but as she sat with difficulty, he backed away. "Damned bitch, you are fuckin' goddamned knocked-up. Never been so close to a gross-out mama." He put his face close to Jackie's. "You ain't runnin' anywhere's are you." He pulled back, "You fuckin' can't. So I just let you be. But don't be havin' that baby here! No way any ambulance comin'." He turned on his heel. "No fuckin' way. I'm gonna lock this door … let you be."

Jackie sat on the single chair, very uncomfortable, pawning off the occasional tightness in her abdomen to the stress of being hijacked, abducted, now held hostage … still clinging to the sweater against her belly, as if hoping Emma somehow could help shield her child from the chaos the October afternoon had become. Lenny continued swearing in the outer room, apparently to himself, no one else seemed to be around. There was an occasional bang as something hit a wall or the floor. She wondered if he was throwing things with some purpose, or if the turn of events was just too overwhelming. Knowing his demeanor toward her could change, she kept still … hoping he'd forget and just leave. After all, he had a perfectly good get-away truck waiting outside.

Time was passing and Jackie was feeling hunger pangs … must be about dinner time. They seemed to come and go. A back ache made her stand to walk around, using only the balls of her feet, hoping to avoid creaking a floorboard. She was also getting tired; the usual late afternoon nap never having happened.

Taking shallow breaths to avoid gulping in the decayed stench of the abandoned room, remnants of binge drinking, smoking weed and doing drugs, wild and mindless sexual carousing … all of years gone by; Jackie tried to ignore the pain recurring in her abdomen. Sitting down again, bending forward, her head pointed toward the floor, arms folded lightly across her stomach.

Memories flooded her mind; long ago memories, of an afternoon when Jackie was fifteen. She had gone with Chloe to

Francois' chateau to visit his ailing grandmother, a woman in her early '90s. *Why am I thinking of this now?*

The grandmother, feisty and strong-headed, originally from a farming family, gained social stature by marrying Francois' grandfather, just as Chloe had stepped up in the French social strata when she married Maurice, Jackie's grandfather. It created a bond between the two women, both outspoken and direct. For some reason, Jackie was at a loss to remember why, the two grandmothers fell into a very frank discussion of childbirth. Chloe mentioned her extended labor when she'd given birth to Jackie's mother; one reason, she said, she'd never had another child, the son Maurice had hoped for.

Francois' grandmother sat back and cackled, open mouthed, stained teeth showing the lack of the modern dental care her generation found so unnecessary. She told the story of her own birth in wartime France, during World War I, when the women of the farming villages were forced to bring in the harvest, all men having been conscripted into the French army. Her mother kept working in the fields until a few weeks before she was due, and feeling some pains of indigestion, headed home alone. On the way her water broke; rushing she just made it to the house before Francois' grandmother was born. Jackie remembered the old woman leaning toward her, looking into her eyes, saying in French, 'When the baby comes, Mon Chere, relax … let your body deliver the baby … tensing up will only make matters worse'.

Francois' grandmother sat back and laughed, "Voila, I was born! Just 'slid out' my mother said." The old woman sat, an open mouthed grin showing her joy in the telling.

The memory, a distraction from the adrenaline rush of the abduction, calmed Jackie. The recollection seemed to tell her to relax; to wait out this gunman. He'd soon feel the need to get away and, hopefully, leave her alone.

Without giving it much thought, Jackie whispered,

Je vous salue, Marie, pleine de grâce.
Le Seigneur est avec vous.
Vous êtes bénie entre toutes les femmes,
et Jésus, le fruit de vos entrailles, est béni.
Sainte Marie, Mère de Dieu,
Priez pour nous, pauvres pécheurs,
maintenant et à l'heure de notre mort.
Amen

She found herself repeating it under her breath, again …
and again … and again.

Chapter 30

Joey walked out of the State Police Command Center, a mobile unit parked next to the Field House. Walking into the crush of people gathered outside, he almost bumped into his uncle. "Thought I'd find you somewhere over here," Nic said. He put his hand on Joey's shoulder and leaned toward him, "Is Jackie okay?"

"We can't find her. I tried to call you back, but it wouldn't complete. Then the police asked me to come in where it's quieter to explore where she might have gone. Everybody's accounted for except Jackie. They've had an alert out on her for a couple of hours now, several counties, going statewide, even into Pennsylvania ... nothing."

Joey glanced away ... thinking. Nic bent closer, catching eye contact, "What can I do?"

"Wish I knew. Norman and Will checked at home, the Clinic, drove around town ... nothing. No sign of her or my pickup."

"This whole thing's a nightmare. Three dead and counting ... well, four with the gunman. Several seriously wounded. You sure Jackie was here?"

"Her cellphone was. The student who picked it up when I called that first time," Joey pointed toward the parking lot, "found it right down there."

"Have you had anything to eat?"

"That sandwich we had for lunch was a long time ago."

Nic gestured to the double doors of the Field House, swung wide open. "They're offering food. Let's get you something to eat."

The two men walked in and joined the end of a line of students hoping for supper, the dining hall of the college still behind Crime Scene tape. Staff and volunteers were rushing to cope ... working as fast as they could. Joey felt a bump on his elbow and turned, facing Hank.

"Where'd you come from?"

"Tryin' to size it up."

"What up?"

"Pieces of the puzzle, put it all together. Saw you were in the police Command Center. They got anything new on the shooter ... or who shot the shooter?"

"That I don't know. Jackie's missing. That's why I was there."

"Wait!" Hank took Joey by the arm and pulled him from the line, out of earshot. "Your wife, Jackie?"

"They want to keep it out of the news right now, afraid she may have been abducted."

"Well, the shooter was killed, right? I mean whoever did that ... quite a shot. But the other guy, didn't I hear he was arrested?"

"What other guy?"

"I saw two of them, on their way to the college. Followed 'em, but lost 'em. Then I heard rapid firing ... too late."

"You suspected somebody before it happened?"

"Nothin' like this! I was down in PA at a gun show. Noticed two guys checkin' out an assault rifle. When they decided to buy it, the one handing over the money was caressing the stock like a lover would a woman's leg ... lust in his eyes. I saw him carrying it out to the parking lot and said, 'Nice choice, that one." He responded with an angry stare, damned near shoved me. Said, 'Fuck off!'

They were driving an old black coupe with New York plates. The left rear fender replaced ... bright yellow ... stood out like a sore thumb. Something pulled at my gut ... wasn't right. I decided to follow. They kept to the back roads; first open field, out in the middle of nowhere, they pull over and out comes the AR-15. Just blasted away. Must a shot up a couple hundred in ammo alone. This afternoon, I'm about 10 miles south of here and see the yellow fender heading north ... didn't realize they were headed to the college until it was too late."

"You know all this and haven't told the cops?"

"Wasn't aware anyone was missing. Problem is they'll hold me for questioning. See being a vet and a trained sniper, they'll think I shot the shooter."

"Did you?"

"Better you wonder about that one."

Curiosity was getting the better of Nic, so he sidled over to the two younger men.

Joey saw him and asked, "Nic, do you know Hank?'

"Oh, Hank. Heard about you … the mystery man on the motorcycle."

"Well, that's the problem with rumors, mostly false. Just a guy tryin' to hold it all together."

Joey turned back, facing Hank directly, "So, these two guys you saw. Are you sure one was the shooter?"

"Well, whoever was had the same firepower I observed in that field."

"So, you took him out?"

"Listen, I think those guys were holed up just a ways south of here … ten miles or so. I was looking for where … but never found it."

Nic stood, listening, hand rubbing his chin, visibly thinking. "Did anybody check the old Simmons place?"

"The where?" Joey asked, "I just went through a list of places with the cops … no Simmons on that list."

"It's an old farmhouse. Way back in … actually in a woods … hard to see. Most people give up on the road into it, looks like a dead end farm track. A tenant farmer bought it from his boss … tried to make a go of it. But it was too small, wrong ground for crops. Years ago a winery bought all the acreage and put it into vines. But back in the woods, they just left the house sit. The hippies found it; made it their playground. Good place to crash as long as anybody wanted. Ihat was a crazy time. Been abandoned ever since."

"How do you know all this?" Joey asked.

"Prior life … I was there. Yeah … stoned out of my mind. So, Hank, you heard of this place?"

"Guess I didn't go in far enough. I went in past a barn and then the road got rough, unused?"

"That's it."

"Yeah, yeah. I rode in there after one of the rains a couple of weeks ago. The ruts were a mud, grabbing my tires, impossible to stay upright. Decided to come back ... never did."

"Well, if there's an accomplice, and he's holed up somewhere south of here, that's where I'd look."

"Okay," Joey said, "let's tell the police."

"No, no, no!" Hank said, "Not with me. They'll question me for hours. No, I'll ride out and check this Simmons place. Won't take half an hour, my cycle's just off-campus. Joey, come with me, if nothin' else is workin', it's the best lead you've got."

Nic said, "Go! Call me either way. I'll deal with the police."

Joey shrugged, "Yeah, I've bugged 'em so much they'll be glad to be rid of me. I need to do something!"

Nic walked over to the Command Center, questioning if anyone had checked the Simmons farm for Jackie's whereabouts. This led to many questions about who he, Nic, was, "...and why are you involved?" Followed by, "On what basis are you sure she was abducted? By an accomplice?"

"I'm not sure of anything. But Jackie's been missing for hours and no one has a clue where she is. I'm just asking if your men have checked the old farmhouse. She's eight months pregnant."

"Yes, her husband has made that very clear."

"Well, he's on his way out there right now?"

"Where? With one of our men?"

"No, on his own, with another guy."

"Who?"

"Hank ... somebody." Never did catch his last name."

"Hank, huh." The deputy frowned, looked over his shoulder toward the back of the trailer. "Wait a minute, don't go anywhere." The deputy walked over to a desk, conferred with a sergeant and the higher ranking man stood and walked back with him. He asked Nic, "You know where this farm is?"

"Yes, of course."

"Well, the sun's set and rather than have some deputies searching around in the dark, would you be willing to ride out and show us how to get there?'

"Sure, be glad to."

"Okay deputy, there's your answer. Take an SUV in case you have to go off-road. Remember, if there is an accomplice, he's probably armed." The sergeant turned to Nic, "Thank you Mr. Kober. Better advise anyone who might worry where you are. This may take a while. And, when you get there hang back …stay well away, out of range."

The deputy radioed a nearby SUV police cruiser and arranged to be picked up in the back parking lot. Walking down the hill toward the lot, Nic heard his name called out and turned to see Father Roy rushing toward him.

"Nic, are you okay? You aren't being arrested are you?"

Nic smiled, waiting for Father Roy to catch up. "No, no. Not like the old days. We're trying to find Jackie."

"Jackie, the girl I just married last month?"

"She's missing."

"Missing! Did she have the baby yet?"

They began to walk, following the deputy. "Not yet … so we're doubly concerned. Heading out to the old Simmons place, remember that?"

"How can one forget … den of iniquity, it was. It's still there? Should have been torn down years ago."

The deputy, his phone to his ear, stopped at the edge of the pavement. "We'll wait right here. He'll be right along."

Nic turned back to Father Roy, "How are you holding up?"

"It's hard, Nic, giving last rights to students; young enough to be my grandkids … if I could have any. Now I'm trying to help those with the internal wounds … the ones who watched their friends die. Takes me back to 'Nam'. With all the guns, our country's becoming a war zone."

A dark blue-gray SUV rushed to stop beside the three men. The deputy reached to open the passenger door, as Nic took Roy's hand. "Hang in their father. You're doing what no one else here can do."

Father Roy shook Nic's hand saying, "And you, be careful." He held out a small card. "Here's my number. Call me anytime."

Hank was pressing his cycle as fast as he dared with a passenger on-board. He could tell Joey was not used to riding. In the waning light, concerned to not pass the road leading back into the Simmons farm, Hank slowed from 80 to 60.

Hard braking into a skid was necessary to miss the red pickup with no lights bolting out of a narrow side road; sliding through a sharp right turn, then heading south. It was evident to Hank the driver didn't see his cycle; he and Joey could easily have been broadsided and wiped out.

Joey shouted, "What the..." then louder, "That's it. My pickup! Follow him, Jackie's inside,"

"Okay. I'm gonna stick like glue." Hank turned off his lights.

Two vehicles, a red pickup and a lone motorcycle, bolted down the highway at breakneck speed, nearly invisible in the deepening twilight. After a few miles the driver of the pickup slowed close to the speed limit and turned on his running lights, as if hoping to avoid attracting attention ... apparently not aware of the still-darkened motorcycle following behind.

At the slower speed, the wind noise lessened so Hank could be heard, "I can't cut him off, he'll sideswipe us."

"There's a town, five or six miles ahead with a light. When he stops pull up on the passenger side and I'll grab Jackie."

"Do you see her? I don't see anyone with him?"

"Probably slumped down. Just don't lose him."

"I'll pull up behind. You go passenger side, me driver. We open the doors at the same time."

"Got it."

A small hamlet with a single stop light under a stark mercury bulb came into view. Instead of slowing the pickup maintained highway speed. The light ahead changed from green to red. The driver of a car stopped at the intersection, given a green light, didn't notice the fast-approaching pickup and began to pull out. Having the intersection blocked, Lenny swerved the truck to head behind the car, barely missing it. A tree loomed in front of his headlights. He swerved back to the left, but sideswiped another car approaching the intersection from the opposite direction, and then back to the right crashing into a car parked at side of the road. A gunshot blasted the windshield into a shower of flying glass fragments

Hank never stopped tailing the rear bumper of the red pickup. When it abruptly stopped, Hank avoided crashing into the rear end by tilting to the left and skidding beside the pickup. Joey ran to the passenger door, Hank to the driver's. They swing the doors open … but no Jackie. Lenny was struggling to get a grip on his rifle. Hank placed a choke hold around his neck, dragging him off the seat and pinning him against the side of the truck.

Joey was immediately beside Hank, his face inches from Lenny's, yelling, "Where's Jackie? Where is she?"

He was greeted by a smirk, "You mean the pregnant bitch?"

Joey brought his arm back and broad handed the man across the face, knocking him sideways, blood spirting from his nose. Hank's tight grip was all that kept him from falling. Joey was raising his hand to strike again, but Hank kneed Lenny in the groin, hard. He relaxed his grip, letting him fall on all fours, in a wheezing gasp of sucking air. Hank used his foot to force him to lie face down on the pavement.

Grasping both hands Hank yelled, "Joey, my saddle bags, duct tape."

Wrapping the wrists of the attacker, Hank leaned down, his lips against his ear. "Let's try this again. Where did you say Jackie was?"

Almost in a whisper. "Left her there ... at the farm. I didn't hurt her."

Hank twisted to look toward the onlookers. "Call 911." He stood, put his hands on his hips, bent to each side making sure the Lenny was well restrained, then turned to the bystanders, "This guy is involved in the shooting at the college. Be careful, he's dangerous. But the woman he held hostage needs help, so we gotta go. Tell the cops we'll be back."

Lenny shouted, "You can't leave me like this! You damned ... damned..." Ignoring him, Hank reached into the cab of the truck, pulled out the rifle and emptied its bullets on the ground, then handed it to the man standing closest to him. "Here, lock this in your trunk and give it to the police when they come. You've called '911' right?"

"My wife's talking to them now."

Hank looked at the woman on the phone, "They're sending someone?"

She nodded 'Yes'.

"Remember, this guy is involved in the shooting at the college." Hank leaned toward Lenny, who was face-down, shouting into the pavement. He yelled, "And you, shut the fuck up!' Turning to Joey, "Come on, we'll go back. I know exactly where to turn. We'll find her."

The two men hopped on the motorcycle and Hank accelerated at full power in the direction they'd come from, leaving a man lying face-down on the pavement, hands bound behind his back, yelling a stream of swear words. Innocent bystanders looked on wondering what-the-hell-is-going-on.

Chapter 31

The quietude of Jackie's prayer in late afternoon warmth lulled her into semi-conscious slumber. A painful belly tightening roused her back to being wide-awake. Stretched out to an almost prone position, Jackie had to use both hands to grasp the seat of the chair and lift to a sitting position. It took a moment to regain her bearings. Amazed at not falling off the chair, she remembered teasing her grandfather, Maurice; napping while sitting up straight, to which he'd jokingly answer, 'reposant mes yeux'. She knew this was more serious, beyond just 'resting my eyes'.

Something was different! Listening closely, silence beyond the door ... nothing, no sound. *Is Lenny gone?*

Her fear had ebbed, that paralyzing sensation felt in the truck, the gun barrel pressed hard against her cheek, erratic driving sure to force a discharge. The scratch on the side of her face no longer bled ... just very sore. Jackie felt calm ... dreamlike hope protecting her baby from harm.

An urgent need to pee led her to open the door a crack. Seeing no one, she hurried to the bathroom. The stench again assaulted her. She wasted no time; but her panties fell to the filth encrusted floor so Jackie stepped out of them, leaving her skirt to provide adequate cover.

Jackie knew dusk would fall soon and looked in the kitchen through the camping gear strewn about for a portable light. She saw a flashlight and grabbed it. Thirsty, she found only empty water bottles; nothing coming from the faucet.

Standing among the clutter, Jackie considered her options. *Stay here or hike out and find help?* Warmth trickled down both legs. *Oh, merde, merde ... Not now ... No!* She stepped back, lifted her skirt and looked down at the puddle on the floor. *The belly pains ... contractions. Mon Dieu!* Fright and panic tried to overwhelm ... she caught herself and took a deep breath. *I have got to get out of here!*

She went into the bedroom to put on Emma's sweater; was out the front door faster than most women who aren't pregnant could make it. It was a clear October evening, still warm … but Jackie knew the air temperature would drop quickly. From everything experienced mothers had been saying there should be time to get to the highway before the baby came. *I am too early, not to term yet. And, first-born labor takes hours.* Jackie started to walk on the farm road leading from the house, the flashlight helping to make out the ruts in her path.

Once clear of the trees, vines ready for harvest bordered the road. Having had no food or water for hours, Jackie grabbed a handful of grapes and sucked their juice to quench thirst, swallowing the pulp. After doing it a second time, an instant wave of nausea made her vomit the grape pulp along with the little left in her stomach from lunchtime. Spitting as much bile as she could left an acrid aftertaste, her mouth dry.

From the dirt road, Jackie heard the swoosh of automobile traffic in the distance, across the rows of vines to the right, not ahead. She stopped and listened. It was clear the shortest path to the state highway was to cut through the vineyard, rather than following the road. Jackie turned and walked between the vines, all five or more feet high; the noise created by an occasional car confirming she was on the right course. In the twilight an enormous yellow-orange orb began to rise over the horizon, a harvest moon stretching a shimmering beacon of reflected light across the lake, reaching up to cast a soft glow on the vineyard.

Her belly wasn't cooperating. The uneven ground made walking very difficult with the baby bulging out in front of her slim frame. The contractions increased in intensity. Jackie bent over, taking deep breaths. She recalled the advice given by Francois' grandmother, *'Relax … let nature help you'.* But, Jackie had no intent of having the baby here, now … *no way!*

Quickening the pace proved futile. The ground too uneven … faster movement too cumbersome. Rushing could easily lead to a turned ankle or worse. Bent more and more, she moved forward toward the highway noise heard from passing cars.

The pain hit hard, causing her to stop, squat ... grab the nearest trellis post for support. Jackie never felt pain like this, belly and back together; she gulped in air ... more deep breaths. She realized birthing was upon her. She slowly exhaled and mouthed a single word through her pain, *'RELAX!'*

The pain ebbed. *How can I relax? I'm supposed to deliver in a hospital, with Joey holding my hand! Alone! In a vineyard, shoddy pruning. Really ... Mon Dieu ... How can I do this?* A new contraction wrenched Jackie's belly, seized her back, the trauma telegraphing through her whole body. She screamed ... but with no one to hear. Easing the waistband of the skirt she let the cloth fall, hoping the long tail of her blouse still covered her thighs.

Sweat broke out across her forehead, face and upper body. She shook off the sweater, dropped it. She shouted, *"Mere de Dieu!"*

Jackie twisted toward the full moon, immense in its early rise, hoping its soft light might ease her pain. She focused on the breathing learned in birthing class.... *'RELAX!'* Hands still gripped the trellis post refusing to let go. She widened her stance, squatting lower. *No! No! I cannot do this ... Jesu ...why me? Here? Now?* Tears streaming down her cheeks, she looked to heaven. *Mon Dieu, sauver moi.*

A hard contraction ratcheted through her, the pain sharper, more pronounced. Jackie screamed, tried to swear, unable to form the words ... her mind receding into chaos. No longer able to grasp the trellis post, she let go, slumping to the ground ... eyes closing, consciousness phasing away.

The next contraction brought back awareness; bright moonlight bathing her face ... thankfully mirrored rather than direct from the sun. Eyes wide, contours of the lunar landscape brilliantly magnified, Jackie continued to take deep breathes. *I will have this baby!* She grabbed the trellis post and grunted, *"Mon Dieu! Mon Dieu!"* into a low squat. *Must it be so damned hard?*

The contractions came frequently. Jackie exhaled in grunts, then yelled through clenched teeth, *"JOEY. WHERE. ARE. YOU?"* The sensation of having the biggest bowel movement ever led to a body shaking wail, a guttural howl of women throughout the ages. Jackie squatted lower, surprised to feel the baby sliding down ... coming ... breach? She reached down and felt skin not her own. Instinctively she took a deep breath and pushed down again; the baby slid out as if in a rush. She put her hand below and caught him beneath his torso, then steadied his head gently into her free hand.

Being off balance she plopped backwards, down onto her skirt, holding the baby. Tears streaming down her cheeks. She stared ... *a son!* ... glistening in amniotic birth fluid. Winded, dazed, she sat immobilized, just wanting to be still. In her head Chloe's voice was impatient and insistent, *"Jacqueline! Jacqueline!"* Jackie gulped in air, the pain in her abdomen and back easing. She wiped her finger over the tiny lips to clear an air passage and heard his first cry ... weak and high pitched ... a keening. Jackie tore her blouse open and held him against her skin, then picked up the sweater and wrapped it over him, gently rocking back and forth. In the soft moonlight, she could not believe the beauty of her newborn son. Emotion shook her body, from fear to joy, thanks to exhilaration.

She sat, the cord still connected, with nothing to cut it ... and afterbirth yet to come out. The baby snuggled against her, unseeing eyes open as if looking at her in wonderment at this new environment. But Jackie wasn't prepared for what to do ... how to cope ... in the middle of a vineyard in full bloom. She moved the sweater to see the beautiful boy she'd lived with for the past eight months ... every detail of his feet and hands, prematurely small, but perfect ... even the wisp of hair on his head. His eyes called to mind her grandfather, Maurice, with his rock-solid stature; her father making his little girl laugh; and Joey ... *this baby looks so much like Joey. He'll grow to be as pleasant and peaceful, strong and competent.* Jackie felt the warmth of Joey that stormy, snowy night more than ever before ... being protected ... fulfilled. *My son's eyes ... Joey's peace and wonder.* Nothing ever meant so much, this baby, in her arms. *Anything for you ... anything! Mon Dieu, Merci, Merci!* She held her baby closer. *But no one will see us in this vineyard; even know we're here...*

Jackie wasn't sure how long they sat before hearing the distinctive sound of a motorcycle. It came from the highway, abated, then was gone. But it soon came back, from the direction of the farm road ... not going very fast. Jackie hollered and reached for the flashlight, grabbed the trellis post, and managed to stand while still holding the baby. She shined the light toward the dirt road. But the cycle passed, so she pointed it upward, hoping whoever was on the cycle would see a shaft of white light. A thin fog had formed, spreading the flashlight beam into a soft glow; the brightness of the moon making it hardly visible.

The cycle proceeded toward the house; then the engine was silent. Jackie hollered as loudly as she could. It was too much; she was forced to sit down again. The baby began to cry. Jackie needed a moment to catch her breath.

Joey and Hank called out to Jackie and ran into the house. They used Hank's small flashlight to avoid falling over the gear and trash scattered on the floor. Finding no one, they came back out on the porch. Joey said, "Now what?"

Hank pressed his elbow against Joey's arm and whispered, "Look and listen."

At first the faint sound was foreign to them. Then, Hank's trained ear recognized it.

"I think there's a baby out there."

"What? A baby?"

"*Shhh!*"

"Yeah, I hear it now. That's not a baby, that's Jackie!"

"... coming from the vineyard."

The moonlight, disbursed by the fog, made it possible for the men to head back down the dirt road; Joey running, Hank limping as fast as he could. Joey stopped to listen, making sure he didn't go too far. *"Yes, there is a baby!"* He turned toward the gulping, raspy sound and saw a faint glow above the vines.

He yelled, "Jackie?" Then heard Jackie scream his name. The contour of the vineyard didn't let him see her; he ran between the rows closest to the glow.

He saw Jackie huddled on the ground, holding the light with one hand, clutching a blanket in the other. He yelled, "Jackie ... Jackie!"

She dropped the light and reached out toward Joey. He rushed and knelt in front of her, encircling her in his arms. "Oh God, Jackie, are you alright?" He drew her close as she exhaled a single deep sob, kissing his neck, then his cheek. She pulled back, "Look! We have a son."

"Oh, my God, you had the baby?"

Out of breath, dizzy, the rows of vines undulating in bright moonlight, unfocused, his head reeling ... Joey pitched back on his heels. He closed his eyes and pressed his fingers against the bridge of his nose, hard. He took a deep breath and exhaled, tears welled in his eyes, "Where? When?"

"Right here, just now."

Joey bent in close, the light of the moon spotlighting the baby's face. "Look at you little guy." He smiled, "You're beautiful!"

"But Joey, I don't know what to do."

Jackie held the baby toward Joey so he could pick him up. "Just be careful of the cord."

Laying her head on Joey's shoulder, she wrenched in gulping sobs. Joey wasn't sure if sorrow, joy ... or just release. Without taking both hands from holding the baby, he pressed tight against her. "Hey, hey, it's okay now. Everything's gonna be okay." He hesitated. "You're shivering."

Hank came up; he stood a few feet away.

Jackie jerked her head up, "Hank! Where did you come from? *Mon Dieu*, you come from nowhere."

"You okay?"

"It's getting chilly out here."

Hank stripped off his leather motorcycle jacket. "Here, put this on". He held it open so she could easily put her arms in.

"We need to get you some attention, pronto! Joey, you're phone's dead right? You keep 'em as warm as you can; I'm gonna trot back and see if I can raise anybody on my radio. If not, I'll ride out and get help."

Hank moved as fast as he could. Coming out of the row of vines onto the farm road, he saw headlights coming toward him. Glad to see a police light bar spanning, the roof, he stood waving his arms. The SUV stopped short of where Hank stood, keeping him in the beam of its headlights. Hank yelled, "The woman you're looking for is out here in the vineyard." Both front doors of the SUV opened and troopers stepped out, guns drawn. Hank instinctively raised his hands, but continued speaking, "She just gave birth to a baby and needs medical help. Call an ambulance?"

The troopers stood taking aim on Hank. "Are you the man who kidnapped her?"

"No, no! I've got his wrists taped together. I'll explain after you call the ambulance."

The driver shouted, "You stay right where you are and keep your hands where I can see them! A newborn baby you say?"

"Yeah, just between the vines, down this row."

The driver grabbed his radio mic and asked for an ambulance and backup.

The troopers approached slowly, "And who are you?"

As soon as Hank divulged his name, the trooper from the passenger side said, "Hank? You're the Hank no one can find? My sergeant wants to talk with you. Listen, I'm gonna frisk you and then cuff you … just so you don't disappear. We'll just take a ride back to the Command Center."

Hank saw Nic getting out of the SUV, a large First Aid kit in hand. Nic shouted, "Hank, where's Jackie? What's this about a baby?"

Still holding his hands high, Hank pointed at the specific row. "Just down there, you'll see her and the baby. Joey's with them. Grab a blanket; she may be in shock. And the baby, I don't know!"

The deputy who'd been driving said to Nic, "Go ahead, I'll grab the blanket and be right behind you."

The first deputy quickly satisfied himself Hank was unarmed and placed handcuffs on his wrists. Hank asked, "Is this legal? I'm a veteran you know; this any way to treat a disabled vet?"

"Yeah, we'll talk legalities later. My sergeant is an ex-Marine too. If I don't get you in front of him, I'll be the one who's toast."

"Oh ... well ... Semper Fi. Recognition for defending our country."

"Listen, I'm only detaining you for questioning. Now where did you say the kidnapper is?"

"I'll explain, but let's get down to the main road so that ambulance doesn't drive on by, they need to get to the mother and baby ... now!"

"Sure, get me away from my partner. Ever hear of GPS; we have it on all our cruisers. The ambulance will come right here. Now, for the last time before I get angry, the kidnapper? You said you had him handcuffed. Where?"

"South on the highway, six or seven miles, there's a traffic light. He's there next to the carjacked pickup truck. I left him lying face down on the pavement. A bystander was calling 911 so the police are probably already there."

The trooper smiled, "No way. I gotta call this in. You better not be kidding me."

"No, no. Go ahead."

The trooper's radio crackled with the voice of his partner. "The mother and baby look okay, but the baby's premature. Have the EMTs bring a stretcher. Advise they seem to be okay, but to hurry. She needs attention, definitely fluids. And the cord, the cord ... I'm gonna wait for the EMTs to cut the cord."

As soon as the trooper called in the update for the ambulance, he continued with the potential to find the kidnapper on the highway to the south. The Command Center confirmed that a County police cruiser did indeed find a man handcuffed face down on the highway and was ordered to bring him in for questioning. After signing off, the trooper looked at Hank. "So you are for real."

"Yeah, why does everyone treat me like a ghost? I was Special Ops, man."

"You must be good … plenty to share with the sergeant." He looked toward the highway. "Hear that? The ambulance…"

Norman hung up the Carriage House landline phone. He'd been holding it for over half an hour trying to get through to the one law enforcement officer he knew, the Chief of Police in Rochester. He shrugged his shoulders, looking at Chloe, Emma and Will, "He's fully briefed on what's going on, even has his force on the lookout for Joey's truck. With the State Police involved, he's sure it'll show up."

Will asked, "How do you know him?"

"Oh, you know, small business owner in the central city … meetings on neighborhood policing, then solicitations for the Mayor's Ball. We rubbed elbows from time-to-time. He's a hard working guy, but with all the guns, drugs and gangs, kinda like shoveling shit against the tide."

"So, what's next?" Will asked. Chloe and Emma sat back, glanced at each other, wishing they had an answer. Norman remained silent.

The loud ringer on the phone interrupted everyone's thought. Will stepped over and answered, "Hello."

After a long pause, he said, "It's Nic Kober. He's with Jackie and Joey."

Into the phone Will said, "What did you say … a baby … what baby?"

Emma shot out of her chair and grabbed the phone from Will's hand. "Nic, Nic, it's Emma. Will can't hear. What are you saying? Is she okay … the baby, is the baby okay?" A broad smile came over her face. Chloe stood to be beside Emma who put her hand over the transmitter and shared, "Jackie had the baby … it's a boy."

311

'Wait Nic, wait. You say they're both okay … Well as far as you know … going to the Clinic … Who? … Oh, EMTs in an ambulance … Just a second."

Emma turned to Chloe and whispered, "Any questions?"

"Is Jackie okay?"

"Yes, Nic, you did say Jackie's okay? She wasn't hurt?" Emma listened, then said, "Okay, we'll head into the Clinic. I don't know how to thank you for calling."

Emma hung up the phone, and threw her arms around Chloe, tears running down her cheeks. As she released her hold, Emma said, "Oh God, Chloe, it may be all right after all."

Chloe wiped a tear from her eye. "Can you and Will give us a ride, we only have the boat."

Will said, "Of course, but there's no emergency as such. I'm sure the doctor will need some time."

Emma said, "Will, get a jacket if you want one."

Chloe stepped over to Norman. Looking up at him, she said, "You have too many guns in your country." She poked him in the chest, hard. "See all the grief they cause. First Vicki, now this. You're lucky Joey found Jackie. And if you say anything other than *D'accord*, I will slap you!

Chapter 32

Emma and Chloe rushed through the entrance of the Clinic. Several people standing in the lobby forced them to weave a path toward the reception desk, their urgency pulling the receptionist's eyes from a computer monitor. Emma breathlessly asked, "Is Jackie O'Donnell here?"

Seasoned in handling emotional situations, the woman frowned and looked over her reading glasses, "And you are?"

"Her grandparents ... both of us."

She smiled under a raised eyebrow, "Oh, Deborah's relations. Nice to meet you. Yes, yes, just a while ago, Jackie and her baby, brought in by ambulance. The doctors are examining them. I'll let Deborah know you're here. Please have a seat."

"Well, do you have any idea how they are?"

"I don't have that information. I'll page."

A few minutes later, Joey's mother came through the double doors marked DO NOT ENTER in large red letters. She smiled as she approached Emma, throwing one arm around her, extending her free hand toward Chloe. "Jackie seems to be okay ... but still more to do." She pulled back to see Emma's face, her smile broadening, "And, you two have a great-grandson ... cute little guy ... underweight being weeks early, but he seems to be fine." Deborah turned to Chloe. "Happily, we can handle everything here; we don't have to transfer to Rochester."

The catch in Emma's throat kept her response to the tears running down her cheeks. Chloe pulled Deborah to her saying, "*Merci, merci!* And you, grand-mere ... *You* are a grand-mere!"

"It's wonderful!" Deborah paused, catching her breath. "I was so concerned about Jackie, and then they brought her in ... with the baby. As soon as we had them situated I had to sit down."

"And Joey, where's Joey?" Emma asked.

"Oh, I'm sorry. He came in the ambulance with his family. He's so excited." Deborah glanced at the many people overflowing the waiting area. "I'd better get back ... we're full ... several people injured in the shooting. I'll keep you posted as soon as we know more."

The too-small waiting area, painted in soft colors muted further by low wattage table lamps, Emma asked Will to stop pacing back and forth, his hands behind his back like a commanding general expecting word on the outcome of a battle. "You're disturbing the other people. They're stressed out too."

Will asked, "What?"

Emma, realizing Will couldn't hear, patted the seat beside her. As Will sat down, Chloe continued to chatter in Emma's other ear about how hard it is to acquire a gun in France. Norman stood against a far wall, overhearing Chloe, but staying away to avoid an argument in public. He wondered why he didn't grab a double scotch before coming into town ... the idle wait amplifying his stress. He came to attention when Chloe asked Emma, "How many people die in the United States of gunshot wounds?"

Emma looked at Will, "Do you know?"

"I've read 30,000 a year."

Chloe leaned forward to look past Emma at Will. "That's terrible ... and you people do nothing about it?"

"Oh, I agree," Will said, "we have far more guns than any developed country, about one per person. Problem is, they tend to be used ... too many innocent people get shot. About 80 people die ... everyday."

"In France, our worry is terrorists; here you have more danger from guns!"

"You're probably right. We have a problem; just don't want to own up to it."

Norman barked, "Chloe, enough about the guns!" Chloe flashed a scowl toward Norman that he'd come to know: *If you want to get laid anytime in the near future, Back Off!*

It seemed a long wait before Joey walked through the double doors. After quick hugs with the women and handshakes with the men, Joey said, "They've got Jackie cleaned up. She was terribly dehydrated ... needs fluids. Now, she's asleep. They'll be keeping her here for observation."

"And the baby?"

"The baby ... diagnostics so far have all been positive. He seems to be a tough little guy coming a month early."

"How much does he weigh?"

"Five pounds, 12 ounces. Normal range for a premature birth. In a while I'll see if we can all go down to the nursery and view him through the window ... they don't want him exposed to outsiders just yet."

Joey glanced at Emma and Chloe. "Jackie's doctor is here. Rushed in when he heard." Joey paused, considering what to say next. "Scarred the crap out of me. Told me vaginal breech, premature ... extremely low success rate. Said we're very, very fortunate. If Jackie'd been anywhere near a hospital he'd have demanded a C-Section He's amazed she did it all by herself ... alone. Just amazed!"

Emma reached back to her chair, "I need to sit down."

Chloe said, "Not so uncommon in France. We often let nature take its course. Hesitate to reach for the scalpel."

Joey, spotting Nic walking through the entrance to the waiting room, turned on his heel, and strode to him, engulfing him in a tight embrace. "Oh, man ... You saved us Nic. You saved us!"

Nic seeming almost embarrassed, smiled, "Na Joey, I didn't do anything."

"Except tell us exactly where to find Jackie. How can we ever thank you?"

"Seeing you like this is thanks enough. Jackie's alright? And the baby?"

"Yes, yes, thanks to you." Joey turned toward the grandmothers, "I was just telling the folks, things look good for both of them so far. Want to stay a while and see the baby all cleaned up?"

"Not right now. I just wanted to make sure they're okay. Let's do it tomorrow. A picking crew's starting up in about six hours, so I'll have a non-stop day."

"Oh yeah. Good luck. I'll be over when I get a chance."

"No you won't! You stay with Jackie, she needs you now. That abduction was traumatic. Don't you leave her side. You hear me? I'll check your crop."

"Just one question, where's Hank?"

Nic smiled, "The police will be questioning Hank for a while. Last I saw him he was being escorted by two troopers into the Command Center. On the ride back with the troopers I got the impression they have a lot of concern over who killed the shooter at the college."

"But, they must be glad it stopped the carnage."

Nic sighed, "Of course, but they still need answers. And, then, there's the kidnapper found at the scene of an accident. One of the troopers asked Hank why he left."

"Yeah," Joey used a defensive tone, "to find Jackie. What would you have done?"

"You're absolutely right. Just pesky laws complicating things. So expect to see the police looking for you."

"Well, right now, I'm staying at Jackie's side."

"As you should. Anyhow, Hank, being Special Forces or whatever in the military, he's probably the only guy around here skilled enough to make a shot that long."

Nic felt a tap on his shoulder. Turning, he said, "Father Roy, good to see you."

"How's everyone doing?"

Joey answered, "Jackie and the baby seem to be fine ... more tests and observation."

"Oh, thank God. I heard Jackie was found and the baby had come. Just want to see if there's anything I can do."

Chloe stood and approached the priest. "Father, since the baby is premature can he be baptized?"

"Tonight? Joey, I thought you said the baby is okay."

"As far as they can tell."

"Well," Chloe continued, "isn't it a good idea. He's underweight."

"I'm certainly not against baptism," Father Roy said, "but the request needs to come from the parents."

"Oh, okay. I hadn't thought of that." Joey said, "Let's go back and see if Jackie's awake."

Nic stepped away saying, "I'm gonna shove off."

Working his way across the waiting room, Father Roy said 'Hello' to Emma, Will and Norman, plus a few parishioners he knew. He promised to come back to one couple when they told him their son was in recovery from surgery. Joey led him through the double doors.

Norman turned to Will. "Believe that? We can't get near her and the priest just saunters in like he owns the place."

"He's with Joey … the husband. Plus, he's well connected."

"How's that?"

"I think the doctors give the clergy some latitude because they know they can't always do it alone. God plays a part. Just believing helps patients heal. And a priest is the most direct link in the belief of the faithful."

"Some power…"

"Reduces the fear and anguish."

"Yeah, still it defies logic."

"I agree. It's a mystery … even in our world demanding answers. We call God 'He' even though we know God exists way beyond any boundaries we set; can't be hemmed in.

"You lost me Will … let's just say priests are given leeway … to break through the barriers."

"That's true, The HIPPA rules probably trimmed their sails a lot, but they still have, as you say, 'leeway'."

"Don't understand it. Never have, never will. To be honest, not sure I want to; priests and ministers with all their 'don't this … don't that'. I get all I can handle from my women.

Joey guided Father Roy past the glassed-in nursery and pointed out his son … an undersized little bundle. "They tell me he's stable, just low weight."

"How low?"

"Five pounds, 12 ounces."

"That isn't too low is it? I mean being early."

"The doctor told me it's in a normal range."

"He sure is a cute little man. Congratulations. I'm glad to see there's no harm done."

Walking to Jackie's room, Father Roy asked, "How is she taking all this?"

"Her focus has been on the baby. She hasn't said anything about the abduction. Thankfully she wasn't hurt; other than a nasty scratch, really a gouge, on her cheek. Hopefully, not serious."

"There may be wounds you can't see. Be extra gentle; and when she starts to talk about it, let her. She may need some counseling to get any deep seated fears out."

"I'll be by her side. I'm not going anywhere."

The men looked into the room. Seeing Jackie asleep, Father Roy turned to Joey and whispered, "Don't wake her. I'll check back in the morning."

In the dim light of the doorway Joey's face gazing at his wife gave Father Roy pause. *Compassion … stress and worry; yearning and affection. Such earnest love; one to another. Akin to our priestly love of the Lord; but with the added risk of human frailty.* Father Roy held out his card, "Call me if you need me … anytime."

"Thanks Father."

"You stay with her now; I'll find my way out."

"Oh, I'd better guide Jackie's grandparents to the nursery and show them the baby or I'll never hear the end of it."

"Good idea. Welcome to being a father."

Leading the way, Joey asked, "Did you ever want to be a father?"

"Of course. It's not an easy decision to be a priest. On days like today, I'm glad I'm here to help. But, as I get older I have to wonder why the Church is so insistent on celibacy. Does ordination have to be exclusive, devoid of the graces and joys marriage and family bring. Anyhow, Joey, you've been blessed. Take care of your family." *Yes, raising a family, the blessed long-term challenge!*

Joey guided the grandmothers to the small nursery, Will and Norman following along. The maternity nurse brought the baby over to the viewing window. She smiled, cradling the baby in her arms. Joey was surprised to see the two grandmothers press forward, side-by-side, Emma exhaling, her voice going from a whisper to a high pitch. "Oh, my my ... isn't he cute." Chloe, in a much lower octave, agreed, "Oh, *oui, oui.* He is a keeper!" The baby, as if on cue, wiggled his mouth into a broad smile, squinting still unseeing eyes as if in greeting.

"Oh my god, look Chloe, he's saying 'Hello' to us"

"You can see, he will be smart."

Emma put her arm around Chloe, giving her a gentle hug. Chloe mirrored the gesture.

Norman and Will edged up to see. "Look Will," Emma said, "isn't he a gem!" The nurse lifted the baby a bit higher so the men could get a better view.

"Yes, yes, of course." He stepped back giving Norman more room.

Norman smiled, "Cute little guy, isn't he."

Chloe glanced Norman's way. "Cute, *oui*, but beautiful ... *magnifique!'*

As soon as the men stepped back the women pressed against the window again making cooing sounds, as if the baby could hear them.

Norman looked at Will and Joey. "Are they always like this ... women with babies?"

Joey shrugged, "Beats me..."

Will sighed, "Yeah, yeah they are ... these two are a little more carried away than usual. All the tension from the trauma of Jackie missing, then the baby coming early." He turned to Joey, "You're really lucky ... Congratulations!"

Norman echoed, "Yes, yes, Congratulations!"

Emma twisted her head toward Will, "I heard that Will. We are not frazzled from before. This is an exceptional baby ... so perfect in every detail."

"You're right there, Emma." Will stepped further away, motioning to Norman and Joey to follow. "I'm always amazed at how fascinating women find newborns... every one is beautiful. Probably from carrying babies to term, becoming their nurturers. It's the only domain men can't take away ... conceiving and giving birth. Best we men stay out of it."

Norman said, "What man would want to get into it?"

"Good point."

Emma and Chloe mouthed, "Thank you" to the nurse and turned toward the men.

"Oh, Joey, he is so beautiful!" Emma said, giving him a kiss on the cheek, "We'll both help in any way we can."

"Yes, thanks."

"Any chance of seeing Jackie?"

"When I checked with Father Roy she was sound asleep. I think we'll have to wait until tomorrow."

"Probably just as well," Norman said, "the great-grand-meres have had a stressful day."

Chloe gave Norman a gentle jab to the ribs. "Must you keep calling me great-grand-mere?"

Joey stayed by Jackie's side after her grandmothers left. Sitting looking at his wife, he wondered if the peaceful expression on her face was a release from the stress of being abducted or satisfaction in giving birth. He dozed off himself; he wasn't sure how long when a loud beep from one of the monitors hooked to Jackie woke him. Jackie was twisting in her hospital bed, moving from stretching her body, then into a fetal position, and back again. Her eyes were closed, but her mouth was working as if in a silent scream. Joey hoped she wasn't having a convulsion.

The clock displayed 2:14.

The night nurse rushed in and put her hand on Jackie's arm while she checked the readings on the monitors. She said to Joey, "A nightmare. I'll just stay here until she wakes up."

Jackie opened her eyes ... wide ... blinked and asked, "*Ou suis-je* ... Uh, where, where am I." Joey stood by her side in her line of vision. Taking her hand he said, "You're in the Clinic, Jackie."

"Oh, *oui* ... yes. And the baby, he is here too?'

"Right down the hall in the nursery."

The nurse said, "Everything looks good Jackie. Do you need anything?"

"Come back in a few minutes."

After the nurse left, Joey asked, "Are you okay?'

"I think so. I dreamt that man who attacked me; he came back and stole our son."

"Oh, no Jackie. He's in jail. The baby is here safe and sound."

Joey leaned in closer to Jackie. She put her head on his shoulder and began to sob, the intensity throwing her body into a paroxysm leading Joey to hold her ever more tightly. Easing onto the bed beside her, he whispered the only words he could find, 'I love you', over and over ... hoping Jackie's fear and anguish would flow out and away.

Chapter 33

The doctors decided to keep Jackie under observation for a few days to be sure there were no internal injuries or any psychological trauma resulting from her kidnapping. Also, a plastic surgeon was scheduled to treat the gouge on her cheek caused by the rifle shoved against her face. Hopefully the repair would leave no scar.

Father Roy stopped in mid-morning as he'd promised. He found Joey at Jackie's side. He avoided bringing up baptism, not wanting to press the parents on the subject. But as soon as Jackie convinced him she and the baby were okay, she asked if her son could be baptized, and soon, given his premature weight. "Of course. I just have a few questions. Since you're both here, is now okay?"

Jackie took the lead in satisfying Father Roy's concern about intending to raise their son in the faith. Then, Father Roy asked, "And, who will be godparents?"

"We'd like to ask Joey's Uncle Nicholas to be godfather, and my cousin Carolyn to be godmother."

"Carolyn is a Catholic?"

"*Oui*, belongs to a parish in Rochester. I know she goes to Mass.

"That being the case, there should be no problem with having her be godmother. But, I know Nicholas, have for years, and while he is a very good and Christian man, he's not a Catholic."

"That's a problem?" Joey asked.

"I'm afraid so. Godparents need to be baptized Catholics and active members of a parish. I know Nicholas is neither. I'm sorry, he can be a witness, but he can't be the godfather."

It was finally decided that Will, a Catholic in good standing, would be godfather … in spite of being a septuagenarian.

Late morning, Jackie's grandmothers came to visit. Jackie sat on the side of the hospital bed, wearing a robe Joey had brought from home. Both grandmothers sat on the straight-backed side chairs provided for family and friends, designed to encourage short visits.

After being assured Jackie felt alright, although still fatigued, Emma asked, "And the baby?"

"Oh, he is better than expected. The doctors are giving him tests this morning; so we can't see him now. And they want to keep him here to be sure he is stable and gaining weight."

"Well, that's good," Emma said. "Joey called and told us the Baptism will be here tomorrow at 3 o'clock. We're glad he's being baptized, aren't we Chloe?"

"D'accord!" Chloe said, "Given his low weight, do it now. The priest agrees?""

"Oui, oui. Father Roy stopped in this morning. He asked only if we intend to raise our son as a Catholic. I told him I intend to pass on the faith to our children. I think my years in the convent school; living with all the ritual, gives him hope I won't abandon it. And Joey said he will be by my side. Father Roy said he trusts we'll do the right thing; he is a very understanding man."

"And well he should," Chloe said, "after all Joey is Catholic and you were married in the Church."

"Do you have any clothes to wear?"

"My clothes from yesterday ... ruined. Joey's bringing fresh from home."

"Have you selected a name yet?" Chloe asked. "You know you will need that for the baptism."

"We had not finished discussing names ... I thought we had three more weeks. So we decided this morning. Our baby is strong, he needs a strong name. We picked Nicholas."

"Oh," Emma said, "I was hoping you'd name him after your father."

We discussed that, but I rejected Ronald, not because it is a bad name ... it just reminds me of so many sad times ... the

way he and mere died. So, the middle name will honor papa …
Nicholas Ronald it will be."

"No Maurice? " Chloe asked.

"Sorry grand-mere. I am not comfortable with Maurice
here in the United States. It sounds too old fashioned. Please
don't take offense."

"Well, it would have been a nice gesture. But why
Nicholas?"

"After Joey's uncle … the fact that without him the baby
and I might not have lived … he knew where to find us.

"Oh," Chloe said, "a life-long commitment by your
grand-pere, dwarfed by a split-second guess?"

"Grand-mere, it is so much more than that … our
vineyard might not have survived without his help … and his
love of nature, his gentle personality."

Joey burst into the room, Jackie's clothes draped over his
arm. "Oh, hello. I didn't expect company so early." He walked
to Jackie to kiss her on the cheek; she found his lips.

Joey turned to the two older women. "I saw Will and
Norman in the waiting room."

"Yes," Chloe said, "we're going to lunch, after we need
to go shopping … a sale ends today. Left alone the men will
have a new plan … *sans* shopping."

Emma smiled, "We'll come back later."

When the grandmothers left, Joey had a look of concern.
"It seemed pretty intense when I walked in."

"Naming our son Nicholas took some explaining. They
would have preferred my *pere* and *grand-pere.*"

"Yeah, I was afraid of that. But I trust you handled it?"

"I think so."

"Probably as well as you answered all Father Roy's
concerns earlier. I was proud of you. I wasn't aware of how
much you know about the Catholic Church."

"Living with the nuns, how does one avoid it?"

"But we never discussed it. Or your interest in having
our son baptized."

"With Emma and Chloe both worrying because Nicholas is premature, better we get it done now. That will put their minds at ease ... no chance of the baby going to 'Limbo'."

"What?"

"You know, Original Sin ... the soul of a baby not yet baptized cannot go to heaven. It is a traditional Catholic teaching. But, at school, one of the younger nuns explained that thinking is no longer correct. Emma and Chloe probably cannot accept that."

"And the baptism will get them off your back?"

"Joey, you read my mind."

Joey was still with Jackie early in the afternoon following a visit with a psychologist when he was advised two State Police investigators were at the desk, asking to see Jackie. He went out to meet them, a man and a woman, middle-aged, dressed in muted grays and blues of plain clothes officers. They showed Joey their badges and introduced themselves. Both carried the non-committal demeanor of asking questions rather than providing answers; poker-faced with flat emotionless voices, but with firm handshakes. "Just a few minutes ... nothing distressing." Reluctantly, Joey allowed them to follow him to Jackie's room. She was in bed, the back raised to a sitting position. After introductions, the woman took the lead, the man receding to the doorway, notebook and pen in hand.

The woman officer smiled, "Congratulations on your new son. He's doing well?"

"*Oui*, he is healthy ... needs to gain weight. One minute I am running, next he is born." Jackie smiled, "I am so happy!"

"We're glad to hear that. And we'll be brief."

Jackie nodded for the officer to continue.

"When you arrived at the college yesterday, did you see anything out of the ordinary?"

"No."

"As you drove into the parking lot, to the space where you intended to park? Anything unusual?"

"As I came to the parking place, some people were coming out of the building.

"Any strangers? Someone you don't know?"

"No, people I've seen before. In the offices where I tutor. They were together."

"Did you see anyone alone?"

"I did not notice."

"A strange car or motorcycle?"

"No. I only go to park. It was hot in the truck and I am big and uncomfortable. I went to the reserved place, gathered my things, pushed down on the door handle to get out. The handle, it is pulled out of my hand and I am shoved across the seat ... a gun pressed against my cheek."

"You mean by the hijacker."

"*Oui*, Lenny."

"We have him in custody. He pointed a hand gun at you?"

"*Non, non*, not a hand gun."

"A pistol?"

"No, a long gun. He needed to get it in the truck. My face was in the way." Jackie pointed to the gauze bandage on her cheek. "He shoved me to the side, the gun made a deep cut."

"The end of the gun ... a rifle?'

"*Oui*, a rifle, pointing up toward the roof, against my cheek."

"We will need to talk about that later; in a separate visit."

Joey thought the interview was ending, but the officer continued. She reached over touching the top of Jackie's hand. "We don't want to overburden you now, but, just bear with us another minute." She stepped back to try a new approach. "Let's go back before that happened, before you were attacked. Please, if you would, close your eyes and try to visualize."

Jackie nodded agreement, closing her eyes.

"You're pulling in to park. Do you see anything out of the ordinary?"

Jackie shook her head 'No'.

"Take your time." Everyone remained quiet. Next, the officer asked, "Strangers … anyone you haven't seen before?"

Jackie says, "No strangers."

"Vehicles parked oddly?"

Jackie opened her eyes and looked at the officer shaking her head, saying, "*Non … non*

"You saw nothing to indicate more people were involved in the attack? Other than the shooter in the tower and Lenny?"

"Only people coming out of the building … people I know. I never saw the shooter. I did not know what was happening."

Joey saw Jackie's face harden, the muscles in her jaw and cheeks tensing up. *I'd better end this … now!* He was about to call a halt when Jackie spoke up. "*Ecouter* … Listen," she said. The strength and inflection of her voice told him he'd better let her continue. "Lenny was yelling, swearing … he drives crazy … away from the college … angry, so angry, even because I am pregnant. If we do not die in a car crash, I am sure he will kill me and the baby."

"So," the officer asked, "You were sitting on the passenger side while all this was happening. He wasn't trying to restrain you?"

Joey saw Jackie's face cloud over. "The gun," she said, "the rifle … its barrel against my cheek the whole time. It pushes me against the door." Jackie sat up straighter; a cold-steel gaze Joey had not seen before directed into the investigator's eyes, her voice stronger, hard, demanding undivided attention. "I cannot move … blood streaming down, dripping off my chin. I am afraid the gun will go off. My whole face … gone!" Jackie paused to catch her breath. She leaned closer to the woman. "What if he locked me in that room? Never left? Nicholas born in that filth … disgusting!" Jackie held the woman's gaze and asked, "How many died?"

"Too many! Happily you weren't injured…"

"No, not this time! My parents, they die when I am nine … a plane crash over Eastern Europe … a bomb. Here, the United States protects from bombs. But guns, you let them flow

327

freely … little control. Not in France," Jackie wagged her finger, *"Non … non!"*

"Well, we have laws…"

Jackie's voice rose, "Ineffective… You investigate after the killing, not control before. So many guns here." Her voice choked up.

Joey realized she was holding back tears. "Yeah," he said, "after every mass shooting, wall-to-wall TV coverage. But no action … no assault weapons ban, no background checks. Congress ignores it."

Jackie stared at the officer, "What about the victims, our rights. It is not safe here."

Joey was seeing a side of Jackie he hadn't seen before. Strength, triggered by her anger. His wife growing into a mature woman. "I don't think Jackie has any more to offer right now."

The officer agreed, "You've been a big help. I hope we can meet again … soon." She reached her hand to touch the top of Jackie's, "Get some rest."

As soon as they left, Joey put his arms around his wife and drew her to him. With tears running down her cheeks, she said, "Thank God we made it out into that vineyard…" Pulling back to look at him, she said, smiling, "Joey, it was a miracle, the birth … so hard; but with the moonlight I could see … Nicholas in the beautiful, beautiful moonlight."

Joey squeezed her shoulders, "I know love … remember that, not what came before."

Joey gave Jackie a kiss and said, "I'm really proud of you. How you got your point across."

"What point? Too many guns … a waste of breath. They do not hear me … I go too far?"

"No, I think they heard you. I'm proud of you."

"So, you do not mind I speak out?"

"You know how you prune vines and canopy leaves differently than I do? I don't question how you do that; and you don't question how I do mine. So, let's just leave it that you speak your mind your way, and I'll speak mine my way. No need to second guess each other. Okay?"

"D'accord."

Joey glanced away in thought. "You know, I don't think those cops realize I'm the guy who was with Hank when we caught up with that Lenny guy."

      ℰ   ℭ

The Baptism was a short, to-the-point ceremony, held in the small room adjacent to the nursery. Jackie sat, holding her son. Joey stood on one side, Carolyn and Will on the other. The grandmothers gathered around; three nurses stood on the sidelines observing. They waited the few minutes until uncle Nic could be present. The baby, perfection in miniature, slept quietly, stirring only when Father Roy poured water over his head and the gently rubbed chrism on his head and chest in the Sign of the Cross … totally unaware of his acceptance into the oldest of Christian communities. All were moved, having this tiny person alive and well; the spiritual dimension of the simple ceremony being particularly significant when Father Roy thanked the Lord for this Gift of Life amidst the pain and loss two days before. Even Norman, observing through the range finder of his camera, was touched.

After the Baptism, with baby Nicholas returned to the nursery, Chloe invited everyone to an early dinner at a nearby restaurant. Nic bumped Will's elbow to get his attention. "I've got to get back … the pickers are working and we can't get behind with the crushing."

"Oh, okay. I'll catch up with you later."

Nic said 'Goodbye' to Jackie and Joey, explaining why he needed to leave and waved to the group.

Dusk was falling when Will drove up to the Kober Vineyards crusher. Nic walked toward his car, opening the door for him to get out. "Perfect timing. We're just taking a quick break. Need to let my crew get something to eat." He gestured toward blue crates neatly stacked near the crush pad. "Afraid it may be a long night; we can't let these grapes sit."

Will joined Nic in leaning against his car. "It's a lot harder than most people think, isn't it … running a vineyard."

"Ya gotta love this business or it'll overwhelm ya."

"Wow, if those crates are all full, that's a lot of grapes."

"Just a fraction of what we picked today. Already crushed the rest. And there's more to come. Long night ahead."

"Listen," Will waited for Nic to look back at him, "I just want to say it's too bad you aren't the godfather. I know Jackie and Joey wanted you. It's nice they named the baby after you, but I was hoping you could be godfather."

Nic looked down in thought. "Well, I'm honored to have a namesake." He looked up at Will, "I was baptized, but not Catholic. So I can't. But don't worry, I'll be a surrogate godfather … keep tabs on little Nicholas and make sure he's okay."

"For some reason I thought you were Catholic."

Nic lightly scratched the side of his head. "Came close, considered converting several years ago, shortly after I found the Lord." He put his hand to his forehead, "But all the rules … in lockstep. Felt like a wedge being driven between me and Jesus. Like I was being asked to worship the Catholic religion … rather than Him. Sapped all the joy."

"I know what you're saying," Will said. "Couple of years ago when the new Mass was introduced, the Vatican had the opportunity to appeal more to teens and young adults. Went the other way. Many complained, but it's like a child talking to a parent when the parent won't listen … or has lost the ability to hear."

Nic put his hand to his side. "I was involved long before that. Couldn't bear how women are treated … clergy kinda puts 'em in the back seat … that way they don't have to pay very close attention. Just look at the mess over birth control."

"That's for sure. Women are pretty smart. But the Church belittles them … ignores their wisdom."

"I also couldn't accept how the divorced are treated. A new God-given love relationship forms, but if no annulment the partners are all but shunned ... the Church says living in sin. Just when the church could offer healing, it shies away. "

Without waiting for a response, Nic continued, "And then the gays ... the pall of being different ... and wrong. Oh, I could go on... But the young ... they aren't blind, they see the flaws and don't accept the rigidity. There's lots of reasons why they don't go to church."

"Yes," Will said, "and they ask 'Why'? The Church doesn't like that. It traps itself in the past; refuses to engage the present. So we leave our real selves at home, where we live, and just bring our proper selves to church. Some accept the unbending rules, others can't and fall away. Families stop going to church together, if at all."

Nicholas smiled, "You're quite the philosopher, Will. I'd a never guessed. Anyhow, you're right on. My hope is in Pope Francis ... puts Jesus front and center ... his joy and love."

"He's got his hands full ... those in power shield themselves in the vestments and ritual of the altar. They aren't about to give up control."

"Where's the love in that?"

Will shrugged, "Damned shame if you ask me."

Nic looked beyond Will, across the vineyard. He gestured to have Will follow his gaze. "This beauty the Lord has given us. Just look at the lake, those hills." He pointed, "See that flock of birds flying home to roost? Almost mystical in this light. It's a gift just to be alive. Let's hope Pope Francis lives a long time."

"Remember though, "Will said, "he's conservative, so he's only gonna go so far."

         ဆ   ಋ

The baby, Nicholas, was discharged from the Clinic a few days later. After a week at home, the first place Jackie and

Joey brought him for a visit was the Carriage House. Prince led Emma and Will to the door. He became still, carefully sniffing the outer shell of the baby carrier and viewing the wee Nicholas lying inside. Looking to Jackie for assurance … his wagging tail confirmed his approval.

Jackie left the baby with Joey as she went to the Manor to invite Maria and Seth over to meet Nicholas. They came running, Vicki not far behind. The kids were fascinated by the little person trying to focus on them; they'd never seen a baby up close. And so small. After ample warnings from Vicki to be careful and "Don't Touch!" the kids sat on the floor next to the baby carrier waiting to see what he'd do next … if anything at all. The baby just looked upward, pursing his lips as if searching for food, then broadening into a smile.

"Is he smiling?" Seth asked.

"No," Jackie said, "Probably just gas."

Jackie offered to let Vicki hold the baby, but she declined. "He's so small."

"He's gained weight. Up to six pounds already."

"Just let's wait until he gets a little bigger."

Joey changed the subject. "So, Vicki, We hear you've been hiking a lot.

"Yes, yes, on the trails. It's very therapeutic … on several levels."

"How so?"

"After a while my mind drops all the cares of my day; I see things differently. My whole body gets into the rhythm of my stride. Everything falls into perspective …no matter how angry or hurt I was when I start. Sunshine shrinks my problems down to size; a canopy of trees protects me; caught in a downpour … my soul is cleansed." Vicki smiled, "Hiking calms better than the damned pills. I feel alive, able to cope."

Emma said, "That's really good, Vicki. But, you are still taking your pills?"

"Of course."

"So, all your hiking ... it's for the good?" Will asked.

"That's one way to say it ... for the good. Things are brighter and happier. Yes, for the good."

Chapter 34

Weeks later, Emma called Jackie mid-morning on a late October day.

"Bonjour."

"How are you Jackie?"

"Nicholas was up during the night. But, he was good, only for an hour."

"You sound exhausted. Are you still having nightmares?""

"Non, non. Not the past two weeks. I get up early with Joey ... I am still tired."

"It may be a while before Nicholas sleeps through." Emma said, "What can I do today? Need anything from the store?"

"Non. Nicholas and I are up in the winery. The Tasting Room is almost finished, but, still, much to prepare. Joey is out in the vineyard . We will be here a while."

"Well, how are you feeling?"

"Is it normal for a mother to be so tired?"

"A new mother ... yes, that's very common. Can I help?"

"Not today. Too much, as you say, 'up in the air'." Jackie continued, "I talked with Joey about the Baptismal party you mentioned. He was surprised; Nicholas being already baptized. He wonders why we have a party now. I explained you just want to have a celebration ... since we never had one at the hospital."

"Yes, a celebration ... just family and close friends. And, as I said, we can have it at the Carriage House, so there'll be no burden on you."

"But Joey, being Joey, he comes up with a different idea. He feels a need, with all the people who helped build the winery and worked the harvest, to have a party. Like a Harvest Party, here, in the Tasting Room. He wants to combine everything into one."

"Well, that's a new one. Never heard of combining a baptism and a harvest."

"I know. Joey's creative though. After giving it some thought, he said, 'It's all about becoming ... new life ... new wine'. I guess he has a good point."

Emma sighed, "I just hope one doesn't get lost in the other."

"*Oui.* Could happen. But, Nicholas will be there to remind everyone."

"Good thinking. A harvest won't trump a baby." Emma paused. "So let's do it ... be easier for both of us. Why don't you come down here for lunch, the three of you? Then if Joey needs to go back you can stay and take a nap. I'll watch Nicholas. I miss him when I don't get to see him."

"*Merci.* But only a sandwich."

"Okay, whenever you're ready, just come down."

Jackie pressed the 'End' icon on her cell phone and looked again at the nearly finished room. She particularly liked the exposed natural oak beams spanning its width, with vertical risers reaching to the cathedral ceiling. Similar beams framed the warm deep ivory color of the walls. In the center four beams jutted above the roof line opening a cupola space with windows on all sides, allowing light to flood the room.

She turned toward the lake and took in the panoramic view through the large windows along the front wall The deck out front would provide a perfect place to sit and sip an exceptional vintage while overlooking the vineyard, the lake and hills in the background.

Heavy broken clouds scooted overhead, occasionally allowing bright sunshine to accentuate a splendor of color only seen during Indian Summer; the vivid yellows and reds of the vineyard foliage in contrast to a deep blue lake. But the bright sunshine was quickly grasped away by clouds bringing threatening grayness. Even though inside, Jackie could tell a stiff breeze heralded more challenging days ahead.

Walking toward the highly polished tasting bar, parallel to the wall of windows, she glanced at Nicholas, asleep in his carrier. He looked so peaceful now, unlike during his nighttime pangs of colic. She'd noticed the men standing in the vineyard, Joey, Nic, and Norman, huddled together, inspecting a trellis of vines. Guessing they'd soon be coming up to the winery, Jackie knew the first thing they'd look for was coffee and hurried to make a fresh pot.

It was only minutes before the door opened and Nic walked in leading the others, saying over his shoulder, "...so if you're willing to take the chance, we'll keep those vines netted to protect from deer and birds. Then when the freeze gets down into the teens, we'll harvest. But, Norman, you've got to understand, if a fungus attacks we could lose the whole crop and have nothing."

Norman asked, "Is that why ice wine is so expensive?"

"That coupled with the fact it takes a lot of hand sorted grapes to make a little wine." Nic smiled, "And, of course, recognition of the skill of the winemaker. But you're gonna like it."

"Joey, have you ever made ice wine?"

"Just once, I helped my grandfather. Several years ago … the climate was just right."

"So," Norman asked, "is it right this year?"

Nic answered, "So far, as good as you're gonna get."

Norman didn't hesitate to answer, "Okay, Joey, if you feel it's a good year for ice wine, go ahead. Wait for the freeze."

Jackie appreciated the fact that Norman, an aggressive man prone to make decisions on his own, deferred to her husband on matters involving the vineyard and winemaking. Her fear that Norman would try to take over, given his investment, seemed misplaced. And Chloe's attention was focused on her new great-grandson; her interest in vineyards dulled since the sale of her chateau in France. Jackie hoped the situation allowing Joey to make his own decisions would last.

ℰↄ　　　　　　　　Ϙʒ

On a crisp November afternoon, Maria and Seth rode up the hill to the winery with Emma and Will. They arrived early to help finish setting-up for the party. Later, when Vicki and Martin walked out of the Manor, she said, "I need to go over to Emma's and get Prince. Will asked me to bring him up to the winery."

"You're bringing the dog?"

"Will doesn't want him left alone."

Martin slowly shook his head.

"Yeah, he's a sociable dog." Vicki said, "People like him."

Vicki went to the door of the Carriage House, stepped inside and came out with Prince on his leash.

The dog came over to Martin, licking his hand in greeting. Martin stroked Prince's head, then stood straight and turned toward his car. "We'll put him in the back."

"No, let's walk."

Martin glanced toward the overcast sky. "I don't know; looks like it might rain."

"We're not gonna melt, Martin."

"Missing your hikes, are you?"

"Yes, I am. And, you can use some exercise beyond pushing papers across your desk."

"I get exercise."

"Not that it does you any good."

"There's been a lot of pressure at the plant. New press, new customer demands. Not a time to be goofing off."

"Yeah, well, here you're still the absentee landlord." Vicki stepped past Martin's SUV, indicating she and Prince were walking up the hill. She asked, "Gotten on a scale lately?" Not waiting for an answer she took a few strides and looked over her shoulder, "Coming with me?"

Martin fell into step beside her. "Every morning."

"And?"

"Damned thing seems a little off."

Vicki smirked, "Yeah, well I'm not off."

"Didn't say you were. You've come a long way since summer."

"My recovery? I'm not talkin' about that." She leaned over and poked Martin in the side, "I'm talkin' about you … in bed. You're heavier when we fuck."

"I wish you wouldn't use that word about our love-making."

"Oh, don't be so sensitive. We make love … sometimes. Fact is, you're heavier … you struggle longer. Not that I mind that … gives me time to get someplace. But, still, old man, you need exercise."

"So I'm getting it now … right?"

"Damned straight!"

Martin had forgotten how steep the grade was, new gravel making walking difficult. As soon as the winery was in view, he stopped and bent forward, catching his breath. Looking up he said, "You know, I haven't been up here in months. Haven't even seen the new building."

Prince came over beside him as if concerned for Martin's well-being. Taking short breaths, Martin said, "Look at that … it's beautiful … exposed beams … portico … deck out front … even a cupola. Nice! That went up fast."

Vicki looked at Martin, "You're in worse shape than I thought. Let your damned paunch get any bigger and you'll be buying all new shirts next spring."

"Yeah, well, let me worry about my paunch." Martin stood straight and inhaled deeply. "Look at you; you're hardly out of breath. I don't have a couple of days every week to take off hiking wherever to get in shape."

"Don't you turn this on me; that's my therapy damn it. No, you look at you! Gonna make it?"

"Yes! I'm gonna make it. Just catchin' some air. I forgot how steep this hill is."

"Great exercise … even makes for a damned good view."

In the Tasting Room, baby Nicholas did what all newborns do without any effort … drawing women like a magnet. He made their interest worthwhile, having the precise miniature features and smooth skin of a six-week-old, capped off by an infectious smile. Nicholas attracted so much attention that Jackie was glad to have to excuse herself and take the baby into an adjoining room for a quiet breast-feed.

Joey found he had to set up a table for gifts, even though 'No Gifts' had been communicated with each invitation. Nicholas was reaffirming that newborns personify our Hope-for-the-Future and every woman present showed she couldn't avoid gushing over how 'cute' and 'beautiful' he was. Meanwhile, Joey accepted handshakes and light punches to the shoulder from the men, as if fathering a child was a monumental accomplishment. He realized those who had children wished him well not so much for his manliness, but for the commitment over years to come ... the real challenge.

There was little furniture in the room except the long tasting bar, so Joey had rented tables and chairs. The early guests tended to mill around greeting one another ... those who didn't know each other taking the liberty of introducing themselves. The room was proving to be a good size for the 50 plus guests, plenty large to easily accommodate everyone comfortably, yet not too big. There was even room at the far end for the young children to play where two teenaged girls created order out of potential chaos.

Mr. Mosbey came up to Joey, his signature unlit cigar clenched between his teeth. He pulled the stub away from his lips, "You've come a long way Joey. A year ago I'd a never dreamed I'd be standing in a setup like this. And ya done a good job, all these fuckin' exposed beams .... Gives the place character ... strength, will last forever. And once ya get customers comin', that septic we put in ... you'll be thankin' me I talked ya into the larger leech field."

"Sure beats doin' odd jobs," Joey said. "And thanks ... thanks for the support. I'm hoping the crew that put this place up comes today ... I'll introduce them."

"No need o' that, I met them when they were buildin'. Snuck up the hill to see what was what. That one fella, on the crane, sure could line up those timbers … the guys puttin' in the pins hardly had to use their mallets. Don't see skill like that much anymore."

Nic approached, "Mosbey, how are you? Glad to see you."

Mosbey pointed his cigar toward Nic, "Son-of-a bitch! I haven't seen you since that spillover."

"Yeah, it's been a year."

"So, anything new on the goddamned hydrofrackin'."

"Oh, the Winery Council monitors the State Legislature … hard to tell since the last election. Upset the balance a bit. But, indications are the State Health Department may have a say."

"I just get pissed when I think of all the regs I need to satisfy," Mosbey said, "while the damned gas companies do whatever they want. Fuckers don't even have to report the important stuff … like what chemicals they're using."

"Feel the same way. At Kober Vineyards we need to report everything we use, keep logs. Even required to have our pond water tested and keep records on that."

"Yeah," Mosbey said, "and now the gas people askin' for a permit to store LP Gas under Seneca Lake … millions and millions of gallons of the damned stuff. When the hell we ever gonna learn?"

"What are you talking about?" Joey asked.

Nic said, "They want to use the salt caverns under the lake to store liquefied petroleum gas They're all for short-term for quick bucks. The hell with any concern for climate change! Not good … not good at all.

"But, getting back to fracking, my brother Tom did mention the Health Department might block it."

"Is he coming?"

"He's invited. But, you never know. I'll call him, make sure he shows up."

Nic turned to find a quiet place and faced Chloe and Norman.

"We just got here," Chloe said.

Norman held out his hand, "Nic, we've got to stop meeting like this."

Nic laughed, "Yeah, it's been almost two weeks." He gestured toward Mosbey, "You know each other, right?"

Norman smiled, "The septic guy. Yes, we've met." He reached toward Chloe, "And this is Chloe, Jackie's grandmother."

Waving a hand toward Chloe, Mosbey said, "Pleased to meet ya."

Nic stepped away saying, "I've got to step out and call my brother.

Mosbey looked back at Norman, "We was just talkin' about the damned frackin' ... still on the table."

"Yeah, "Norman said, "That's still up in the air, isn't it?"

"Not for me," Joey said, "No hydrofracking anywhere near our vines."

'Well, I wouldn't be so quick to conclude that." Norman said, "Remember those acres high on the hill that you said were no good for growing vines. All you need is five acres for a well pad. And the money would be fantastic."

Before Joey could answer, Chloe barged between the men, facing Norman. "Are you that crazy? A gas well near a vineyard! I thought you listened before. Did I not tell you all of France bans hydrofracking? Why do they do that? Because we must protect the vines. And you want to set one up next to Joey's vineyard. Do I even know you?"

"Chloe, I ... I was just thinking out loud."

"Do not think ... even in silence. You thinking convinces me I should return to France!" Chloe turned to Joey, "I must find Jacqueline."

Chloe strode off, then seeing Emma and Will, veered over to them.

"Oh, that man!"

Emma asked, "What happened? What man?"

"Norman. Why do I live with him ... sleep with him?"

Will held in a smirk, asking, "What did he do now?"

"He suggests Joey allow hydrofracking on the acreage up the hill."

"Joey can't do that." Will said. "The noise alone would destroy the value in this place. The traffic, the pollution…"

"And the terroir," Chloe stated, "It will ruin the grapes … the wine."

Joey circulated among the guests … family, friends, builders, harvest pickers. He'd accepted the offer of two volunteers to work behind the bar making sure everyone had a glass of wine, or, if they preferred, a beer in hand. The caterer he'd hired had hot and cold hors d'oeuvres set out, enough so anyone could have a meal if they wanted.

Seth heard Joey tapping a fork against a wine glass and noticed a sudden drop in the level of adult conversation. Grabbing Maria's hand, he led her through the maze of adult legs toward the front of the gathering, to where Joey was standing. He sat and motioned Maria to join him. Both children looked up in anticipation. Prince followed them and lay down at their feet.

Joey stood and gestured toward Jackie, who sat at a table next to him holding the baby. "Jackie and I thank you all for coming. Although we said 'No Gifts' I see a table overflowing in the corner. We thank you for that … Nicholas thanks you."

Someone loudly said, "You're welcome." Joey pointed toward the speaker, smiling, "Never realized how much stuff a baby needs."

"That's okay, Daddy. You'll learn." The retort was accompanied by laughter.

Joey continued, "We'd have had a party right after Nic's baptism if it had been at church, but with Nicholas and Jackie still in the hospital we were limited. So we're catchin' up today. Plus, in the weeks since, we've been able to finish this building and complete the harvest. A lot to celebrate…"

Joey looked over at Father Roy, "Father, want to get us started with a prayer?"

Roy smiled and stepped next to Joey. "All the warmth and good wishes in this room are a good start; a prayer in itself.

Everyone, let's take a moment to bow our heads in thanksgiving for the many blessings bestowed on us. We thank you Lord Jesus, especially for Nicholas' birth and health, for the success in constructing this beautiful building, and for a bountiful first harvest. For all this thank you, Lord. You have carefully watched over us, and for that we are truly grateful. We ask you to give us enduring guidance and grace as we go forward. And, bless us Lord Jesus, each of us gathered in this room. Amen."

Father Roy stepped back, placing his hand on Joey's shoulder. "So, Joey, please, so much has happened ... your insights?"

"Well, Father, Jackie and I offer special thanks to you for your help with our wedding and the baptism ... all along the way."

Joey put his hands on his hips, as if in thought, and looked around the room. "If you saw this vineyard a year ago, just after the tornado, you'd never have dreamed we'd be standing here today. Just look at this beautiful Tasting Room." He pointed toward Bruce, the architect, and Aaron, the builder, who happened to be standing beside each other. "Bruce ... Aaron ... terrific job! And everyone else who worked construction and helped finish this building, please raise your hands." A few hands were raised to applause rippling across the room. "You all made it look so easy.

"But, Aaron, your father with that large mallet he calls the Commander." Joey looked at the gathering, "Unfortunately, Aaron's father isn't here today." He gestured upward toward the ceiling and the massive beams, exposed in their static show of strength. "You see all those mortise and tenons joining the beams. Each beam was precut by computer controlled machinery in a factory. Using a crane, the very abled crew standing among you raised the frame of the building, piece by piece, in a very specific order. But often the alignment on the job varies just a bit from the factory, so a joint refuses to easily go together. That's when Aaron's father and his Commander came into play. He'd get himself situated next to the joint, so the angle of his blow would be just so, and *'thwack!'*, he'd hit it with just the right amount of force making the joint snap together. It looked so easy," Joey swung an imaginary mallet with both hands, "*Thwack!* But Aaron explained that too little force and the joint wouldn't budge, might even be damaged; too much force and the joint could be split. Aaron's father didn't miss a one."

Joey paused a moment. "It reminded me of my grandfather, when I helped him plant the vineyard across the road. All the drainage tiles had to be placed just so. He drove his mantra of 'Do it right the first time' deep into my skull. And he kept emphasizing 'Do it right the first time' as he strove to get the essence of wine making through to my distracted teenaged brain. He explained how so often in making wine, we only get one chance, just one, if we want the exceptional vintage."

Joey hesitated, lightly scratching the side of his forehead. "Well, I must have done something right. We haven't had a drainage problem over the past 10 years. The vineyard was planted as my grandfather's after-retirement project, to continue exploring the characteristics of various European varieties in our climate. That's why, those of you who helped with the harvest heard so often, 'Pick this, that'll come later." I know it was tedious and frustrating. But thanks to all of you … please raise your hands. You stuck with it and Jackie and I really appreciate that."

Again, light applause.

Joey held up his glass, pointing at Nic. "And uncle Nic, my daily guide, so essential to success. Your vigilance on deciding when to pick each variety; your constant advice and encouragement as the hand picking proceeded. On my own, first time around, I would have botched it."

Nic held up his wine glass in acknowledgement. "You'd have done all right."

Joey continued, "As it is we've captured a limited harvest, hopefully to become exceptional wine. Unfortunately, we don't have any vintages from the vineyard you worked in to share today; but Nic has made sure we've got plenty of Kober

Vineyards Riesling and Vignoles to enjoy; and for a red, the latest Kober Cabernet Franc, just released."

Light applause gave Joey the break he hoped for. He looked at Jackie. He smiled, and looked back at the guests. "But, enough about the winery and the harvest. The most significant moment of the past few months ... no, of my life ...was that evening when we didn't know what had happened to Jackie. I was frantic! Running through that vineyard toward the cries, seeing Jackie sitting between two rows of vines, realizing she was holding a baby; our baby. She'd been missing for hours ... I was lost without her." Joey's voice had tightened and he took a moment to regain composure. "And there she was, the moonlight upon her face, and she held Nicholas toward me. I gotta tell you, the sight of him floored me." A single tear began to ease down Joey's cheek. He looked at his guests and let it be. "I'll never forget. I realized, nothing else can be that important."

Joey smiled as pent up emotion of the guests erupted in applause, shouts and laughter.

Joey wiped his cheek and raised his hands asking for attention. "I have just one final item. Everyone asks, 'What is the name of your vineyard.' Currently on the regulatory documents submitted to the State of New York we're known only by a number. We need to rectify that ... I want to rectify that.

"As you all know, a year ago the experiments I was working on were destroyed in the storm." Joey paused, looked down, softly saying, "My good friend and partner, Harry, even lost his life." He looked up, his voice strong again, "It was about that time that Jackie also came into my life. She was the inspiration that led me to carry on. But, without Harry, I soon realized I couldn't replicate the experiments ... he was the chemist ... to some extent alchemist. Then my uncle Nic came to help out and reminded me of the wonderful legacy his father, my grandfather, left us. So with Jackie, I decided to rebuild, along more traditional viniculture. And through her, I came to know Norman ... he made it financially possible to rebuild quickly, to afford a winery on this scale."

Joey held up his glass toward the ceiling, then lowered it in Norman's direction. "Thank You."

Speaking over light applause, Norman nodded in the recognition, "Just make the wine…"

"For those of you who were at our wedding reception, some unexpected excitement was provided. I'm hoping never to be repeated again … ever."

There was a lilt of soft laughter across the room.

"But, seriously, we appreciate your patience and understanding."

Joey hesitated, collecting his thoughts. "So, it was quite a year … a lot happened. After our wedding Jackie and I looked forward to a few peaceful months before the birth of our child and a successful harvest. Then, just over a month ago, Jackie went through that horrifying experience. It ended, thank God, with Nicholas coming into our world.

Joey paused to look at his wife and baby again. "Look at the thread winding through it all, Jackie is at the center."

He glanced at two servers standing behind the bar. "So, how do I rectify the question of what to call this winery?" Joey held his wine glass out toward Jackie. "I propose we call it '*Vin Jacqueline*'.

The two men behind the bar raised a long sign with the name *Vin Jacqueline!* painted across its surface in a rich burgundy red over a bright ivory background. Applause and shouts filled the room.

During the applause, one of the guests held up a camera, so Joey took the baby from Jackie and guided her to stand beside him in front of the sign being held above the young family. Jackie threw her arms around Joey's neck and kissed him gently on the cheek … her nonverbal way of saying 'Thank You!'

Joey quietly said to Jackie, "You can change the colors if you want."

After many congratulations on the new name, as the noise returned to a more normal level, Joey recognized the distinctive note of Hank's motorcycle as it labored up the grade to the winery. Since he had not been able to contact Hank with an invitation, Joey walked to the front door in greeting. Not seeing anybody, Joey stepped out. Hank wasn't in sight. Joey turned back into the Tasting Room and was met by Hank walking across the room toward him.

Hank asked, "Did you hear?"

"How did you get in here?"

"Back door. Left my cycle out back."

"You on the run or something?'

"Hard to tell. Listen, have you heard?"

"Heard what?"

"Hydrofracking may be banned after all. Not decided yet, but leaning that way. They're not gonna approve it."

"Nic and some others were saying that earlier, that maybe the Health Department will have a say. If that's so, you won't have to fight it anymore."

"Oh, I'm still fightin' it ... in PA. State Police can warn me all they want; I'm fightin' back. And up here in New York, even if it is banned, litigation will go on for years ... the industry won't give up."

"Be careful Hank. You know those companies have a lot of clout."

"Yeah, well maybe I can bring them down a peg or two. Make 'em think twice."

"Just be careful. Don't do anything crazy."

"Naw ... all up-and-up. Nothing beyond what a gas company would do."

"That's too much. A gas company has money to fight it and nobody goes to jail. While you, the lone ranger, you go to jail. No question of it. Listen, Pennsylvania is used to drilling. What do you hope to accomplish?"

"I'll take my chances. Need to for my own self-respect. It's my mission, my purpose."

The Tasting Room proved to be a comfortable place for the party ... many, strangers to each other when they first came, became more and more comfortable as wine and beer were

347

poured. The bar was christened and food was consumed at a pace denying servers any break.

Dusk began to set in when the headlights of a car approached the winery. It stopped, blocking in several cars. Two Sheriff's deputies, a male and a female, stepped out and preceded up the stairs directly to the winery entrance. They walked and stood inside the door surveying the guests … evidently looking for someone. One nudged the other and the deputies proceeded down the length of the bar toward where Hank was standing. Their presence brought many conversations in the room to a standstill.

Hank took notice and stepped back into the shadows, toward the parking lot. He turned and quick-stepped to the exit. Opening the door he found his passage blocked. A State Trooper, about 6'3" tall with girth to match filled the space, the broad brim of his hat blocking the sky. Hank looked up to his face, raising his hands in surrender. "Lookin' for me?"

"You got it. Let's keep it peaceful."

The Sheriff's deputies came up behind Hank. Keeping his hands high, Hank stepped sideways so he could see them. "So what did I do now?"

The male deputy said, "You shot up some gas drilling equipment this morning."

"No, you got the wrong man. There isn't any drilling gear to shoot at around here."

The male deputy patted Hank down. "Nice try. No, just down across the border … got you on camera this time. Even a view of you leaving the scene on your motorcycle."

"What's that prove?"

"You'll be under arrest in Pennsylvania for vandalism and unlawful discharge of a fire arm."

"I doubt that'll stick."

"We'll let their Grand Jury figure that out. The DA in Pennsylvania may have more charges to come."

"Okay, okay. I don't want to ruin this party."

"Yes," the female deputy said, "peaceful would be nice."

Hank held his arms behind his back, making his wrists available for handcuffs.

The trooper slid the cuffs on and clicked them closed.

"They gotta be so tight?"

The deputy began the standard chant, "You have the right to remain silent, anything you say may…" As soon as she was finished, the male deputy and State Trooper each took one of Hank's arms and started to escort him around the side of the winery toward the front where the Sheriff's car was parked. Joey and Norman followed them, staying within earshot.

Joey said, "Hank, sorry. Don't worry about your bike." Norman stepped closer, saying, "Hank, I'm calling my lawyer … I'll have him meet you."

"No problem. I've been expecting this. Getting' lazy I guess."

"Don't say anything!' Norman said, "Wait for my lawyer." He turned to the female deputy, "Where are you taking him?"

"For now, the County jail."

Nic fell in step beside Norman. "If you follow him to the jail, I'll come with you. We need to have Hank's back … any way we can."

Guests moved out onto the front porch. They watched the arrest march to the patrol car, Hank's limp was pronounced as he kept pace with the lawmen. One of the guests who'd attended the wedding reception whispered to another who'd also been there, "Not nearly as exciting as the wedding, but how many baptismal parties you been to where somebody gets dragged out in handcuffs?"

Chapter 35

Hank's departure became the topic of conversation: 'Who is he?'... 'Did you see the handcuffs?'... 'Wonder what happens next?'

Norman nudged Joey on the elbow. "My lawyer's gonna talk with Hank. I'm meeting him at the jail."

"Should I come too?"

"No way. Nic's comin' with me. You can't leave your party. Every woman in the family will have my neck ... blame me for taking you away. Keep an eye on Chloe. Make sure she goes down to the Carriage House with Emma. I'll pick her up there."

Cloud cover in afternoon twilight shrouded the hillside promising a moonless evening. Guests continued congratulating Jackie and Joey on their first harvest, "...and the Tasting Room; the hardwood beams and the picture windows. Makes us feel like we're outside." But, the real star was Nicholas ... the women couldn't stop fussing over him.

As dusk fell, many helped take down the tables and chairs; doing the cleanup necessary after a large gathering. As soon as the tables were folded and chairs stacked, Martin told Vicki to collect Seth and Maria. In saying 'Goodbye' the kids surrendered to tight one armed hugs from Jackie, then stood looking at Nicholas cradled in her arm. They returned the baby's wide-eyed gaze, the unblinking stare only young children seem to understand.

Will approached Martin, "It's pretty dark outside. Let me give you a ride down the hill."

Vicki overheard the offer. "I have my trail light. We'll be okay."

"You sure. There's no moon."

"Will, on the trail, we walk in - we walk out. Here, we walked up - we walk down ... no shortcuts."

"But, it's probably gonna rain."

"So we get wet. Good trail lesson for the children."

Martin just shrugged; avoiding disagreement leading to an argument he was bound to lose. He knew Vicki would stand firm, poised in her new resolve of recently found self-respect. He raised his eyebrows and accepted Will's handshake, acknowledging his nod of male-to-male understanding.

Across the room, Emma pulled up a chair and gestured Chloe to join her. "Let's let the young folks wrap-up. I don't know about you, but I need to sit down."

"*D'accord.*" Chloe said, joining her, "A long afternoon … too much standing."

Emma quietly asked, "You didn't mean what you said to Norman before … about moving back to France?"

Looking down, Chloe said, "*Oui,* some, I mean some. Behind the bravado, Norman is a good man. Even though he craves money from fracking, he helps Hank, who fights to stop the wells. Norman told me, 'Hank helped save Jackie. We owe him.' And we do. That's how he is." Chloe raised her eyes to meet Emma's. "Just don't cross him."

'Without Hank's help rescuing Jackie … I don't even want to think about it."

"At times Norman, he infuriates me … but he has, how do you say, 'Got under my skin'. Should have never let him do that. I have friends in France you know."

"Oh, I can imagine. But, forgive me for saying, Norman needs you. Will is the same; needing me."

"It happened so fast. Only weeks it took … and like a drug, I become dependent. I soften, overlook faults … realize he won't change … only a little, if at all."

"Yes, yes … they won't change, the men … at our age they are who they are. So we have to cope."

"*Oui,* cope ... if I walk out in anger … where do I go? Live alone. When we were in France I realized I want to be with him, I do not care where. So, I cope; we cope … overlook … even forgive. I get angry at myself for letting him." Chloe brought her face close to Emma's, almost whispering, "His touch, Emma, it is his touch. He soothes my turmoil."

Emma smiled, "I know what you mean…" But she was unwilling to share more about the intimacy she enjoyed with Will.

"So, yes, I may well go back to France … but I know damned well I will return." She hesitated, then continued, "Norman is like a magnet to me. *Mon Dieu*, I sound like a school girl. *Excusez moi.*"

Emma put her arm on Chloe's, "No, no. You're family … and always welcome. Just know that we care for you and Norman … you need each other. Like Will and I need each other … more as we get older. Life is so crazy these days."

Chloe was silent for a moment, then spoke with conviction. "That Norman, I will not let him ruin *les enfants* with the fracking; not near this vineyard."

"You mean the new vines across the road?"

"*Oui* … young vines; the vineyard Jackie has worked so hard to train. The vines they are like babies entrusted to our care. So, no, I cannot stay in France. I leave … *Voila*, Norman will lease. Up the hill, above those vines. No, no … Norman cannot lease for a well … not while I am here."

"But what if fracking is banned altogether?"

Chloe smiled, "Then I find another excuse to stay."

"Chloe, my dear, you are a love…"

Jackie walked over, "So how are the great-grandmothers?"

Chloe pursed her lips; Emma looked up, "I wish you would stop reminding us of that."

"I say it in respect. How do they say, 'Wisdom, Age and Grace'.

"Yes," Emma said, "we certainly have the Age, still searching for the Wisdom … and Grace, I don't know … maybe for Chloe?"

Chloe's reaction came more as a snort through her nose than the laugh she intended. "Emma. If you have no Grace, I am doomed for eternity!"

When the last friends and grandparents departed, Joey checked to see each door was locked. Standing at the far end of the Tasting Room, holding Nicholas, Jackie watched her husband walk the perimeter of the room. He came to her side and took the sleeping baby in his arms. They stood silently for a few moments, bathed in the soft glow of dimmed hanging lights. "It's as nice as I'd imagined," Joey said. He slowly put Nicholas into his carrier, careful not to wake him.

"*Oui.* I think a good size. And the noise, it is not too bad, even when crowded."

Hands on hips, looking around the room, Joey said, "Maybe the high ceiling and beams help absorb the sound. I don't know. Beautiful though! I guess we done good."

"*Oui, oui, c'est bon* … this room." Jackie entwined her arm within Joey's and leaned in close. Smiling, she said, "Being together … married, so good. But best is Nicholas!"

Joey looked at Jackie. "So, should we try again … not right away, but soon?"

Jackie reached over to adjust Nicholas' blanket. "We better or this one will be spoiled. Soon! But, *s'il vous plais*, not in a vineyard!"

The young couple stood, enjoying the quiet beauty of the moment … the contentment of their child … being with each other. They touched their heads together.

Joey pulled away enough to look at Jackie. "You've been wonderful through a very tough year … prepping the wedding, the reception … and the fire. As if that wasn't enough," he gently ran his index finger over the remnants of the scar on Jackie's cheek, "the day Nicholas came. You've been so brave through it all."

Jackie put her hand behind his head, pulling his ear close to her lips, saying softly, "You can say it Joey, the shootings, me being hostage… You can say it, talk about it. Or, put it away, all of it. I have! To me, we find each other, *Dieu Merci!* Soulmates! We are married, our wonderful honeymoon; our baby, he is healthy."

Joey didn't move, he whispered, "You're right, we are lucky."

"Blessed! To be here, like this ... we are blessed."

"Next year, I'll have the winery finished ... the crusher, tanks, all the equipment installed ... we'll make our wine here. Yes, next year will be a more peaceful year."

Jackie pulled away, laughing. "I think you said that last year after the storm tore up the vineyard. You the optimist...."

"Yeah, well, my love, this time I mean it. We can only hope."

Jackie kissed him on the cheek and again put her head beside his, "*D'accord*, my love .... *D'accord.*"

Prince led Will and Emma into the Carriage House. Walking into the kitchen Will said, "Good day. I'm glad to see how far Jackie and Joey have come in just a year. Who would have guessed?"

"Me ... she's my granddaughter. Brings the best out in Joey." Turning on a lamp, Emma looked at Will, "Hungry?"

"Not really. Ate more than I should have at the party. I'll just catch up with the news on TV."

An hour later, Emma and Will retired ... it had been a long day. Will was asleep almost as soon as his head hit the pillow, a trait Emma envied. Prince lay next to the bed, following his master's lead. Emma propped herself on pillows against the head board, reading. After a short nap, Will awoke. He reached over and touched her hip, allowing his hand to slowly caress her smooth skin. She shifted her body inviting his touch, knowing his hand would wander; Will wordlessly seeking sexual intimacy. Emma put her book down and eased closer, their interplay following a comfortable pattern... although somewhat repetitious, never boring; always drawing them closer together.

It was fine with her that the timeframe between sexual encounters was lengthening ... she was getting older too. This evening, she became satisfied, but Will only came to the edge of climax. He cried out, "Oh, my love!" but couldn't physically finish. It had happened before. Emma pulled Will tight against her, helping him to come down, ease off psychologically. She heard him quietly groan, "My body should get in sync with my brain!" After a few moments, he added, "One of the joys of getting older."

Once he caught his breath, instead of falling into what he called 'The Sleep of the Gods', Will let his fingers almost float over Emma's skin, whispering, "I have never felt so one with another as I do with you ... in this instant ... now! Is this what 'Two shall be one' means?"

"I think so ... it's so, so ... intense"

"So much to discover of our love together. Always wins out over material stuff. When the chips are down, we grasp for the essential ... our relationship."

"I love you," Emma said, "more than I can say."

"Getting older, being aware limited time is left ... does that deepen our feeling?"

"Probably. We've done what we're gonna do. We just hope to be with each other."

"No pinnacles left to conquer..."

Emma and Will laid side-by-side, enjoying the silence of the moment.

"I guess we're forced to slow down," Will said. "I used to be able to complete one project after another. Now, I finish one and have to sit a while, or worse yet, take a nap. And canoeing ... this season my range became shorter ... closer. Maybe only one cottage a week shorter, but the long paddles I used to take at dawn ... just aren't that long anymore. You must notice me coming in earlier."

"I didn't want to say anything. You're still gone plenty long. I walk out on the dock and look down the lake.

355

Sometimes you're only a spot on the water. When you hug so close to shore that I can't see you, then I begin to worry."

"It's only natural we have to cut back, not act like we're 40 anymore. I guess I'm lucky to be able to go as far as I can. To even balance my canoe."

"We should enjoy, and thank God for what we can do."

Will lay back in thought. But, not for long. At his age, he wasn't allowed to just lay in bed … always the need to pee.

When he came back, Emma had resumed reading. She looked up from her book, questioning what he was thinking with her eyes. "Oh," Will said, "I'm just thinking of that fella, Hank."

"Hank?" She lowered the book to her lap, "What makes you think of Hank, now?" Emma was getting used to Will needing to talk; unfulfilled sexual energy having to dissipate.

"Quite a character if you think of it. Been sneakin' around this area for months and the cops couldn't find him. Maybe even shootin' up gas company equipment down in PA. I don't know, maybe he is the guy who stopped that shooter over at the college. And what's in it for him … any of it?"

"I doubt he's comfortable away from a war zone."

"That's a hard one to call."

"Oh," Emma said, "he's still over there, Iraq or Afghanistan, wherever he was; or he'd like to be. His injury took him out; but he needs the danger of the chase, whether he's pursuing or being pursued. I just hope he isn't in too much trouble."

"All the guy seems to be trying to do is keep fracking away from the lakes and the vineyards … protect our environment. Joey's uncle Nic is always thanking and praising the Lord for the beauty, the bounty of nature … the terroir. Hank protects it with his motorcycle and rifle."

"Is that wrong?"

"I don't think so. I'm comfortable with it."

"Even though you're all for gun control."

"Yeah control. Keep guns out of the hands of crazies. Hank's a responsible guy. He knows what he's doing. Never fires when anybody's around. Still, I wish he'd ditch the gun."

"Yeah, he's breaking the law?"

"Simple case of the ends justify the means. He's stickin' his neck out, makin' a statement tryin' to slow down ... stop ... the damage. While so many others ignore the harm. We've misused nature for centuries ... messed it up ... but nothing like the last hundred years or so. Just thumbin' our nose at it."

Prince stood and stretched. Will reached down, patting his flank. "Yes, old dog ... you know what I'm talkin' about."

"Yep, "Will continued, "We're obsessed with screwing up this earth God gave us; and we hurt each other in the process. We blast the shale to smithereens to get the trapped gas. Ruin our water. Pollute the air. Keep burning fossil fuel. Kinda like how we live. Take advantage ... grasp at power ... gotta get ahead of the other guy."

"Not everybody. Most folks just want to have a better life."

"I suppose, but we want to get our own way ... even at the expense of others. I mean, how do you explain the proliferation of guns? Our gun culture has become like a religious commodity. Look at how easy it was for Vicki to get one. The gun advocates say for safety and protection. Tell that to the parents of the kids killed over at the college. Think they'll ever be the same? Or, the injured who'll live with their disabilities?"

"That was a tragedy. The shooter was mentally ill."

"Maybe so, or just use a gun to confirm our convictions ... put the other guy down ... literally. My point is, life would be so much easier if we'd just smarten up and stop exploiting each other."

Emma set her book on the bedside table. "Will, most people are just trying to get by. Raise a family, do a job, go to church if they want."

"Yeah, the Church ... creates a lot of strife. Hell, half the people don't go anymore. It needs to loosen up, realize our modern day lives ... our work, our caring, how we treat each other ... that's our prayer."

"Oh, I agree." Emma paused, her eyes widening in anger. "But, the clergy will still put women down, ignore our insights, keep us in our place."

"I don't know, that might change…"

"Dream on…" She patted the sheet. "Come, get back in bed. It's been a long day and I'm tired."

Will laid back and was quiet. After a few minutes, Emma softly asked, "Are you asleep?"

"No … just thinking. What if we kept the earth with the care that Jackie, Joey and Nic give their vineyards? Our planet would be so beautiful, so healthy."

Will exhaled and lay back. After a moment he spoke toward the ceiling. "Well, Jackie and Joey'll get up tomorrow and continue working to finish the winery; Uncle Nic will be at Kober's fussin' over a new vintage; Chloe and Norman … who knows what those two'll be up to. Hell, I'd go canoeing if it wasn't so cold out. But in spite of all the problems and frustrations, we place our hope in the young … baby Nicholas, Seth and Maria. They're our hope for the future … they'll be around to see it. God help 'em!"

Emma heard the fatigue in Will's voice. Experience taught her his monologue would continue down seemingly disconnected paths. Paths she'd be unable to follow. "I agree. That baby is our blessing. He'll keep us going. Now get some rest." She reached over and switched off her reading lamp; nestled her body against his. Her lips found the scar on his forehead; she kissed it tenderly. "Maybe in the morning, my love, maybe after a night's rest, things will look brighter."

Will opened his eyes, he turned his head to look over at Emma. "Ah, maybe even sex at dawn?"

"Just go to sleep, Will. Please, just go to sleep."

End

358

Acknowledgements

Heartfelt thanks to those who made this novel possible:

Elaine Powell, the 'first reader', who suffered through my early rough drafts; often handing pages back saying, "You can do better."

The Webster Writers Group: Paul Bagdon, our leader, a prolific published author himself, taught me how to write fiction. Joe Callan, Bonnie Frankenburger, Willow Kirchner, Roz Pullara, Michael J. Scott and Sid O'Connor listened chapter-by-chapter and gave me myriad suggestions for improvement. Also, Blanca Mastbaum-Kane, (1962-2015) always urged more emotion; she left us much too soon.

Winery owners Oscar Bynke of Hermann J. Wiemer Wineries, Len and Judy Wiltberger of Keuka Springs Vineyards and Morton and Lisa Hallgren of Ravines Wine Cellars for patiently answering my many questions about vineyards and making wine. Their help was essential … errors are mine.

Once the manuscript was written, Liz Webster, my sister, became the principal grammatical editor. She also guided me on current sacramental practices of the Catholic Church.

Howard Angione suggested needed improvement in the early chapters.

Anna Powell designed and produced a distinctive cover.

Photo of author on back cover by Ginger Graham; cover photo by author

Rob Maurer, my son, developed the manuscript into published form.

My daughter, Christine Gallion, and son, Peter Maurer, keep my PC operable.

My family, who patiently endured my distraction during all the times I've been in-the-book!

And, to all readers of *Twisted Vines* who encouraged me to write this sequel.

Finally, let me not forget my high school English teacher, Father James Malone SJ, who planted the seed all those years ago that perhaps I should consider writing.

My Thanks to All

శి   ౪

Art Maurer is married and the father of seven children. Retired from Frontier/Rochester Tel, he lives in Penfield, NY. This is his second novel ... sequel to *Twisted Vines*.

Email: amaurer40@frontier.com